H-HAR WARS

"...it may not be friendly"

PETER MELVILLE

Tellwell Talent
www.tellwell.ca

ISBN
978-1-7635432-1-8 (Hardcover)
978-1-7635432-0-1 (Paperback)
978-1-7635432-2-5 (eBook)

Table of Contents

VOLUME 2:   THE MOTHERSHIP

PART 6:   ALONE AGAIN

PART 7:   THE WAIT

PART 8:   MOTHERSHIP

PART 9:   SHORTEST WAR IN HISTORY

A big thank you to my dear wife, Enone,
who humoured, encouraged,
and tolerated me during the writing of this book.

PROLOGUE – The World at 2070

It is seventy years into the twenty-first century, and the world faces the most threatening conflict period since the darkest days of the Cold War.

The United States of America remains the most dominant political and military power. However, like other democracies, it is recovering from generations of profound leadership failures. Fraudulent ideological earnestness, driven by an intolerant, patronising, and aloof ruling establishment, has produced polarised and fractured societies and driven a foreign policy more concerned with global virtue signalling and ineffective international institutions than traditional great-power diplomacy, leaving the world plagued by chaos, threats, and conflicts.

China, by brutally imitating a market-oriented economy, edged close to the US as the world's largest economy. However, a harsher global financial system, poor international politics, increased Communist Party centrality, steep demographic decline, and lack of property rights preventing the development of an innovative and dynamic private sector have caused prolonged stagnation.

China's economic and military shadow looms large over many nations. Its use of troops to siege and operate "threatened assets and investments" in Africa and its persistent threats to take

Taiwan have both added tensions to its multi-decade Cold War rivalry with the US and most of the world.

Germany, Poland, and Ukraine dominate the new European Free Trade Organisation. The EFTO is without a socio-political union movement to avoid the failures of the dissolved European Union, which tried to wipe out national identities and unify Europe under a friendly version of a Napoleon-Hitler Empire.

Russia's pseudo-tsarist regime once again threatens Eastern Europe. Although its economy is too small to support its ambitions, Russia has been building up its nuclear and non-nuclear arsenal since the failed invasion of Ukraine. Many provinces, although still loyal to and dependent on Moscow, operate under their own laws. However, those with growing Chinese populations increasingly look to China for protection and culture.

Tensions between India and Pakistan remain high. A nuclear escalation was narrowly avoided after each country exchanged a tactical nuclear weapon during a punitive Indian military incursion into Pakistan against terrorist groups. China supported Pakistan by increasing troop numbers along the Doklam border and Southern Tibet.

Japan has re-emerged as a major military power in the Western Pacific, closely aligned with the US, India, and Australia to counter Chinese assertiveness.

In Indonesia and Turkey, Islamic-aligned presidents have taken their countries down the path of religious intolerance, causing regional instability.

Religious and traditional conservatism in Southeast Asia and the Middle East have led to rising illiberalism. The wealthy elite and many businesses see this as an opportunity to influence their governments. Although no country has yet firmly aligned itself with China, the possibility could intensify US-China rivalry.

Jihadist violence continues to rage across the Middle East and Africa. A stolen Pakistani tactical nuclear weapon was recovered while being trucked to Israel for detonation. Other weapons were traded on the black market for months before they were recovered. The airline industry was virtually shut down after handheld anti-aircraft missiles were used against civilian jets.

Africa remains a continent of failed states, with its people impoverished, dispossessed of their land by their governments, and without a future.

South America is as unpredictable and politically insignificant as ever. Politically swinging from left to right, led by charismatic politicians mired in scandals.

An antibiotic-resistant plague last decade infected half of the world's population and killed 260 million people of all ages. Panicked governments shutdown economies, closed public places, and prohibited travel. Virtual police states existed in many countries. After three years, an antimicrobial brought the pandemic to an end, but economic, psychological, and social problems and broken communities persist.

The risk of a man-made global catastrophe is growing. Weapons of mass destruction are widespread. The world's digital economies are controlled by inexperienced, complex computer algorithms. High-energy physics experiments may have unknown diabolical consequences. Artificial intelligence could spiral out of human control. Synthetic life could become pathogenic or something even worse.

The myth of catastrophic anthropogenic global warming has been finally dispelled. Historians marvel at how flawed science, proxy data, expert partisanship, and unbridled alarmism were accepted so readily for almost eighty years by know-nothing, acquiescent governments, news media, businesses, and the public, condemning third world nations to decades of poverty and famine, and advanced nations to economic hardships and environmental damage.

Technological change is increasing. Humans cannot compete against faster, cheaper, and accident-free automation. Consequently, production costs depend less on labour rates, and manufacturing locations are determined more by local infrastructure, regulations, taxes, quality of life, and political stability. Underemployment pressures are worsening, making societies less resilient, divided, and more dependent on governments. Liberties are being sacrificed for the promised benefits of a safer and more ordered society.

The world's population peaked at nine billion during the last decade, then slowly declined, creating a large aging population.

Despite government regulations, genome editing is set to enhance the characteristics of newborns.

The first human landings on Mars showed that robotic explorers are the only feasible long-term option. Two and a half years of exposure to cosmic radiation outside of Earth's atmospheric and magnetic embrace, and the damaging effects of partial gravity showed the enormous health problems associated with long-term human space exploration.

Space tourism is growing, with week-long trips around the far side of the Moon being the most popular. But they are not without risks, as several disastrous failures have demonstrated.

The most thorough survey of the skies for extraterrestrial life has just been completed. If a spacefaring civilisation colonised just one of the millions of galaxies studied, their activities would be detectable at radio and infrared wavelengths. If there were just one other earthlike planet in our galaxy, its water and oxygen abundant atmosphere or other bio-signatures would be detectable from spectroscopic observations. Yet, no evidence of alien life has been found. After more than a hundred years of searching, nothing. Only the indisputable and unsettling "Great Silence".

Although many scientists are mystified by this, believing there should be many earthlike planets, some much older than Earth, most now accept that the universe is a lonely place full of dead rocks.

A leading astrobiologist wrote:

"It took ten billion years for the Earth to form and stabilise its orbit around the Sun, a billion years for the creation of life, two billion years for multicellular organisms, and another billion years for intelligent life. This is almost the entire lifetime of the universe, 13.8 billion years. If this process had taken just ten percent longer, humans would never have existed, because, in another billion years, the Sun's increasing luminosity would make the Earth uninhabitable.

"The conditions needed for life to emerge are an almost impossible combination and sequencing of astrophysical, geological, and biological events. Time estimates for the occurrence of these events exceed the lifetime of the universe by many orders of magnitude. So, unless there is an unknown process to explain these rare chance events, life on Earth is an unresolved miracle, and the rest of the universe is just background scenery. If alien life does exist, it would unlikely be within our local galactic group or even within the visible universe, which could be a blessing, because it may not be friendly."

VOLUME 1

CONTACT

PART 1

NO LONGER ALONE

"… shielding was not designed to protect any life forms …."

Chapter 1   The First Arrival

East Africa – A Million Years Ago

A male ape-hominin emerges cautiously from a grove of small trees into the milky light of dawn. Naked, scarred, and moving like a worn-out athlete, his breath puffs out in the frigid air. With a survivor's unblinking intensity, he pushes up on his spear to peer over the endless sea of softly swaying, tall savannah grass for any threat. There's the ever present and always menacing hyenas in nearby trees and some distant vultures circling, but nothing else. He angles his head and turns into the breeze. His face contorts; it's just strong enough to carry their scent.

Gesturing his tribe to follow, he climbs down to an open, dry riverbed, where they feverishly dig for water. This time, they're lucky. It's smelly and dirty, makes them sick, but it keeps them alive. They gulp as much as their weak bodies can hold. They're too far away to see the lion and leopard paw prints on the opposite side of the riverbed.

The never-ending drought is forcing them to migrate north in search of food and water.

Predators, starvation, a drying climate, diseases, mishaps, and disputes have reduced their tribe to only twenty-eight breeding pairs. Their global numbers are less than two thousand breeding pairs. Their race is on the brink of extinction.

Their feet crunch a slow and steady pace through the grass. They spot a tribe of other ape-hominins in the distance, their first sighting of others in over ten months. These Others have longer and stronger spears. Although they have no concept of numbers, the Others' tribe size looks similar to their own. In this highly competitive struggle for survival, the two tribes instinctively avoid each other.

Through the shimmering mid-day heat haze, the tree ape-hominins notice unusual patterns crisscrossing the rippling grass behind them. Their fears intensify. It could be the wind, but it could also be ape-eaters stalking them. No way of telling. The patterns suddenly merge, pick up speed, and head directly towards them. They grab their children and desperately flee in terror, their hearts pounding, their skins shredding on the sharp, entwined grass. But the trail of breaking grass quickly catches up. Weak with hunger and armed with only light clubs and flimsy spears, the ape-hominins spin around in horror to confront three huge leopards, their wet tongues dangling in anticipation. The hominins form a protective circle but still look very vulnerable. They've learned from previous encounters to attack the predators' eyes. Males on the outside, then females, then young ones in the centre with the fire pot and other precious possessions. Another ferocious battle for survival is about to commence.

The ape-hominins frantically shriek and wildly pound their weapons, partly in panic but also in an attempt to scare off the starving carnivores. Undaunted, the leopards furiously pounce with tooth and claw. The hominins stab their spears, but they may as well be poking at tree trunks. A hominin in the outer ring is dragged off screaming, leaving a trail of blood as his fingers scratch the dirt. A young male hominin moves to replace him in the circle, but an elder female knows better and pulls him back. Another hominin is taken. The rest can only watch helplessly.

The leopards, satisfied with their meals, eventually depart, leaving silence broken only by the hominins panting and groaning. Overwhelmed by familiar inexpressible grief, the hominins are bloodied, gashed, beaten, and in disarray. And yet, they are still defiant and determined to survive. They wipe the blood from their faces, sharpen their spears and vigorously screech to each other about the battle. They'll defend themselves better next time. Herding together, they continue their journey. Life goes on.

Before long, fear grips them again. Something large is breaking the grass towards them. They take off in a blood-curdling panic and unexpectedly burst upon the Others hiding in a small clearing.

The two tribes stare at each other in frozen confrontation before their heads snap to the bestial roars of ten gigantic lions exploding from the brush. Blazing eyes, giant teeth, and ripping claws.

The hungry beasts immediately spread out, circling the apes, breathing heavily, sniffing, drooling, savouring the scent of the meal to come.

The two tribes, in the face of terror, close ranks but remain separate.

The lions attack in a whirling blur of horror.

A tree hominin is grabbed by huge jaws and tumbles over. His panicked scream soon expires. Another is dragged off in a flurry of violence, predator teeth deep into his neck.

The other hominin tribe, without an organised formation, quickly loses three apes. A crying juvenile hugging her knees is taken. An adult hominin tries to save the child, only to be seized and dragged away screaming.

The ape-eaters, roused into a mad frenzy of killing, are nowhere near finished.

Faced with annihilation, the two tribes come together and merge. The extra numbers and the Others' longer and stronger spears add depth to the tree hominins' defensive formation. Their protective circle is suddenly complete and decisively unmoving. With their hearts racing, the apes screech in new-found defiance.

The snarling carnivores start suffering serious injuries, but their hunger drives them on. One carnivore frantically climbs over the rest and leaps, only to impale itself on a wall of spears. Its crazed eyes remain focused on the nearest ape, and its claws keep raking the air until it drops limply to the ground.

The lions hesitate, doubt showing in their eyes, while the hominins gain confidence. Finally, they challenge the lion's gaze, and the lions have little choice but to withdraw, their wounded animal cries waning into the whispering grass. They'll be wary of attacking these hominins again. The two tribes, exhausted, cut, and bloodied, lower their spears. They are surprised, thrilled, elated by their newfound power over the ape-eaters. They form a collaborative bond and continue northward into parts unknown, daunted but feeling safer united.

***

One night, as the little hominin camp lies doused in moonlight and hidden within scrub, a young girl wanders out alone beyond the flickering fire glow and looks out over the ghostly grassland. The full moon is particularly large and luminous tonight, pretty but unsettling. She knows to fear it; it's a time when the large carnivores come hunting. She rubs the small, developing bulge in her lower abdomen but takes little notice of it.

A cold breeze brushes the girl's face as she looks skyward, her eyes sparkling in the moonlight, her white breath escaping into the darkness. There's something in her gaze, something deep and unusual for her species, something almost alien. A kind of conscious curiosity or fascination. Her ape brain cannot grasp the incomprehensible, big, empty world in front of her. Almost beyond her imagination, she wonders if there will come a time when all tribes like hers unite and are safe from predators, when food and shelter are plentiful, and when someone knows what the strange twinkling lights in the night sky are. A dim indication of an intelligence that will take another million years to flourish.

There is something different about this child. She carries a mutated genetic code, one that will spread quickly throughout the small numbers of her species. Hers is one of many in a long and necessary chain of events that will eventually give her species intellection and the universe morality.

But she is not alone. Two huge yellow eyes lie low in the dark moon-shadow of the foliage, waiting, watching. They focus on the girl's figure, silhouetted against the brilliant stars, with a predator's unwavering attention. They narrow and inch closer. The predator's hot breath is white in the cold air but cunningly concealed in the moon-shadows. The darkness and eerie silence are all encompassing. Then, the sound of a twig snapping. The young girl turns instantly, every sense suddenly on high alert. Choking with fright, she stands frozen, listening, waiting, breath held, staring out at the shimmering moonlight running along the crests of the swaying grass until it eventually dissolves into blackness. A cloud passes over the Moon. The shadow moves across her stricken face. The obliteration of her planet a million years from now depends on what happens in the next few seconds. The girl turns just in time and hurries back to the relative safety of her tribe's camp.

Meanwhile, a metallic object is slowing from a high speed as it approaches the Moon. It gently lands, then lies inert.

Chapter 2   The Second Arrival

Eastern Europe – Thirteen Thousand Years Ago

A gap between two snow-capped mountain peaks shows a small group of humans wrapped in goatskins struggling up a narrow, icy mountain path. The way ahead is hidden by thick mist. They have all their possessions with them: plants, seeds, tools, water containers, and animals.

A boy with fair skin and dark eyes turns as a small stream trickles down the mountainside and stares back in apprehension at the breathtaking, vast, wooden valley below. A village of two hundred people straddles the banks of a swiftly flowing river, sunlight glinting off the water's surface. There are boats, mudbrick huts, smoky fires, and fields of wild cereal crops and legumes. People, domesticated dogs, goats, and sheep move about – not more than dots. "Are you sure we have to leave?" he asks.

"Yes, the great green plains beyond have plenty of new fertile farming lands for us," answers his father.

The boy continues gazing at the village.

"Come on, son. We have a long journey ahead."

Their instincts push them westward into an unknown wilderness. They're excited but also anxious, as only colonisers of new lands can be.

Their new farming techniques, suited to a warming planet with receding ice sheets, will enable communities to expand quickly and spread ideas that will be absolutely necessary for defending their planet against a future extraterrestrial threat.

Meanwhile, two metallic objects enter Earth's orbit. Four hundred years later, they relocate to a large asteroid, radio their status, and wait.

Chapter 3   Signals – Year 2070

A computer beeped, a backpack fell, a breath held, footsteps quickened, a chair scraped, and eyes widened.

"O my God … another signal!"

Tingles of goosebumps washed over her.

Thirty-six seconds later, the signal stopped.

Pushing herself away from the desk, her chair again scraping, she fumbled for her phone.

"Locky!" Even speaking to a machine, her excitement forced a breath pause. "A third signal … wow! I can't believe it!"

A text message came back impressively quickly: *That's awesome, Anya. I'm on my way.*

She squealed excitedly and circled the room. *So much for the weekend.* She stopped at the computer and replayed the signal. For the very first time, her eyes flickered with uncertainty, and a hint of concern crossed her face.

Anya Connell and Lochlan McLean were research scientists at the Massachusetts Space Corporation – Hydrogen Line project, MSC-HL. Utilising hypersensitive radio detectors on independent space probes, delving into the mysteries of the distant universe. A year ago, they added software to identify any unnatural signals. Nothing had been detected until now.

Signal filtering and correlation made errors almost impossible. Nonetheless, they initially suspected the first signal to be an aberration. However, after further investigation and the reception of the second signal, their reservations disappeared.

***

Anya Connell was born in 2047. With the body of a ballet dancer, short, sandy blonde hair, a full, natural smile, and intelligent blue eyes, she was attractive in a way that wouldn't stop a party but would surely pause a few conversations. She was quietly independent and at times introverted, but there was strength and fierceness within her that even she was unaware of. Anya turned her childhood love of astronomy and science fiction into a PhD in xenobiology.

Lochlan McLean, born in 2046, was a lanky, unkempt academic with scruffy, mousy hair and a mischievous grin. He was too much of a die-hard science nerd to score dates at university. One rejecter told him his face had attractive alertness, and he was geekishly sexy in his own peculiar way.

Slightly hyper and lacking patience, nothing in life happened quick enough for Lochlan, which explained the large number of motorbike speeding tickets. Once his Irish temperament took over, he was often overly assertive and outspoken.

Enthralled by a universe filled with scientific wonder, Lochlan graduated with honours in astrophysics. His intellectual arrogance was soon tempered by the disappointing realisation that there were researchers smarter than him.

Lochlan and Anya had worked together on the MSC-HL project for two years, forming a strong, dynamic duo. A close and loyal friendship developed, and it seemed they could – or at least should – have been lovers. Their likes and needs were similar, and they often had meaningful discussions. But strangely enough, it never ended with a gaze into each other's eyes, an indulgent smile, or a proposition. Perhaps if they had met outside of work, it may have been different.

***

Lochlan arrived in his usual mode, casual haste.

Anya grabbed him and dragged him to her computer. "I've removed the space and time distortions. And look … the same header and tail section as the two previous signals. So, it must be another encapsulated message."

Lochlan shook his head. "Amazing. We should have enough data now to locate the source."

"Yeah."

"Let's get started, Anya."

"What, now!? It's Friday night!"

"We're in a hurry, and there's so much to do."

"You'll be the death of me, Locky. I'm sure of it."

By Saturday lunchtime, they realised it would take much longer than a few gruelling hours. Two months later, they were still working on it.

After another week, a breakthrough. "That confirms it, Locky," said Anya, releasing a wide smile.

"Yeah, the first two signals are from Io, and the third from Europa."

"Two separate sources make little sense." Anya's smile faded.

"Yeah …" Lochlan turned to his computer. "And we still have that strange non-linear spatial and time distortion."

"That's crazy too. We need to find out what this distortion is. It might help us find the source."

Working late one night, Anya stared one-eyed at her monitor. Three cups of cold coffee stood next to her. Around her, the lab equipment looked like strange creatures in the semi-darkness – the HV injection unit silhouetting an eerie alien-like form. She mumbled thoughts to herself and slouched as her other eye slowly closed. A moment later, both eyes snapped open. She spun in her seat to face Lochlan. "Hey!" She suddenly paused, her thoughts occupied. "Y'know what? These distortions resemble a 2D surface projection onto a 3D sphere."

Lochlan's bloodshot eyes suddenly widened. "Yes, of course! You're absolutely brilliant!"

Anya tilted her head, brushing off the compliment.

"Why didn't I think of that?" Lochlan gave a brief, innocent grin. "The signals are echoes off Jupiter's moons from another source."

They became so excited they talked over each other.

"So," Anya said, "they're reflections from a directional Earth transmitter, but—"

"But Io was hidden from Earth by Jupiter at—"

"At the time of the second signal. So, a satellite transmitter in orbit around Jupiter, maybe? But then—"

"But then we'd have reflections from many moons."

They were struck silent for a minute.

"This is getting really scary," said Anya with a slight shudder.

They tediously studied the ephemeris of Jupiter's moons and the asteroid belt, plotting their celestial movements. Finally, after another week, Lochlan announced, "Pallas! It has to be."

"Yes." Anya was a bit hesitant, looking like someone who had just turned on a light in a room full of snakes. "It's the only sizeable object that could source all three signals. You realise what this means?"

"Yeah. We've detected signals directed away from Earth from an asteroid way out in the solar system. And—"

"And our detectors just happened to be in the right place at the right time, pointing in the right direction. That's … that's one chance in a million, Locky, one chance—"

"In a million!"

They stared at each other for some time before Anya finally asked. "Sooo … what have we found, Locky? Some secret government space probe?"

"Y'know what?" Lochlan shifted in his chair and scratched his head. "I don't think these signals have anything to do with Earth." His eyes showed little doubt about what he was thinking.

Anya's blank expression turned into a worried frown. She stared at him like he was a stranger.

"Don't worry, Anya." Lochlan reassured with a smile. "It's awesome, but it's time we got help to interpret these signals."

Anya parroted the smile and slowly nodded. "Okay, but where do we start?"

Lochlan gave a little smirk.

Anya choked on a laugh and swung a circle. "Jeevan Partha!?" she asked, spitting it out as if it were poison in her mouth. "You're joking, right?"

"I know. He doesn't know shit from clay, but he's our starting point."

Anya groaned. "Uggh, he's just a tacky, flashy, arse licking, sweaty palmed phoney. He's so infuriatingly dumb, frustratingly annoying, and … and …" Anya ran out of words, eventually exhaling a sharp breath.

"And useless," Lochlan finished for her.

"About as *useless* as an ash tray on your motorbike." Anya flashed a jovial smile. "I bet you ten bucks at five-to-one odds that Jeevan will be a waste of time."

"Hmm …"

"C'mon, dare you!" urged Anya.

"Hmm … nah, don't want to lose ten dollars."

***

Jeevan Partha was the project coordinator. A rodent-like man with a thin moustache and a permanent, untrustworthy smirk. He looked like an overdressed accountant, implying either a burning but delusional desire to impress management or an imbecile. A loud and rapid speaker, he appeared energetic and enthusiastic, but this was just a facade to hide a slow learner, poor performer, and weak character. Socially likeable but intolerable to work with.

Partha's brief engineering career was a catastrophic disaster. One employer was sued when Partha commissioned a lift that failed shortly afterwards, trapping residents for five hours. He then completed a cheap correspondence MBA and excessively bloated his online credentials attempting to land a high-flying management role. After spending a long time in the wilderness, he found a temporary position in his current job. Unable to comprehend negative feedback, he was unlikely to ever improve.

***

They set off to find Partha. But the man who had been nowhere, and who was going nowhere, was nowhere to be found. And his phone wasn't answering.

"Off to one of his many God-knows-where places," Lochlan said with a wry smirk as their eyes swept over Partha's empty workstation.

They nudged each other and flashed the tiniest look of complicity.

"Something's not right here," Anya said with a wry smirk of her own.

Lochlan needed little encouragement. "I know what you mean. The tabletop, it's completely bare, except for"—he moved closer without touching anything—"a perfectly clean coffee cup, a blank sheet of paper with a pen, and an ornamental picture of his wife and dog. All perfectly aligned and neat. A clear indication of the day's activities."

"Note the computer screen at an unusual angle," Anya added, "so no one can see it."

"Good observation, *Mrs Holmes*," Lochlan complimented with mock amusement. "I suspect it isn't a busy desk."

"Not a busy desk at all, *Dr Watson*." Anya leaned forward. "Note the window shade, lifted just above eye level, allowing a daydreamer's view of the outside world."

"Yes. And note how his chair is angled and pulled away from his desk."

"I do, doctor," Anya said, nodding knowingly. "And its unparked position suggests the owner just stepped out for a moment, intending to return shortly."

"But I suspect this was staged to give that impression," Lochlan proposed. "I therefore submit, *Mrs Holmes*, that the owner won't return today."

"Hmm. Interesting theory, Dr Watson. But it's the only logical conclusion."

They wandered off, both shaking with laughter.

***

"Good morning to you both," routinely greeted the overly charged and shifty deadwood that was Partha. His squeezed-out, welcoming smile glowed like a cut-priced insurance salesman. But it soon faded along with his shallow patience when Anya and Lochlan began describing their discovery.

"And that means what to me?" Partha repeatedly interrupted, huffing, puffing, and giving death stares.

Anya could tell he wasn't following any of this. She shook her head and remained patient while Lochlan looked like his annoyance was on slow burn.

Finally, Partha scratched his head in condescending aloofness and said, "Our manager, Mr Hughes, is a busy man. I can't disturb him with this so-called discovery of yours. He—"

His attention suddenly shifted to the other end of the office. "Why is that chair being moved?" he shouted, frowning disapprovingly.

Lochlan's annoyance boiled over. "Stop being an arsehole, Jeevan."

Partha turned with a cold stare.

"What did you just say?"

"Hey, chill out, Jeevan," Anya said before Lochlan could repeat anything. "Don't worry, we can go directly to Ethan Hughes."

"That's a great idea, Anya," Lochlan said.

The blithe and obtuse Partha, speechless and blank-faced, conceived in the only comprehending part of his brain that this might look bad for him.

"All right then, I'll see Ethan Hughes," he said.

"Thank you," Anya muttered. *Stupid bastard, but no need to make a scene.*

Two days later, Partha reported with a melodramatic, cartoonish grin, "Ethan's not interested."

Lochlan and Anya tossed a glance at each other and walked off, muttering and shaking their heads.

"Y'know, it's fun being your friend, Locky," Anya said as a gleam of satisfaction lit her face. "I get to say 'I told you so' a lot."

"C'mon, Anya, let's go see Ethan."

Chapter 4   Terry Dittmar

Ethan Hughes's workload methodology was an unmitigated disaster. Months, maybe even years, of unopened emails that could never conceivably be answered. An action list so large, he himself didn't know where to start.

"Hi, Ethan," Anya and Lochlan greeted as they entered his office, a sea of piled papers, scattered folders, and overflowing boxes.

Hughes glanced up just as his phone rang. "Goddam it! Who the hell is it now?" Without even looking at the caller ID, he cancelled the call, mumbled something to himself, and hunched back over his computer, busily engrossed in something they couldn't see, clearly irked by any interruption.

A crooked notice on top of a pile of papers on his shambolic desk read: THERE'S NEVER ENOUGH TIME, SO DON'T WASTE MINE.

Lochlan and Anya traded a puzzled look. Lochlan held his hands in front of his eyes and glanced down at his body as if to say "we must be invisible".

Anya gave a slight grin and turned to Hughes. "Excuse me, Ethan, we need to talk to you about the signals Jeevan Partha mentioned."

Hughes, deep in thought and eyes glued to his screen, continued tapping away on his keyboard. Moments passed. Finally, without looking up, he muttered absently, "Uh, signals?"

"Yeah, signals. He did mention it to you, didn't he?" Anya asked.

More moments passed. Still without looking up, Hughes replied. "Um? … yeah, some problem with your equipment." He frowned at something on his screen, lifted his head, and added, "He didn't really have any idea. He just said it was too complicated to explain. I told him to leave it with you two. Why?" Hughes looked back at his computer, far too busy to wait for any response.

They decided it was time to enter his busy world of whatever. Anya was about to say "excuse me, but I think we have something a bit more important than whatever you're staring at", when Lochlan came out with it. "We've discovered unexplained signals from outer space, and we don't believe they're from a human source."

Hughes's head sprang up with a blank expression. His eyes darted between them.

"You're not joking, are you?"

"No," they answered in unison.

Hughes's default blank expression suddenly changed to shock.

"Holy shit!" he burst out, jumping up to close the door.

Anya smiled to herself. *Well, that did the trick.*

Hughes slowly returned to his chair, stroking his chin. He looked up at them intensely. "Are you saying you've found *aliens*?"

The word "aliens" lingered for a few seconds, a word Lochlan and Anya had avoided. They then explained their discovery. Hughes listened, undistracted. Afterwards, he took a deep breath, rubbed the back of his neck, scrutinised their faces again, and asked, "Okay, what now?"

"We need to keep listening," Anya immediately answered.

"And get statistical and encryption experts to analyse our signals," Lochlan added.

"SETI?" asked Hughes.

"No!" Lochlan shook his head. "They're too political and populist. After a hundred years and millions of dollars of speculation, they've found nothing. They'll just take over and grandstand everything."

"We have some contacts at MIT," Anya said.

"Good." Hughes hesitated for a minute, then added, "But let's just keep this in-house for the time being, until we know more."

"Yep," Lochlan said.

Anya nodded in agreement, then frowned. "What about Jeevan Partha?"

"Jeevan?" Hughes gave a little dismissive cough. "Don't worry, I'll talk to him."

Lochlan and Anya excitedly exchanged thumbs-ups and left.

***

MIT identified the signals as intelligent but indecipherable.

"We really have found something, y'know, Locky." Uncertainty flickered across Anya's face. "And it may not be warm and fuzzy."

"We need to find out what it is first. We can worry about the implications later."

"We need to be careful," Anya said, chewing on a thumbnail.

Armed with MIT's report, Hughes arranged a meeting with the general manager, Terry Dittmar.

Anya, Lochlan, and Hughes waited for Dittmar in his plush meeting room on the top floor of an elegant, high-rise glass building in the posh part of town.

Lochlan helped himself to the cappuccino machine. Like a kid sneaking chocolate, he half glanced over his shoulder as if he were doing something that, obscurely, he shouldn't be.

He took a wary sip. "Hmmm … not bad."

He wandered to a window that took up the entire wall – an unimpeded, commanding view of the city. He took it all in. He had heard stories and wondered if Dittmar would stare down at all those little people toiling below and speculate whether they could be better utilised for profit. *Nah, I'm being too cynical.*

Anya examined an old, framed picture on the wall. Two teenage boys holding a large tennis trophy. The description read: "Terry Dittmar and Chuck Brookes, national junior doubles champions – 2037". Another picture, only six months old, showed two men smiling at the camera as spectators at a tennis tournament. This description read: "US President Chuck Brookes and Terry Dittmar".

Gee! They go way back. Anya looked closer at the second picture, at a tall and lean man with hooked eyebrows, lived-in skin, and a hawk nose. *So that's Terry Dittmar. His looks certainly match his reputation. Cranky, impatient, intimidating, and devouring people who waste his time. But also seductive and charming.* Anya was anxious about what to expect.

Anya and Lochlan settled into chairs next to Hughes, who was busily reading emails on his phone. They faced a large, circular table. The chair at one end was different – a dominating, high-backed, expensive executive type. They assumed it was Dittmar's and instinctively adjusted themselves to face it.

Anya skimmed through the news headlines on her phone: *Chinese Navy Exercising in Greater Numbers Closer to Taiwan's Shores. Democracies Disunited About What to Do.* She sighed and put the phone away.

Twenty-four minutes later Dittmar arrived in mid-conversation with a corporate-type assistant scurrying alongside him. He pulled out his chair, sat down heavily, leaned back with his legs crossed, joined his fingertips, and imposingly stared across the table at the three visitors, not unlike a hanging judge about to give a sentence.

"I'm listening," he said.

The absence of formalities caused a moment of confusion before Hughes began. "As we discussed on the phone, Lochlan and Anya,"—he gestured towards them—"have discovered inexplicable signals from Pallas. It's—"

"Mr Hughes ..." said Dittmar, his face blank with incomprehension. He took his time speaking, knowing no one would interrupt his gravelly voice. "Your group is a complete mystery to me. I inherited it during the company merger. So please tell me again, this time in plain English, what is a palace? Actually, I'd like to hear it from the young couple here. Straight from the horse's mouth, so to speak."

Lochlan volunteered. "Pallas, spelled P-a-l-l-a-s, is—"

Dittmar's phone rattled across the table. He grabbed it, held it close to his ear, turned away, and spoke softly. "Slow down, and just tell me what happened." His voice then became inaudible. The conversation looked close to ending several times. Finally, Dittmar was heard to say, "I can't discuss this now. I'll be there within an hour."

He turned back to the meeting. "Sorry," he said unconvincingly, "where were we?" He pulled his chair in and placed his phone on the table.

Lochlan resumed. "I was explaining that Pallas is a five-hundred-kilometre asteroid, the second largest in the asteroid belt, which is a ring of rocks and ice that orbits the Sun between Mars and Jupiter. Very little is known about Pallas. The JWST orbital telescope has taken images, but the resolution is—"

"Whoa, whoa. Mr McLean." Dittmar's voice was slow and slightly impatient. "I'll put it bluntly." His gaze switched between Lochlan and Anya. "Please assume I know less about what you are talking about than ... that goldfish over there." He pointed across the room. "So please talk to me as you would talk to a simpleton. And I'm the only one in this room you need to convince."

There were no doubts now about this guy; his reputation for toughness was justified. Anya and Lochlan restarted the presentation, ignoring Dittmar's persistent glances at his phone.

They talked about the three signals from Pallas: how they were directed away from Earth, their unnatural characteristics, how no record exists of any Earth radio transmitter on Pallas, and how measurement errors were negligible. And, finally, how the signals could be alien.

All eyes turned expectantly to Dittmar. He tapped a rhythm with his fingers on the desk, stood up, and walked to inspect his goldfish swimming around in a large spherical bowl.

Was his mind even on the presentation, or was it on something else? Perhaps his phone messages?

He slowly returned to his seat, seemingly distracted. After clearing his throat, he simply said, "I see."

The unimpressible Dittmar was only slightly impressed.

After another pause, which seemed to be for effect only, he turned to Hughes, as did everyone else. "Mr Hughes, now that this—"

Dittmar's head turned to the door, where an office junior was quietly waiting. "No coffee orders today, thank you," Dittmar said with a disapproving look. The junior hastily retreated.

Dittmar resumed. "Where were we? Oh yeah. Now that this smart couple here have made this *discovery*, the ball's in your court, Mr Hughes, as they say. So what plan do you have for us?"

Before Hughes could say anything, Dittmar's phone rang. "Yes?" he impatiently answered. "I know, I know. Just tell her I'm not contactable." He placed his phone back on the table.

Hughes waited for Dittmar's attention, but Anya beat him to it. "We need management support in the form of work prioritisation, equipment upgrades, signal deciphering, public media interfaces, and—"

Dittmar's phone chirped. He quickly grabbed it, pushed back his chair, and got up as if about to leave. No one else seemed to think the meeting was over. He slowly walked to the door and stood there, reading his phone. A minute later, he returned and sat on the front edge of his chair, still reading his phone. Everyone waited.

I swear he's mocking us, Anya thought. Any moment now, he'll put his fingertips together and reveal how this will hinder his plans for world domination.

Dittmar eventually lifted his head and, with the phone still in his hand, finally spoke. "Anya and Lochlan, I understand this is exciting for you." His strained facial expression indicated what was coming. "But this company cannot support such an investment. So, and this is a question for you, Mr Hughes. How will we get someone else to pay for it?"

That's an under-reaction if ever I saw one, Anya thought. We've just discovered aliens in our solar system, and he describes it as exciting but not worth paying for.

"We can lobby the space or defence organisations," Hughes suggested rather awkwardly.

Dittmar remained silent as he tapped a finger on his lips. It was clear he didn't consider this financially viable.

Anya's optimism withered.

"And how would we do that, Mr Hughes?" Dittmar asked. Hughes's mouth was dry, and for a moment he hesitated. It was only a short moment, but a moment too long for Dittmar's patience.

Dittmar straightened and peered restlessly down the table. "I understand as much as I need to. I think we can end it there. I'll postpone my decision and let you know. In the meantime, I'll ask everyone not to discuss any of this until then." It wasn't a question, so it was met with muted, compliant stares.

Dittmar rose casually from his chair, his task finished, and headed towards the door.

Anya watched him with raised eyebrows. *What! He must be joking. I don't—*

"Excuse me, Terry," Lochlan said rather emphatically, leaning forward with a confused frown.

Dittmar stopped and looked at the young man inscrutably.

"I don't think you understand the significance of this discovery," Lochlan continued strongly. "There's something on Pallas that's not from Earth, and it could be the greatest discovery in mankind's history with significant economic implications. A big opportunity to miss out on."

Good on you, Locky.

Dittmar gave Lochlan a ghost of a smile. Suddenly, he seemed much less frightening and intimidating. Was this a change of heart?

"Dear Anya, Lochlan, and Ethan," Dittmar said gently. His face and tone then returned to their nonconciliatory state. "This discovery is just speculation. There are many other considerations here, and I don't want to wake up in the morning pregnant because of something we did the night before."

No one asked what these "other considerations" were.

After a shallow goodbye grin, Dittmar turned again for the door, his phone already at his ear. Stunned gazes burned into his back as he disappeared, his assistant in tow.

***

A week later, nothing from Dittmar. When Anya and Lochlan contacted his office, they were told to leave a message. They left messages daily for another week, but nothing. Finally, an email from Dittmar:

In view of the uncertainties associated with the current company restructure, further investments in ill-defined, non-core activities cannot be supported. Thus, work on this discovery is to immediately cease.

"Ill-defined, non-core activities! What the hell?" Anya pulled a face. A little girl who had just been told her biggest dream in life would never happen. "So, where does that leave us, Locky?"

"We'll just take our business elsewhere, Anya."

Ethan Hughes transferred to another division. Jeevan Partha carried a smug grin after hearing about the meeting with Terry Dittmar, but it disappeared when his name didn't appear in the restructure.

Chapter 5   Farmer

The MSC-HL equipment was dismantled. Lochlan and Anya left the company to lobby for support for their Pallas discovery. But with tough funding competition from other research groups, it was not going well.

After five months, they reconsidered approaching SETI and accepted an opportunity to speak at their annual open forum conference at Florida University. This was a popular event for the media, sponsors, and renowned scientists.

At the conference, the speaker before Lochlan and Anya claimed he had seen secret alien artefacts as a government researcher. As he spoke, his fingers tapped against his side, his voice trembled, and his deeply watchful eyes nervously surveyed the room.

Before Lochlan and Anya could even leave their seats to begin their presentation, a man dressed as a farmer leaped up. "A pinkish flying saucer hovered over my farm," he said, edging his way onto the podium. He downplayed the previous speaker's story about alien artefacts, claiming he himself had a whole yard full.

Amazingly charismatic, well-spoken, unnerved, and with a captivating tone, the farmer continued. "Okay. Okay … God. I know what you're thinking, but a tractor beam lifted my car and dropped it. The tyres burst, and the hood and boot opened. I jumped out and heard really scary, outer space-themed music. A tall being that looked like a werewolf hovered in midair near my car. It had an eight-pointed star medallion on its chest. My poor dog, Spotty, was vaporised when he growled and bared his teeth. Then a strange blue beam sucked all information out of my brain."

Some attendees left, accusing the forum of becoming a circus. However, most just listened, humoured by the story. A few laughed. The farmer finished off. "I was abducted and saw a 3D star map showing a planned invasion of Earth. I was physically examined with probes and had sore cavities for weeks. It also stole my biggest pig. The police said I was crazy, but I'm a good Christian and don't lie."

Later, in a dimly lit corner outside the forum door, a lone, lingering figure watched with hawklike concentration as people left. He didn't seem to belong there, but no one paid him any attention. He quietly identified the nervous speaker from a photo on his phone and followed him to his car. Two large men moved in and, with trained precision, hooded the nervous speaker's head and forced him into the car. The kidnappers were joined by the "farmer". The car drove off and vanished, just like that.

Lochlan and Anya's presentation received some interest on SETI's website. MIT re-examined the signals but concluded they were too convoluted to be useful. NASA pointed an antenna at Pallas for two weeks before losing interest. Other opportunities were pursued, but military tensions with China gave funding preference to military projects.

Nine months after the SETI presentation and sixteen months after the third signal detection, Lochlan and Anya's lobbying efforts were going nowhere. They were forced to move on to new jobs, but they never gave up hope for an opportunity to prove there was something on Pallas.

Chapter 6   MOT

A seemingly insignificant event was about to change everything for Anya and Lochlan.

Kevin Garrett, the operations manager for the recently commissioned Martian Orbital Telescope, MOT, worked out of Sydney, Australia.

While deleting his unread emails, Garrett paused at a two-week-old one from a colleague. Something told him to check this one.

It contained an internet link that led him to an article on SETI's website: Unexplained Signals from Pallas by Lochlan McLean and Anya Connell.

After reading the article, he emailed the authors and arranged a video call.

"We could use some free MOT time to view Pallas," Garrett told them.

"That's absolutely fantastic," Lochlan said.

"This is terribly exciting," Anya added.

Garrett took an instant liking to them and arranged flights to Sydney to discuss their discovery.

Two days later, Garrett bounced across reception in three long strides to greet them. With a beaming grin, he gave them the warmest of handshakes, grasping their shoulders as if to protect them from further disappointments. He guided them with his big hands on their elbows into a meeting room and waved them to sit as his technical officer arrived. Everyone was smiling.

In his mid-forties, Kevin Garrett oozed confidence, vigour, and authority, even a sense of controlled power. He leaned in his chair towards them and listened intently to their story.

"Well," Garrett said, leaning back in his chair. "I really am impressed." His eyes switched between them. "There's never been a Pallas fly-by?"

"No," Anya said. "Very little is known about its surface geography. It was photographed by Hubble in 2007 and James Webb in 2028, but the resolution was insufficient to identify any features."

"The MOT is a hundred times more powerful than the JWST and a lot closer to Pallas," Garrett boasted. "We'll get one point six metres per pixel. Any object larger than ten metres, my MOT will see it."

He regarded them for a second, then spoke softly. "I'll be honest with you. Some of my colleagues thought you were just a couple of nerdy science geeks with uncorroborated messages from outer space. And I know if you gaze too long into the abyss, the abyss will gaze back at you. But somehow I suspected you were onto something, and now I'm convinced. Assuming our technical expert here can't find any problems with your data."

Garrett looked at his colleague, who nodded acknowledgement. He then turned back to Anya and Lochlan with an assuring smile, as if saving the best for last. "Then I can find some free operating time on the MOT that we can use to spot your mystery signal transmitter on Pallas."

Lochlan grabbed and shook Garrett's hand. "That's absolutely awesome."

Anya did the same. "Thank you so much, Kevin."

"My only concern now is," said Garrett, oh-so-slowly while raising an eyebrow, "what will we find?" It didn't sound like a question, more like a warning, but it paused the enthusiasm.

"Yeah," Anya said. "That's my concern as well."

"Well, hopefully we'll find out," Lochlan said hastily. "When will the MOT be ready to view Pallas?"

Garrett checked his computer. "About three months from now." A confident smile surfaced, not unlike a boxer accepting a challenge.

Anya and Lochlan spent two days enjoying the city and their companionship before flying out, excited about returning in three months when the MOT would be pointed at Pallas. These three months were carefree and jaunty. A time of hope, expectation, and suspense. An innocence, a simplicity that a world soon to be shattered would stomp out.

***

Lochlan, Anya, Garrett, and some MOT staff faced a large wall screen in the conference room. Expectations were high. More staff arrived, requesting to be present. Their attendance added to the suspense.

Lochlan sprang from his seat, full of nervous energy, and paced the room. "This waiting is killing me," he grumbled before flopping back down.

Silence again overtook the room, as everyone waited expectantly, uneasily, and, especially in Anya's case, with some apprehension.

Garrett's phone rang. He quickly grabbed it, the others keenly watching for a reaction. "They're sending the enhanced pictures through now," he said, sounding slightly despondent. "They couldn't see anything unusual except for an outline on picture 17, which they said could be shadows."

"Shadows?" Lochlan heaved an anguished sigh. "Bullshit!"

"Let's just wait and see," Anya said, turning to the blank wall screen where Lochlan's reflected face showed a picture of impending failure.

Picture 17 suddenly flicked onto the screen. Lochlan moved closer and studied it like a pirate with a treasure map. His finger traced out a ghostly shape in a dark shadow. "I see what they mean. The shadows are so deep it could be something, or it could be nothing."

Anya's eyes filled up. "Are you sure there's nothing on the other photos?"

"Yeah," Garrett said. "Pallas rotates, and this is the only picture covering this region. Unfortunately, the Sun's angle wasn't quite right."

Lochlan rested his hand on Anya's shoulder, distress clear in both their eyes. "There must be something else we can do with the MOT?" he asked.

Garrett turned to his computer. "I was about to check. Um … yep, if I reschedule a few things, we can get a six-minute window in four days. Um … let's see." Garrett checked again. "We should get a full sunlit view of the relevant region at a good angle. After that, there's nothing for two years."

Lochlan hooked his arm around Anya and turned to Garrett, smiling. "Let's grab it."

***

It was a restless four days. All their efforts and expectations were coming to a climax. They killed time walking along the tree-studded shores of Sydney Harbour in the beautiful spring weather.

With one day to go, Lochlan sat alone, cross-legged on a grassy slope in a harbour park facing the foreshore. His mind was occupied. A gentle morning breeze stirred the leaves, punctuating the silence. Up high, fluffy, white clouds drifted across the sky. A great white seabird glided along moist air currents. On the ground, eager seagulls surrounded him, squawking at each other, inching closer to his hot chips, testing his generosity.

Anya approached from behind, slid down the slope, and sat next to him, her long, skinny legs landing close to his, but not touching.

"Hi …" she said, beaming. "One day to go."

A game seagull took the opportunity to steal a chip. Lochlan shooed it off, then glared at Anya as if it were somehow her fault.

"Whatcha doin'?" she asked, ignoring his accusation.

Lochlan turned back to the harbour. A cloud cast a large shadow over it. "If the pictures tomorrow show nothing, then there must be something hidden under the surface, and we'll never find it. What do you think?"

Anya waited as a swarm of white dandelion seeds whirled past. "All the evidence tells us there's something there," she said in a voice leaden with months of worry and anxiety. "But what it might be is the scary part."

"I'm still going for an alien artefact," Lochlan said. "It's just far enough from Earth to remain hidden, but close enough to observe us. And the signals were aimed away from Earth."

"I agree."

They sat quietly for a minute, then Lochlan swirled around to Anya. "Hey! Remember that strange farmer guy at the SETI open forum at Florida University?"

Anya wrinkled her forehead. "Yeah, he was weird. He kept demanding to be heard, even though no one was stopping him. He ruined the forum's credibility."

"He raved on about a flying saucer the size of the Moon behind his barn. Y'know, I've been thinking, I reckon that was too weird to just happen."

"What?" Anya turned with a serious stare. "You're not suggesting he was planted?"

"He was too well presented and too well rehearsed to be a poor farmer."

"But … but that means someone is hiding something, and that's scary." Her face became alarmed. "And what did Terry Dittmar mean when he said 'other considerations'?"

"I think Dittmar was a lot smarter than he let on. He's a friend of President Brookes and could be the next defence secretary."

"So he did know something?"

"If there's some cover-up, why would he be involved?"

"Sometimes I wish this would all just go away."

Lochlan turned to Anya with a raised eyebrow. "Are you telling me you don't need to know what's on Pallas?"

"No, I'm not. I want to solve this more than anything. But—"

"We can't stop now." Lochlan turned back to the harbour.

"Locky, can I tell you something?" Anya's voice sounded troubled.

"Sure, go ahead."

"My mother told me this story about my nine-year-old great-great-grandmother. Her name was Maja. She lived in Poland during the Second World War. They were Jewish, and a friend warned them the Nazis were arresting all Jews the next morning. So they fled. The family split, three one way and three the other.

"They planned to meet in two days and cross into Soviet-occupied territory. The other group didn't make it. They waited two days, but with the Nazis closing in, they … uh … they had to leave. They—"

Anya's head dropped as a single tear slid down her cheek. She looked up, her eyes met by Lochlan.

"Jesus! You okay?" Lochlan gave a reassuring hug.

Anya took a sip of Lochlan's Coke. "Yeah," she said, letting out a shaky breath before continuing. "They were soon caught by the Soviets, treated as criminals, and imprisoned in Siberia. The Soviets would tie three people together, mortally wounding one, then throw them all into the river to freeze or drown. Maja saw her brother die this way. She fell ill many times and almost froze to death, only surviving by befriending the guards, who still raped her several times. She eventually escaped through Asia and reached America in the 1950s. She would still talk to her family at night, knowing they were listening."

Anya sighed as she wiped away another tear. "That story's been haunting me lately." It almost came out as a sob.

"And if we find aliens on Pallas, you think this terror will return?"

"Yes, maybe even worse." Anya's voice tightened further. "And if they're hiding, that suggests intent."

"Look, if they're aliens, I think they'll be friendly." This was a lie; Lochlan had his own suspicions.

"And if they're not friendly?"

"Well … then it's better we find out sooner rather than later, don't you think?"

Anya nodded slowly. "Yeah, I guess so." She didn't sound the least bit assured.

They sat in silence.

***

Anya, Lochlan, Garrett, and a few MOT staff were again in the conference room, facing the big screen in unnerving silence. No one knew the world was about to change.

Garrett's phone rang loudly. "Yes … okay, thanks." He turned blank-faced to the others, who were staring in anticipation, all trying to read his expression. "They're sending the pictures through now. They haven't viewed them yet."

As all heads swung sharply back to the big screen, it ignited with the first picture.

Everyone slowly rose to their feet, staring in awe.

"Oh … my … God!" Garratt was the first to speak, his voice an odd mixture of wonder and fear. "What have we found?"

Anya's eyes widened in shock. She covered her mouth, as though something terrible had just happened or was about to.

Dropping her hands in apprehension, she took a deep breath and turned away to conceal her dismay.

Lochlan smiled triumphantly, caught up in the magic of the moment. He looked across at Anya, alarmed that she seemed so frightened.

The picture was earth-shattering – two large tubular, cylindrical, metallic objects sparkling in full sunlight.

"They're alien spaceships!" someone said.

The pictures were immediately posted online and went viral. It was front-page news, unstoppable, and ominous. Billions stopped to grapple with their significance, and the inevitable dawn of an uncertain new era.

Chapter 7   Secrets

A man in a plush office sat quietly, casually sipping his coffee. Thirty minutes after the discovery, a news headline flashed across his phone: *Alien Spaceships Discovered.*

"Ha-ha, another bullshit UFO story."

He snickered and readied himself for a good laugh as he opened the link. Coffee suddenly spluttered from his mouth, his phone dropped from his flaccid grip, and his scepticism instantly vanished. His shaking hand missed the table, splashing coffee on the floor.

He recovered his phone and flicked through the Pallas pictures, coffee dripping from his clothing.

He fumbled for the call button. "Get me the president … then wake him up!" He called out to his secretary just outside the door. "Get me Agent Riley immediately."

He breathed hard and slowly whispered to himself, "The day has finally come."

***

After the discovery, Garrett, Anya, and Lochlan turned off their phones, had dinner together, and stayed in a hotel to escape the media. No one could sleep.

The next morning, Garrett pushed through a gauntlet of overly excited news reporters outside his office building. Microphones and cameras swung his way as they all shouted questions at him. *Feels like I'm a suspect escaping from a crime scene.*

Although his mind buzzed, fully aware that nothing would ever be the same again, he was completely unprepared for what was to come.

In his office, two dark-suited men awaited, their solemn expressions indicating this was no social visit. Garrett cast a surprised and wary eye over them. "Can I help you?"

One suit closed the door and stood in front of it. The other watched, then turned to Garrett. He was a big man, taking up most of the space at one end of the desk. "Kevin," he firmly addressed with a strong American accent. "I'm Special Agent Riley from Section 3 of the United States National Security Organisation, NSO. This is Special Agent Russell."

Agent Russell nodded with a forced grin.

Agent Riley handed Garrett a business card. One side had a phone number, the other was blank. Garrett's eyes widened in bewilderment. "This is obviously about the Pallas photos. What's the problem?"

Agent Riley opened his coat and placed his hands on his hips. "You have done nothing illegal. However, we're requesting you, as well as Lochlan McLean and Anya Connell, to immediately accompany us to our Section 3 headquarters in the US for a briefing. We have a plane waiting, and we have an agreement from your Australian government."

"*WHAT!* ... now? ... No! ... I can't go! I mean ... um ... I have things to do," said a shaken Garrett.

"You'll be back in three days. Any business you have will have to wait, Mr Garrett. Those Pallas objects are not just scientific curiosities."

Garrett gave Agent Riley a hard stare. The last bit convinced him to go, although he wasn't sure he had any choice. "What's the plan?"

"Can you call and advise Dr McLean and Dr Connell to expect immediate contact from our agents? Convince them to accompany these agents and meet us at the airport. They can make phone calls on the way, but ask them not to talk to the media."

Garrett took a long look at the two men. "Can you verify your identity?"

On Agent Riley's suggestion, Garrett called the Australian Security Organisation's main phone number. After some bureaucratic transfers, he was convinced of their authenticity.

***

Anya, Lochlan, and Garrett pressed against their windows in curiosity as their black hummer approached a security gate through a razor wire perimeter, hidden in the US countryside. A stern guard snapped Agent Riley a recognition salute and lowered huge hydraulic barricades. The SUV passed security cameras and armed soldiers with guard dogs, then pulled into an empty spot near a windowless, concrete building.

"Looks about as welcoming as the KGB headquarters," Lochlan joked as they entered the building. Anya gave him a worried squint.

Agent Riley led them down a featureless hallway. Anya's heels echoed off the walls. They passed through a series of checkpoints, more armed guards, more cameras, and wall posters warning about cyberattacks and personal security.

They were introduced to Agent Powell, an African American in his fifties. His unkempt hair, crumpled T-shirt, and worn jeans gave the appearance of a nerdy professional student, isolated for too long from the outside world.

The five of them walked without a word through steel security doors, into a lift, and down to a briefing room in the belly of the building. There, the three baffled visitors were asked to wait and left alone until the arrival of another agent, Agent Haggett, who apparently was always late.

"What are we doing here, Kevin? What?" Lochlan asked.

"I don't know, but it's obviously something big."

Lochlan walked to a large wall mirror, which seemed completely out of place. "Hmm … interesting," he commented, casting a glance at the other two. He couldn't resist the urge to press his nose against it, blocking out the light around his face with his hands.

"See anything, Locky?" asked Anya with an amused grin.

"Yeah, there're a couple of guys watching us with machine guns."

"Yeah, right, you bullshit artist." Anya smiled wryly, then studied his face just to make sure he was joking.

They took up seats around the table.

"Why were we in such a big hurry to get here when we've now got to wait?" Lochlan asked.

"Seems a bit disorganised," Anya said.

"I know disorganisation when I see it," said Garrett. "This is tight security. They're probably watching us right now, gauging our attitude, briefing themselves."

Agent Riley and Agent Powell finally returned with Agent Haggett, a humourless, intense-looking man in desert camo fatigues with a marine-style flat-top.

Clutching a takeaway meal, Agent Haggett was obviously agitated. "I got caught at a fucking failed traffic light. All I could see was an endless string of white headlights and red taillights. The rough street kids with their squeegees had a field day."

He lifted his head, looking through everyone except Anya, whom he checked out with an uncouth stare.

Anya returned a "what are you looking at, arsehole?" frosty look.

Agent Haggett's eyes darted to his phone. "Let's get started. I've got a busy day."

Garrett looked at Agent Riley, expecting an explanation, apology, or anything. He got nothing.

Lochlan, always suspicious but now bordering on paranoid, suspected Agent Haggett's unusual behaviour must be for some unknown purpose.

Agents Riley, Powell, and Haggett sat across from the trio. Agent Riley's hand firmly rested on two zip-locked folders in front of him, as if guarding them. One was particularly old and worn.

"Thanks for coming." Agent Riley spoke softly and conversationally, as though trying to project an easy-going manner.

The trio exchanged a puzzled look. Lochlan wondered if they really had any choice.

Agent Riley continued. "Let's start … Oh, it almost slipped my mind. You'll need to sign a confidentiality and zero-footprint agreement. This agreement forbids discussion of, or leaving traces of, anything relating to this meeting. Breaking the agreement is punishable by imprisonment without trial."

The threesome checked each other's expressions – alarmed.

Agent Riley elaborated. "What we will reveal to you relates to global security. We've already completed security checks on you folks to make sure there are no skeletons in the closet."

Lochlan did a quick recollection of his life, focusing on the darker corners. He was sure the others were doing the same.

Garrett turned sharply to Agent Riley with a questioning eye. "Security checks? What sort of security checks?"

Agent Haggett flashed him a grin, but it wasn't obvious what merited it.

"Just the usual checks," answered Agent Riley.

"Like?" persisted Garrett with attitude.

"Checks to identify vulnerability to manipulation, blackmail, or coercion. DNA characteristics, criminal convictions, family backgrounds, education, financial and credit histories, residential addresses, internet, email and phone histories, employment and unemployment, litigation, whistleblowing, medical, drug, driving record, purchases, sexual preferences, travel, social activities. I don't want to be more specific. We use this information to assess your ability to conceal classified security material. Your information is protected, of course."

"You did all that in one day?" Lochlan queried. "That's difficult to believe."

Agent Riley opened the newer folder on the desk. "Let me see … Lochlan … warehouse break-in."

Anya shot Lochlan a glare. "Huh?"

"I was cleared of that."

"Kevin … stole a government bus and tried to outrun the police."

"You stole a bus, Kevin?" Anya blurted out, cracking a shocked smile.

"I was only twelve."

"Anya … assault on a boyfriend."

Anya's smile quickly dissipated.

"What?" Lochlan almost shouted, his eyes wide with intrigue.

"He was abusive, and I was also cleared."

"There are other, shall we say, *incidents*," Agent Riley stated.

This caused a bewildered silence until Garrett asked, "What happens if we don't sign?" There was more attitude in his voice.

"Then you are free to leave and go home. But you'll never find out why you're here."

Puzzled looks and more bewildered silence followed.

"We'd like to discuss it privately between ourselves," said Garrett, leaning forward.

Agent Riley gestured to a side door. "You can go in there."

"Is that room bugged too?" Lochlan was compelled to ask as he moved towards the door.

"None of these rooms are bugged, sir," said Agent Riley humourlessly.

The room was small and boxlike, with only a table and two chairs fixed to the floor. Lochlan continued to amuse himself by bug-hunting.

"I doubt you'd even recognise one," Garrett said.

"I can just feel a lens twitching."

"Don't worry about him, Kevin," Anya said. "He's like this quite often."

The little group congregated in the centre. Garrett gestured with his hands to move closer and talk softly.

"I'm not very good at keeping secrets," whispered Anya, her voice shaky. "And I'm afraid I might end up in some clandestine federal prison. Maybe we need lawyers."

"If we just go home," Garrett said, "do you really think they'll leave us alone?"

"I'd always be sleeping with one eye open," Lochlan said.

They stood silently, looking at each other. Lochlan rubbed his mouth and blinked several times.

"Locky?"

"Look, we can't just go home."

Anya hesitated for a second, then deliberated for another. "You're right. After all we've been through."

Their eyes shifted expectantly to Garrett, who was scratching his head. He slowly nodded, then muttered an unconvincing, "Okay. Let's sign."

They returned to find Agent Riley alone, facing the other way, talking on his phone. His voice was low but clearly audible. "The situation is under control, Mr President. sir, in my opinion—" Agent Riley slowly turned. "They're back. I'll call later." He pushed the papers towards them. "Read the section 'penalties for disclosure' carefully. Then we can start." He somehow knew of their decision to sign.

Agent Riley waited for the signatures, then began. "We knew nothing about the two spaceships on Pallas, but we're certain they're a threat to the future of the human race ... to the entire planet." Agent Riley's troubled face left no doubt about the accuracy of his words.

Lochlan's eyes widened, Anya's face paled, and Garrett blew out his cheeks. They gaped at Agent Riley for an explanation.

"You're looking at me as if I'm crazy. Well, I'm not. From now on, you'll be constantly doubting mankind's future."

"M-mankind's future?" Lochlan had to check.

"Oh yes," Agent Riley quickly confirmed. "Mankind's future."

"I knew it. I … I just knew it," said Anya.

Agent Riley turned on a large screen. "This is your MOT photo of Pallas, showing two alien spaceships."

The trio was silent, listening, transfixed.

"Now, look at this picture."

Lochlan let out a confused groan. Garrett raised his head. Anya grabbed a glass of water, fumbling it to her lips.

Garrett was the first to recover. "It's … it's one of the spaceships taken from the surface of Pallas, but … but you said you knew nothing about them?"

"This object is *not* on Pallas," Agent Riley revealed. "It was discovered on the *Moon*, twenty years ago."

Anya swallowed half her drink, almost choking. The other half spilled over the table. Lochlan sucked in a deep breath. Garrett's eyes widened and bounced between Riley, Anya, and Lochlan. Leaden silence endured until one of them cried out, "The Moon!"

Agent Riley watched them curiously, offering no immediate response. Eventually, he confirmed, "Yes, the Moon."

He opened the older folder, almost reverently, and slowly slid it across the table without releasing it. Lochlan craned his neck with some annoyance to look over Agent Riley's hand. The trio eyed the folder eagerly.

"ALIEN MOON-SHIP – TOP-SECRET" was clearly visible in large lettering at the top of the first page. Several sections of smaller text below were circled in red: … "hidden in a deep crater" … "one million years ago" … "valuable alien technology" … "highly weaponised" … "extremely dangerous" …

Agent Riley retracted the folder and closed it.

"Hang on a minute!" protested Garrett. "We're still reading it."

"As the title states, it's top-secret."

The questions poured out.

"What are you telling us?" Garrett asked.

"What does all this mean?" Anya asked.

"Are we at war with aliens?" Lochlan asked.

"Not yet …" Agent Riley replied. "A robotic mining pod discovered this alien spaceship while mapping the floor of a large crater near the lunar south pole. These craters are deep and always in icy darkness, so this discovery was extremely fortunate. We estimated it landed a million years ago."

Agent Riley paused as three stunned faces glared at him with unsettling intensity. He slowly continued. "Because of potential dangers, the ship was kept and studied on the Moon for the first five years."

"Dangers?" asked Garrett.

"Imagine a nineteenth-century scientist studying a nuclear weapon. If he disassembles it without blowing himself up, the radiation would kill him along with everybody else. Also, there may have been booby traps, dangerous systems, weapons, or even an auto-destruct. But progress was too slow, so we brought parts of the ship to Earth. Agent Powell can explain things better. He spent two months on the Moon in the early stages, and he's been part of the study team ever since."

The dumbfounded visitors shifted in their seats to face Agent Powell.

Lochlan noticed Anya still holding her empty glass, frozen midway between her mouth and the table. He touched her shoulder. "It's empty," he said.

"Oh …" Anya grinned weakly, gently placing the glass on the table. "Thanks."

Agent Powell cleared his throat and, in a casual voice, said. "We still have over 150 scientists and engineers masquerading as miners at a supposedly disease-infected camp on the Moon. They're covertly studying what's left of the Moon-ship. On Earth, there are tens of thousands of researchers. To say 'progress is very slow' would be a gross overstatement. We're still neophytes, probing the very limits of what is knowable."

The visitors hung on every word. Agent Powell briefly paused to allow them to take it all in. "The ship was concealed and completely intact. So, it had to be functioning when it landed, after which everything shut down.

"It's possible that the Moon-ship was hibernating. A dormant crypt, waiting to be activated by some event or signal. How this Moon-ship relates to the two spaceships you found on Pallas, we don't know.

"What we do know is the Moon-ship carried weapons that posed an existential threat to our planet. And it's likely that the two identical spaceships on Pallas pose the same threat that—"

"That's about as far as we can go." Agent Riley jumped in as if the words came out of Agent Powell's mouth.

The trio turned to Agent Riley with bewildered looks.

"Come on, mate," Garrett said in a firm voice. "What else can you tell us?"

"You can't stop there," Anya added.

"Yeah, this is not where we want to end," Lochlan said.

Agent Riley waited for a moment, then gently nodded to Agent Powell to continue. "Remember, Agent Powell," he said, "they have no security classification."

"Okay. Um … the spaceship's hull, especially the front ablation shield, showed considerable ionisation and corrosion from cosmic radiation and collisions with high-speed space hydrogen, dust, and micrometeoroids. Based on this, we estimated the ship had been travelling at a very high speed for about six hundred million Earth years."

"Six hundred million years!" The words burst out of Lochlan in disbelief. "How is that even possible?"

Again, Agent Riley cut off further discussions.

"Tell me," pressed Garrett, "just how long do you think you'll be able to keep all of this a secret? The public has a right to know."

"And how will they find out, Kevin? From you?" asked the late-arriving Agent Haggett, who had been sitting at the end of the table, tapping on his computer, and making the odd sotto voce comment to no one. He couldn't have looked more bored. Slowly raising his head, he gave the trio his full attention for the first time. The underlighting from his computer screen made his face appear creepy.

Garrett gave a penetrating stare; his patience was clearly wearing thin. Agent Haggett, unperturbed, stood up, cracked his knuckles, and wandered around the table. "Your Pallas pictures show we have an enormous problem." He glared at the trio like a general intimidating new recruits and expecting an explanation for a misdeed. "There are movement marks around your Pallas spaceships, so the occupants are active, unlike the Moon site."

Agent Haggett came up behind Garrett, leaning close to his ear as if he were about to impart some wisdom. Instead, he contemptuously demanded, "We want all your data and the use of your telescope for further study of Pallas."

Garrett turned slowly in his chair, his eyes narrowing. He locked Agent Haggett with a very defiant and challenging stare, and in his broad Australian accent, he made his feelings clear. "You've got *Buckley's chance* of getting my telescope with that bloody attitude, mate!"

Agent Haggett continued his tough guy demeanour as if Garrett hadn't spoken. "Your discovery was a complete surprise to us."

"Don't mention it," Lochlan said.

Agent Haggett gave Lochlan a long look, then continued. "And recklessly circulating your Pallas photos on the internet threw our security protocols out the window, revealed to the world there are aliens on our doorstep, and probably alerted these aliens to the fact we know they're there. If the public ever finds out these beings are hostile and they were once on the Moon, we'll have a mass panic. You've put us all in unimaginable peril."

The trio stared at Agent Haggett with worried wonder on their faces.

"Are you accusing us of something?" asked Anya.

Agent Haggett ignored the question and continued to assault them with dire predictions about their discovery. "The public has enough to worry about with China threatening a world war over Taiwan. Other countries are sceptical of our story about the Moon epidemic. We even found a Chinese spy robot creeping around five kilometres from our Moon-ship site. And cyberhacks are everywhere."

"Well," commented Garrett with a thin, sarcastic smile. "You might think jewels in a safe are protected, but thieves know jewels are kept in safes."

Agent Haggett shot Garrett a dark look and wandered around the table towards him. "Now that you're here, we can shut this thing down, sit on as much information as possible, and not share it with our enemies." He stopped very close to Garrett's blindside with an undecipherable smirk, like he was about to either kiss or murder him. He placed a hand on Garrett's shoulder. "So, we need to restrict all MOT information about Pallas being distributed to the public."

Garrett stared at Agent Haggett's hand until it dropped limply. "You can take that suggestion back to the shit hole it came from," he growled.

"I can see you're not a team player," Agent Haggett said. "So, you're not going to cooperate with us, Kevin?" The last word sounded threatening.

Lochlan knew Garrett was not the type to be intimidated, and certainly not by this guy. He knew what was coming.

Garrett looked up at Agent Haggett and forcefully stated, "Not while you're being such a big arsehole, mate."

Agent Haggett continued unruffled. "You served in Saudi Arabia with the Australian military forces as an intelligence officer."

Garrett stiffened while holding Agent Haggett's stare.

"You and a colleague were captured, but only you survived."

Garrett didn't respond.

"Why was that, Kevin? Why you and not him? Did they consider you in some way more useful to them alive?"

Silence from Garrett.

"Do you need me to repeat the question?"

Garrett pushed his chair back and stood up, anger bubbling over, blazing eyes locked on the man in front of him. "None of your bloody business, mate." The moment froze as Garrett looked ready for the final showdown.

Agent Haggett raised his hands and stepped back. "Okay, Kevin. Stay cool."

Lochlan noticed Agent Riley was now a little uneasy. There was something not quite right about this Agent Haggett guy. Lochlan glanced at Anya, knowing she would be stressed out – not only because their big discovery was a threat to the entire world but also about the way this meeting was progressing. She caught Lochlan's glance and gave a "let's get the hell out of here" head and eye motion.

Lochlan nodded back.

Just then, Garrett turned sharply to Agent Riley with a rebellious stare. "You know what?" he said, letting it hang there for a few seconds. "I don't have to listen to this crap anymore. I'm—"

"Let's have a coffee break before we do anything else," Agent Riley quickly suggested, leaping to his feet and gesturing to the door. The first trace of a genuine smile crossed his face. It was a conciliatory one at that.

Lochlan quickly agreed to the coffee, worried that Garrett was about to tell Agent Riley to "fuck your coffee".

An expressionless Agent Haggett propped open the door. Garrett passed with a cold, lethal stare. Lochlan's was blank. As Anya approached, Agent Haggett's eyes wandered down her lean figure. Pitched to her ears only, he uttered a sound as if he were about to say something. But Anya gave him a wide berth, shooting past with a "don't even try it, arsehole" chilling glare.

Agent Haggett's eyes followed her with an amused expression that implied "yes, I am an arsehole".

Sensing something, Lochlan glanced back to see Agent Riley whispering to Agent Haggett with a serious look. Lochlan had already judged that Agent Haggett didn't quite fit in and suspected he was just a bad cop plant.

When the meeting resumed, Agent Riley eagerly informed them that Agent Haggett had left for another engagement.

"So, the man of mystery has departed," said Lochlan with his characteristic sarcastic grin.

Agent Riley returned a brief humorous grunt and asked, "Do you folks have any questions?"

Now it's good cop time, reasoned Lochlan.

"Can you tell us more about the Moon-ship?" asked Anya.

Agent Riley nodded to Agent Powell to answer. "When I first saw the ship, I gaped in superstitious awe at the huge amount of potential knowledge that lay only a few metres from me. This made it look evil, threatening, and unimaginably powerful, like a sleeping beast about to wake at any moment and destroy the world. It was the only time I could hear my heartbeat.

"It was days before I was allowed to touch it. I wondered if I'd recognise the purpose of anything I saw, but I didn't. Well, not immediately. Everything was so alien. The military—"

Agent Riley coughed delicately.

Garrett's eyes switched to Agent Riley. "You're not stopping now, are you?"

"What are you not telling us?" Lochlan added. "What was the ship made of?"

"Tell us about the occupants," Anya also added.

A hesitant nod from Agent Riley allowed Agent Powell to continue.

"The outer shell was a super hard aggregated nanorod material. The first investigators could see the outline of a door but couldn't open it. It took them a week to thermally cut through it. Inside was a gold mine of extraterrestrial artefacts, including over eight hundred deactivated humanoid robots."

"Robots!" Anya's knee bounced up and down. Lochlan placed his hand on her knee to stop it. "Thanks," she said.

"They were probably the crew, not the cargo," Agent Powell said.

Anya took a nervous breath and asked, "Was there anything that resembled life?"

"No. The radiation and bremsstrahlung shielding were not designed to protect any life forms. The ship was like a giant computer. There was very little free space."

For Lochlan, the truth about Pallas had finally surfaced, and the evidence was there in front of him – in the pictures and in this whole amazing story. But he knew that for Anya, it was a whole lot more. Despite her calm public persona, he knew this was exactly what she feared. Sensing her discomfort, he asked, "You okay?"

"Yeah, I'm fine." Anya sounded so upbeat, and her smile was so convincing that Lochlan accepted her response, even though her eyes were so troubled.

Agent Riley abruptly concluded the meeting and said, "You know, I'd like to get to know you folks better."

The trio looked at each other, concerned, then turned back to Agent Riley for clarification.

"That's an employment invitation."

Lochlan's eyes widened in shock. "You've gotta be kidding me, right?"

"I'll take that as a yes," said Agent Riley. "We need to build new radio and telescopic stations to monitor Pallas."

After some hesitation, Lochlan shrugged and said, "What the heck? That sounds too good to miss."

Anya stared at him as if he were crazy. "I think you're getting a bit ahead of yourself, Locky. We don't know enough about all of this yet."

"What have we got to lose?" Lochlan gave a persuasive smile. "But—"

"It's a great opportunity. Come on, Anya." Lochlan gave her *the look*.

Anya slowly forced an artificial smile. "Oh, what the hell," she murmured, "count me in." Then, immediately losing her smile, she added, "I better not regret this, Locky."

Garrett appeared to be hesitating. Lochlan watched him, hoping he would accept but not thinking he would. "I'll let you know in forty-eight hours," Garrett said.

"I'll call you," Agent Riley replied. "And don't worry about Agent Haggett. You'll never see him again."

As they were being ushered out of the building, Lochlan casually glanced at a small group passing in the hallway. One of them looked familiar. It took a moment to strike him. *That's the farmer from the SETI forum.* He continued walking, almost in a state of shock, resisting a strong urge to look back. He waited until they were well clear of the building before telling Anya and Garrett, his voice slightly quivering.

Anya burst out a shocked laugh. "So, they were on to us."

"I don't think so; otherwise, they would've stopped us long ago."

"Well, they must have been onto someone," Anya replied.

"Let's get the hell out of here while we can," Garrett said.

"Yeah," agreed Anya, shooting a questioning glare at Lochlan that said "what the hell have you got me into?"

Chapter 8   Reactions

Apprehension and fear swept the Earth. Even without knowledge of the Moon-ship, the world was all too aware of the implications of extraterrestrials secretly taking up residence in the solar system. But the media loved it. "People of Earth, sorry to disturb your slumber, but something out there has been watching us for some time."

Celebrity scientists popped up everywhere, making predictions. Many travelled on lecture tours postulating about who or what they are; where they come from; what they would look like; how long they have been watching us; how will we communicate with them; will they help us live longer.

"The aliens must be hostile," claimed some alien experts. "Intelligence demands a large brain, which requires a large calorie intake, which requires a species to be carnivorous, which requires predatory behaviour, which requires aggressive instincts."

"The aliens must be friendly," claimed other alien experts. "Any spacefaring civilisation controls great destructive powers. They must have evolved beyond any brutal compulsions, otherwise they would have wiped themselves out. They will teach us a tremendous amount about science, the arts, and the humanities."

"The aliens are here to study us," others claimed. "They're forbidden to contact us. Otherwise, they would have done so by now. They're not here to colonise Earth; they're too biologically incompatible. They're not here to enslave us; automation is better.

They're not here for our oceans or raw materials; these are more readily available elsewhere. And they aren't here for our women; they have their own."

"It's bad news no matter what the reason for them being here," claimed another group. "Being discovered by a technologically superior alien civilisation means we've lost our destiny and uniqueness; our society will demoralise and eventually collapse; modern humans in Europe led to the end of the Neanderthals; farming communities resulted in the decline of hunter-gatherer cultures; and industrialisation caused the decay of pre-industrial civilisations."

Many new movies were scripted around alien lovers, aliens in skin suits, government cover-ups, secret alien treaties, abductions, alien invasions, and other similar themes. Alien welcoming groups held ET dress parties and even end-of-world festivals. Hawkers had a field day selling alien glowing green heads, ray guns, four-eyed mugs, eight-legged toys, cute teddy bears, and other alien products.

Science funding and global stock markets crashed. The aliens would give away undreamed knowledge and technology and all the universe's secrets for free or obliterate everything.

Despite initial concerns about the collapse of religion, theologians discovered their scriptures allowed for the coming of aliens after all, and therefore people's faith should be unaltered. However, secretly, they feared that an advanced alien religion would triumph over the Earthcentric ones.

The Moon-ship remained top-secret, safeguarded by the threat of imprisonment. The authorities made sure any information breaches were lost in the many crackpot stories being told.

Meanwhile, the question of who should represent humanity remained unresolved. Governments and corporations with space capabilities discussed the aliens in terms of their own interests. Concerns about the monopolisation of alien technology increased global tensions and led to fierce competition to be the first to fly a spaceship to Pallas. The United Nations proposed an international council to decide Earth's foreign policy and representation, but it received scant support.

Chapter 9   Something Bigger

*A young girl running with her mother. Nazis, Soviets, no …
they're aliens chasing; death is coming.* Anya, momentarily lost in a
mental flashback to last night's nightmare, quietly snapped out of
it. She discreetly looked around, relieved that Lochlan and Agent
Powell had not noticed her.

"From our limited but not unintelligible comprehension," said
Agent Powell during a second meeting with Lochlan and Anya at
Section 3 of NSO, "the Moon-ship was not built for exploration.
It was built for planetary destruction."

Anya stiffened. This was exactly what she feared. This was
exactly what her secret nightmares were all about.

"You mean it had cannons, bombs, a secret army?" asked
Lochlan.

"No, they aren't that primitive," Agent Powell replied
flippantly with an amused grin. But Anya wasn't amused. From
her expression, she wasn't even close.

"Sorry, Anya. I didn't mean to, um …" Agent Powell gave
a sympathetic grin, then continued. "The Moon-ship had laser
weapons for space combat, and we found laser rifles inside. These
used a property of light we didn't even know about. But the
real threat was the equipment it carried. We believe they were
components to assemble a relativistic impact weapon that could
bombard and destroy any planet from its moon."

Anya again stiffened. "Is … is that why the ship was on the Moon?" Her grim expression was becoming permanent.

"It's likely, and the occupants were waiting for an activation to begin construction."

"If they had a big, planet-destroying weapon," Lochlan said, "then why would they have laser rifles?"

"We don't know. Maybe they have lots of internal conflicts."

"How could the ship still be functional after six hundred million years of space travel?" Lochlan asked with a slight tone of disbelief.

"The ship was constantly renewed to repair damage."

Anya shook her head. "You mean these renewals can keep the ship operational forever?"

"No, not forever. No renewal process is perfect. Undetectable errors, no matter how slight, will worsen over time, especially if they're in the control system itself. After six hundred million years of exposure to cosmic background radiation and thousands of renewals, some systems may not work properly or even at all. Whoever or whatever built these ships couldn't have anticipated such a long journey. Even though their technology is orders of magnitude above our own, their machines, weapons, and systems could be irreparably damaged."

"Could they be doing a renewal on Pallas?" Anya asked.

"We don't know."

Lochlan scratched his head. "Was there something like a black box recorder on the Moon-ship?"

"Well …" Agent Powell lowered his eyes and hesitated. "I'm not sure I should even be mentioning this, but we think we've found data storage devices or DSDs."

Lochlan's and Anya's eyes widened and stared at Agent Powell blankly.

"If we could read that," said Lochlan, his voice full of awe, "imagine the knowledge we could learn."

"All their history, science, and technology." Anya's voice was also full of awe.

Agent Powell leaned back. "I can't reveal more."

Anya asked the question that had been on her mind for some time. "Is there any evidence that the Pallas ships had contact with the Moon-ship?"

Agent Powell shook his head. "No." His expression then darkened. "But there is something else you should know." He glanced back and forth between them, as if he were about to reveal something big.

"We believe there's another much larger spaceship out there somewhere."

Anya made several choking noises, while Lochlan gave a short, nervous laugh.

Agent Powell continued. "The space weathering on only one side of the Moon-ship and the fixings on the hull indicate that for most of its journey through space, it was fixed to a much larger ship – a mothership. Your Pallas spaceships were also carried by it."

"Maybe the Moon-ship and the two Pallas ships are waiting for this mothership?" Lochlan asked.

Agent Powell did not respond.

All the blood in Anya's face had drained. Emotion filled her. She took a ragged breath. "All this, and we still don't know what they're doing on Pallas." She slumped in her seat then hesitantly asked the question she had been dreading. "And how will they respond now that we've discovered them?" She didn't sound like she wanted an answer.

No one gave her one. Anya knew the nightmare had only just begun.

Chapter 10   Threat of World War

As earth-shattering as the Pallas discovery was, incredibly, it had done nothing to reduce the risk of a major war between long-standing rival powers.

The totalitarian nations of China, Russia, Turkey, and Pakistan, brought together by a common goal of territorial ambitions and forming a new, yet undefined, world order, have formed a loose partnership of strategic convenience known as the "club of monocracies". Each one, led by the cult of a single personality, regarded the democracies as their common enemy.

China's president, Shen Yin, believed success in his expansionist pursuits would dampen domestic problems and prolong his leadership. An arrest of Chinese "fishermen" in Japanese waters spiralled into a series of naval and aerial confrontations. China threatened to teach Vietnam a lesson after it installed advanced US defence weaponry along its northern border.

The main danger was Taiwan, where China threatened invasion. "We can win a war with anyone, including the US. So, we dare them to interfere."

Taiwan's defiant president, Chen Yung-fu, responded. "We have a distinct Taiwanese culture, and we don't feel any attachment to Communist China. President Yin believes the Han Chinese are the superior race, and all of East Asia should tremble and kowtow to Beijing's divine authority. We'll fight to the last person to preserve our existence."

Trying to firm up support, President Chen Yung-fu warned the US president, Chuck Brookes, during a heated phone discussion, "President Yin will risk a conflict, even if he's not sure about the outcome. And the loss of Taiwan would upend the world's geopolitical landscape."

***

President Chuck Brookes and recently appointed US Defence Secretary Terry Dittmar stood facing each other across a shiny desk, empty except for a single phone. Weak sunlight filtered through the windows, giving the room the appearance of a cathedral's nave.

"So, what you're telling me, Chuck," said Dittmar, "is that Taiwan wants us to provoke China to draw some fire away from itself?"

"I'm not sure I'd put it that way, Terry," said President Brookes.

"Considering what Taiwan has to lose, it's not an unreasonable request," Dittmar said bluntly. "We've already moved up our surface and submarine fleets. And we've warned China we'll seize their assets if they invade."

A long, tense look passed between them.

"I know I hauled you out of your plush business job for this, and I know you want to go back there as soon as possible. But believe me, you're the best man for the job, and one of the few people whose judgements I trust. And that goes back to our tennis days."

"In this conflict, the most committed will win. A little more provocation would show the Chinese we're united and strong," Dittmar said forcefully, even insistently.

Another tense look between them.

"I haven't given up on a conciliatory outcome."

Dittmar nodded. He knew better than to try to talk him out of anything at this stage. But he also knew he'd get there in the end. He always did.

***

The problems around Taiwan encouraged tensions elsewhere.

Russia's president, Zaur Donskoy, put aside, at least for the time being, his country's deep anxieties over China's slow encroachment from the south and identified a strategic advantage in temporarily aligning with China against the democracies.

"Fifty years ago, NATO prevented our nationalist leader, President Putin, from reclaiming our eastern empire," Donskoy said. "They won't stop us this time."

Large Russian and NATO military forces faced each other across the borders of the Baltic States, Ukraine, and Poland.

President Sarper Aytekin of Turkey slowly implemented neo-Islamic autocratic rule, and the country descended into ethnic terrorism, corruption, and despotism. He blamed the democracies and ethnic minorities for Turkey's problems, and promised to return to the glory days of the Ottoman Empire and unite all Turkic speaking people.

Indian and Pakistani rivalry over Kashmir was again at a flashpoint. Encouraged by Chinese support, Pakistan promised to solve the problem by force. Indian fighter jets scrambled on a regular basis against Pakistani jets nearing their airspace. Muslim insurgencies in India were at their highest levels in decades.

Iran was also aligning with the club of monocracies after China promised military support against Israel, Saudi Arabia, and Egypt.

Hostilities in the Taiwan Strait could easily trigger a series of major conflicts, leading to a world war between democracies and monocracies. This possibility was given little consideration by the Chinese, whose wargame scenarios were based on Taiwan falling in two days. A fait accompli victory. Thereafter, any attempt to retake Taiwan would have enormous attrition costs.

"The US public," concluded China's President Yin, "will accept that Taiwan is lost and demand peace talks. The US will withdraw from Asia, not unlike the 1970s."

***

Unbeknown to the Chinese, their wargame scenarios were anachronistic, as General Fields explained to Secretary Terry Dittmar and the deputy defence secretary. "After twenty years of intensive study of the alien Moon-ship, we are now ready to deploy some outstanding alien-based weapons."

"And, general, that interests me because?"

"Well, Mr Secretary," said Fields, his voice steady and convincing, "if we could deploy our laser weapons on Taiwan's coastline, it would end any Chinese invasion. It's as simple as that. The president's approval is the only thing stopping us."

A slight frown appeared on the deputy defence secretary's face. "The president has prohibited alien weapons outside of the US homeland. If they were to fall into enemy hands, then not only would we lose the military advantage, but it would confirm what all US presidents have constantly denied: that we're hiding alien artefacts."

Dittmar looked at General Fields deeply. "I was told three years ago, before I knew about the Moon-ship, that there were aliens on Pallas. I discounted it as fantasy, not accepting the evidence." He turned to the deputy defence secretary. "Denying the existence of these alien artefacts be damned; preventing World War III is more important." He turned back to General Fields. "I need to get the president's approval for what exactly, general? And for heaven's sake, keep it simple; don't get technical on me."

***

"Have you decided on a strategy to defuse this Taiwanese crisis, Chuck?" Dittmar asked.

The president walked slowly to the window behind his desk, rubbing his hand along his arm. "No, not yet," he said simply and bleakly, without turning. He looked off into the distance. Dittmar could see he was seriously grappling for a solution.

"We have to be honest with ourselves," Dittmar said. "Without direct involvement, we're just encouraging China. They won't stop until they're forced to. They'll claim territorial waters over our undersea cables and Taiwan's strategic position, and that's disastrous for business."

"Yes, Terry, I know." The president slowly turned, a strained expression on his face. "But is maintaining the current global status quo worth a possible out-of-control nuclear war?"

"It's not just Taiwan," said Dittmar, his haggard and drawn face tightening. "The world will change as we know it."

The president responded sharply. "I'd be willing to actively defend Taiwan if I were sure we would win quickly, before possible escalation."

"That's the reason I've come here to see you."

The president eyed Dittmar curiously. "Well, go on."

"General Fields just informed me that our military has a newly developed weapon." Dittmar pulled out his phone and read. "A photon tunnelling laser weapon system or LaWS, developed from the alien Moon-ship. It's ready to be used in Taiwan. I'm told it'll destroy the entire Chinese invasion force in thirty seconds."

President Brookes stared in shocked silence.

Dittmar's hooked eyebrows arched. "Chuck, this is just what we need."

The president walked to the window, this time in deep concentration. He turned quickly, enthusiasm all over his face. "This means we can defend Taiwan without committing our entire defence force and end the show before it starts."

"We need to act quickly, Chuck."

"Yes, I know." After a short pause, he went on. "If we deploy these weapons, an *absolute condition* must be that they remain a complete secret from everyone, including the Taiwanese. And they must be immediately removable under any situation. We must be able to deny that this technology exists. This is just as critical as the preservation of Taiwan itself." He gave Dittmar a hard, penetrating look. "Can you give me these assurances, Terry?"

"That's exactly what I'm about to explain. The escape route will be via low-flying helicopters and submarines off Taiwan's south-east coast."

"And you're recommending we use these weapons?"

"Yes," answered Dittmar with calm confidence.

"Good. That's good, Terry."

President Brookes appeared thrilled at the sudden change in circumstances. He took a long breath and stiffened as his expression changed to that of the hard-arsed leader of the free world. "Okay," he said, standing sternly. "You have my authorisation to *deploy* these alien weapons on Taiwanese soil. But I will *only* authorise their use as an absolute last resort."

Dittmar allowed himself a hint of a smile. "Yes, Mr President."

*****

High in the upper stratosphere just east of Taiwan, a stealthy, autonomous airship with super-surveillance sensors communicated with the US military by undetectable lasers along an ionised-air waveguide.

Deployed in the rugged Chung-yang Shan mountains overlooking Taiwan's western coastline facing China were the most lethal alien weapons of all – two 200 MW high-energy LaWS. Using the stored energy in hafnium's metastable isomer nuclei to instantly release an intensive gamma-ray laser burst, these LaWS could eliminate any number of incoming threats. A nine-metre diameter, hemispherical, molecularly manufactured armoured encasement made each LaWS indestructible against conventional weapons.

The LaWS and encasements could be quickly disassembled and helicoptered to autonomous submarines off the south and east Taiwanese coasts. The submarine's armour, photonic 3D integrated circuits, and stealth operation rendered them virtually unassailable.

After weeks of worsening rhetoric and heightened tensions, the club of monocracies agreed to a bold plan: swiftly occupy the contested territories with overwhelming force while not directly threatening the main powers, then sue for peace.

Once China established a secure beachhead on Taiwan, Russia would invade Ukraine. Turkey would invade Iraq and Syria with assistance from Chinese troops. Pakistan would attack southern Kashmir and South Tibet, also with assistance from Chinese troops. Iran would remain neutral, with the option of occupying parts of Iraq.

The plan was risky. Although all forces had a "no nuclear first" policy, conditions could easily change and quickly escalate. Not since World War I have military alliances been so dangerous.

As the world neared a global war, it was still unaware that a discovery made seven months earlier represented an extinction threat so serious that the only chance of survival was a united planetary defence. President Brookes considered informing China's President Yin about the Moon-ship to avoid war, but Dittmar convinced him otherwise. "Let me tell you what this Yin will do," Dittmar told Brookes. "If he thinks the new weapons have not been deployed, he'll immediately attack. And if he thinks they have been deployed, he'll try to capture them."

President Yin, although aware that China had never won an offensive war in over five hundred years, even against lesser opponents, was now confident enough to roll the dice. He implemented a naval and aerial blockade of Taiwan while simultaneously launching a massive pre-emptive attack on Taiwan's military facilities in preparation for an invasion.

Arrest warrants for Taiwanese officials were issued. Having passed the point of no return, Yin strangely hesitated. Something flickered in his mind; something missed. Doubt? Regret? He shook it off.

Next came the cyberattacks. Operators on both sides choked on their coffee as their screens suddenly turned static, forcing a switch to more secure but less informative systems. Then satellite-destroying missiles eliminated orbital surveillance intelligence for each side. Only the US stealth airship remained operational, making everything below stand out like a well-lit Christmas tree.

Yin, told that Taiwan's defences had been neutralised and the blockade was holding, launched the first wave of airborne and amphibious forces. However, large numbers of Taiwanese mobile strike missiles and sea mines survived, causing heavy Chinese losses and delays. Short-range missiles targeted Chinese drones and prevented helicopters from dispatching storm troopers behind enemy lines.

President Yin, furious when the first wave was aborted, was delighted with reports from the invasion fleet's admiral that the path was now cleared for the second amphibious wave, which carried the main force. A secure landing was expected within eight hours.

It was eight hours that would bring the world to the brink of an all-out nuclear war.

Yin was greatly concerned to hear that enemy submarines off Taiwan's south and east coasts had destroyed a large part of their blockading force. Panicking, thinking that this could be part of an elaborate counteroffensive by foreign forces, Yin widened his flanks by sieging the Senkaku Islands, an act of aggression against Japan. He escalated further by attacking Japanese freighters and US carrier groups outside the war zone. The US and Japan countered with missile attacks on China's Paracel and Spratly

Islands military bases. Chinese shipping through the Strait of Malacca was blocked.

General Fields, stressed and frustrated by the lack of US action, called Secretary Dittmar. "Terry, the situation is desperate. You need to get the president to be presidential and authorise the use of these goddam LaWS."

"He's aware that this matter needs urgent attention, general."

"C'mon, for Chrissakes. Does he? Tell him we can't wait. Another six hours, and all weapons will have to be evacuated."

Dittmar grimaced, but his voice stayed cool. "Keep us informed. Thank you, general."

President Yin, alarmed at the conflict's escalation, desperately sought support from his club of monocracies partners. Advising them that China was close to landing on Taiwan, he called on them to start their attacks as planned. However, Russia, Turkey, and Pakistan decided to wait for evidence of a secure landing before entering the conflict.

As large concentrations of opposing forces assembled across borders, the enormous advantage of a pre-emptive nuclear strike against vulnerable front line troops and military assets became obvious. Little thought was given to the risk that such a strike could quickly escalate into a full strategic nuclear exchange.

Israel, recognising the danger, warned that it would massively retaliate by "all means available". India claimed its retaliatory nuclear weapons would survive any attack by Pakistan and China. Russia's nuclear arsenal was "ready to go". And NATO announced that its military doctrine justified retaliatory nuclear weapons to prevent defeat.

The US confirmed its extended deterrence commitment to NATO and Quad, warning that "any nuclear attack on the US or its allies will be met with a full retaliatory response."

Suddenly, the prospect of an all-out global nuclear war was very real.

Meanwhile, the second wave of the Chinese invasion fleet continued unabated.

President Yin was updated: "Our invasion fleet is nearing Taiwan's west coast. Losses are manageable." Yin suspected the real situation was worse.

Taiwan's President Yung-fu updated President Brookes. "The Taiwanese Army is preparing for a ground battle, but we can't win against the might of China."

President Yin, believing a landing and final victory were now assured, was seemingly unaware of the global catastrophe he risked. He again called for his partners to start their invasions. They instead chose to wait.

India prepared for its own nuclear strike against Pakistani and Chinese forces as soon as they crossed the border. Japan announced its submarines would survive any nuclear attack, and they carried aerosolised biological weapons targeting Chinese major cities. Russia broadcast a message claiming that mounting threats from NATO would lead to total war, and it had nuclear-armed submarines deep under the Arctic ice and off the US coast. Russia was deeply worried it would not detect a first strike from US stealth missiles and considered its own pre-emptive options.

The US president was advised that "everyone has an itchy finger on the button, and all that's needed for a global nuclear shootout is a nervous hand".

Some US news outlets opposed defending Taiwan. "Taiwan is more important to China than to us. It makes no sense to risk our existence." However, national pride was now in control.

China ordered its Moon and Martian stations to break contact with other stations and find whatever weapons they could. Iran confirmed its neutrality and called for calm.

Off Scotland's western coast, the Royal Navy dropped warning depth charges to force an unknown submarine out of territorial waters.

"Captain," said the Russian submarine's second-in-command, "we're under attack. You must follow orders and turn the key."

"I want goddam confirmation from fleet command before I kill half the planet!"

Around them stood their terror-stricken crew.

"Captain, this is not a request. It's procedure. Comms cannot contact fleet command; they've probably been wiped out."

"I told you. I want goddam confirmation."

"Turn the key, captain. *Now.*"

The captain turned to see a pistol pointed at him.

"Now, captain!"

***

In Washington, the Sun peeked out over the monument, a new day. Defence Secretary Dittmar checked on his wife. *Still asleep. If a war starts, it's better she dies peacefully.*

He stepped into the study, stretched, scratched his torso, and sat down with his phone. A video call came through.

"Yes, General Fields," he said. "I guess I'm not the only one who's been up all night."

"An hour ago, a Russian submarine off the Scottish coast came dangerously close to launching a nuclear strike. It was only prevented by a vigilant captain and last-minute confirmation from fleet command that they weren't being attacked."

Dittmar appeared a little shaken. "Anything else, General Fields?"

"Yes. We have to evacuate the lasers in two hours, Terry, unless the president authorises their use."

"He's fully up to date with the situation, general."

"Beggin' your pardon, Mr Secretary, but I don't think he is. Conventional weapons won't stop the Chinese. The goddam fuse is burning. What's he waiting for?" Fields brazenly stared at Dittmar's image on his screen, long and hard.

Dittmar returned his stare. "General, do you know why I'm defence secretary?"

"Excuse me, Mr Secretary?"

"For one reason, and one reason only. And it's not because of my good looks, I can assure you of that. I listen to advice, pick the best one, and make sure the president follows it. But the ultimate decision is his, no one else's, general. If your weapons are as effective as you say, and you have definitely convinced me of that, then we still have ninety minutes."

The phone call ended. Dittmar gazed out the window. The morning sunlight seeped through the trees like honey, washing softly over his worn face.

Brookes, alone at the White House, was also looking through his window. The same morning light was creeping onto his front lawn. He glanced at the time, buttoned his shirt, and wiped the sweat from his brow.

Dittmar's eyes tracked across to the kitchen. The Sun's rays were reflecting off the chrome taps, producing a rainbow of colours. He leaned back in his chair, waiting.

Brookes wandered across to the hall window, pulled back the curtains, and peered outside. He checked the time.

Dittmar's gaze drifted farther, to a yellow tennis ball on the kitchen table. He walked over, picked it up, and returned to his chair.

President Brookes leaned against a wall and checked the time. There was enough sunshine pouring through the open windows now to switch off the lights.

Dittmar repeatedly threw the tennis ball up, catching it. He missed one. The ball rolled along the floor under a table. He left it.

Brookes removed his dressing gown, dropped it on the lounge, wiped his brow again, and looked at his phone.

Dittmar looked away from the tennis ball to the window. His phone rang. He grabbed it immediately. "Yes, Chuck," he answered.

"Chinese landing vessels are a kilometre from the Taiwanese coast. I need to decide now what to do."

"Yes, Chuck."

"It's my decision, and I'll make it, but I need your advice, and I need it now."

***

Five minutes later, a Taiwanese news reporter described the scene. "I can see the approaching Chinese invasion force. Flashes of light … must be missile launches. I'm preparing for impact; any second now … Hold on! … Hold on! Wait! What's happening? Aircraft are falling out of the sky. Ships are on fire, dead in the water. I don't understand it."

The inexplicable destruction of China's invasion fleet prevented Russia, Pakistan, and Turkey from acting. In desperation, President Yin ordered a non-nuclear missile attack on military bases in Guam, Pearl Harbour, and on the Japanese mainland. The coalition retaliated by striking China's overseas naval bases, occupying their port facilities in the Pacific and Africa, and hunting their submarines and surface vessels.

The Chinese Communist Party, worried about the escalation, famine, and collapse of their economy from a lengthy blockade, arrested President Yin and others in a bloodless coup, charging them with corruption and inhumane crimes against the Chinese people. The new moderate Chinese president sued for peace.

The coalition agreed.

After the relief and jubilation, the world was curious about this mysterious weapon, which seemed to come out of nowhere. There was no trace of its incremental development, nor even a theoretical basis. No conceptual parallel weapon existed anywhere else. How could the US be so far ahead?

***

Two days later, President Brookes reflected with Defence Secretary Dittmar.

"Do you think we'll ever achieve peace and unity on Earth, Terry?" he asked, leaning back wearily in his chair. "We've had Germany, Japan, the Soviet Union, and now China."

"Peace? Only when there are no totalitarian states left." His hooked eyebrows furrowed. "Unity? Not without a common challenge to keep us focused. Otherwise, societies will become complacent, dysfunctional, and fractured."

"The UN has shown us that."

"Exactly."

"When I was a kid,"—the president's eyes squinted to the side, remembering—"our history teacher told us Hitler's Germany was defeated just before the atom bomb was developed, and this was remarkably fortunate. He said it would be too horrible to contemplate what the world would be like if atom bomb technology had been known sooner."

A questioning look crossed Dittmar's face. "So … you're drawing an inverse analogy to Taiwan? Where alien technology was available just in time to save the world."

"Well, what if the LaWS wasn't available for another two weeks?"

"Are you suggesting, Chuck, that some godlike being is looking after us, helping us to survive?"

"No, of course not, Terry. That would be ridiculous."

PART 2

FIRST CONTACT

"But … but why would any rational being
want to destroy this planet?"

Chapter 11   To Pallas

The public expected contact with the mysterious objects on Pallas to be just a formality. However, despite two years of directional radio broadcasting, there had been no reply. Not even signals similar to those detected by Anya and Lochlan.

One "alien expert" explained, "Just as insects can't comprehend human behaviour, we can't grasp the behaviour of an advanced alien race. They may, for example, experience time and space in a much more complex way, in a way we can't even perceive."

Another speculated, "They could be hiding on a mission of strategic information reconnaissance or as outlaws on the run."

The perpetual silence added to the mounting concern that these objects may not be friendly.

While international efforts stalled, space companies competed to be the first to send a rocket to Pallas. The earliest launch was scheduled for ten months, which was optimistic given the huge distance involved.

The world was shocked and wary, but also excited, when, five months later, the Chinese government announced they had a spacecraft heading towards Pallas by slingshotting an existing rocket around Mars. Eight months later and twelve light minutes from Earth, the Chinese probe entered Pallas's orbit, live on world news media. It was about to orbit Pallas for the second time and focus its cameras on the alien site when all communications were lost.

Kevin Garrett's MOT and other optical telescopes detected a distinct flash.

Other missions to Pallas were immediately cancelled. The three Martian bases prepared for evacuation, but this would take eighteen months.

Protesters gathered outside Chinese embassies, believing China had provoked the aliens. After not commenting for almost three days, the Chinese went on the offensive, accusing the US of concealing alien technology.

Earth was worried about the aliens' response. Governments mobilised their militaries and instructed the public to remain calm. There was no international agreement on what to do. Some world leaders were relieved that the monopolisation of the aliens by one nation was now unlikely. Despite episodes of anarchy, fear, and hysteria, the public's faith in the social status quo generally held up.

Two weeks after the destruction of the Chinese probe, the two alien spaceships left Pallas and headed for Mars. Despite increased attempts to communicate with them, there was no response. Three weeks later, contact was lost with two of the three Martian villages. Five hours later, the third village detected the approaching Pallas ships. A fixed camera transmitting directly to Earth gave a live account in grotesque detail of what followed.

It showed a peaceful, defenceless village at the foot of a Martian mountain range. Some humans were outside, looking skyward, waving at the two descending spaceships.

Moments later, a rain of laser beams shredded the village. Two cylindrical spaceships dropped into view and landed. Large, dark humanoid figures emerged. They hunted down all the remaining humans with a large rifle-like laser weapon.

A shadowy blur swept past the camera, only millimetres from the lens. Seconds later, transmission was lost. Twenty-seven years of mankind's presence on Mars ended abruptly and brutally.

The destruction of the Chinese probe could no longer be a misunderstanding. The world was horrified at the prospect of war against an alien race. People headed for the hills, built bomb shelters, sandbagged buildings, and rushed supermarkets.

Although panicked governments added to the crisis, they were finally prodded into international action. Long-running ideological conflicts between liberal and illiberal states were put aside. World unity seemed possible. The Earth Defence Organisation, or EDO, was established to protect humanity from an alien attack, whatever that meant.

The US begrudgingly acknowledged to the EDO the existence of the alien Moon-ship and the extensive technological research being undertaken. But not all of it was disclosed, and what was revealed was classified. The public was still in the dark about most things.

Chapter 12   MSR-1

Thirteen months later, when Mars was in solar conjunction, a cargo transport rocket lifted off from Earth.

The rocket entered Mars's retrograde orbit by a trajectory always obscured from Mars by the Sun. There, it cooled its engines to the undetectable cosmic temperature and waited for the arrival of Mars. Its approach would be well outside of the detection zone for objects travelling directly from Earth.

Eight months later, the rocket ignited a short, and hopefully undetectable, metallic hydrogen thruster and coasted towards the south pole of Mars, below the aliens' horizon. At thirty-three kilometres from the alien site and two kilometres above the ground, it dropped a small lander rocket. The main rocket kept going, eventually crashing into a deep valley thirty-two kilometres away.

The lander rocket fell rapidly through the Martian atmosphere. At a hundred metres from the ground, its scorched heat shield dropped off, its descent engines ignited, and its lander petals opened, touching down gently on the surface. The engine flare quickly faded until all that was left was a tiny, unnoticeable dark speck amidst a sea of dark rocks.

A robotic rover with "MSR-1" stencilled on its side emerged and slowly set off over the rocky terrain and along a dry riverbed towards the aliens. A blower on the back cleared any tracks left in the fine dust. The multi-wheeled Martian Spy Rover-1 was on its way.

Forty-seven hours later, MSR-1 concealed itself at a well-known outcrop two kilometres from the alien site. It now had an unobstructed line-of-sight to both the alien spaceships and the comms relay station on the lander rocket. Its anti-reflective solar array and anti-infrared emission venting made it virtually undetectable.

***

Kevin Garrett tried to ignore the excited murmurings in the EDO operations room. Despite his previous refusals to join Section 3, he eventually accepted an offer from the EDO when the aliens destroyed his MOT. He now headed the Observation and Analysis Group and suddenly found himself part of MSR-1's ambitious plan to spy on the Martian aliens.

Testing was about to start.

The comms relay station unfolded its hi-gain, hi-directional antenna, aimed it at Earth, and tested its radio packaging equipment – everything worked. The comms relay station and MSR-1 adjusted their alignments and tested their narrow laser comms link – everything worked.

MSR-1 extended and switched on its telescopic camera snouts and sensors, pointing them towards the aliens, the rising Sun reflecting in their black lenses. Garrett wondered whether the aliens would still be there.

Tense silence reigned in the ops room while images and data were collected, compacted neatly into thirty-five second pulses, and transmitted to Earth. Everyone had the same thought: *Is this damn thing going to work?*

People crowded around the large, blank screen, anxiously waiting. Peripheral data streams indicated an imminent video connection. Agonising seconds passed, then minutes. The screen suddenly flickered to life, showing white streaks, a blurred, red horizon, then a smudge of mountains. As the camera searched, Garrett looked like he was about to see the holy grail. The camera finally zoomed in and focused on the two alien spaceships. Several figures moved about. Everything was in clear HD. The room erupted in applause. Even the MSR-1 images seemed to quiver with excitement.

Celebrations quickly quietened as everyone turned to the screen, transfixed by the images.

Chapter 13   Alien Intel

Kevin Garrett hated these high-level UN intelligence briefings. So much restricted information to hide.

This particular meeting was special. Firstly, Lochlan McLean would be present to "meet some of the main players". And secondly, Garrett was finally authorised to disclose the existence of MSR-1.

Garrett and Lochlan greeted each other across the table. Garrett wondered how much things had changed since their Pallas discovery, including himself. He was looking forward to catching up afterwards.

"MSR-1 is a living miracle," Garrett said. "It's been continuously operating now for the past six months, transmitting invaluable images and data from the Martian site. The aliens have no idea they're being spied on."

After a moment of shocked speechlessness, where one head shook in scepticism and a few surprised sighs were heard, a shaky voice came from Garrett's right. "What information is gathered?"

"As much as we can, Elyse. Day-to-day movements of the aliens, their behaviour, relationships, skills, radio transmissions. We've completed a psychological dossier on each identifiable alien."

With an even shakier voice, Elyse asked, "What can you tell us?"

"What I'm about to tell you will be made public tomorrow. The only image of these aliens released to the public is that famous blurred humanoid figure from the Martian village camera. This image doesn't show that these aliens are machines."

After a sharp, audible intake of breaths, the room settled into an uneasy quiet.

Garrett lit up a large overhead screen. "These creatures are two and a half metres tall. Their exterior covering is normally a light grey, soft material. When threatened, they transform into a dark, armoured shell. Their powerful physique is obvious. As you can see from this picture, the head has two eyes set at the front. There's no nose, mouth, or ears. We're calling them H-HARs, Hostile Humanoid Alien Robots."

A video advanced through a series of frames identifying the H-HARs like a school yearbook.

"The H-HARs," Garrett continued, "look identical except for two things: a ranking colour on their right arm and an individual identifier marking on their left arm. They have three ranks: the overlord red-armband, the manager green-armbands, and the slave blue-armbands. These ranks are very rigid and severe. We believe there are hundreds, maybe even thousands, of deactivated H-HARs inside the spaceships. Only the numbers they currently need are activated.

"They're intelligent and self-aware, with each having its own characteristic personality. We have pictures."

Picture 1 showed an H-HAR watching from the spaceship doorway: "This is the red-armband. It's the overlord or master H-HAR. There's only one red-armband."

Picture 2 showed an H-HAR pointing: "This is a green-armband. These are like project managers. We've counted thirty-four of them. They're subservient to the red-armband, but subjugate the blue-armbands. When not directed by the red-armband, they have free rein."

Picture 3 showed several H-HARs carrying a large cylinder: "These are the blue-armbands. They're the slaves. We've identified one hundred and twelve that are currently active. When a green-armband is not present, their behaviour is more instinctive than slavish. One observation that could be extremely useful in any future conflict was that a blue-armband was terminated when a displeased green-armband hit it on the left side of its neck. We believe this ultimate punishment keeps the blue-armbands subservient."

Garrett showed another video. "We've also counted four dog-like unintelligent robots. We're unsure of their purpose."

While more videos and pictures flashed by, Garrett was asked, "How do these things communicate without mouths or ears?"

"I was wondering when someone would ask that question, Glenn. Mouths and ears are useless in a vacuum. They communicate by short-range wireless. MSR-1 sometimes picks up their chatter. Their colour armbands and individual markings indicate that they still use visual identification."

One representative looked more than a little apprehensive. "They're doing something to the spaceship on the left. Could they be preparing to attack Earth?"

"Hang on, mate," replied Garrett, a little stumped. "There're more assumptions to that question than days in February. At this stage, we can't even speculate."

At the table's end, an unknown representative, whose presence was obscured by the Sun's glare through the window, had been listening with singular and unblinking interest to every word. "Tell us about the Moon-ship?" she asked.

Garrett's eyes shifted to the end of the table. "Um … Oenone, from Greece?"

"Correct, Mr Garrett."

"Hi, Oenone." Garrett gestured with an open hand across the table. "We have Agent Powell from Section 3 of NSO visiting us today. I'm going to ask him to answer this."

All heads swivelled expectantly to Agent Powell, who sat next to Lochlan. To everyone's astonishment, Powell gave the briefest possible narrative, stating only the year it was discovered and that it appeared identical to the Pallas ships. Everyone wanted more, but Agent Powell was not prepared to give it and handed the narrative back to Garrett.

Oenone rose inconspicuously, walked to the chilled water machine, filled a cup, and stood there sipping, hanging back, waiting.

When Garrett paused, Oenone jumped in. "Sorry … um, Agent Powell … um, you made a passing reference, perhaps inadvertently, to Moon-ship renewals. How are these carried out?"

The question sounded innocent enough to Garrett.

"Well …" said Agent Powell, glimpsing at his computer to recall her name. "Oenone. Every million years or so, a major renewal is required. Thousands of fabricating nano-machines work in tandem with disassembler nano-machines that break up raw materials from a moon or an asteroid. It's a molecule-by-molecule process that can take many thousands of years."

Oenone shot Agent Powell a sideways glance with a suspicious grin. "But …" she said, returning to her seat in short, deliberate steps. "But this requires a lot of specialised know-how, don't you think, Mr Agent Powell?"

Garrett's ears popped up. *That's an intentionally precise question. Why would she ask that?*

Agent Powell hesitated before answering. "Yes, of course."

Oenone immediately responded, her grin vanishing. "So, these aliens, or H-HARs as you call them, must have information storage devices for equipment servicing and renewals. These devices might even be a complete library or encyclopedia of their technology or even their civilisation. Tell me, Mr Agent Powell, have you found such storage devices?"

Garrett's eyes slowly turned to Agent Powell. *Let's see how much he reveals about the data storage devices.*

Agent Powell took a measured sip of water – not too fast, not too slow. He drifted a wary eye to Garrett. Both men's practised poker faces gave nothing away. "You don't ask for much, do you?"

said Agent Powell, not sounding defensive at all. "We've found a lot of equipment. Most of it we're still trying to identify."

My God thought Garrett. *How much truth did he leave out of that answer?*

Oenone gave Agent Powell a searching look. "So, you're telling me you could have found their information storage device?" Her eyes insisted on a "yes".

Garrett leaned back and watched with growing amusement at Agent Powell's elusiveness. He looked at Lochlan, who also appeared somewhat fascinated.

"No, I'm not saying that." Agent Powell sagged back into his chair, holding Oenone's gaze, bluffing it out. "I'm saying we don't know what we've found."

"And if you did find such a device, you would share it with the rest of the world, wouldn't you, Mr Agent Powell?"

Garrett silently agreed. He, Lochlan, and Anya had previously discussed how long this secret could remain hidden.

"I can't speculate on hypotheticals, Oenone," Agent Powell replied.

"You don't have an opinion?"

"My opinion is irrelevant."

"If there is to be a war against these H-HARs, then deciphering their library of information is perhaps our only hope, and this needs to be a global effort." Oenone's voice was now full of suspicion. "Do you know where all the alien artefacts from the Moon-ship are stored?"

"No one knows that, Oenone. They're spread out in any number of different, unknown locations."

Garrett knew Agent Powell was telling the truth about this. Agent Powell once told him that he was taken blindfolded, some time ago, to study artefacts at a remote, unknown army base.

Chapter 14   Fort Bush

Two and a half years after the aliens relocated to Mars from Pallas and seven months after MSR-1 started streaming live videos, one of the two alien ships lifted off from the red planet. Tracking stations confirmed its destination – Earth. Fear and panic swept across the globe.

Military forces were on high alert. All lunar stations – surface and orbital – were evacuated. Thirty-one days later, the spaceship entered Earth's orbit and dropped an ovoid-shaped landing craft. The drop-craft decelerated heavily through the atmosphere, leaving a long trail of frictional sparks. It was tracked to a football field inside Fort Bush, a remote US Army base on the edge of a desert. All contact with the fort had been lost earlier, just after the detection of a microwave nuclear explosion.

Two drone reconnaissance jets sent to investigate vanished near the fort. A second flyover was cancelled.

A platoon of armed soldiers, who had just left the fort for a two-day exercise, were ordered to return and investigate. Twenty-five minutes later, wild rye whipped about in the wind of pulsating rotor blades as their helicopters touched down in a shallow valley, nine hundred metres outside the smoking fort. Forty-two troops quickly alighted with twelve Combat Autonomous Robots, or CARs.

First Lieutenant Allan Templeton, the commander, briefed his soldiers. "An alien spacecraft has landed in our fort. Our orders are to assess the situation and avoid conflict. Do not engage unless fired upon. Our military is still guarding the cities, so it will take at least five hours for support to arrive, which, unfortunately, will be after sundown. We have no information on what they are doing here, their numbers, or if they are armed. All we're told is that they will be an enemy like no other in human history."

Lieutenant Templeton, a man in his forties and tough enough for anything, formed three teams: Alpha, Bravo, and Charlie. They cut through the perimeter fence, fanned out, and proceeded through the army base along different routes towards the alien drop-craft.

"Dead soldiers strewn everywhere," reported the medical officer, his voice wavering with emotion. "Twenty-two hundred killed instantly by dielectric heating of their central nervous system. Their swollen faces covered with lesions and hardly recognisable. Horrible beyond description. We only avoided this fate by leaving before it happened. Buildings are mostly intact, but the streets are littered with pipes, metal, vehicles, trees, and other debris. The only thing stirring is debris blown by the occasional wind gusts. If this place resembles anything at all, it's the aftermath of a terrorist attack. Our dosimeters are reading zero."

Bravo team passed a World War II obelisk at the centre of the army base, where they had done their military parade and daily foot drills the day before. On a normal day, they would take in the spectacular view beyond the main gate, where a single road split the arid landscape, and distant mountains rose to meet a blazing blue sky with fluffy, drifting clouds.

But this was far from a normal day.

Templeton's Charlie team passed a Humvee that had crashed through a fence, its driver slumped over the steering wheel. He then passed the many simple but orderly rows of dormitory buildings. Templeton checked their doorways. One building was carpeted with bodies, many of whom he would have known. He whispered his heartfelt condolences.

Bravo and Charlie quickly made their way to within sight of the drop-craft. There, eighty metres away, stood two humanoid figures. Templeton tensed and stared in wonder. *Aliens. What the hell do we do now? Talk to them?*

The soldiers were oblivious to the danger until, in a shocking and horrific scene, one soldier's head slid off his shoulders, his body falling to its knees and collapsing. It took another victim before they ducked for cover. The carnage continued as the mysterious alien beam weapon silently cut through everything in its path.

The CARs were slower than the soldiers and almost wiped out. The head of one rolled down the street before spinning to rest, face up.

With no time to recover, two robot dogs leaped onto the soldiers. Black, slippery, and with eyes piercing, they resembled giant jaguars, only considerably quicker and stronger. While body armour provided some protection for the soldiers, the razor-sharp teeth and talons of the dogs tore into their arms and legs with incredible ferocity. Bullets harmlessly pinged off their hideous bodies, ricocheting only millimetres from the soldiers.

The horror persisted as the dogs sprang from soldier to soldier, knocking them to the ground, wildly ripping and tearing at them in a homicidal rage, blood and flesh splattering everywhere. One soldier was knocked to the ground with an agonising yell of pain, his body flung from side to side as the creature savaged him. Behind him, another soldier screamed in anguish and terror, "Get it off me! Get it off me!"

The soldiers converged, desperately struggling to fend off the dogs. But they were being picked off one by one, only moments away from a mauling death. The dogs seemed impossible to stop.

"Shoot them down the throat," yelled Templeton through the clamour. After several attempts, a rifle muzzle was plunged into a dog's gaping maw, and the magazine emptied. The dog slumped to the ground, motionless, its rage spent. The second dog was stopped the same way.

The soldiers, bruised, battered, and soaked in sweat, panted like steam engines. Their expressions a mixture of horror and confusion. This was far beyond their training. Templeton regained control over what remained of Bravo and Charlie and established a defensive perimeter against further dog attacks.

Operations HQ radioed in. "Commander Templeton, a Delta Force squadron of one hundred troops is three and a half hours away."

"These aliens could well be gone by then," Templeton said. He had no doubts about what to do. He called in a missile air strike and quickly evacuated the troops and CARs outside the blast zone.

***

Alpha team, commanded by Second Lieutenant Walter Meitner, was still making its way to the drop-craft after diverting to an apparent false alien sighting. Aware of the attacks on Bravo and Charlie, Meitner proceeded with added caution. He turned into Perryville Street, a long, wide street he knew well, and instantly paused. He examined the street thoroughly. There were the familiar shops and recreation facilities lining both sides. But he had never seen this street without people and movement. It's as if they're hiding, watching from the windows. It was even strangely free of debris and bodies. The western half of the street lay in deep shadow. Only a large pile of metal drums near the end prevented a clear view of the street's entire length. After a lifetime in the army, he thought nothing could faze him. But the eerie emptiness of this street was unnerving.

"It's too open, and there's no cover," Meitner said. "Private Wiggins, do a recon. And take Private Tryon with you."

"Yes, sir," said Wiggins, turning to Tryon. "Come on, let's move."

As Wiggins and Tryon progressed down Perryville Street without incident, Meitner signalled Alpha team to follow. Then, a building door crashed onto the road like a drawbridge near the metal drums, and a large figure suddenly emerged. Wiggins's radio erupted with mayhem cries. Meitner quickly pulled Alpha team back and yelled into his radio, "Wiggins, Tryon, what's happening?"

He looked down the street through binoculars. "Wiggins?" he yelled again into his microphone.

Tortured screams came back, followed by some mutterings from Wiggins.

"Wiggins, did you say Tryon is dead? ... Wiggins?"

No answer.

Meitner looked again through his binoculars. "Wiggins, the alien is walking away from you; stay put."

"I've got this fucker," Wiggins said. "It's mine."

"No, Wiggins! Let it go ... Wiggins?"

Seconds later, pinging bullets and a scream echoed down the street. All Meitner could do was listen in horror.

***

Wiggins and Tryon ducked behind the metal drums when the Perryville alien unexpectedly appeared.

"Wiggins, it saw us!" Tryon said, his voice trembling, his eyes full of fear.

"Keep your head down," Wiggins whispered.

Meitner's voice came through their radios: "Wiggins, Tryon, what's happening?"

A laser beam suddenly sliced through the drums. Wiggins dived onto his stomach. The terrible beam missed him. But not Tryon, slicing into his waist, it burned through his armour, cloth, flesh, and bone with no ignition or smoke. Tryon's spine protruded through his back.

Wiggins caught Tryon's eye in a terrible, frozen instant and turned away. He could still hear the desperate screams, choking sounds, and his partner's ragged last breath. The metallic scent of oozing blood was sickening.

Wiggins turned back to take a final glance at Tryon, whose body was now a grotesque mass of bleeding flesh. He heard Meitner's voice on the radio: "Wiggins?"

"Tryon is dead," Wiggins murmured.

Saturated with blood, all Wiggins cared about was payback. He uncontrollably yelled at the earless creature.

Realising he had to calm down, Wiggins swallowed and steadied his breathing to contain his fury. He heard Meitner's voice on his radio, but the words were missed. "I've got this fucker, sir," Wiggins said. "It's mine."

He stayed low, quietly simmering, blood running into his eyes. He let it. The creature's footsteps neared, hitting the road hard and kicking away debris. They passed and receded. Wiggins tightened his grip on his rifle and rose up in reckless, savage anger. His wrath had boiled over.

"Time to die, motherfucker!" Wiggins shook in pure rage as he opened up, hitting Perryville everywhere. He emptied his entire magazine before the creature stopped and slowly turned, as if it had finally decided to do something about this irritation. Wiggins's piercing scream was brief.

***

Meitner radioed Templeton. "Lieutenant, we have an alien in Perryville Street, about a hundred metres from us. It just killed Privates Wiggins and Tryon. It's huge, armed, and wearing a green band on its left arm. It's heading our way but seems to be searching for something in every building. It's about to enter—"

Terror struck. The Perryville alien opened up with its laser, hitting two soldiers. Meitner returned fire. But the hail of bullets just pinged off the alien, ripping through buildings and walls, tearing them to shreds, and creating a cloud of debris. The alien kept coming, firing, forcing Alpha team to retreat further. As the thunderous echoes of gunfire faded, Meitner shook his head in disbelief and radioed Templeton. "It's unstoppable. Our armour-piercing shells just ricochet off in a shower of sparks. I've seen nothing like it. Its weapon can cut through anything, so it's little use taking cover if it knows where you're hiding."

Through the fury of dirt and flaming debris, Perryville rose to its feet undamaged and resumed searching each building in Meitner's direction. Meitner clasped his helmet as his stomach tightened. A fearless, unflappable man had just discovered what it was like to be afraid. Turning to his soldiers, his eyes had a haunted look. So much so that it even startled some of them.

Meitner had no choice but to leave the injured and fall back further. Taking a deep breath, he stood up to signal. It was his last.

Sergeant Cole, a tough, no-nonsense career soldier, took over command of Alpha team. Commander Templeton ordered Cole and Alpha team to continue towards the alien drop-craft and join him there. Cole left Corporal Thompson, or Thommo, behind with four soldiers to watch Perryville with the orders: "Do not hinder; stay out of sight and fall back as it approaches."

***

Operations HQ radioed in. "Commander Templeton, be advised the airstrike is two minutes away. Please confirm we are clear to proceed."

"Affirmative. Proceed with strike."

Nineteen kilometres away, a drone jet fighter descended through broken clouds, releasing a missile. The missile followed a low-altitude trajectory along the valley floor. It banked hard, reaching hypersonic velocity over the three-kilometre desert scrub crossing to the fort.

Templeton and his soldiers lay flat on the ground, their heads buried in their helmets, bracing themselves as best they could.

There was no escaping the heat of the flash, the jolt of the blast, the deafening thunderclap, and the shower of burning debris. The explosion echoed off the distant mountains twenty seconds later.

Templeton rose slowly, slightly disorientated. As the dust settled, he surveyed the devastation. Where the alien drop-craft had been was now a huge crater. *A direct hit! Surely nothing could survive that* – or so he thought. As more and more dust settled, the drop-craft became visible, displaced by five metres, slightly tilted in a mound of debris, but still in one piece. The two alien sentries had resumed their positions with their weapons, looking just as ominous as before.

"What the hell's going on here?" Templeton struggled for answers. "How can we fight these things?"

He received a radio reply from operations HQ. "We're frantically trying to find out, Commander." They sounded just as desperate.

News of the battle had reached Section 3, and they immediately established a direct line to Fort Bush. "Yes, this better be damn important," Templeton answered the radio call sharply. "We're in the middle of a battle here." His face was frozen in a stone-cold frown, and his clothes were dirty and blood spattered.

"This information is critical, Commander. The H-HARs – I mean, the alien humanoids – have indestructible, molecularly manufactured armour that stops any ballistic weapon. It's useless trying to shoot or blow them up. However, they have a vulnerable spot on the left side of their necks. If you hit this spot with a bullet, it should terminate them. The spot can be seen as a small indentation, about the size of a dime. Only a direct hit will have any effect, so several shots may be necessary."

"How the hell do you know this?"

"From our research on the Moon-ship aliens, Commander."

"Moon-ship what?" Templeton shouted. "What on Earth are you yammering about?"

"Don't worry about that now, Commander. Also, shooting the back of a knee should cripple the leg. One more thing, and I'm not sure if this is helpful, but their eyes are sunken. Paint bullets bursting near their eyes should blind or impair their vision. I must add, Commander, that this information is speculative."

Templeton fell silent, awkwardly scratching the back of his neck, as if not completely convinced. His eyes slowly narrowed. "Okay … I'm going to put lives at risk based on this information. I hope for our sake it's correct." He paused, again scratching the back of his neck. "How about the dogs? Anything else apart from shooting down their throats?"

"No, Commander, the dogs have no other weaknesses, only a paint-like substance in their eyes, like the H-HARs. Sorry."

Templeton broadcast the new information and ordered Cole to take Alpha team back to confront Perryville and any other aliens they encountered. He stayed with Bravo and Charlie to engage the aliens guarding the drop-craft. Templeton could see from his soldiers' faces that this was a different fight now.

***

Private Alex Zyga was the youngest and most inexperienced soldier in the group. This was his first combat assignment. Sergeant Cole ordered him to join Thommo and assist in attacking Perryville. On the way, he rounded a corner into Vicksburg Street just as a dark figure exited a building. "*SHIT*!" He threw himself back and scrambled to the nearest hiding place. He didn't think it saw him, but *who knows? Maybe it has superpowers.*

Cold fear slammed through him as he heard heavy footsteps approaching. They stopped. The silence unsettled him. *It must be searching for me.* He took a nervous breath and listened, trying to regain control and make sense of it all. He spoke softly into his radio. "Sergeant Cole! Sergeant Cole! An-an alien! What do—"

"Zyga! Listen to me. Shadow it until backup arrives. You are not to lose it under any circumstances. Understand me?"

Cole's words sounded plainly in Zyga's ears, but they didn't coalesce. "Yessir, yessir," he said. He thought about what happened to Wiggins and turned off his radio, worried about the Vicksburg alien detecting it. *How am I supposed to follow this monster without getting killed?*

A loud bang from across the street startled him. He dropped his shoulders, but immediately raised them again. *Come on, get up. I'm a soldier. My orders are to follow this thing.* But his muscles tightened.

Another ominous bang filled the air. Zyga waited, listening to the eerie stillness that followed. *I can feel that creature sneaking around me, behind me, above me, about to pounce. I need to look.* But his muscles still wouldn't move, a rabbit frozen in the presence of a wolf.

He continued to hesitate: two minutes, three minutes. Realising the danger was too real to ignore any longer, he stumbled to his feet and raised his head to look. *Shit! … it's gone! … vanished to God knows where. It could be anywhere.*

Wiping the dirt from his mouth, he radioed Sergeant Cole, which was nearly as frightening as the alien. "Sir, sir …" Zyga said, swallowing a lump in his throat. "I-I've lost it … I lost the alien creature. It's … it's gone." His dry throat burned on every word.

"Gone?! … Gone! What the fuck do you mean? Now you've put us all in danger. Goddam you, Zyga. Get your useless ass to Thommo. And if you find that motherfucker on the way, follow it. And when I say follow it, I mean keep your fuckin' head out of your ass, Zyga, and stick to it like shit … Are you hearing me, Zyga?" Cole's voice could almost be heard without a radio.

"Yes, yessir … yes, yessir, I am."

Cole signed off. Zyga grabbed his helmet in dismay and cursed incoherently to himself. Gathering all his courage, he turned to face whatever nightmare awaited him.

He stepped out onto the street, a solitary figure among the wreckage and bodies, and listened. Every sound – creaking structures, blowing debris, gas hissing from a pipe – was magnified. Only regular noises, nothing to worry about. His eyes roved around, checking.

He headed off as silent as a ghost, one step at a time, tiptoeing around things only he could see. The Sun was low, so he clung to the dark side of the street to hide his shadow. Outrage crossed his face as he passed more blistered bodies. A terrible crime had been committed here. He almost wanted to encounter this alien to serve some justice.

He sensed a chilling presence and spun around, his ears listening, his eyes scanning – the shadows, the corners, the windows, the doors – but nothing was there, a false alarm.

He moved on quietly, listening and watching, making sure it was safe before darting to the next shadow. A narrow lane ahead paused him. *Take the lane or continue to the T-intersection? I don't like either.* He looked both ways. *The lane might be safer.* He headed towards it. Then a noise, an unnatural noise. Sounded like it came from the lane. He stopped, cocked his head warily, and listened – nothing. Yet he was sure he had heard something. His eyes searched left, right, behind – nothing. He wiped his brow with a trembling hand. A breeze blew up, strangely from nowhere. The Coca-Cola sign across the street squeaked, and a large piece of paper blew against his leg. He shook it off. The paper soared skyward, circling him before floating to the ground. Then that noise again. He strained his ears. Apart from the distinctive sound of the breeze, there was something else.

Is the wind playing tricks on me, or is that noise coming from that monster? He changed his mind and decided to stay on the street, crossing it like a minefield, his rifle up, ready. The noise stopped. He reconsidered. *Lane or street? I'll stay with the street.* He shook off a chill and creeped towards the T-intersection, his shadow inching along the building walls. He was almost there.

What if the creature is lurking just around the corner? His breathing quickened. He reached it and cautiously leaned out, looking left, then right. A car park, a Humvee ambulance, some rubble, and a few bodies, but no sound, and no sign of Vicksburg. He exhaled a frozen breath and stepped out just as a loud bang came from the church across the street.

He quickly backtracked to the corner and headed for the lane. A loud, shattering noise stopped him dead. He looked back at the corner he had just left. *Shit! What the hell was that? The church wall being smashed out?* All went quiet. He turned and started off again, each step faster than the last.

Then, from the corner, came footsteps on wooden boards. Hard enough to be heard. Too heavy to be a human. Every muscle tensed, but Zyga kept moving, faster and faster. He glanced back at the corner. A ground shadow was emerging – a head. He glanced again – shoulders. Zyga raced to the nearest door as quickly as possible over the rubble. *Please, God, don't be locked.* It wasn't. He hurried inside, taking a final panicked look at the enormous, elongated shadow, now almost complete, before quietly pushing the door back.

The room was dark and smelled of death. A single slash of light through a slit above the window curtain revealed a soldier slouched across a desk. His body was red, oozing blood. It made Zyga nauseated. He stood in the far corner, petrified, staring at the door. Then he suddenly realised: *I'm trapped.*

He switched off his radio and waited. Outside, the only sound was a distant hissing gas pipe. But Zyga needed to strain to even hear that. *Did that monster see me come in here?* Then those heavy footsteps again. A door smashed across the road. Quietness resumed: ten seconds, twenty seconds. *Maybe I should run for it? … No, no time.*

He needed to look to be certain it was Vicksburg. He forced himself to the window; his hand shook as he gently lifted the curtain an eye crack. It was Vicksburg all right – a green band on its arm, carrying a weapon, and standing menacingly in the middle of the road. He carefully lowered the curtain but not before the creature's head abruptly shifted in his direction.

Shit ... Shit!

He lifted the curtain again. This time the creature's black, pupilless eyes stared directly at him with a deadly gaze that said "I'm coming for you".

Fuck ... Fuck!

He dropped the curtain and jumped back in terror. "Now I'm really screwed."

Footsteps neared. Vicksburg's huge shadow swept across the curtain towards the door, which Zyga had left ajar. He couldn't risk the 'click' it would make closing it.

What to do? His eyes searched desperately, only one possible hiding place. He rushed to it as the wooden floor outside creaked under a heavy weight, barely audible over his heartbeat. The shape outside blocked the dirty beams of sunlight leaking around the door. The creaking stopped. Under the door, two wide shadows appeared from planted feet.

Zyga waited, numbed, white-knuckling his rifle. Everything was so quiet. Then, with an ear-splitting crash, the door exploded inwards, splintering against the opposite wall. Zyga squinted as the light flooded in. Vicksburg's humanoid yet inhuman shadow fell across the floor and onto the opposite wall. Zyga stood statue-like, just inside the door, pressed flat against the wall, not really out of sight. He knew he was dead the moment this thing laid eyes on him.

He wasn't sure about the instructions to kill this thing. *Was it the right or left side of its neck? Left side, I think. Yes ... I'm on the alien's left side ... Oh, thank God for that.*

His crude rifle seemed frighteningly inadequate, yet it was his only hope. He raised it above his head, slowly, weakly, as high as his arms could reach, which he estimated to be about Vicksburg's neck height. The muzzle was poised across the entrance, safety catch was off, and his finger was on the trigger. But his body trembled, and blood pounded in his ears. His sweaty hands couldn't hold the rifle firmly.

Vicksburg dipped its head and stepped through the doorway, looking straight ahead, seemingly oblivious to Zyga. It stood still, poised like a colossus, blocking any escape, its eyes surveying everything in front of it without moving its head. Zyga's rifle muzzle was almost touching a small indentation on the creature's neck. All he had to do was pull the trigger. But his trembling finger wouldn't squeeze, paralysed by fear.

The creature swung its head to the right, away from Zyga. Its eyes still surveying. Vomit rose from Zyga's throat. He swallowed it down.

The alien's head swung forward again. Any second now, it will swing left and discover Zyga. In that frozen second, something clicked inside Zyga's head. The growing doom steadied him. The trembling stopped, and he stiffened. With an unfamiliar, deadly calmness, he corrected the position of his rifle's muzzle just a fraction to the indentation on its neck and pulled the trigger.

Vicksburg instantly collapsed to the floor.

Zyga recoiled, recovered, jumped over Vicksburg, and charged out the door. He sprinted wildly down the street, his eyes wide, and his chest heaving. He suddenly stopped, but not out of exhaustion.

"Shit! Fuck!" he yelled, realising Sergeant Cole would demand to know if this thing was dead or not. He warily looked back. All was quiet. He raised his rifle. A moment passed. He took a very reluctant step back, then another. Ready to flee in an instant.

He peered through the doorway, his breath catching in his throat. The creature's carcass lay where it had fallen. Its head hung back, one arm still clutching its weapon, while the other was cupped behind its back. Its hips were twisted, with one leg cocked beneath the other. Its unclosed eyes were deep, beady, and black.

Zyga cautiously studied it in the fading sunlight. *Looks like some evil being from a horror movie. It doesn't even look dead.* Zyga half expected it to suddenly rise at any moment.

Its dark skin abruptly turned to light grey.

"H-holy shit!" Zyga fell back through the door. His mouth opened in speechless horror.

Taking a cautious step forward again, he prodded it with his rifle – nothing. He kicked it, then kicked it harder – no response. Zyga was as sure as he could be that this thing, this abomination, this … whatever it was, was now dead.

He warily set off to rejoin Cole and Thommo, his eyes squinting in the sunlight as he rounded the corner and raced past the church. He reached for his radio, only to be stopped by another unnatural noise from the next corner. "Holy shit … don't tell me there are more of these fucking things." A bead of sweat trickled down his temple. He wiped it off, jumped into the nearby Humvee ambulance, climbed over the seats, and crouched in the back to peer out the rear window.

The noise kept getting closer. Silhouetted figures approached against the sinking glow of the crimson sunset.

"That's just fucking great. A whole fucking army of these things!" He looked again. "Oh, thank God."

It was Sergeant Cole.

***

While the conflict at Fort Bush raged, the alien spaceship in Earth's orbit attacked other targets. All the world's major space launch facilities were destroyed, except for one in Japan and one in Ukraine, where the warheads failed to detonate.

***

Commander Templeton concluded there were only two alien scouts: Vicksburg and Perryville. Vicksburg was terminated by Zyga, and Alpha team was about to confront Perryville. That left the two alien sentries at the drop-craft to be dealt with. He set up snipers with the remaining soldiers to protect them against dog attacks.

"We know they can return fire almost immediately," warned Templeton. "Two quick, consecutive shots, then move on."

Using explosive shrapnel rounds mixed with streamers of tracer fire, the snipers opened fire. Bullets pinged off the alien sentries from all angles. One soldier lingered too long after his first shot and paid the consequences, then another fell.

Templeton watched the shootout in horror, but Zyga's success against Vicksburg encouraged him to persist. After another soldier fell, he was about to end the engagement when an alien sentry suddenly dropped limply to the ground. Templeton let out a deep breath of relief.

"Well done, soldiers," he shouted. "Let's get the other one."

The remaining alien covered its neck with its left hand before disappearing into the drop-craft.

"Hold fire," Templeton ordered, breathing another sigh of relief. The shootout lasted three minutes.

Meanwhile, Cole and Alpha team caught up with Thommo, who was still shadowing Perryville.

"It just came out of the admin building, sir," said Thommo to Cole. "It ignores us as long as we're out of sight and keeping our distance." Both men craned their necks to look.

"It's in a hurry," said Cole.

"Yeah, looks like it's given up on the search and heading back to the drop-craft, sir. Maybe it's found what it was looking for."

"It's not carrying anything," said Cole, looking through binoculars. "Let's give the son of a bitch hell."

Struggling to keep up, Cole, Thommo, and Alpha team followed Perryville as it headed back towards the drop-craft. As

Perryville smashed through a fence onto the football field, with the drop-craft in sight, a barrage of bullets from Templeton's Bravo and Charlie teams hit it. Perryville covered its neck with a hand and kept moving. The soldiers went for its knees, crippling its left leg. Perryville limped on but returned fire, forcing the soldiers to shift their firing positions.

When Cole's Alpha team arrived and added to the gunfire hailing down on Perryville, its armband changed from green to blue. In a whirl of viciousness, an alien dog unexpectedly emerged from nowhere, injuring one soldier before jumping onto two others. After a struggle to get a rifle in its mouth, it was terminated. When they returned their attention to Perryville, it had vanished into the drop-craft.

Templeton expected a violent reprisal. "Stop taking useless pot shots at the drop-craft and move well back on the double," he yelled. And just as well. A sweeping laser beam decimated everything within a hundred and fifty metres. The magnitude of the destruction shocked Templeton. The soldiers remained out of sight, now also behind a screen of fire, smoke, and dust. Miraculously, there were no serious injuries.

As a gentle breeze cleared the air, an eerie stillness hung over the drop-craft. "Maybe it's damaged," Templeton said, picking up the radio. "I'm ordering another air strike." He dropped the microphone as the drop-craft suddenly lifted off and quickly disappeared high into the evening sky.

The Sun had now sunk behind the western mountains, leaving an orange glow beneath the darkening sky. The sudden disappearance of the breeze allowed the smoke plumes to float to a considerable height before dissipating in midair, creating a scene as strange as an alien planet.

Templeton couldn't quite believe the nightmare was over. Nonetheless, he wanted to inspect the alien corpse at the landing site. Wearily picking up their gear, the troops followed him over the smouldering debris. What they saw would haunt them forever.

The alien figure was almost completely adsorbed by the dark, even with torches shining at it.

Templeton stared at it in total incomprehension. *This is like being stuck in a nightmare – an awful, frightening nightmare.*

"What the hell are you?" a soldier asked. "And what are you doing here?"

No one wanted to even try for an answer.

The medical officer took a step closer. "Um … four fingers, a thumb, no fingernails, head slightly reptilian, two sunken black eyes. There's no mouth, no nose, and no ears." He moved his torch closer. "Its skin is not like normal blackness, more like a hole or absence of matter." He shone the torch into the unblinking blackness of its eyes and immediately pulled back. "What the fuck… I swear it stared back at me."

"Zyga?" yelled Templeton, looking around. "Where the hell is Zyga?"

"Here, sir," said Zyga, just arriving.

"Zyga, you said Vicksburg's skin transformed to a coarse, light-greyish material after you killed it, right?"

"Yes, sir," Zyga answered, looking at the alien. "This one should too."

Zyga crouched down, touching it. "It's smooth, slippery, and—" The soldiers suddenly stumbled back as the alien changed colour. They pointed their rifles at it, anxiously watching it. But not Zyga, who rose slowly. "That's what happened to Vicksburg."

Templeton turned to his soldiers. "Duckett and Curran, fire another round into this alien's neck and all the dogs to make sure they're dead. Zyga and Santner, go back to Vicksburg and do the same thing. The rest, move the wounded to the helicopters. Delta Force will be here in two hours, be ready for evacuation."

The soldiers, dirt-encrusted, bloodied, and exhausted, were finally starting to relax in a grassy clearing near the heliport. The moonless sky was a spray of stars, and patches of light clouds stretched to the horizon. The startling sound of a choked-off scream shattered the lull. A soldier fell to the ground, his head and upper torso separated from the rest of his body.

Everyone ducked except for one lonely figure who stood facing the darkness, his weapon dropped, his shoulders slouched.

"Curran!" Templeton whispered.

No response.

"Curran!" Templeton repeated, a bit louder.

Curran slowly turned, his face pale and blank, blood flowing from his neck. He suddenly collapsed.

Templeton checked Curran's live-monitor. "Curran is dead. Everyone stay down."

The soldiers huddled together in a phalanx formation, their weapons levelled. Terror had returned. No one moved, faces were tight with fear, and eyes intensely focused. Although nerves were frayed, whatever was out there, they were as ready for it as they could be.

Templeton peered into the gloom as a light fog settled on the low ground surrounding them. The deep silence added to the eeriness. "Delta Force will be here in just over an hour. We'll do nothing 'til then." There was fear in his eyes and a waver in his voice. The soldiers were witnessing a first: a scared Templeton. "Let's hope the wait isn't too long." Templeton slowly looked across his soldiers' faces. "I need five volunteers to stay behind to assist the new troops."

Zyga was the first to raise a hand.

***

A thorough and cautious night search convinced Templeton and the US Army Delta Force captain, Andrew Mackenzie, that there were no aliens within the fort. The colours of sunrise made everything look surprisingly peaceful. An aerial surveillance drone found a single blue-armband alien four kilometres away, heading towards the mountains.

The mountains were rocky, steep, and lightly wooded. Templeton, with half of the Delta Force squadron, set off to pursue the marooned alien after being dropped by helicopters as close as they dared. Mackenzie and the other half-squadron were dropped three kilometres in front of Marooned. Briefed by Templeton on the previous day's battle and warned that his task would likely be bloody, Mackenzie took up hidden positions on Rigby Ridge and waited.

Later that day, Templeton lost three soldiers in a disastrous firefight and was forced to drop back. Marooned quickly disappeared into the distance. It was unnaturally quick, crawling through gaps like an insect and leaping over obstacles with the agility of a graceful wildcat. *Where's it heading?* Templeton's solemn stare showed his desperation. It was difficult enough to kill this thing during the day, he didn't want to be still hunting it after sunset.

Snapping tree branches and swaying shrubs alerted Mackenzie to the creature's approach. It leaped onto a large rock, where a hail of bullets from Mackenzie's half-squadron funnelled it into a narrow valley.

With Templeton closing in from the rear and bullet after bullet peppering its neck, Marooned attempted a desperate escape past Rigby Ridge. Its swiftness, deadly laser, and impregnable armour made this a distinct possibility. However, Mackenzie's trap held, and an array of withering gunfire from a hundred soldiers unrelentingly pinged from the creature's neck and knees.

Marooned's left knee collapsed, sending the creature tumbling down a steep slope and slamming hard against a large boulder. It immediately leaped up on one leg, its right hand against the boulder, its left hand clamped over its neck. Its weapon was missing.

"Cease fire!" yelled Templeton, dropping his rifle, taking a step towards Marooned, and holding up both hands. If he was afraid, he wasn't showing it. The creature ignored him, its eyes combing the ground for its weapon. Templeton knew that Marooned could still kill them all if it regained its weapon, and there was nothing they could do to prevent it while the creature's hand protected its neck. If it didn't surrender, he needed to distract it enough for it to remove its hand.

Templeton took several steps forward, stopping at thirty metres. Marooned's attention finally snapped to him. It hunched, as if about to pounce towards him. Templeton stood still, more like rigid with fear. The two figures stood there, as if frozen in time.

The soldiers watched in horror, bracing themselves, gripping their rifles.

"What's he doing?" asked one Delta Force soldier, his voice taut.

"Trying to get himself killed," answered another.

"Keep your sights on its neck, and be ready to fire when ordered," Mackenzie broadcast over the radio.

Marooned's eyes slowly drifted off Templeton and again searched for its weapon.

"Be careful, cap'n," yelled Mackenzie. "It's planning something."

Templeton spotted the weapon six metres behind Marooned in tall grass. Mackenzie also spotted it and moved slowly towards it. Then Marooned saw it and instantly sprang for it, using both arms to balance. Mackenzie tried to reach it first, but backed off when he couldn't.

Templeton had enough. "Shoot the beast!" he shouted. "Shoot the H-HAR!"

Every soldier opened fire at its exposed neck. Marooned's luck finally ran out. A bullet struck home, and its body slumped to the ground.

The soldiers gathered around, looking at the lifeless anomaly. Shadows now covered the entire landscape. Darkness was moving in, and a gentle breeze picked up around them.

"We're lucky there were so few of them, captain," Zyga said.

Templeton's eyes looked up at the angry orange sky. "I suspect our next encounter will be far more devastating."

Chapter 15   Why Fort Bush?

"No one seems to know what they were searching for at Fort Bush," said the overwhelmed UN Secretary General. "We need to find out."

To a few within the EDO, there was only one possibility. Nineteen years earlier, Fort Bush was the secret landing site for the Moon transport rockets carrying the DSDs.

The official EDO response to the attack on Fort Bush was, "We don't know what the H-HARs were searching for, if indeed they were searching for anything. This is under investigation." For most spokespersons, this was the truth. They really didn't know.

The media was largely sceptical of the US government's denials about alien artefacts at Fort Bush. Other governments joined the media chorus in demanding that any artefacts be returned to the aliens as a sign of goodwill.

With media headlines increasingly predicting imminent doom and the US government's failure to debunk rumours, public anxiety quickly turned into near panic.

Persistent and credible security leaks eventually forced the US government and the EDO to publicly acknowledge the discovery of extraterrestrial relics on the Moon. There was no disclosure of what these relics were nor any indication that it was an entire spaceship.

Within days, noisy news media and capitulating governments called on the US to return the relics. The public's desire to appease the H-HARs grew.

"We should give them part of the Earth to avoid conflict," one politician said. "That's better than annihilation. Perhaps South America."

Those within the EDO who knew about the existence of the DSDs were secretly asking, "Why would the H-HARs want to get hold of the Moon-ship DSDs?"

Kevin Garrett, who, after three years in the EDO, had become one of its strongest hawks, was sure he knew the answer. He told an EDO committee: "To negate the accumulated information errors on their own DSDs and obtain an accurate and complete set of instructions to quickly build a relativistic impact weapon."

The media and public continued to harass governments to return the relic, whatever it was. And it was gaining further political support, with some politicians claiming that the EDO was just trying to satisfy its scientific curiosity, regardless of the risk. "We can't give it back," Garrett argued. "The consequences would be too dire to contemplate."

Ultimately, politicians had the final say, and they decided to give the DSDs – known to the public only as "the relic" – back to the H-HARs.

Meanwhile, a thorough investigation concluded that the DSDs were exposed at least once outside of their electromagnetic proof enclosure at Fort Bush. That was the only location where this occurred, and they must have been detected by the H-HARs on Pallas during this period.

Chapter 16   DSDs Returned

Six months after the Fort Bush attacks, in terrain flat and barren as far as the eye could see, a circle of red flags ruffled in the breeze. At the centre were the DSDs, removed from their electromagnetic proof enclosures. The remoteness and emptiness of the surroundings, and the absence of humans, reflected a feeling of trepidation and perplexity.

Two days later, an H-HAR spaceship lifted off from Mars. Earth braced itself for another attack. Thirty-one days later, it entered Earth's orbit. Emergency sirens sounded around the world. A small drop-craft emerged. Within minutes, its shadow swam over the featureless landscape and landed adjacent to the DSDs.

Hidden cameras showed the H-HARs transferring the DSDs into their drop-craft.

Next to the DSDs was another item: a gold-plated aluminium tablet with pictorial drawings and symbols indicating Earth was friendly and welcoming. A green-armband glanced at it with the stolid indifference of someone walking past cow dung.

The drop-craft returned to its spaceship, which immediately launched missiles at the Japanese and Ukrainian rocket launching facilities; the two sites the H-HARs failed to destroy on their first visit. This time, however, the missiles were intercepted by a new defence system.

Instead of Mars, the spaceship headed towards the Moon, destroying six hundred Earth orbital satellites along the way.

Although all crewed lunar facilities were abandoned months earlier, the H-HARs made no attempt to check their occupancy.

The world's media asked in horrified anticipation, "Why the Moon?"

***

This second visit generated many UFO stories.

A mining engineer on a lonely road, forty kilometres east of the collection site, saw an egg shaped, metallic object hovering fifty metres above the ground and 1.5 kilometres off the road. "It was clearly visible in the setting Sun. I could see a faint thrust from its engines. It moved away in a westerly direction and disappeared. I reported it to the local police."

A remote camper, fifty kilometres east of the collection site, was preparing dinner. "I heard a weird, whistling sound. About one kilometre away, a long, thick object was flying low. It shot past me at high speed and quickly disappeared."

Chapter 17   RIW

Kevin Garrett's suspicions were correct. He looked horrified. In an email, he wrote:

> Intel has just identified the structures being assembled by the H-HARs on the Moon, and it's the worst scenario. A doomsday Relativistic Impact Weapon, or RIW, to target Earth with projectiles travelling at relativistic velocities. Such a bombardment would eradicate all life, including the most resilient bacteria. Our planet's surface would be completely barren.

At a subsequent media announcement, Garrett braced himself as the world's gaze fell upon him. "This weapon shoots a projectile close to the speed of light." His voice had a tone of urgency mixed with primal fear. "At eighty-five per cent of light speed, or 0.85 c, the kinetic energy of the projectile impacting the Earth is equal to its rest mass, that is, $E=mc^2$. The weapon being built by the H-HARs could be as high as this."

Nervous glances spread across the room, then everyone's attention immediately returned to Garrett.

"To give you some understanding, the world's most powerful nuclear explosion was the Soviet Union's Tsar hydrogen bomb in 1961. It destroyed everything within a fifty-kilometre radius, caused third-degree burns a hundred kilometres away and shock waves seven hundred kilometres away. The explosion could be seen and heard from a thousand kilometres away."

Garrett's expression darkened, and his tone became more ominous. "If just one of the hundred and sixty-kilogram tube projectiles we can see on the lunar surface were to impact the Earth at even 0.7 c, the devastation would be thirty times that of the Tsar bomb. And they can produce thousands of these projectiles, with an estimated firing rate of one per day."

Garrett paused to allow the fear to sink in. "Most of the destruction will be from the mechanical blast, but there will also be deadly radiation."

Shock and despair shot across the room. Garrett had just prophesied the end of the world.

A reporter questioned, "But … but why would any rational being want to destroy this planet?"

"These beings are not rational, mate," Garrett answered bluntly, surprised this question was still being asked.

"Could you be wrong about the weapon? Could they be building something else, something we can't comprehend?" another reporter asked.

"No, mate!" Garrett shook his head bleakly. "The evidence is irrefutable. The site's location on the lunar equator, the coils, the storage ultracapacitors, the boron-11 storage tanks, the fusion power generators, and the cooling towers – it's all there. The most damning of all are the rod projectiles and the four-metre-wide barrel pointing directly at us. All this is visible through ultra-high resolution telescopes. They obviously want us to see the very thing that will destroy us. We're sitting ducks."

When the same question was asked again, Garrett was confused. His previous response must have somehow been inadequate. Focusing his stare, he wanted to leave no doubt this time.

"Listen. It's absolutely certain that the H-HARs are building this weapon, and I mean absolutely. Anyone who argues otherwise is wasting their time and, more importantly, everyone else's time. Time we simply don't have. Once this weapon fires, it'll be the end of us, the end of everything. If we don't stop them, then you can kiss your arse and everybody else's arse goodbye."

The question wasn't raised again.

"How can we stop them?" another reporter asked.

Garrett initially ignored the question. He wanted, when he finally did answer, to keep any hint of hopelessness from showing on his face, but also to shock the world into action.

"The only thing we can do is somehow destroy the weapon before they use it and prevent them from building another one." He said the words without any belief in the possibility.

"How about the Kessler barrier?" a reporter asked.

"When the H-HARs destroyed our satellites," Garrett explained, "the wreckage formed a Kessler barrier around Earth. This means we cannot launch any space operations for three years."

"How long before the weapon can fire?" another reporter asked.

"It's … uhh … it's hard to say …"

"Could we already be doomed?"

"The weapon is extremely complex," Garrett said. "However, in just seven months, they're well into the major structures. If they maintain this rate of progress, the weapon could be ready in four years."

Garrett stopped taking questions. The reporters were overly excited, and he couldn't offer any more information or hope. However, he wasn't done. He made an unequivocal statement. Whether it was calculated or not was unclear, but it would soon rock governments around the world.

"The *relic*," he said, "that our governments gave back to the H-HARs were digital storage devices. We're sure that the H-HARs are using information from these DSDs to build their weapon.

Without this information, we believe it would have taken them hundreds, even thousands, of years."

Earth now understood the magnitude of the H-HAR threat – extinction.

***

Meanwhile, at 10 Downing Street:

"He didn't?"

"Yes, Mr Prime Minister. I'm afraid he did."

"Get the inner cabinet in here right away," the PM demanded, his face tightening. "We need to downplay this; otherwise, this government is finished."

At the White House:

"He what?"

"Yes, Mr President. On live media. He just announced to the world that the H-HARs are using the *relic* we gave back to them to build their RIW weapon."

"I knew that son of a bitch Australian couldn't be trusted." The president tried to stifle his shock, well aware of the ramifications for his administration.

Chapter 18   Any Plan

"They're planning to wipe us out with some giant space bug spray," said Belgium's representative, summing up the mood of the UN General Assembly session on planetary defence. "And what can we do? Nothing. They're aliens." He sounded as if it were inevitable.

Despite the negativity, the session concluded with the EDO being directed to devise a plan to save Earth, no matter how unlikely it may appear.

Outside, among the confusion of delegates arriving and leaving, police supervised a huge crowd. Most applauded the decision, but at the back, an angry mob of fanatical dissenters and the dispossessed shook banners and screamed obscenities. They were about to light a huge bonfire.

Terry Dittmar, a delegate but no longer defence secretary, approached them. "You people sound like eulogists for the human race. Can you explain to me what the problem is here?"

One wild-eyed protester waved her arms furiously, ranting, raving, and spitting out words. "We're outraged at these trumpedup, hoaxed-up alien invasion bullshit stori—"

"Whoa …" Dittmar said. "You've lost me on the trumped-up, hoaxed-up bit."

"What!? … They want us to willingly bundle together under a single world dictatorial government, and this is all part of it." She scornfully pointed at the UN building. "These inbred—"

"Now you've lost me again."

"What are you talking about, mister?"

"What I'm guessing," Dittmar said, "and give me some slack here, is that what's being done to save the planet from annihilation by the H-HARs doesn't quite make sense to you?"

"Huh? … Look, you corrupt, ruling elite think everyone is your servant. The web of deceit in this whole conspiracy is unbelievable. You're preparing us for something really big. I can tell by all these bullshit stories popping up everywhere."

"Well," said Dittmar, staring bewilderedly. "I really wish at least a little bit of what you said was correct."

***

The news media picked up Kevin Garrett's story about the H-HARs using the DSDs to build their weapon. The same media that demanded their leaders return the alien relic now labelled them as incompetent and reckless for doing so.

Many countries that voted to return the *relic* now claimed they were unaware of its significance. Russia would not work with any state leader responsible for this "catastrophic misjudgement". The French President's attempt to dodge questions on live media in a last-ditch effort to save his government was a disaster. He looked like a man caught beating his dog.

Dissent threatened to drive the global alliance apart.

Within five months, all major governments involved with returning the DSDs lost office. The global alliance only survived thanks to Terry Dittmar's careful diplomacy.

Dittmar was also instrumental in forming an international advisory group of military and civilian experts to find the most feasible plan to save Earth. The group was locked away, with Terry Dittmar as chairman. After five days, Dittmar asked for more experts and locked everyone away again.

The daily reports indicated nothing. Then the daily reports stopped; only verbal messages from Dittmar that they had no time to provide them.

On the twelfth day, Dittmar issued a plan to the UN with a simple preamble: "This represents our best and only hope."

The plan was: "Secretly land a large assault force on the Moon to destroy their weapon, wipe out the H-HARs, and capture the DSDs."

Despite doubts about its viability, the plan was immediately accepted.

Soon after, Dittmar announced he was returning full time to his business interests.

Chapter 19   Desperation

"Mr President, Mr Prime Minister," addressed the Indian defence minister, immediately after returning from the clatter and clamour of the UN. Nodding courteously to each, he continued in an indoctrinated tone of hopelessness. "As you are aware, we voted to send an attack force to the Moon, and—"

"Yes, we know that." The prime minister was irritated, impatient, and anxious for answers. "Did we have a choice?"

It was a question, a statement, and an expression of defeat. And it was silently accepted as such.

"What about preliminary planning?" the prime minister asked.

"Nothing! Mr Prime Minister," the defence minister hesitantly advised, shaking his head. "Absolutely nothing."

The prime minister stared impatiently for elaboration. The defence minister plunged into explanations. "There are no Moon rockets for troop transportation, no heavy equipment or life support systems, no touchdown sites, and no Moon transport vehicles. Troops require training. Combat drones, Moon equipment, and weapons need to be built and tested. New strategies developed. Earth launch facilities need rebuilding …" He gave up.

The prime minister's face was bewildered. He pulled his hard stare to the president, keeping it there for some time, then back to the defence minister. "I heard they had a plan to reach the Moon without these aliens knowing?"

The defence minister blinked rapidly. "Well, yes and no … I mean … they don't know if it'll work." He paused for a second before going on hesitantly. "Basically, the plan is to launch the rockets during a penumbral lunar eclipse … um, when the Sun, Earth, and Moon align. This will allow the rockets to travel to the Moon's orbit behind the Earth so that the aliens, or H-HARs – Hostile Humanoid Alien Robots – as they are now called, on the Moon won't see them. The rockets then travel along the Moon's retrograde orbit to the Moon, with the Sun's glare directly behind them, hopefully concealing them from the H-HARs. It'll depend on a lot of H-HAR complacency."

"Bloody hell!" said the president, his mouth agape as he paced to the other side of the room before turning. "It's not much of a plan."

"Well, Mr President, as the prime minister mentioned, this is the only plan they could come up with. The advisory group almost broke up several times in a state of hopelessness. It was only the brilliant skills of the US chairman, Mr Terry Dittmar, that kept everyone there and focused."

"Dittmar? The former US defence minister?"

"Yeah, him."

"Okay, okay," said the prime minister, nodding approvingly. "Terry's a good man. While I understand we can't just do nothing and await our fate, surely other options were considered?"

"There is a Plan B and Plan C. Both involve nuclear warheads. Both are likely to be intercepted by the H-HARs since they won't have Sun cover. Plan B is a launch from the Moon's surface if our troops get that far, and Plan C is an Earth launch. But neither includes recovery of the DSDs."

"But my understanding is that we need the DSDs to have any chance against these H-HARs."

"That's correct, Mr Prime Minister."

The president and prime minister exchanged a hard look.

The defence minister continued. "Preparations are starting immediately, and it'll require unprecedented cooperation between all countries."

"Yeah, well, tell that to the Pakistanis and the Chinese," said the prime minister. "What's the completion estimate for the alien weapon? And when are they planning to launch this attack?"

"They estimate the doomsday RIW will be finished in four years, which is the minimum time they indicated is required for preparations and training for the attack. By then, the Kessler barrier should be traversable."

The prime minister's shoulders dropped, and his arms fell by his side, strengthless. A knot tightened in his gut. He turned away, stepped to the window, and gazed out at the Sun quenched parliamentary lawns. "This could all be gone in a sea of flames soon," he murmured as a tear almost rose in one eye.

"Mr Prime Minister?"

The prime minister waited for any sign of the tear to disappear, then turned to face the other two. "God help us all," he managed before quickly leaving the room.

***

After the initial worldwide panic, governments and the public eventually overcame their defeatism and strengthened their commitments. Celebrity performances, movies, documentaries, songs, ads, books, stories, musicals, and plays all focused on a united Earth defending the planet in a total war against an evil alien menace.

PART 3

CONFRONTATON ON THE MOON – OPERATION THEIA

"Let's hope you guys aren't the last humans alive."

Chapter 20   To the Moon

Nineteen spaceplanes accelerated along the runway centreline before climbing steeply through the sunlit sky. Tension was high. The Earthlings were finally on their seemingly damned journey to confront their nemesis on the Moon after almost four years of planning, building, testing, and training.

Their first stop – the inclined Earth Orbital Transfer Station.

Rapid construction progress by the H-HARs forced the mission to be brought forward 29.5 days to the preceding penumbral lunar eclipse. This meant that, after emerging from behind the Earth, the rockets would now have to cross a five-degree gap of clear space before the Sun's glare is behind them.

The spaceplanes carried 312 combat troops, 294 CARs, 32 engineers, 19 support personnel, 10 medics, 6 scientific officers, 2 historians, and 2 videographers.

Also on board was Lieutenant Alex Zyga. While he was confronting Vicksburg at Fort Bush, his entire family was killed during the attack on the Texas space launch facilities. He immediately volunteered for future H-HAR operations.

The spaceplanes arrived at the transfer station three hours later.

Assembled in space from prefabricated segments when the Kessler barrier dissipated, the transfer station orbited the Earth opposite the Moon in the Moon's orbit at the Earth-Moon

L3 Lagrange point. Its discovery by the H-HARs would have guaranteed a sad ending for humanity.

During the one-day stopover, troops and equipment were transferred onto Moon-transports.

"If you're sending a message home, do it now," advised videographer Penny. "Radio silence is about to start."

"I said my goodbyes on Earth," videographer Tony replied.

Penny turned, catching Tony's eye. "I didn't realise we were saying our goodbyes!" Thin, nervous grins slowly spread across their faces.

Right on schedule, the operations officer announced, "All systems are A-okay; transports are ready to go."

Fourteen troop and eight support transports accelerated from the transfer station, pressing heavily on their passengers. Their next stop – the Moon.

***

A medic on the transfer station watched wide-eyed, as the Moon-transports pushed away from their berths, turned outwards, shrank to dots, and vanished. "It's all up to them now," her whispered voice drowned out by the noisy hum of the station's power plant.

Strangely, behind her, a voice whispered back. "What do you think their chances are?"

Without the slightest thought about who she was talking to, she whispered instinctively. "Probably about one in a thousand, I reckon."

Again, a whispered reply, "History will tell."

She stood there for some time, mesmerised by the stars. Her job now was to prepare for their return, a task she hoped wouldn't prove unwarranted.

***

The transports continued to accelerate hard along the Moon's retrograde orbit. They were about to emerge from behind Earth and enter the Earth-to-Sun gap of clear space. The engines were shut down and cooled with slush hydrogen to prevent IR detection. And just in time. The Moon, cold, remote, and fear-inducing, suddenly appeared. They would be easily visible to the aliens on the Moon for the next two hours. That is, if the aliens bothered to look.

Everything fell quiet, only the whirr of the life support blowers could be heard. At any moment, without warning, the journey could abruptly end in the flash of a deadly laser beam.

Videographer Penny, in Transport-03, pointed alarmingly through the side window. "We're off course! Look at the Moon; we're heading into outer space!"

"It's okay, Penny," Lieutenant Alex Zyga reassured. "We'll turn towards the Moon as we move along its orbit."

The tension was also too much for videographer Tony. "These transports are just fucking glorified coffins. The aliens will spot us for sure." His rapid breathing betrayed his inner terror. "Where the hell is Transport-02? It was just out there!" A sergeant tried to calm him, but he pulled away, chewed on a nail, and muttered, "I'm fine."

The transports pressed on across the gap, the last minutes seemingly endless. At last, over the intercom, "Ladies and gentlemen, this is the pilot. The gap is bridged!"

"Hallelujah!" One relieved soldier called out. The rest cheered.

Although they were still in the H-HARs' direct line of sight, at least now they had the Sun's glare directly behind them.

Two and a half days later, with a much larger Moon visible through the front window and the transports hidden below the alien's western horizon, everyone started to relax, if only a little. Although awed by the ever-nearing, sunlit Moon, the next four days passed in total monotony.

The following day, after flying low over the Moon's dark surface, the transports approached the touch down point, an evacuated mining village on the western side of crater Cyrillus, four hundred kilometres from the H-HARs.

Transport-08 was the first to land. It vibrated fiercely when the landing computer failed, fifty metres above the surface. The backup computer assumed control, but four metres from touch down the descent engines failed. The crew braced themselves as the transport slammed onto the surface, its landing gear reduced to a mangled wreck. The comms engineer rushed to a window, but all he saw was dust.

Transport-07, carrying commander-in-charge Colonel Andrew Mackenzie, was the last to land. It hit the surface with a heavy jar. He broadcast a sobering message to all transports. "Training starts in twelve hours. Six-hour periods every twenty-four hours until we leave in fourteen days. It will be tough, demanding, and extremely dangerous. But I can assure you, it will not prepare us for the tough unknowns ahead." His voice was surprisingly calm.

The soldiers, now suited up, were anxious to disembark; it had been a long journey. Alex Zyga was waiting at the exit door, helmet on, leading the way.

Videographer Tony was the last passenger to exit his transport. He hesitantly stepped onto the gangplank and stopped. Night had just fallen, and it would be another fourteen Earth days until sunrise. The ghostly moonscape slowly emerged before him in the dim, eerie glow of Earthlight. Rocks and craters of every shape and size filled the terrain, and the sky was black with a billion stars. It looked cold, lifeless, and alien. Tony checked the outside temperature: minus 170 degrees Celsius. He couldn't believe it would rise to 120 degrees Celsius during the day. It was only pushing from behind by a crewman that moved him on.

Chapter 21   The Force

After the battle at Fort Bush, Andrew Mackenzie was selected to train three thousand elite soldiers for future combat operations against the H-HARs. This earned him the rank of colonel. The tall, heavily built American was an obvious choice to lead the Moon's multi-national assault force.

Following in the footsteps of his great-great-grandfather, who landed at Normandy on D-Day during World War II, Mackenzie entered the U.S. Military Academy at West Point. His disregard for authority caused initial conflict; however, he eventually accepted the military's no-nonsense demeanour.

A natural leader who radiated authority, physical power, and intelligence, he gained a reputation for offensive actions. He rated politicians as the most failed professionals. They quickly forgot about the dead and injured, claimed victories while denying defeats, shifted from alarmism to denialism, and were so engrossed in their comfortable lives that they had little regard for the suffering and sacrifices on the battlefields. Re-election opportunities for them were death, injury, and consoling families for him. He insisted on being a part of any political decision that affected his soldiers.

Major Philip Saunders, deputy commander, was the 'old man' of the team. He fought alongside Mackenzie in the Saudi Arabian War. The deep creases in his face, the scar tissue over his body, burn scars on his left cheek and arm, a bullet wound, and a half dozen bone fractures that never properly healed implied a street brawler. However, an arm full of stripes and a special forces tattoo implied something else. A bull-necked, capable, and intense soldier, he had a reputation for toughness, and there was certainly no lack of respect for his authority. Secretly, he suffered from severe back pain, but lately it had eased and miraculously vanished under stressful conditions.

Like the others, Saunders spent the night before his departure with his family. The mission was a tight secret, but his face and the struggle to avoid questions gave much away. The following morning, his wife, Angel, pulled him back with a tight hug. "Don't you think you've done enough?" she asked in a trembling voice. "They know you're the best. That's why they keep asking you. But why, for God's sake, can't it be someone else?"

Saunders held her close, then turned and left, torn between his heart and duty. He could give all the logical reasons, but none would mean anything to her. Like any man heading off to war, he knew he might never see his family again.

The soldiers who came to fight in this unearthly place were the finest Earth had to offer. Mackenzie saw to that. No doubts about volunteering. No concerns about national interests. They were part of the most justifiable battle in human history. Earth's final unification was symbolised by their left shoulder patches depicting a blue-white Earth and the initials LEF – Lunar Expeditionary Force.

They were resourceful, dedicated, and aggressive. Mackenzie was certain they were exactly what he needed to defeat the H-HARs. He insisted on each soldier receiving a full retirement pension, including all medical and counselling costs. If they did not return, all benefits would pass to their families.

The soldiers' bodysuits and helmets were contoured layers of lightweight, body-fitting, smart fabric providing the agility of normal clothing. The outside layer, a shear-thickening fluid built from nanocomposite particles, instantly hardened around any impact area and repaired minor breaches. This protected them from solar radiation, alien attack dogs, micrometeoroids, and ballistics, but not the alien lasers. The recycling rebreather only required a small oxygen tank. Life support systems were powered by forty-eight-hour capacitors housed in two hip packs. The helmet display provided 3D mapping, target identification, and other battlefield data.

The primary assault weapon was the semi-automatic MW-7 gauss rifle. The automatic aiming adjustment and the narrow profiled, depleted uranium pellets that shatter on impact should make the H-HARs' necks and knees far more vulnerable than at Fort Bush.

They also carried the four H-HAR hafnium-laser rifles captured from Fort Bush. This was all they had; the weapons were too technically complicated to reverse engineer. The Moonship lasers were deactivated and unusable. Each soldier carried an adaptor device that would clip onto a seized H-HAR laser weapon, allowing them to use it.

A high-powered handgun was carried for terminating H-HARs at close quarters and easy insertion into the mouths of alien attack dogs.

The CARs were far superior to those at Fort Bush. Their ultracapacitors provided over forty-eight hours of continuous combat action, with nearly equal mobility to a human. They had no single point of failure and were sufficiently intelligent to perform simple operations without human intervention.

The NA-30 shoulder-fired rocket launcher was one of two options to destroy the H-HARs' doomsday weapon. It had an eighty-metre surface blast zone, but firing required a visual. The second was a hafnium-178 nuclear grenade, with explosive equivalency to 30 tons of TNT.

Coffee-cup sized Mini Melting Robots, or MMRs, were designed to crawl towards an H-HAR, spring onto its body, and ignite dicyanoacetylene, producing a mass at five thousand degrees Celsius to melt through the H-HARs' armour and disable it.

Bursting field grenades would distribute superdense, ultrafine, laser-diffusing crystals and smoke to conceal oncoming soldiers and CARs.

Other weapons included rocket-operated overhead surveillance cameras, paint grenades, paint bullets, and radiofrequency jammers to disrupt communications between H-HARs.

Chapter 22   Lunar Night

Cyrillus was a Helium-3 pilot processing plant, evacuated just before the attack on Fort Bush. Recommissioned and made functional again, the village was a transient island of life in a hostile and changeless wilderness, a human outpost in a silent world of inky darkness.

Videographer Penny recorded: "… bunker-like concrete shells buried under the regolith and connected by tunnels. It's crowded, claustrophobic, and the air smells of piss. Our water comes from melting ice, which is steel hard and razor sharp. It's easy to imagine why someone would go crazy here. But it seems like a safe place to hide.

"At the first sign of sunrise, the soldiers will board surface transports to launch an attack to determine the future of the human race. We will be there to record it all. Cyrillus village will once again be abandoned. Maybe forever."

***

"Andrew, Plan C is ready to be launched," said General Clive Fischer from Supreme Command during a video briefing.

Mackenzie's stern expression said it all. "What are the final details?" He already had a good idea.

"Once contact is made with the enemy, two nuclear missiles will be launched from Earth. They'll take only 28.5 hours to reach the H-HAR site. But without the Sun's background protection, they may be detected." Fischer's voice lowered ominously. "So that's all the time you have, Andrew. If you complete your mission, we'll disarm the missiles before they reach you. If not …"

"Can't say I'm thrilled about being killed by friendly fire, general," Mackenzie said, feeling a tightness in his chest. "It's not much time."

"Andrew." Fischer moved closer to the camera. His face was stone. "We don't have much time. The weapon is almost ready."

The tightness in Mackenzie's chest just got tighter. "Okay, general. I'll talk to the soldiers." Concern coloured his tone.

"How did the laser penetration test go, Andrew?"

"They confirmed the lab results, general. The vaporising gas and resolidification of Moon rock and regolith effectively limited laser penetration to about a metre."

"That's excellent news. Is Plan B all set?"

"Yes, general. Two missiles will be launched from Cyrillus mining village should our mission fail. However, with open terrain and the H-HARs' laser defences, their chances of getting through are low."

Plans B and C were not Mackenzie's main concern; there wasn't even time to think about them. Training had not gone exactly as planned, and time had run out. Troops were bored, their time at Cyrillus in the dark had been an eternity, and they wanted to go. Soon, lives would be at stake in a battle like never before – an alien foe in an alien environment, with every decision determining humanity's fate.

***

Lieutenant Alex Zyga sat at the end of a cold steel table on a wobbly steel chair, poking at his breakfast. Around him, other soldiers were wolfing theirs down.

"This time tomorrow, Alex, we'll be on our way," Mackenzie remarked casually as he sat beside him.

"Oh, hi, sir … Good. We're all eager to get going." Zyga's vacant eyes revealed the heavy toll the H-HARs had taken on him.

"If I've learned anything from the military, it's how to wait patiently."

"I'm still learning that, sir." Zyga dug his fork into a container of food.

"Alex, I wanted to thank you for helping with the training. You've been invaluable, being the only one with real combat experience against these aliens."

"Thanks, sir. But it'll be a different battle here than Fort Bush."

"Yes, but we're prepared this time. The key issue will be capturing more of their laser rifles."

"Do you think they'll be waiting for us, sir?"

"I don't know. But they've been trained to destroy worlds with a planetary weapon, not by ground combat. And I'm predicting their rigid command structure won't lend itself to dynamic battle conditions."

"That's good to hear, sir."

Mackenzie blew over his coffee, then slowly spoke. "I'm sorry about your family. I'd like to hear what happened."

Zyga took a moment, but his voice was firm. "I haven't talked about it much."

Mackenzie simply nodded, a simpatico presence.

"A chopper flew me home to Texas the night we terminated Marooned. The space launch facility was a wasteland after the H-HAR attack. Buildings were blown away. Blankets, sheets, and clothes hung everywhere. Bodies were all over, but not like Fort Bush; these were burned to cinders. The smell of burning flesh was everywhere, and white ash covered everything. First responders were searching for survivors. I was heading towards my house when a building suddenly collapsed. There was screaming from the wreckage, so I hurried to help."

Zyga paused as the soldiers left after their breakfast. "Do you have to leave, sir?" he asked.

"No, please keep going."

Zyga closed his eyes and took a deep breath. "This is harder than I thought."

By now, the canteen was deserted.

"A firefighter was trapped. His right arm was missing. I can still see his face." Zyga's voice was still firm. "I lifted the rubble off him, then this crazy guy came up and wanted to move him. I told him, 'No, he'll bleed to death.' He insisted on moving him. Then I thought, this guy needs to fuck off, and I told him, 'Okay, go get something like a stretcher.' He left.

"An ambulance soon arrived and took over. I heard a soft 'thank you' from the firefighter as I left."

Zyga pushed away his half-finished breakfast; it no longer agreed with him.

"I continued towards my house. Another ambulance stopped; I waved it on. My street looked like a bombed-out war zone. When I reached home, I found the burned remains of my mother, younger brother, and sister. My father worked at the launch facility, so I knew he would be dead. They never had a chance to fight. Never had a chance to defend themselves. All they had acquired in a lifetime was destroyed. On their behalf, I want to *kill* as many of these H-HAR murderers as possible." Zyga's hand slowly curled into a fist, his haunted eyes showing something Mackenzie had only witnessed a few times before: an intense, unrelenting, vengeful quest, and a willingness to die for it.

"Well, you'll get that opportunity real soon, Alex," said Mackenzie.

Mackenzie put a hand on his shoulder as they left.

Chapter 23   Moving Out

Mackenzie stirred lazily. He could feel his stiff joints from too many nights on this hard pallet bunk. He sat up on an elbow as a soft murmur passed by his door, an indication that others were already up and packing.

Pushing himself up, his bleary eyes stumbled upon the now-familiar wall poster on the door: WIN A DREAM HOLIDAY TO PARADISE. He could almost hear the surf crashing on the sunny beach and feel the gentle breeze blowing open the pages of the magazine on the sand, beckoning him to a well-deserved rest.

His fantasy suddenly collapsed as his mind returned to his task. To the reason he had come to this place. He ran through his plan again in his head – so many weaknesses, so many unknowns. His greatest fear was that the enemy would be waiting for them.

Suiting up, he grabbed his gear and headed down the narrow corridors, holding up his helmet to allow oncoming traffic to pass and ducking his head every few steps to avoid the low sectional joints. The village was a hive of activity.

Catching up with Saunders, they exchanged grins. The lunar night was ending, and it was time to move out.

"No matter how well the pieces have fitted together so far, Andrew," Saunders said, "I can't believe we've gotten this far."

Mackenzie nodded.

They contacted General Clive Fischer for an update. "The H-HARs have made considerable progress over the last eight days, Andrew. The weapon appears to be finished."

Mackenzie and Saunders exchanged despairing looks.

"How's your situation?" asked Fischer.

Mackenzie cleared his throat. "We're all suited up and about to board the surface transports. We'll take the quickest route, rather than concealment. ETA to the H-HAR site is twenty-five hours."

"Let's hope you guys aren't the last humans alive," Fischer remarked bluntly. "Our estimate has been updated to eight hundred H-HARs."

"Eight hundred!" Mackenzie and Saunders exclaimed.

"It's going to be tough, Andrew. We expect them to vigorously defend their weapon and spaceship once your presence becomes known. The good news is that there's still nothing to indicate they suspect anything."

"We have to go now, general," Mackenzie said, looking outside. "Is there anything else, sir?"

"No. We'll be monitoring your progress. Good luck, Andrew and Philip. They don't know it, but the world is counting on you."

Mackenzie signed off.

After fitting their helmets and packs, they picked up their weapons and stepped outside.

Mackenzie stopped, daunted. The long-awaited Sun was peeking over the horizon, lighting the very tops of the craters and giving a fresh, breathtaking unreality to the moonscape. The village plateau, now visible as grey and powdery, was worn and marked by mining. It ended abruptly on three sides with steep, towering ridges, their texture still hidden by darkness. The northern side disappeared into a deep chasm. *It's so quiet and still, so lonely and distant, so timeless and mindless, and ... so deadly.* It wasn't that long ago that he only comprehended this world as a small, two-dimensional yellow disc.

Saunders stopped some way ahead and turned. "Andrew?"

"I'm coming."

They rounded the maintenance building to a large open area and stopped to watch the soldiers queueing to board transport trailers. The trailers were made from the Moon-transports, fitted with wheels and towing fittings.

The boarding controller was gesturing in all directions, urging the soldiers to board quickly. It was a scene of frantic activity. He glanced across to Mackenzie and Saunders and waved. "Colonel Mackenzie, sir," he radioed. "We've just coupled the last trailer. Three trains, each with three trailers. Each train is hauled by an eight-wheeled all-terrain harvester."

"I hope they all make the distance," said Saunders.

"So do I," replied the boarding controller. "Each trailer has forty-five soldiers, so it's going to be crammed."

"When they're pressurised, we can take our helmets off," Mackenzie said. "That'll help."

One of the queues became restless. Saunders walked over to assist the controller.

Mackenzie was left to his thoughts. *My God! What a moment in history. These soldiers would be intimidating anywhere else. But here, it might be like a primitive warrior with a spear not knowing the enemy has a tank. These H-HARs could have some wonder weapon that'll just zap us. Maybe that's why our presence hasn't been detected. They might not even care that we're here.*

McKenzie was aware he should be afraid, yet he was numb to it. The mission was all that mattered, and it had to be completed no matter what the cost, even if it meant sacrificing himself and everyone around him.

Saunders is a godsend; asking him to join this mission wasn't easy, but it was essential. He'll finish the job if anything happens to me. Mackenzie turned back towards the trailers. *Speak of the devil.*

"They'll be ready for us to board in a few minutes, Andrew."

"Okay. Thanks, Phil."

Mackenzie looked up at the half-Earth floating in the starry blackness. "It's so fragile," he murmured.

Saunders looked up. "Well, it has some big problems that need fixing."

"Yeah. Problems that delayed this operation so much it almost didn't happen."

"Which leaves me worried about our future."

"Most people are followers, Phil," Mackenzie said. "All that's needed is a strong leader with clear vision, conviction, and good judgement, and the world will unite."

"You should go into politics, Andrew, because that person sounds like you."

Mackenzie shook his head and smiled. It was a pretty good smile too, given the circumstances. "Politics! Politics is just showbiz for ugly people, and my mum swears I'm not ugly. Besides, I'll be happy just to survive the next forty-eight hours."

Saunders looked to check on the transport trailers. "What do you make of all this red-green-blue-armband stuff?"

"It's a legacy of their culture: terror, totalitarianism, paranoia, and supremacy. This makes them very dangerous."

"The blue-armbands greatly outnumber the greens. I wonder what's preventing them from rebelling."

"The threat of permanent termination, I guess. And maybe an opportunity to become a green if they show outstanding loyalty."

"Well, it seems to work." Saunders glanced at the trailers.

"At Fort Bush, a green that was in danger of termination changed to a blue. Our experts believe this identity swap also included consciousness, so that a blue-armband would get terminated instead of a green one. They also believe that the swap indicates the red- and green-armbands backup their consciousness and memories, probably in the spaceship, making them almost digitally immortal."

Saunders turned to Mackenzie with a bewildered expression. "So, what happens if the red- and green-armbands are unharmed but their brain backups in the spaceship get wiped out?"

"I don't think anybody knows. Maybe their individual paranoia overrides their collective paranoia. Hopefully, we'll get to find out."

"I wonder what they think of us."

"They think nothing of us," Mackenzie answered blankly.

Saunders acknowledged a hand signal from the controller and picked up his gear. "Time to board, Andrew."

Mackenzie climbed into the second trailer of the first train, and Saunders climbed into the first trailer of the same train.

***

Videographer Tony pressed his face against the window, steaming it. He elbowed the soldier next to him. "You know, Scott, there's something dangerous about that man. It shows in everything he does."

"Mackenzie?"

"Yeah."

"He can be mean and pragmatic; harsh, demanding, and overbearing, and many hate him for it. But he's the best commander I've ever had; smart, leads from the front, and if we have any chance against these H-HARs, he's our best."

"Was that the Saudi War?"

"Yeah." Scott's eyes lowered, not warming to the recollections. "We lost six good soldiers and were forced to evacuate. The whole operation was a stuff-up by our commander. We almost shot him ourselves. Mackenzie was flown in. We all thought, another dumbass commander, but he immediately took control. The first thing he told us was, 'These bastards think we're pussies. We'll show them who the pussies are. Stay tight, watch your flanks, tell me what you see, and listen to me carefully.' We headed back out with Mackenzie and wiped out the same motherfuckers that kicked our arses earlier, and without losing anyone. We showed them who the pussies were."

Tony slowly nodded as they settled into the reflective silence of a long and anxious journey.

***

As the door closed behind him, Mackenzie could see uncertainty in the soldiers' eyes, but also an eagerness to go. He gave each one a sharp, encouraging look and a reassuring nod, conveying a confidence he didn't feel.

"Next stop, the H-HARs' camp," he said as they moved off.

The CARs, equipment, and supply trains followed.

With the Sun still rising and the transports departing in semi-darkness, Mackenzie's mind filled with doubts. *Was this possibility adequately addressed? Was this underestimated? Will the H-HARs' necks and knees still be vulnerable?* Despite his efforts to remain positive, he couldn't help but worry about the unknowns.

His mentor's words flashed across his mind: "First contact with the enemy is like sex with a stranger. You never know what's going to happen."

He shook all distracting thoughts out of his head. *We can only make the best of the hand we're dealt.*

Mackenzie didn't have the time or resources to fight for every hill. He had to advance quickly and relentlessly at every opportunity, regardless of losses. His plan was to use smoke grenades to diffuse the H-HARs' lasers, cross the open areas, and eliminate them with point-blank shots to their necks.

Destroying the doomsday weapon is not enough. We must ensure that another one can never be built. If this means destroying their spaceship and endangering the DSDs, then so be it. But maybe, just maybe, we won't have to.

Lunar dust hazed their wheels as the transports bobbed and weaved over the Moon's tortured surface. They travelled south-west across relatively open ground to crater Tacitus, swerving around smaller craters without slowing. Turning west, they zig-zagged through the rugged gaps and broken ridges between crater Abulfeda to the north and crater Almanon to the south.

The Sun made its first appearance as the transports emerged from the shadows like beasts from a cave, casting long, dark shadows across the sides of the craters. There was no colour, just black and white.

Passengers were told to grab the "Jesus-bar" as they braced themselves against the bench seats. But the rigours of the journey bounced them up and down like toys. They continued westward past a flat ridge north of Abulfeda F, then along Abulfeda A and an unnamed chain of small craters on their left. Winding through a shallow valley that curved to the right in an elongated arc around small ridges, they crossed into more open terrain until they passed within ten kilometres of the southern edge of crater Burnham. From there to the drop-off point, the terrain was broken only by low, sharp-edged crater ridges and depressions.

Passengers on the first train received a tour commentary over the PA system from the pilot. She described crater Abulfeda as: "A gigantic sixty-five-kilometre-wide crater with steep, three-kilometre-high sides. The floor is basalt and relatively smooth. You can see that most of the south wall is marked with small craters, and there's a small landslide on the south-western side if it's not still in the dark shadows. This crater marks the northern end of a long chain of craters extending for two hundred and forty kilometres."

A soldier asked how she knew all these landmarks. "On and off, I spent eighteen months at the Cyrillus mine site," she explained, "until we were evacuated over four years ago. For the last three years, I've been studying contour maps and planning this route."

The transports finally reached the drop-off point, just north-east of crater Vogel B. The H-HARs were on the northern side of crater Vogel A, only 3.4 kilometres away, within a flat depression just south and east of the rising slopes of crater Albategnius. Being dropped off so close was a risk, but time was paramount. They unloaded the trailers and established a local operation and casualty station.

Radio silence would be maintained until contact was made with the H-HARs, but local voice communication was still available via a visual red light comms channel between helmets.

Mackenzie tensed, finally reacting to years of stress. He knew the others would be feeling the same. After a brief orientation and equipment check, he moved among his soldiers, looking into their faces, grabbing their shoulders firmly, and reassuring them they were ready.

"Scott, okay?" "Yes, sir."

"Packer, okay?" "Yes, sir."

"Zyga?" "Yes, sir." …

Mackenzie turned in the direction of the H-HARs, held up a hand, and pointed forward. Tiny, insignificant figures moved north along the base of a tall crater.

Saunders brought up the rear.

The H-HAR site spanned over seven hundred metres square. An immersive 3D simulation of the area taught the soldiers to identify and locate every structure. The doomsday weapon was the northernmost object, with the power stations and energy storage capacitors just to the south. Further south was a large open work area. Two hundred metres south-west of the weapon was the spaceship's nozzle. The ship lay flat on the ground, its nose cone was another two hundred and sixty metres due south. The ship was thirty-two metres wide. Scattered around the site were several buildings, mostly within six hundred metres of the weapon.

At 2.4 kilometres from their objective, they came across an H-HAR's footprint trail. This instantly changed everything. Their surroundings were now more menacing; every shadow was a source of danger, every turn a possible confrontation.

After another one hundred metres, Mackenzie stopped to separate the soldiers into company-sized units to encircle the H-HARs as planned.

The main forces would be led by Mackenzie and Saunders: Mackenzie's company of 120 soldiers and 119 CARs would advance from the east, and Saunders's company of 120 soldiers and 118 CARs from the west. Diversionary forces of 33 soldiers and 21 CARs commanded by Captain Yao Zhang would advance from the north, and 33 soldiers and 26 CARs commanded by Captain Finja Graf from the south. Small units would patrol the flanks around the entire perimeter. There would be no reserves.

Mackenzie and Saunders exchanged a parting look and respectfully tilted their helmets, a sign born out of years of duty together. With that, the companies separated, well aware of the uncertainties that awaited them.

As they advanced, more footprints were sighted. The inevitable face-to-face encounter was getting closer, and their apprehension grew with every step.

At 1.1 kilometres from the doomsday weapon, Saunders's company came across several small metallic objects resembling machine components scattered over the lunar soil.

"Landmines?" asked a soldier.

"Unlikely," said Saunders, bending down to look closer. "Probably just litter. Keep going, and don't disturb anything."

Mackenzie's company came to what looked like a quarry; high vertical walls, cut rock along the bottom, and mysterious alien equipment around the rim. He signalled the leading soldiers to survey the area. They scanned every rock, every shadow, every ridge, and every edge.

Mackenzie was about to break cover when infrared was detected a hundred and seventy metres away. He zoomed his helmet camera at the source. Two grey H-HARs. One rounded a rock and disappeared. The other abruptly stopped and turned their way.

"It's seen us," murmured a soldier, also zooming his camera.

The H-HAR walked towards them, picked up something, turned, and followed the first H-HAR behind the rock.

Everyone exhaled slowly.

Mackenzie's body shook, but he remained steady. The sight of these alien creatures brought back chilling memories. He ordered two soldiers armed with laser rifles to the front; years of earthside training had taught them how to sweep the deadly beam across the enemy. The rest followed in a tactical formation. Every eye was trained on the slightest sign of movement.

***

Meanwhile on Earth: A tenacious caterpillar slowly crawled from one lush, green leaf to another. The melodious murmur of a cold, crystal-clear brook over smoothed stones filled the wilderness as it disappeared into a dark gorge. A newlywed couple gazed deeply into each other's eyes and kissed intimately. A determined salmon sprang into the air, splashing into a turquoise pool atop a two-metre waterfall. A gigantic, water-laden leaf dipped and dripped its load.

Chapter 24　Battle for the Moon

At 650 metres east of the doomsday weapon and 200 more to the spaceship, the lead soldier in Mackenzie's company rounded a rock and came face to face with six light grey, blue-armband H-HARs. The creatures stood still, as if trying to comprehend the peculiar figure before them.

The soldier stepped back and terminated two H-HARs with his gauss rifle before a H-HAR fatally knocked him to the ground. One H-HAR rushed away. The three remaining H-HARs transitioned into combat armour and charged at a CAR that had just appeared. The CAR fired for a full two seconds before the H-HARs reached and disabled it.

The rest of Mackenzie's company joined the fight. In a hail of ricocheting bullets, the three H-HARs were terminated. One soldier was injured.

Mackenzie broadcast a message to his Lunar Expeditionary Force. "This is command with eastern. Be advised: contact made with enemy. I repeat, contact made with enemy. Necks and knees are still vulnerable, and shatter bullets are very effective. Be on your guard, and stay on comms. Out."

Mackenzie's company rushed forward, spreading out to obtain good crossfire on any H-HAR.

Videographer Tony stood still, frozen in immovable terror. Suddenly realising the lonely and shadowy environment that surrounded him, he raced in panicked horror to catch up with the others.

Mackenzie's eastern company gained a hundred metres when rocks started exploding around them. Three H-HARs, forty metres away, blocked their path. One soldier was cut in two, his blood freezing on the regolith in the icy shadow of a crater. Another fell, curling into a foetal ball. Four CARs were dismembered, their parts falling over the moonscape.

The Earthlings dispersed behind craters. The H-HARs charged across open ground, one almost reaching Mackenzie's position before being brought down in a rain of crossfire on their necks.

Mackenzie counted another fifteen blue-armband H-HARs passively congregating around the craters ahead. A green-armband arrived, pointed at the Earthlings, and pushed the H-HARs out to attack.

Mackenzie launched smoke grenades, which instantly halted the H-HARs. Guided by their helmet displays, the Earthlings charged into the smoke, blasting the H-HARs' necks at point-blank range.

Videographer Tony, now sticking to the soldiers like gum, aimlessly followed them through the smoke, straight into a shadowy H-HAR. Spellbound by its sightless eyes, his knees gave way. As the smoke cleared, the creature raised a foot to crush him. But before it could, it collapsed, terminated by a CAR's shot to its neck. Tony gave the CAR a look of gratitude, but it had already moved on.

Mackenzie gained another crater, fifty metres, before being stopped again. This time, the H-HARs spread out as a countermeasure against smoke grenades.

***

Meanwhile, Saunders's western company reached 450 metres from the spaceship when a lone H-HAR spotted them. It disappeared without engagement. The sighting chilled Sanders but didn't slow him. He gained another fifty metres before being stopped.

He radioed Mackenzie. "We're pinned down by a small but well-positioned number of hostiles, Andrew." His voice was cold and methodical. "There's a small crater about twenty metres to our left. Maps indicate it may be a way around. Over."

"Keep moving, Phil. And it's critical to capture their laser rifles. Over."

"Copy that. Over."

"The Plan C nukes have been launched. They'll hit in twenty-nine hours. Over."

Saunders exhaled deeply. "All we can do is get this fucking business over with. Over."

"Out."

Under the cover of smoke grenades, Saunders ordered five soldiers and six CARs over the crater. But the ridge was steeper, and the smoke screen dissipated quicker than expected. Earth's future could have ended on that small crater if not for one soldier, Lieutenant Alex Zyga, the only one to make it. With laser beams tracking him and only millimetres from death, Zyga's incredible agility and lightning speed propelled him up and over the rim.

Quickly gaining his bearings, Zyga emerged unnoticed behind the H-HARs. He lifted his laser rifle. It was heavy and awkward, but it gave him all the power he needed to kill these aliens. Seven blue-armbands were immediately visible, but there were sure to be more. His face hardened into a look of pure, defiant hatred. He couldn't terminate them all in a single sweep; it had to be done one by one. Calm, calculating, and purposeful, unrecognisable from the soldier at Fort Bush, he moved in close and stealthily terminated four of them with a laser pulse to the back of their heads. Diverting to the rocks, he found and terminated another five, then returned to finish off the remaining three. Another H-HAR appeared, then two more. But Zyga was ready. A single laser sweep wiped out two. The other tried to run, but Zyga's laser sliced off its leg and head.

"The way ahead is clear, sir," he reported.

Saunders saw everything on his helmet display. "Well done, Zyga," was all he said on a private channel. Switching back to broadcast mode, he ordered, "Everyone, go."

They quickly advanced another fifty metres to the next crater. They were now 350 metres west of the spaceship.

***

Mackenzie also had some success. Blue-armband H-HARs again congregated behind rocks. Mackenzie attacked. First with paint grenades and exploding paint bullets, then smoke grenades and a frontal charge. The H-HARs, blinded by paint and smoke, stood motionless, easy prey to the fierceness of the advancing Earthlings.

One blind H-HAR scratched at its eyes, shook its head, bumped into a rock, and fell to its knees. Struggling to its feet, it took a few halting steps before collapsing to its knees again and lying flat on the ground. A CAR terminated it.

Mackenzie, however, was not satisfied. The smoke screen's duration was too short, and its coverage was too limited. He looked back through the falling smoke and saw many H-HAR carcasses, but also many human bodies. He kept moving, knowing there was no time for sentimentality. He seized the next crater, gaining fifty metres and several laser weapons. They were now 450 metres east of the doomsday weapon.

A soldier pointed ominously at a laser scorch mark on Mackenzie's helmet. "That's life number eight," Mackenzie muttered dismissively. "Still got one to go."

***

Zhang's northern platoon, still advancing south undetected, spotted two grey H-HARs. The H-HARs rounded a crater and disappeared. Not sure whether they were spotted or not, Zhang waited and moved his only laser trooper to the front. Nothing. They cautiously continued until a soldier pointed to a dark shape a hundred and ten metres away.

Zhang checked the IR scanner. "There's definitely something there." He checked again, then ordered, "Fire!"

A hellish blast of bullets brought the figure to life. A dark, unarmed H-HAR charged at them. The continuous rain of bullets could not stop it. At forty metres, the laser trooper fired, amputating its right arm. It kept charging. The trooper fired again, severing its neck. The headless carcass crashed to the ground among the soldiers, producing a dusty cloud.

Shortly afterwards, Graf's southern platoon also reported enemy contact.

Meanwhile, the command centre on Earth watched, in tense silence, live video from each soldier and CAR.

***

Mackenzie radioed Saunders. "Phil, what's your status? Over."

"Pinned down again, sir," said Saunders, glancing around and swallowing hard. "Twenty metres of open ground to the next crater, and every metre is covered by hostiles. Longer distances on our flanks. Over."

"Copy that, Phil. You must keep moving. Advance again in ten minutes. The nukes will hit in twenty-four hours. Over."

Saunders took a moment to respond. "Affirmative. Over."

"Northern and southern, keep occupying as much of the enemy's resources as possible. Zhang, Graf, do you copy? Over."

"Copy that, sir," said Zhang and Graf.

"Copy that also," Saunders said. "Still no sign of their dogs or any new weapons. Over."

"No, and thank God for that," Mackenzie said, shuddering at the thought. "Out."

Mackenzie and Saunders attacked again and again. But the H-HARs were learning, moving around during the smoke attacks, making it difficult to locate them. As the smoke cleared, the Earthlings had to scramble for cover, leaving them out of position and suffering casualties without gaining any ground.

The paint weapons were also less effective; the H-HARs simply covered their eyes. The MMRs were easily destroyed crossing open ground, and the RF jammers were ineffective against autonomously acting H-HARs.

After struggling for six hours with different tactical combinations, Mackenzie advanced only a hundred metres and Saunders only fifty metres. Losses were unsustainable, and time was running out.

Mackenzie, exhausted but unwavering, paused for an update. "Phil, what's your status? Over."

Saunders took a second to catch his breath. "We're at a complete standstill, sir, almost in survival mode. Troops are exhausted, low on ammunition and life support, CARs need charging. I've ordered new supplies. Hostiles are defending better but can't understand their failure to counterattack. Over."

"Copy that." Mackenzie took a breath, his voice returning a bit tighter. "Earth is detecting large amounts of heat from the doomsday gun. It could be charging up for a test fire. Over."

Saunders sucked in a gasp. "Fucking hell …"

"There's more," Mackenzie said, his jaw tightening. "The H-HARs have destroyed the Plan C nuclear missiles, and I have little confidence in our Plan B missiles getting through. So, it's just us. And that doesn't mean we've got much more time. Over."

Saunders gazed up at the Earth and gave no response.

"We must keep moving, Phil. Over," Mackenzie said.

"Yes, but how? They've effectively negated our smoke and paint weapons. Over."

Mackenzie paused momentarily. Then, with the bearing of a man in full command, he said, "We'll advance on a much wider front around these hills of excavated dirt. The H-HARs will be forced to cover more approaches. Our captured laser rifles will be the deciding factor. Zhang and Graf will launch major diversionary attacks to draw away their numbers. We'll talk again in five minutes. Out."

Mackenzie caught a glimpse of Saunders's tormented face between camera switches. The tremendous stress was clear, but so was Saunders's characteristic determination and incredible strength.

***

The humans rested while supplies were replenished. They then grouped in formation for the offensive, with laser troopers moving to the front.

Mackenzie's company of 77 troops and 90 CARs attacked from the east, while Saunders's company of 79 troops and 94 CARs attacked from the west.

Saunders's attack failed before it even began; there were just too many H-HARs.

In desperaton, he ordered four soldiers and six CARs over an excavation embankment. The soldiers exchanged a long look with Saunders, an awareness of the suicidal futility they were ordered to attempt. Saunders's jaw only tightened.

Deadly laser fire immediately tore across the regolith. The body parts of every soldier and CAR on that embankment came tumbling back down as shredded flesh, bone, and metal.

The tattered body of one soldier stopped in front of videographer Penny. She raised an eye from the camera and glimpsed the nightmarish world she was recording. A splash of blood caught her helmet visor, partially obscuring her view of the mess that was once a soldier's face. She sank back, pale and gasping.

Saunders turned to the next four, about to order, "*You're next.*"

He couldn't. He didn't. Numbed and dazed, he turned away from his soldiers. The battle, no, the war, was being lost. He knew it. And all his soldiers facing him knew it. He immediately stifled his doubts and turned to address them. "The Earth is depending on us. Why us? … Because we're the best the Earth has, and we carry its vision for the future of our families, our grandchildren, our great-great-grandchildren, and our species. Right now, it's just simple numbers. They have more. But they don't have Mackenzie, we do. So be prepared to move out."

Everyone responded. "We're ready, sir." And saluted.

***

Mackenzie's eastern company was also having problems. After five hours, they had advanced only one tailing hill, thirty metres. The last five attacks failed to gain any ground. Mackenzie called off the attacks. He needed to preserve whatever resources he had.

There were also signs of a possible counterattack, and the troops needed to prepare.

Mackenzie called Saunders for an update.

"We're cornered, Andrew." There was plenty of strain in Saunders's voice. "Any H-HAR offensive will wipe us out. Over."

"I'm relying on their inability to attack us just a little longer. Over."

"Are you close enough to hit the RIW with a rocket, Andrew?"

"Negative!" Mackenzie replied bluntly. "We're 310 metres from it, and the opening is obscured. We need to get close enough to use a hafnium grenade."

"What's on your mind? Over," Saunders asked.

"We'll start with the usual smoke grenades, using all of them to extend the smoke screen for as long as possible." Mackenzie spoke with more conviction than he felt. "The enemy will reposition themselves as usual, but this time we'll rush past them and keep going. Break." Mackenzie waited for Graf to join comms. "Graf, I need you to push hard from the south just before we attack. Zhang will do the same. We start in ten minutes. We have enough laser rifles now to make a big difference. Over."

"Copy that. Out," said Graf.

Saunders hesitated. "Okay. We'll be ready. Out."

Mackenzie and Saunders attacked simultaneously, with the longest smoke bombardment so far. They rushed past the H-HARs, dropping MMRs. As the smoke cleared, the MMRs sprang up, not only burning into the H-HARs but boiling through them. The RF jammers kept the surviving H-HARs ignorant of what was happening, and hidden laser troopers kept them occupied.

Mackenzie's company emerged from the smoke cloud to surprise at least sixty unarmed H-HAR workers. The gauss rifles easily smashed their grey skins while the laser rifles bisected the few that had transitioned to combat armour. The Earthlings raced on, past several outbuildings, no time to catch their breath. The top of the doomsday weapon and the spaceship were now visible above the craters and buildings. Mackenzie couldn't believe they were almost there.

They gained a hundred metres before passing a tailings mound and rushing into a forty-metre gap, known as clearing-24. It was an ambush. Crisscrossing laser beams lanced out from flanking H-HARs, instantly ripping apart a dozen soldiers. Panic was evident for the first time as the soldiers scrambled back to the tailings mound. Screams filled their comms, formations broke, joints froze, and shadows became targets.

"Clear my line of fire!" yelled a soldier.

"Get out of the way!" yelled another.

Mackenzie and three of his platoons remained trapped behind a few large rocks. Unable to withdraw, they were being steadily picked off.

With increasing H-HAR numbers edging his flanks and his force too spread out, Mackenzie's entire company was in imminent danger of annihilation.

He surveyed the battlefield and took control. Studying the terrain, he ordered, "Wolf and Bear Platoons, provide suppressing fire to your right only. Those at the tailings mound, to your left only. Fox Platoon, with—"

A laser skimmed his biosuit, cutting into his flesh. He fell to the ground, still yelling orders. "Fox Platoon, withdraw on the double to the tailings mound now. Come on. Move it! Go!"

Mackenzie refused to let others stop for him, ordering them to go. The biosuit sealed itself, and he limped to the tailings mound with Fox Platoon.

Thirty-nine soldiers and twenty-seven CARs of Wolf and Bear Platoons were still stranded and suffering casualties.

"Give them cover fire left and right," ordered Mackenzie. The soldiers and CARs at the tailings mound immediately opened fire with gauss and laser rifles.

"Wolf and Bear. Go! Go! Go!" yelled Mackenzie.

The stranded soldiers scrambled for their lives back to the tailings mound. Their legs buckled, their boots slipped, their breathing was hysterical, and their equipment pulled them back. Most made it, but many didn't. Mackenzie could now, at least momentarily, hold his current position.

The faces of the wounded, writhing in pain, were visible through his helmet display. "Hang on," he told them. They would have to wait for the medics after he had moved on.

He looked across clearing-24. Two green-armbands were circulating among the H-HARs pushing and hitting them. Suddenly, seventy-armed blue-armbands charged across clearing-24 towards the Earthlings. The laser troopers opened up, but H-HAR covering fire hindered them. Forty H-HARs crossed the halfway point, twenty metres from the Earthlings.

"Hold your positions and keep firing," ordered Mackenzie.

The last three H-HARs closed within two metres of the Earthlings before being terminated. Eleven troopers died, including the squad sergeant alongside Mackenzie. Hit and bleeding heavily, the sergeant's biosuit was too damaged to repair itself. Mackenzie called for a medic while pressing against the wound and taping up the biosuit. "Hang on, son," he said with a sympathetic gaze.

The sergeant looked back. "I'm sorry, sir." He knew.

"Sorry? What for?"

"For not killing more of them."

"Don't worry about that; we're going to kill them all."

Before anything could be done, the sergeant choked and died. Mackenzie turned away and yelled, "Shit."

Eighteen more armed H-HARs charged across clearing-24. The Earthlings stopped them, losing two soldiers and five CARs. The closest H-HAR fell to the ground without legs, its arms swinging. A laser trooper finished it off. There was now a pile of H-HAR black and grey carcasses along the entire length of clearing-24.

Mackenzie again surveyed the battlefield. Although he was only 210 metres east of the doomsday weapon, he was trapped.

***

Saunders's company also had some initial success on the western flank until growing H-HARs defenders halted them 180 metres west of the spaceship.

159

Mackenzie's grim voice came through his comms unit. "Phil, what's your situation? Over."

Saunders took a deep breath before answering. "We can't hold this position, Andrew. Over." He sounded equally grim, with no illusions about their fate.

"Here's the plan." Mackenzie became calmer, his voice showed it. "Northern and southern platoons are breaking their positions. Northern will approach us from the north-east, and southern will approach you from the south-west. The H-HARs are gathering in uncoordinated groups, maybe because of our RF jamming. Zhang and Graf will distract them, hopefully enough for us to breakout. If we don't get to that doomsday weapon very soon, nothing else matters. Over."

Saunders was not totally convinced. "Let's get going," he eventually said. "Out."

***

As Mackenzie waited for Zhang's northern platoon, he watched in mounting horror as the enemy's head count grew. Across clearing-24, one hundred, two hundred … A sea of countless alien heads, all ducking and weaving. This looked like the end, there was no way out.

"We're all gonna die," yelled videographer Tony.

"Shut the fuck up!" a soldier yelled back.

Meanwhile, Graf reported in. "We can't reach Saunders, sir. We're trapped with heavy casualties. Over."

"Can you hold your position? Over."

"At the moment, yes, sir. Over."

"Keep me informed. Out."

Mackenzie looked despairingly at the Earth. His eyes slowly narrowed, his chilling gaze lowered, and his vision focused sharply on his adversaries. A burning resolve gripped him.

He turned to his terrified soldiers with a defiant look. "Stand your ground and await my instructions." His tone was rock-solid and commanding.

"Yes, sir," they all replied.

After years of comradeship, Mackenzie knew they would follow him into hell, and now they were about to do exactly that.

As the H-HARs edged to encircle them, they unexpectedly stopped. Mackenzie was baffled. A green-armband pushed its way to the front. Several blue-armbands pointed at Mackenzie across clearing-24. The green-armband grabbed a laser rifle and focused its dark eyes on him. It had apparently decided, "Mackenzie is mine."

The green-armband shifted to several hidden locations and fired several laser pulses at Mackenzie's position. One pulse burned through seven hundred millimetres of tailing mound, missing Mackenzie by millimetres.

This delayed hell just long enough for Zhang's platoon to reach the exposed rear of the besieging H-HARs. All H-HAR cohesion surprisingly evaporated. They tore across clearing-24 in a panicked stampede, where Mackenzie's laser troopers were waiting with desperate determination. A maze of criss-crossing laser beams swung across the H-HARs, cutting them to pieces. Fleeing H-HARs had to scramble over the top of a pile of H-HAR carcasses where they were hit, adding to its height. The struggling movements of H-HARs on the pile made crossing difficult and the H-HARs more exposed. Clearing-24 became an H-HAR killing field.

The fleeing H-HARs then turned back towards Zhang, who was forced to fall back to defensive positions and let them pass. Mackenzie and what was left of his company advanced over clearing-24, over the pile of H-HAR carcasses. They then passed between two craters towards the weapon. Twenty-three unarmed grey H-HAR workers at an outbuilding started transitioning at the sight of Mackenzie's Earthlings racing towards them. But they were easy prey for the Earthlings, now fully armed with laser rifles.

***

Meanwhile, Saunders reported in: "Andrew, some H-HARs are leaving their positions and heading your way. This has opened an under-defended gap on our right; we can try for a breakout. Over."

"Copy that, Phil. Out."

"Let's go!" yelled Saunders, his eyes filled with purpose. They advanced to within sight of the spaceship, 130 metres, before being forced into a crater.

Saunders glanced back at the human bodies and CAR parts strewn everywhere. *This is a scene straight out of hell.*

The spaceship's surface was blast-proof against everything except a hafnium-178 nuclear grenade. But this would devastate the entire site. They needed to get a high-explosive device inside the door on the other side to limit the damage and have any chance of salvaging the DSDs.

***

Mackenzie, still on the move, was close to exhaustion. Knowing Saunders was only five hundred metres away on the other side of the spaceship was encouraging.

Suddenly, the moonscape lit up, and a soundless lightning bolt flashed high into space. The ground jolted and rumbled. Earthlings and H-HARs steadied themselves until it subsided. Then a shower of pebbles, thrown into the sky by the flash, bounced off everything.

"What the fuck was that!?" Mackenzie shouted, his eyes darting.

"Uh!? … What the fuck!?" Saunders's eyes were also darting.

"Felt like a hafnium grenade going off!" Mackenzie was still searching for the cause.

"L-look, look at the Earth!" yelled a horrified soldier, pointing upwards.

Eyes shot skyward to see a circle of white fire, like God's wrath itself, widening just off the South American east coast. Expanding rapidly, it was soon hundreds of kilometres wide, looking like the end of the world. A spine-chilling sight.

Mackenzie stood dazed, disbelieving what his eyes were seeing.

"It can't be!" said Saunders. "It can't be working yet!" His voice was devoid of all hope.

"It's a test fire." Mackenzie's eyes darkened as he struggled to control the rage he felt towards these monsters.

As the realisation sank in, fury replaced fear on the faces of the battered soldiers. There was something different about them now – a new desperation, a deeper hatred.

***

An injured soldier lay on the Moon's surface, semi-conscious, his eyelids slit open on the wounded Earth. The medic was fighting a losing battle. The soldier's eyes flicked to a dark figure in the distance – an H-HAR. His focus instantly sharpened, and hatred possessed him. He rose to his feet, his life-support equipment ripping out. Grabbing a gauss rifle, he turned to go after the H-HAR but fell to the ground. The medic tried to stop him, but the soldier pushed him off, dragging himself across the ground towards the long-gone H-HAR. A minute later, he was dead.

***

Mackenzie kept everyone moving.

Ahead lay the doomsday weapon, only a hundred and seventy metres to the west. Its headframe visible between two rock excavation dumps. Fifteen armed H-HARs appeared from the south. The laser-armed Earthlings ripped through them with all the cold-blooded hatred they could muster.

Reinforced by Zhang's northern platoon, Mackenzie sprinted past outbuildings, rock dumps, strange alien machinery, and into a clearing. The doomsday weapon's entire headframe was now visible. Its six, four-metre-high, concrete columns surrounded the rim of the vertical barrel shaft. A thick, circular metal ring joined the tops of each column.

They crossed the last one hundred metres and stood under the weapon's headframe. Nine armed H-HARs guarded the weapon, but they were unprepared and offered little resistance. Mackenzie peered down into the depths of the bottomless barrel shaft from a metal grating on its funnelled rim. It glowed cherry red from the firing, the heat forcing him back.

"Jackson, blow this fucker," Mackenzie ordered, pointing down the shaft.

He turned towards the spaceship, two hundred metres away. "Let's go!" he yelled. His face was filled with brutal determination as he picked up pace. The soldiers followed in his wake.

A hafnium-178 nuclear grenade was dropped down the shaft as the troops ran and ducked for cover. They squinted as a forty forty-metre-high fireball exploded silently into the dark sky like a furious volcano, lighting up the moonscape. The sight was oddly beautiful. Dirt and rocks showered down, the soldiers' armoured biosuits protecting them. "That's one fucker gone!" Mackenzie shouted as he glanced back, the dying fireball reflecting in his helmet visor. "Now for the spaceship."

With bloodlust in their eyes, the soldiers raced forward between the craters, rocks, and alien equipment, oblivious to the sporadic, distant laser fire now targeting them. Mackenzie tripped, quickly recovered, and relentlessly resumed running. Others also fell, some permanently, but there was no time to stop and help.

The sporadic fire intensified, forcing Mackenzie and his soldiers to take cover in numerous small craters.

"The enemy is re-massing," Mackenzie said as he peered over the crater rim, laser beams burning into the regolith around him. He looked towards the spaceship. "I can see faint blue light." He looked closer. "I don't believe it. The spaceship's door is still open!"

Wild hope returned. He radioed Saunders. "Phil, we're launching a rocket through the spaceship door. It may damage the DSDs, but we're out of options. Keep the H-HAR snipers off my left flank. Over"

"Copy that. Over."

"The shot will be difficult. It's over a hundred and twenty metres, the door is narrow, the angle is sharp, and we're under intense fire. We've only got one attempt at this, Phil. If we miss, the H-HARs will close the door. Then our only option is a hafnium grenade. Over."

"Which will destroy us and the DSDs. Over."

"As I said, Phil. It's our only option. Out."

A soldier mounted his NA-30 rocket launcher and turned it towards the spaceship door. Just as his finger found the trigger, a laser beam hit him. Mackenzie pulled the body away and ordered another soldier to take the shot. But he too was hit. Mackenzie picked up the NA-30. As he lifted it over the crater's rim to take aim, an explosive inferno ripped from the spaceship. Flames and heat surged from the door like an apocalyptic eruption, blowing a dust cloud over the entire site.

Mackenzie fell back, dazed and confused. As the dust cleared, he pulled himself up, wiping dirt from his visor. He could see a reddish glow radiating from the doorway. To a crater on his right, a soldier dropped a NA-30. Mackenzie stared at him in disbelief. "Zyga!?" he whispered to himself. "How the hell …?" He then yelled into his radio. "Zyga! Zyga! You've done it. You're unbelievable!" The relief on Mackenzie's face was enormous.

He checked his timer: thirty-seven minutes past the scheduled arrival of the Plan C nuclear missiles. He silently thanked the H-HARs for destroying them.

With the spaceship engulfed in flames, strange things were happening with the H-HARs. Instead of continuing the battle against the Earthlings, they ruthlessly annihilated each other like a mutinous mob. They had no sides, cohesion, or authority. It was as if the spaceship were the only source of their unity. The scene was brutal. Hundreds of H-HARs hitting and shooting. Only a few seemed to be avoiding the violence. One by one, their numbers reduced.

The Earthlings stayed under cover, turned off their radios, and waited, Mackenzie east of the spaceship and Saunders west. Two unarmed H-HARs fought hand-to-hand just metres from Mackenzie's crater. The nervous soldiers watched with laser rifles pointed. The fight lasted ten minutes before a third unarmed H-HAR joined in, on no one's side. One H-HAR fell limp to the ground, its neck twisted. The other two continued to battle until they were spotted by an armed H-HAR and terminated. The H-HAR also spotted the Earthlings and turned its weapon towards them. Three laser troopers terminated it.

Another armed H-HAR walked uncomfortably close to the Earthlings. A soldier lifted his laser rifle and looked at Mackenzie, who shook his head to signal "no, let it go".

Within half an hour, only the armed H-HARs remained. Most formed rival groups of up to four H-HARs. A green-armband was seen within one group, but it had no more authority than others in the group. The groups fought each other. No group lasted more than ten minutes before being violently wiped out.

After three hours, the civil war was over, although small numbers of H-HARs were still wandering around, occasionally fighting each other when their paths crossed.

The Earthlings turned on their radios, and Mackenzie ordered, "Let's go. Take prisoners if you can; otherwise, terminate them. Do not risk your own life. No H-HARs are to escape. Remember to keep an eye out for the leader; it may be a red-armband, or any colour other than green or blue."

Saunders, Mackenzie, and their companies finally reunited. Mackenzie gave a weary smile and put a hand on Saunders's shoulder. "Let's finish here and go home," he said.

Saunders returned the smile and gave a nod.

The Earthlings searched cautiously from building to building, crater to crater, and mound to mound. After three hours, it was finally over. No H-HAR allowed itself to be captured; they senselessly battled the Earthlings to the very end. The remains of a headless yellow-armband were found lying among a shredded, mangled mess of H-HARs. It was assumed to be the leader of the H-HARs on the Moon.

The area around the spaceship was a desolate battlefield, littered with H-HAR carcasses.

Together, Mackenzie and Saunders headed towards the spaceship door. It was still too hot to enter. A distant, unseen green-armband watched. It raised a laser rifle, focused its blank eyes on them, and fired. A beam hit the soil behind Mackenzie and Saunders and tracked towards them. They dived for cover, but Mackenzie took a hit on the hip, cutting open his biosuit. He tried to get up but stumbled. Saunders and a soldier pulled him to safety.

"Medic!" Saunders called out, crouching over him.

"A sniper," said a soldier, pointing across a long clearing to a distant rock.

Saunders called up his best laser trooper. "Zyga, you'll have to use a single pulse. The sniper will see a sweeping beam and duck."

"Yes, sir, I can do it," said Zyga, moving into position with his laser rifle. The others moved back, giving him space. Zyga lay on his stomach and propped his rifle on a tripod in front of him.

He attached a telescopic lens with a small screen to the top of the rifle and zoomed in on a green-armband's head protruding from a rock four hundred metres away. Shifting the rifle some distance to the left of the H-HAR, he fired onto a rock then calibrated the crosshairs on the screen. "That should do it," he said. Zyga moved the crosshairs back to the H-HAR. His finger slid to the adaptor trigger. Pausing for a second and keeping his eye on the screen, Zyga gradually squeezed the trigger. The H-HAR slumped forward.

***

Saunders accompanied Mackenzie to one of the medical treatment modules, which had just arrived from the drop-off point. Soul weary and totally drained by the battle, he stood vigil. He heard murmurings from Mackenzie and placed an ear to his lips.

"Phil …" Mackenzie groaned, barely audible, his eyes finding focus. "I won't be taken here." Mackenzie grabbed Saunders's shirt and, with a pain-filled grunt, pulled him close. "These monsters will be back …" Pulling Saunders even closer, he made a commitment that would later dominate his life. "And so will I, so help me, God."

Saunders stopped at every wounded soldier and obtained a briefing from the medic. He spoke to those who could respond. After, he reviewed the battle report: "One hundred and sixty dead soldiers and sixty-eight wounded. Eight hundred and twenty-three H-HARs destroyed. Two hundred and forty-one CARs non-functional."

He inspected the battlefields. Body bags were being loaded onto trailers. He turned away and stared at his glove, the ground, the sky, anywhere else. The grisly scenes would remain in his memory forever. So affected by the experience, he disappeared and couldn't be found, returning with only minutes of live support left.

Saunders insisted on being the last soldier to be evacuated. As he reached up for the transport, a shooting pain pierced his lower back. Cursing, he stood still and waited for it to ease. While he waited, he looked up at the devastation inflicted upon the Earth. The incandescent fireball had darkened. The impact zone was hidden by a huge storm of dirt, smoke, and water vapour, part of which had drifted east towards Africa. The Argentinian coastline looked different.

***

The scientific teams quickly studied whatever intelligence they could find. There wasn't much left of the RIW doomsday gun, but it was still possible to confirm its operating concepts. The barrel cavity extended sixteen kilometres underground and pointed directly at Earth. Before firing, gas was jetted seventeen kilometres above the barrel cavity. A powerful laser cleared a path through the gas, ionising it into a conducting plasma. The projectile was fired via a powerful, ultra-accelerating magnetic field from the base of the barrel cavity to the end of the ionised gas. This field acted on every atom of the projectile, eliminating differential stresses. The laser now illuminated the back of the projectile, causing millions of non-thermal Li6D fusing propulsion pulses. The projectile would ultimately reach thirty-eight per cent of light speed.

There were nine hundred projectiles, each weighing a hundred and eighty kilograms, stockpiled and ready to be deployed. The best estimate predicted one could be fired every second day. Each impact was equivalent to sixteen hundred megatons, or over thirty times larger than the Tsar bomb. Earth was close to destruction.

All DSDs were found intact.

The public was told the story. The victory was a huge morale boost and showed the possibilities of a united Earth. Reprisals from the H-HARs were expected. Earth and Mars would soon be in proximity, and there were no shortages of catastrophists' predictions.

The soldiers, dead and alive, returned to a hero's welcome. A monument was built on the site to honour them and the human spirit that shone for thirty-seven hours.

Chapter 25   Victims

Although the RIW fired at only a fraction of its potential, it still left a large part of the Earth a wasteland strewn with two hundred million corpses.

In Brazil, Marta left her office early to spend the warm summer afternoon at the beach with her boyfriend. Like everyone else, she was unaware her future was dependent on a battle currently taking place on the Moon.

She wandered through the jubilant town square. People everywhere, coming and going, sitting in cafes, or browsing in shops. She rewarded a street busker for playing music. The music gradually softened as she moved further down the mall, replaced by the cheerful sounds of kids rushing out of school to start their holidays. Two jumped up to greet their mother. A wilful girl ran past her with a bag of lollies, chased by a young boy. Marta had to step sideways to avoid the boy. They were apprehended at the kerb by an adult. Marta gave herself a happy smile.

Stopping at an intersection, she gazed up at the brilliant blue sky, then across at a pale Moon. A tiny dot of light with an intensely bright tail caught her eye. Before her brain had time to formulate a thought, the sky exploded. A hellish white flash, hotter than the Sun's surface, instantly incinerated her and everything around her. All this in less than four seconds after the tiny dot left the Moon. A thunderous shock wave blew her embers to the wind.

Marta was more than three hundred kilometres from the explosion. Everyone within four hundred kilometres was fried by a microwave burst – thirty million people. The air blast severely damaged buildings within six hundred kilometres, covering the entire area with brown ash. No one had the chance to scream. Death came too quickly to comprehend.

***

Christiane was 820 kilometres away. An intense, searing flash formed a second shadow of herself in front of her. By the time she turned, the source was gone. People facing the other way were blinded – some for weeks, some for life.

PART 4

H-HARs AND THEIR TECHNOLOGY

"It begins on a planet … in a very distant galaxy, about four hundred million light years away, a long, long time ago, about six hundred million years ago."

Chapter 26   Reverse Engineering

After the Battle for the Moon, the EDO publicly revealed that in addition to the *relic*, an entire H-HAR spaceship was found on the Moon thirty-one years ago, and every part had been disassembled, reassembled, examined, analysed, and categorised.

The news brought shock but also hope. Hope that with reverse engineering, the technological gap with the H-HARs, who were still present on Mars, could be partially bridged. To the researchers, this gap, although immense, was never considered uncrossable. However, progress was slow, and the huge potential remained untapped. With a second H-HAR spaceship to study and most security restrictions relaxed, progress was expected to gain pace. The race was on to reverse engineer H-HAR technologies for advanced weapon systems.

In homes, schools, universities, industries, and governments, science, technology, engineering, and mathematics were seen as humanity's saviours. Such a dramatic expansion of state and military patronage of STEM had not been seen since the end of the Cold War.

Chapter 27   Alien Technology – The DSDs

The Moon-ship DSDs were returned to the H-HARs after twenty-seven years, then recovered after the Battle for the Moon four years later, where an additional set from a Pallas spaceship was also captured.

It would be a disaster if they could not be deciphered. Two years after the Battle for the Moon, a DSD Decipher Organisation was formed for this very purpose. This was part of the EDO, which had taken over all functions of Section 3.

Lochlan McLean, after thirteen years in Section 3, had gained a reputation for getting results out of scientific groups. He was selected to head this new organisation.

The night before his first day, Lochlan was excited, restless, and couldn't sleep. He switched on the AR-TV and watched a promotional advertisement encouraging students to enter science. A student contemplating engineering was asked what was her preferred field of study. "I'm undecided," she hesitantly replied, her face perplexed. "The fields are too wide. My father suggested wormholes, warp drives, massless neutrino drives, antimatter containment, bottom quark fusion, or dark boson exploitation. My mother suggested metastable isomers, neuro-networks, superheavy stable nuclei, near-Planck-size black holes, or relativistic thermodynamics. However, my friends are doing quantum entangled computing, molecular ionomer manufacturing, and Sakharov's emergent spacetime/gravity."

Shaking his head, Lochlan switched to another channel where a theist asked, "What do you think it feels like to realise that everything you believed in is utterly wrong? To witness your beloved faith destroyed before your very eyes?"

He turned it off and reflected on how quickly the world had changed during his lifetime.

***

Am I out of my depth?

Lochlan's eyes widened with anticipation as people shuffled in and found seats, some nodding cursory hellos. The meeting room was unremarkable – bare brick walls, a drab table, and a dozen shaky chairs. There was a workplace safety poster on one wall. On another, a wide window overlooked the car park. This was his first meeting with the organisation's technical heavyweights. Resisting an inclination to scratch his head, he looked around the table. Hair uncombed, plain coloured T-shirts or cardigans, jeans, dirty coffee cups, worn shoes, no one conversing, taciturn, and little eye contact. *Okay, they must all be engineers or scientists.*

After an around-the-table introduction, Professor Marcel Holmes spoke up. "It's a pleasure to meet you, Lochlan. Welcome."

Lochlan smiled brightly.

"Thank you, Marcel. This group has a huge responsibility in this H-HAR war. Could we start with a briefing on the current DSD status?"

Holmes had a glow of excitement in his eyes. "I've been working on the DSDs longer than most, so I can start. It's quite a story. On the Moon-ship we found three identical rectangular prisms." He pointed to a model on the table. "Like this, each one is 133 by 133 by 340 millimetres."

"So small ..." Lochlan shook his head in amazement.

"For the first two years, we had no idea what they were. It was like feeling unknown objects in the dark. We eventually concluded that they must be memory devices operating in triple redundancy. Each device had three physically distinct media sections. Unfortunately, the information in one section of all three devices was lost to decoherence long ago. But the other two sections looked like they still contained information."

Lochlan's eyes glistened with amazement.

"Both were *write-once, read-many-times* memories. One was a quantum medium, probably written during fabrication. We called it Nanofabricated Written Information Storage, or NWIS. The other was a classical medium, written after fabrication, which we called Field Written Information Storage, or FWIS."

Lochlan gave an expression of "*Holy shit*," causing Holmes to stop.

"Am I getting too detailed?" asked Holmes.

"No, please go on."

"This story still raises hairs on my neck." Holmes took a deep breath and continued. "If you think it's amazing so far, just wait 'til you hear this. First the NWIS medium. The 3D imagery revealed the medium is a nanostructured, monolayered lattice comprising silicon, carbon, and tungsten ditelluride. The fluid-like electron interactions between these components produce a quantum insulator where a huge amount of stabilised information can be stored. The information is retrievable by a reference electron beam, which interacts with the electrons in the storage medium."

Lochlan cleared his throat, raking a hand through his hair. "That's incredible."

"That was just the beginning. We assumed the information was stored in the electron wave function. But we couldn't determine whether it was an analogue with virtually any value, or a long string of ones or zeroes. An absolutely brilliant researcher, Dr George Cumberlege, using heuristic techniques that no one understood, somehow discovered it to be a vector representing a thirty-two bit word. George was only thirty-one years old. Unfortunately, he had to leave us. He was a professor at the University of Chicago for a while, but no one knows where he is now."

"Maybe we should get him back," Lochlan suggested. This caused a strong reaction around the table.

"Get him back! No … I don't think so. He was extremely difficult, but he showed that this medium can store almost unlimited information. Now, you're probably wondering how the electron quantum wave function has remained stable for so long?"

"I wasn't … but how?"

"The electron coupling of both the silicon and the tungsten ditelluride creates a low-energy, triangular-shaped state of carbon-12, which basically consists of three alpha particles, thereby indefinitely stabilising the quantum wave function. So, apart from six hundred million years of radiation, long-term chemical reactions, metal migration, and Rydberg-Rydberg interaction damage, data storage is permanent. It was like seeing Saturn's rings for the first time."

"That's amazing progress. Any idea about the medium's information?"

"We're pretty sure it was written on their home planet using some unknown process and likely contains their libraries, history, science, literature, et cetera." Holmes turned to Warren Elliott, another long-time researcher. "Warren, can you tell us about the FWIS?"

"Yep," Elliott said. "Unlike the NWIS Marcel just described, the FWIS information was stored *after* fabrication. It could contain the entire history of the H-HARs' journey through space, their route, their stopovers, their entire timeline on the spaceship."

Lochlan excitedly glanced around the table, then asked, "How is the FWIS information stored?"

"A laser pulse excites the bonding electrons between two adjacent memory atoms, causing them to switch into one of thirty-six distinct intermediary states between a long amorphous bond and a short crystalline bond. This gives thirty-six bits of information per atom pair, or an estimated eighty Xenottabytes. About sixty per cent of the media is used to store data. We don't know its quality."

"This is unbelievable," Lochlan said. No one at the table showed the slightest sign of surprise. *They must all know this information.* "So, what's the next step?"

"Next?" Holmes scratched his ear. "Well, uh, that's a difficult question. We know the information is there, but accessing and interpreting it are the big problems."

Lochlan nodded slowly. "Have you tried using the H-HAR interface?"

"Yes, but nothing. We can't even turn it on." Holmes paused, shaking his head in frustration. His characteristic enthusiasm had disappeared. "Some think the NWIS conversion uses qubits, some think there's a deeper level involving nuclear spin, and others believe entanglement has a role. At this stage, it's almost unknowable. The solution may be beyond our grasp, at least within my grandchildren's lifetime."

"This war with the H-HARs won't wait that long," Lochlan said. "So, when we get past this hurdle, what's next?" His look beckoned the professor to speculate.

Holmes grunted and gazed off into the distance. "The theoretical next step is we match the code to a grapheme and logogram, and then to their language, that is, if they have one, finally translating it into something we can understand."

"Grapheme? Logogram?"

"Grapheme. It's the smallest contrastive linguistic unit that causes a change of meaning, like a letter of the alphabet. A logogram is a linguistic unit, like a word or phrase."

"Okay," said Lochlan, understanding slightly.

The meeting ended with Lochlan daunted by the enormous challenges ahead.

Chapter 28   Dinner

Anya Connell arrived early to claim a corner table near the window. She bubbled with excitement at the thought of catching up with her old friend. Although they had been in close contact on social media, they hadn't seen each other for years. She picked up the menu but couldn't concentrate enough to read it. Her eyes anxiously checked the time and glanced towards the door. *Not here yet.* She then gazed at the rock music posters and pictures of famous singers from over a hundred years ago that covered the back wall of a darkened stage.

Dressed in a short, red dress that hugged every curve, she looked as good as ever. She pulled a wry face at her reflection in the window and slid the short sleeves of her dress down, exposing her shoulders. *That's better.*

Another reflection in the window instantly turned her head.

"Locky!" she called out, waving and opening a big smile, her eyes twinkling.

Lochlan spun around and hurriedly squeezed between the tables to reach her, his face wreathed in smiles, his hair combed. "Hello, Anya."

They kissed each other's cheeks and embraced.

"I can't believe it's you," Anya said, her large mermaid eyes sparkling.

"It's great to see you. It's been so long. How are you, Anya?" A huge smile lit Lochlan's face.

"I'm going really well. Back with EDO and so busy with work, my daughter, and … But how are you?"

"Good."

Silence stretched as they stared at each other.

The region around their table suddenly darkened, and their seats appeared to be floating in outer space. A dazzling 3D simulation of thousands of heavenly bodies emerged just beyond their fingertips.

"Wow … what's this?" Lochlan excitedly asked.

"It's an astronomical setting for our dinner. I knew you'd like it." As Anya pointed, the images whizzed towards them like they were swirling through space.

"Give me a go."

"Go for it, Locky."

Leaving a blue and white Earth behind, Lochlan zoomed off. Past the Moon, Mars, Saturn's rings, and beyond. A comet overtook him. Extending his finger farther, Lochlan chased it, riding its luminous tail of gas and dust. He kept going, faster and faster, farther and farther. Past Pluto, a harsh world of ice mountains and frozen plains, and into interplanetary space. A large, bulging star within a ring of glowing dust dashed past. "Must be Vega," he said.

His finger turned towards a starburst nebula with a small, white dot in the centre. He shot through it.

"The Ring Nebula," Anya said.

He rocketed past a black sphere, visible only by the distortion of light from behind. Past a neutron star, its rapidly rotating light sweeping the simulation. The majestic, spiralling disc of the Milky Way sped away into the distance. Clusters of galaxies appeared ahead. Then, far-off galactic superclusters emerged, forming filaments spanning vast voids, becoming denser and denser, forming a continuous wall.

"I could spend all night playing with this," Lochlan said.

Their gazes met, and they shared a shy smile before turning back to the simulation.

Anya chanced a quick, intrigued glance at Lochlan. *Hmm, strange how we're such good friends but never became lovers.*

The simulation ended, and they exchanged another smile, sharing the easy intimacy of their earlier time together.

"How's Jenny?" Lochlan asked.

"Great. She's three now and growing up quickly. How's Ben?"

"Same. He'll be three next week."

They talked for forty minutes with easy familiarity, two old friends who knew each other well. No time to even look at the menu; their waitress gave up asking. The conversation drifted effortlessly from people to work, science to technology, and onto other things. Other things, except the H-HARs. They weren't even mentioned.

"So, things with your ex didn't work out?" Lochlan asked.

Anya rolled her blue eyes. "No. But I'm totally over it, and I have a wonderful daughter."

Lochlan casually rubbed his nose and asked, very coolly, "What happened to that other guy? Um … what's his name?"

"Darren?"

"Yeah, Darren … You two seemed pretty serious." He hid a sly, knowing grin while watching closely for a reaction.

After a dramatic eye roll and a deep sigh that denied nothing, Anya bit her lip and gazed into her glass of water.

"He was nice, but so mainstream he was almost invisible." She looked up from her glass after a thoughtful pause, squeezing out a little, reminiscent smile. "Anyway, how about you? Sorry to hear about your breakup with Lydia."

"Yeah, well, that didn't work out either. I'm also totally over it, but it gave me a son."

They smiled at the waitress and inspected their meals, resulting in a short lull. After which, Anya remarked, "I hear you're working on the DSDs, Dr McLean."

Lochlan shook his head. "I just keep everyone happy."

"Like Jeevan Partha?"

Lochlan pulled a face and laughed. "No! Nothing like him."

"Here's to Partha," Anya said. They clinked glasses and quietly sipped their drinks.

Lochlan leaned towards Anya and lowered his voice. "We're deciphering the H-HAR language. Then we'll find out who they are, where they came from, and how they got here. We may even be able to decode those three signals we recorded at MSC-HL."

"What the f—?" Everything went quiet. Anya straightened and slowly glanced at the other tables. Wary looks and hushed tones were everywhere. She dropped her shoulders, breathed deeply, composed herself, tilted towards Lochlan, and whispered, still excitedly. "That's absolutely amazing."

Lochlan stayed silent, rocking back in his chair, grinning, and calmly sipping his wine.

Anya slipped him a smile. *Hmm, this must be top-secret. I'll beat about the bush and see if he can tell me anything.* "I bet you're making huge progress."

Lochlan leaned forward, slowly chewing on the last of his meal. He held up a finger while swallowing. "We are, but there's still a long way to go – years, maybe decades. We've got the smartest people working around the clock. They're all stressed out, but they realise this is the biggest thing in their lives. And working towards a common goal gives them a purpose."

"True," Anya said. *He's not giving anything away.* "What are these people like?"

"Unusual."

Lochlan opened a new wine bottle. The waitress collected their empty plates and asked if they wanted dessert.

"No, thanks."

When the waitress was out of earshot, Lochlan softly continued. "We had this professor who thought he had solved a major mathematical problem called the Hodge Conjecture. Last year, he realised his proof was wrong. He fell into depression and disappeared."

"Poor guy," Anya said, putting her glass to her lips.

"Yeah, well … this guy couldn't get along with anyone and had to work alone. To everyone's amazement, he found a method to identify complex sections of the DSD's memory code. He then became obsessed with the idea that ultra-intelligent machines and GM humans were as much of a threat as the H-HARs."

"That's a complicated guy."

"There was another mathematician who was so devoted to his work that he left home, lived in the office out of a suitcase, and only slept two hours a night. He had great trouble understanding the limitations of others. The funny thing is, he couldn't complete the simplest of tasks."

Anya shook her head while reaching for her glass. "Hmm …"

"Then there was this remarkably gifted cryptanalyst. She categorised alien word characters from markings found on the Moon-ship, which embarrassed a lot of people who had been working on this problem for ages. She later claimed some of her co-workers were aliens, and they were watching her. She left on medical grounds and founded her own religion."

"It takes all types," Anya said.

"Yeah."

Anya looked at him with a troubled expression. "So much has happened since Pallas, Locky."

"Are these H-HARs still spooking you?"

Anya tried to force a smile but failed.

"Anya?"

She gave a look that said "yes". "I'm a professional worrier. I can't get over the fact that the aliens we discovered are trying to destroy us."

Lochlan appeared surprised that she still carried this guilt. He shifted his chair closer, resting his hand gently on hers. "Look …" Lochlan moved closer, his knee touching hers. "If we didn't find these aliens, they'd be plotting our destruction, and we wouldn't be prepared."

"Well, maybe." Anya took a little breath and gazed out the window into nothingness. "It's easy for you. You've never worried about them."

"I do worry about them. I'd be foolish not to. Look, I'm sure the DSDs will show us they aren't invincible."

"Why didn't they destroy Earth thousands of years ago?"

"We don't know. They had plenty of time. As Kevin Garrett said, it would only take them a thousand years to build a RIW without the Moon-ship DSDs."

"We seem to owe our existence to so many favourable events, Locky. As if some supreme entity were watching over us."

"It's just a mysterious, quirky coincidence, that's all." Lochlan gave her hand a little squeeze.

Anya placed her other hand over his, softly caressing it. Their eyes met. Strangely, after all this time, they were finally being drawn together.

Anya shyly looked away, gazing again through the window.

Lochlan's eyes slowly tracked down her face to her lips. "You okay now, Anya?"

She turned back and unleashed the warmest of smiles. Bright again, as if the fear somehow locked itself away deep within her. "Kevin Garrett's going well," she said in a strong voice.

"Yeah, I haven't spoken to him for about a year." Lochlan removed his hand from Anya's to stir his coffee. "But we chat on social media."

"He must be used to all the secrecy stuff by now after heading the Observation and Analysis Group for nine years."

Suddenly the stage lit up, and a Billy Ocean look-alike started singing *No More Love on the Run*.

Anya pulled her seat out and turned. "I just adore these old songs."

Lochlan watched her as she crossed her legs.

Some people started dancing.

Anya swung back to Lochlan. "You know what? I've never seen you dance," she said excitedly.

Lochlan hesitated for a moment, then said, "I happen to be a good dancer." He took Anya's hand and led her onto the dance floor.

Awkward at first, but both soon relaxed, gaining confidence, finding each other's rhythm, mimicking each other's moves. The lyrics of the song seemed to highlight their experiences over the many lost years since they last met, causing their gazes to lock.

The music pumped louder. They kept dancing, watching each other's movements. Their bodies synchronised as they drew closer, pressing against each other. Their looks and smiles suggested they could dance forever. The troubles of the world seemed distant, giving a sense of a more joyful one. They danced until the music ended, and the restaurant closed. The buzz of excitement was electric. The night couldn't end there.

As they left, Anya shoved Lochlan's shoulder, causing him to briefly lose his balance. "You little jerk," she said with a chuckle. "I know you too well. I know all your old tricks."

"What?"

"You know exactly what I'm talking about."

"No!"

"Darren! That's what. You knew his name all the time. You were just teasing me."

A lame smile spread across Lochlan's face. "Oh, yeah, that. Sorry ... couldn't help myself."

She gave him another bump – but not hard enough to push him away. "You super-jerk." Her eyes were lit with a dazzling gleam.

They walked down the street together, laughing and totally themselves with each other.

As they slowed to cross a road, Lochlan hung back, his eyes following Anya's swaying body, considering. She turned unexpectedly and caught him, giving him a flirting smile.

"Where are you staying?" he asked, strangely sounding a bit nervous.

"The Four Seasons just down this street. Why?"

Lochlan didn't answer.

They kept walking, gravitating together, gently colliding. Anya suddenly stopped him. "Why?" Her smoky eyes were alive and luminous.

"You know why," Lochlan said.

She blew a strand of hair out of her eyes and offered him a seductive smile.

"Tell me to leave," Lochlan said.

"Leave!"

"No!"

Anya kissed him.

Chapter 29   DSD Breakthroughs

One quiet morning in a DSD deciphering laboratory, while dozens of researchers were studying all types of fluctuating data on computer screens, a loud, ecstatic cry broke the tranquillity. "Holy fuck. They're entangled bonding. Now it all makes sense."

The digital coding method used on the NWIS was finally uncovered thirty-five years after the discovery of the Moon-ship, and it changed the course of history. Many paradoxes that had baffled researchers for years disappeared. When a spokesperson made the official announcement, it was like Moses himself reading the ten commandments.

Unfortunately, Professor Marcel Holmes never got to hear the news. He died three days before the discovery.

Further progress over the next year showed the H-HARs' language consisted of ninety-three graphemes. The spotlight shifted to the cryptographists to translate these into a comprehensible referent.

When asked how long this process would take, Lochlan answered, "We don't know. Its structure is bound to be profoundly different from any human language, something totally, uh-huh … well, totally alien. Is it phonetic or visual? Is it graphemic or logographic? Is it one or more characters per sound, object, lexigram, or sentence? Is it modality dependant? Is it just one language? What about semantics and cognition? Is it an antiquated language? It may not even be a written language. It may be, say, computer codes, video protocols, databases, or anything else."

Two years of intensive study yielded no discernible progress. However, Aleksandr Borodin, a mathematician from Saint Petersburg University, and Gopal Suraj, a linguistic anthropologist from the University of Delhi, showed promise.

Aleksandr Borodin was one of the youngest chess grandmasters in history. He rejected a Stanford mathematics professorship to pursue his interest in hyperdimensional transformation topology, where he proved several conjectures in dimensions higher than seven. Borodin always dressed shabbily, with bitten nails, torn jeans, and dirty shirts. Pessimistic and disenchanted, his life showed on his face – every woman, every failure, and every disappointment.

Gopal Suraj was an expert on extinct languages and orthography. "Language influences how speaker perceives reality," he once said. He founded the Association for the Preservation of Endangered Languages and claimed, "In a hundred years, there will only be four living human languages." With his youthful face, he was often mistaken for an undergraduate.

There was a friendly rivalry between the two men. During one of their many philosophical discussions, Suraj asked, "Can thought exist without language?"

Borodin pondered, then replied, "Which came first, proteins or RNA molecules?"

What followed was a four-hour, loud, and lively debate, which lasted until the pub closed.

Together, they analysed the grapheme units using statistical coherence ensembles. Utilising a new supercomputer that Suraj described as "large enough to have a complicated personality but small enough to be quantum", they ran billions of calculations and transformations, matching data to identify specific complex patterns.

When asked why they needed so much computer power, Borodin answered, "The complexity of the task can only be conquered by using computational transformations. As you are surely aware, this is the fourth pillar of any deciphering method, complementing reasoning, guesswork, and luck."

After four and a half years of research and several inexplicable guesses, they casually walked into the manager's office one evening and announced they had found a correlation. When asked to explain what that meant, Borodin calmly elaborated, "We've found the solution everyone's been searching for, so now you can tell them to stop."

They found that the current set of graphemes was an intermediate code. They also discovered the transformation function required to convert this into the actual H-HAR grapheme units.

This was the breakthrough that was so sorely needed. Soon to follow were language parsing, semantics, syntax, phonology, morphology, and finally, the H-HARs' dictionary.

Lochlan was astonished by the discovery and jokingly questioned Borodin and Suraj's sanity. "I don't understand it. It's like a hand drawing itself."

Chapter 30   Q&A

The DSDs quickly started divulging information about the H-HARs. To control the flood of fake news and alarmist theories, the shroud of public secrecy was being lifted.

***

On a popular Wednesday night live-media Q&A program, Nainkin, the host, peered up at the audience from behind his desk on the podium. He smiled to himself. Every one of the two hundred seats in the theatre-like venue was occupied. The progressively elevated herringbone seating gave each person a clear view of the podium. *They're getting impatient. And why not? Tonight's episode should be mind-boggling.*

Nainkin was still a little concerned about the new format, where audience members would not be registered or selected, and questions would not be filtered. This was insisted on by the managing producer, who was furious about the show finishing second for the last seven months and wanted to "sex it up" to boost this month's ratings by appealing to the "non-scientific" public.

Well, we'll see how that goes. At least I get to choose the questioners. Nainkin looked across at the managing producer, who was sitting in his favourite seat at the far end of the first row. *Hmm … he doesn't look all that confident.*

Nainkin pulled up his collar, checked his perfectly parted hair with a hand, and took a breath … He was ready. With his usual comforting grin, agreeable voice, and charismatic presence, he said, "Welcome everybody to The Nainkin Report, where we put you at the centre of the debate. I'm Tommy Nainkin, and tonight is one of our most important episodes. Yesterday's media release on the H-HARs was a world show stopper. We have three guests on our panel tonight to explain what it all means." Nainkin turned to his right to face the end section of the desk that angled forward. "The husband and wife team, Lochlan McLean and Anya Connell. Together they discovered the two Pallas alien spaceships … what? … twenty-one years ago?"

Lochlan and Anya nodded with a smile while the audience clapped.

"Lochlan, for the past eight years, has been head of the organisation responsible for decoding the alien digital storage devices. Anya has been an EDO public affairs representative and works in various EDO groups." Nainkin then turned to his left, where the end section of the desk also angled forward. "We also have Dayle Davis, who heads the Earth Defence Scientific and Military Advisory Body. I thank them for attending The Nainkin Report.

"Lochlan, can you give us a summary of what we know about the aliens? Then we can go straight to audience questions. To allow for as many participants as possible, each person is limited to one question. And please state your name before asking your question." He then turned to Lochlan and let out a sigh, as if preparing himself to be overwhelmed.

"Firstly," Lochlan said, looking uncomfortable wearing a suit, "I acknowledge the many brilliant individuals who have given their souls to deciphering the DSDs.

"Now, everybody, please sit back for this amazing and disturbing story. It begins on a planet the inhabitants called Yerte, in a very distant galaxy, about four hundred million light-years away, and a long time ago, about six hundred million years ago. The Yertians were technologically much more advanced than us, their civilisation a thousand times older. They were divided into two totalitarian confederations, the Dautjatas and the Guarnums.

"They were fanatically and ideologically opposed, and a permanent Cold War existed between them. An extremely paranoid, aggressive, and genetically modified subspecies appeared among the Dautjatas and dominated their leadership. This removed phylogenetic affinity between the two confederations, and a full-scale nuclear war left both sides devastated. There wasn't a clear victor, and the war continued. The worst was yet to come."

Soft, excited murmuring slowly rippled across the room.

"The war shifted to one of gaining territory, which led to the use of millions of advanced combat robots called Igwemaws. These Igwemaws razed the planet with what we call a scorched Earth policy. Plague and environmental devastation brought the two sides close to extinction. But the war continued."

The audience oohed and aahed.

Lochlan sipped water and waited for quiet. "The Dautjatas eventually won and exterminated the Guarnums. The Igwemaws were abandoned and fell into disuse.

"Three hundred years later, the Dautjatas' civilisation had all but crumbled. Reason degenerated into paranoia, knowledge disintegrated into superstition, and scientific progress ceased. Slavery was rampant, so van Loon's law was probably still a huge factor.

"At about this time, a radical minority group with an extreme religious and political ideology called the Kectors emerged. They resurrected and reprogrammed the Igwemaws as a terror weapon against the remaining Dautjatas for control of what was left of the dead planet.

"The Kectors programmed their ideology into the Igwemaws, thinking this affinity would protect them. However, their perverted madness backfired. The modifications removed safeguards against higher consciousness and independent behaviour."

The audience gasped, their arms waving to ask questions.

Lochlan took a deep breath and waited for the rumbling of voices to fade. "An Igwemaw leader emerged and selected its own goals. Top of the list was to make itself a supreme-god. Second was the elimination of all threats to its existence. This led to the total extermination of all organic intelligent entities on the planet. There was no effective defence against the mass killings that followed.

"Its next goal was to modify the Igwemaws from a purely military machine to one more able to serve the supreme-god. After thousands of years of modifications, they eventually developed into the H-HARs that threaten us today. We don't know much more about the supreme-god. It's hidden in mystery."

Nainkin sipped some water while waiting to see if Lochlan had finished. He held up a hand to silence the room. "Wow! That's … that's quite a story. We've witnessed from recent history how a mad regime can obtain control over a technological, industrial state."

Lochlan nodded gently, then continued. "Even after everything was destroyed, their programmed paranoia grew to be the main characteristic of their civilisation. There was a distant colony on mega-computers located deep underground on an outer planet. Billions of individual, virtual conscious entities lived undisturbed and isolated in a simulated reality for over two and a half thousand years. A haven from constant wars on their home planet. A fringe society, content with being a peaceful entity and slowly progressing their computational powers, which were far more advanced than the Igwemaws. They had little need for interaction with the rest of the universe and just wanted to be left alone to live as immortals within a digital paradise.

"But the Igwemaws wiped them out, and the supreme-god prohibited the existence of any conscious machine outside of the Igwemaws themselves.

"Driven by a constant fear that an unknown, hostile civilisation would unexpectedly appear on their doorstep, they used existing technology to build starships for the sole purpose of finding and eradicating all life."

"And now they've found us?" Nainkin asked.

"That's correct." Lochlan nodded solemnly. "They never intended to travel this far or this long, so their weapons are old but still capable of destroying planets. According to the DSD records, the H-HARs have passed and scanned over one hundred thousand galaxies. The Milky Way was the only one with life."

Nainkin shook his head in bewilderment. "Thank you, Lochlan, for that excellent introduction. Without taking any time to catch our breath, we'll take questions now from the audience."

Several people were out of their seats, waving their hands. Nainkin pointed to an intense looking, androgynously dressed woman in a great looking pant suit. A smile stretched her face at being selected for the first question.

"My name is Izzy Devine, and my question is: It's been ten years since the Battle for the Moon and nothing from the H-HARs on Mars. What are they doing? Their presence on Mars is unsettling the entire world."

Davis made a "we don't know" hand gesture. He looked very alpha in his tailored suit, polished smile, and three hundred dollar haircut. Young, charismatic, political, well connected, and ruthless with a bravado attitude, he had ridden the corporate wave of the alien industry further than even he thought possible. "We simply don't know," he said. "Our telescopes are not—"

"What's being done about them?" the questioner called out. Her lost smile insisted on a direct answer.

"Well," Davis continued, "I was about to say the best answer is from yesterday's report. I have it here. 'The H-HARs are sophisticated machines representing a hostile, totalitarian, and xenophobic civilisation. Don't expect them to have ethics, sympathy, morality, or empathy. To them, all life is a threat to their very existence. Their mission is to sterilise any planet that has or may develop life. The weapons on their spaceships, as well as information from the DSDs, confirm this was their intention from the very start of their voyage and not some offshoot from a more benign origin.' So, my answer to your question is that we need to confront and stop them before they again attempt to destroy us."

The audience waved, shifted, and talked to each other all at once.

Nainkin waited for silence, then asked, "I have a question for our guests. Could the H-HARs on Mars be waiting for reinforcements?"

"That's a good question," Davis said. "Those three H-HAR spaceships were carried by a larger ship, a mothership, which could be anywhere. And, yes, the H-HARs on Mars could be waiting for it."

"This is kind of frightening," Nainkin said, turning towards Davis and holding him with a steady gaze. "I mean, this is really frightening. Is there any way we can find out?"

Davis directed the question to Lochlan and Anya.

Lochlan offered Anya the chance to answer.

Anya took a while to get started but quickly gained pace. "The mothership is much larger, so you would expect it to be more formidable than the three spaceships we've seen so far. We've got the entire sky covered with radio, laser, and even pulsed gravity detectors, but so far there's been no sign of it."

Nainkin pointed to a jovial looking man of indeterminate age for the next question. The man flashed a dazed smile, giving him the air of a gypsy. "My name is Danior Abraw. According to one report, part of Fort Bush was infected with self-replicating miniature nanobots. Is that why the area was carpet bombed?"

"Jesus Christ!" uttered the previous questioner to herself. But everyone overheard and turned towards her. She responded by glancing up at the ceiling and exhaling a loud, exasperated sigh.

Is this guy serious? Nainkin wondered, slowly turning right and left to his three guests.

Lochlan slowly leaned forward, putting his arms on the table, as if he were about to speak, but Davis jumped in.

"There were no nanobots, and there was no carpet bombing. I might add just as a general comment, and this in no way alludes to your question, but there're a lot of people claiming to see footprints where the H-HARs have never passed. We get numerous stories, and we take them all seriously. However, believe me, some stories are just so ridiculous, they're nothing more than that, just stories."

"Do you think these aliens are listening to this program?" asked Nainkin.

"To tell you the truth," Davis quickly replied, "I don't think they care in the slightest about anything we do."

Nainkin pointed to a man in a charcoal shirt with a golfer's tan, a mullet, and a neatly squared goatee. The man smiled excitedly. "Hi, I'm Samuel De Jong. On Earth, some things live forever, such as tardigrades, immortal jellyfish, cancer cells, bacteria, and yeast. Is there any truth that these H-HARs are eternal?"

"There are three classes of H-HARs," Anya said, "identified by a coloured band on their arms. The red is the king, the greens are like the guards, and the blues are the workers. There is evidence that each one is a self-contained, conscious, objective-thinking, and self-protecting individual with its own memory and sophisticated personality. The red and the greens have an updated backup copy of themselves on a computer in their spaceship. If their physical body is destroyed, they simply download their entire identity into another body and carry on. The backup information is only data; it's not conscious. If their body and their backup in the spaceship are both destroyed, they die."

Nainkin shook his head. The whole thing was becoming too much. "This is unbelievable." He gave the desk a light tap with his pen. "We better take another question." He picked a young Afro-American female with a carefree appearance and a fixed smile that was laughing either with you or at you; he couldn't tell.

"My name is Kayla Stack. According to yesterday's release, these Yertians were humanoid-shaped reptiles. Do you mean like a humanoid dinosaur?"

Anya spoke first. "That's one way of putting it. They had an upright humanoid posture, two arms, bipedal locomotion, forward-facing stereoscopic eyes, two ears, a nose, and other human features. We understand they were carbon based, with a vaguely similar flesh and blood biology to ours. They would have evolved by the same universal Darwinian laws that governed our evolution. Where we evolved as mammals, they evolved with reptilian characteristics under the conditions of their planet. Convergence gave both of us a lot in common. Our biologists use the term 'humanoid reptilians.' They never lost their predatory instincts. We know this because game hunting was their main sport right to the very end. We also know that each male had many female mates."

Nainkin pointed to an ungroomed woman, who looked as though she had just been roused from a sleep and wasn't sure where she was. "My name is Tiffany Mattox. Um … you're saying they're like us, with our tendencies towards violence and exploitation? Do you know anything about their language?"

Lochlan answered. "Firstly, they aren't like us at all. They're nothing like us. And I don't think I need to explain that. As for their language, it's phonetic with a long written history. The lack of multiple embeddings suggests short-term memory limitations. Sorry, we don't know much more."

"Te Yibing is my name," said the next questioner as a black forelock of hair from his broad comb-over fell across his oriental features. "Dinosaurs dominated Earth for millions of years. Why didn't they evolve intelligence like the Yertians?"

"Intelligence isn't the goal of evolution," Anya said, smiling pleasantly. "If dinosaurs could thrive and successfully compete without intelligence, which they did, as evident by their diversity in form and size, then intelligence won't evolve."

The next questioner pulled back his hair while waiting for the microphone, revealing a rectangular-shaped head. "Tyler Robinson is my name, and I would like to ask if you know anything about their home planet?" His accent was European, but hard to place.

"We sure do," Lochlan answered. "Basically, it was terrestrial, orbiting an orange dwarf star. Its mass was twenty per cent larger than Earth's, making it extremely difficult to launch chemical rockets into space due to higher gravity. Its year was seventeen Earth months long and had four seasons. Its days were twenty-eight Earth hours long."

The next question came from a strikingly pretty, fresh-faced young woman in tight clothes. Many in the front rows turned to check her out. "My name is Sara Brand. You talk about their planet in the past tense. Is there any reason for that?"

"Good question," Lochlan complimented. "Our most powerful radio telescopes have been pointed at their home planet for years, listening for signals. Don't forget it takes four hundred million years for these signals to reach us, and that's two hundred million years after the H-HARs left their home planet. If they were still a living, radio-based civilisation, then our telescopes should have detected signals. But there's been nothing. The H-HARs' civilisation could be long gone, making these visiting H-HARs worldless."

The last questioner smiled persuasively at Nainkin and motioned for the microphone to be returned. Her smile quickly vanished with a huff when the host ignored her and turned to Lochlan, asking, "Six hundred million years! Good heavens! What were they doing in their spaceship all that time?"

"Probably nothing. They just turn themselves off until something happens. It would seem like only a few years to them."

"Only a few years! Ha," repeated Nainkin. He shook his head while holding his pen just above the tabletop. "Okay, so when they landed on the Moon or Pallas, an alarm clock woke them up?"

"Well, maybe," Lochlan said, "but only some of them. On the Moon-ship, the alarm clock didn't go off for some reason."

The host gave the next question to a rebel-cool looking, jewellery-festooned woman with short, teased hair and purple lipstick that went well with her misfit jacket covered with yellow stickers. "Heidi Schiffer. My question is: We were so lonely and wanted badly to find other intelligent life. And now we have, only to find they want to kill us. How … how did they find us?" She wiped away a tear and leaned against the girl beside her for a supportive hug.

"They knew exactly where to look," said Anya.

Nainkin's eyes grew wide. "You mean they came straight for us?"

"Well, yeah. Once within our local group of galaxies, the chemical composition of our atmosphere would lead them to our galaxy, then to Earth. Even without their spectrum detection instruments, they would still notice our unique location for the development of life."

"What do you mean?" asked Nainkin.

"Our local group of galaxies is far enough away from the energetic Shapley Supercluster to allow delicate organics to form. Inside our local group of galaxies, the H-HARs would notice an undisturbed, large spiral galaxy with a central black hole of just the right size for stability. This, by the way, rules out Andromeda. Then they would observe an unusually quiet, low density, habitable outer zone in a synchronised, stable, highly circular galactic orbit, rich in heavy elements from previous star generations, and other heavier elements and phosphorus from neutron star collisions."

"That's amazing," said Nainkin.

"Well, there's more. Once in the habitable zone of our galaxy, the H-HARs would notice a stable, long-lived yellow dwarf star with a remarkably low luminosity variation. They would notice a solar system containing a giant, gaseous, outer planet with a stable orbit, providing asteroid protection and water distribution to the smaller inner planets. They would see a rocky, rotating planet with a tilted axis for creating seasons, located in the stellar habitable zone, sized to hold a suitable atmosphere, and a molten core heated by radioactivity to produce a protective magnetic field and active plate tectonics that produce fertile, high-lying continents and favourable chemical compositions in the lithosphere, atmosphere, and oceans. Then, finally, they would notice an unusually large moon, providing the planet with a thin crust, orbital stability, and tides."

Lochlan pulled his shoulders back and proudly grinned.

Davis's mouth slowly fell open.

Nainkin's pen fell from his open hand onto the table and rolled onto the floor. "So … so the deadly mothership that's out there somewhere could easily find us?"

"Yes, but it probably already knows the location of its smaller ships anyway."

"Okay …" Nainkin turned his gaze from Anya to the audience. "We'll take another question." He pointed to a man with longish, salt-and-pepper grey, windswept hair and moustache. An Einstein lookalike.

"Hi everybody. My name is Pierre Bolelli. They've been in our solar system for a long time. Why do they now want to destroy us?" He talked with a lot of wild hand-waving.

"That's an excellent question, and thank you," Davis said. The questioner grinned as if he'd just received a medal. Davis continued, "Maybe because they've been discovered."

Anya's pleasant look dimmed a bit, but she quickly regained it.

Nainkin recovered his pen and looked up at the audience. He pointed to an old-world-looking lady with long hair that hung over her shoulders like a thick curtain.

"Hello. My name is Joanne Wood. Lochlan, one of your previous answers indicated we know where they came from. Is this true?"

"Yes. The DSDs suggest their home planet is in a previously unnamed galaxy, in the A2179E cluster of galaxies in the Hercules Supercluster."

The next questioner was a weathered man with an advancing waistline and sandy blond hair that greyed around the ears. "My name is Maya Kamamoto. Are these H-HARs on a one-way suicide mission?"

"You could say that," answered Lochlan. "It's highly unlikely they'll ever return to their home planet. The distances are too vast. Only the larger mothership, if it still exists, is capable of extended intergalactic travel. And it's highly unlikely it would survive another six hundred million years in space."

Nainkin chose for the next question a slightly overweight woman, who looked to be trying too hard at youth, wearing a short black, enigmatic, Gothic dress. "My name is Melanie Latimer. You mentioned earlier that we were the only life the H-HARs had found. Does that mean there's no other life apart from the H-HARs and us?"

"No," Lochlan answered. "It means we're the only life between here and the H-HARs' home planet. It's a large slice of space but still only a small fraction of the visible universe."

"The creation and evolution of life depends on a very large number of highly unlikely factors," Anya added. "Intelligent life is even more unlikely. The latest Life Equation gives the probable separation between two life-evolving planets at more than a billion light-years."

Nainkin was a bit overwhelmed. He turned slowly to the audience and selected the next questioner.

A short and chunky man with a skirt of white hair around a polished bald crown that shone under the studio lights smiled widely and asked, "Thank you. My name is Denis Golovan. Given that the Americans had found one of their spaceships and hidden it for many decades, is it possible the H-HARs just wanted their artefacts back?"

That's a good question, Nainkin thought. I should have asked it.

"If that were the case," Davis said, "they wouldn't be trying to destroy the entire planet, since that would destroy their artefacts."

"We have time for one more question," said Nainkin, peering into the audience. His eyes were drawn to an overly eager young woman. Simply dressed in black, skinny with untamed, dyed red hair, a pierced eyebrow, and a large, tattooed spider on her neck, she was the scariest looking person in the room. Against his better judgement, he picked her.

"My question is—"

"Can we have your name first, please?" asked Nainkin.

"My name is Jorge Sundhage. My question is for all three guests," she said with a gravelled voice. "Who gave you scripted lines to recite like trained seals to mislead us?"

"No-no! I'm sorry," Nainkin said, talking louder to be heard over the booing and titters of laughter. "That's not a fair question; our guests have been very honest and open. We'll take another question."

Davis jumped in. "I'm happy to answer that. Lochlan and Anya are more than capable of speaking for themselves. So, on my behalf and for the record, no one coached me on what to say or not to say with the intent to mislead on this program."

Anya's pleasant look faded again for an instant. "No one knows all the answers, and no one has access to all classified information, including us. At no stage was I directed to toe a certain line."

"I'm a little surprised by your question," Lochlan added. "And you may have a good reason for asking. But I've always believed news should be shared without censorship, and that happened tonight."

"Before we finish," Nainkin said, "I'll just ask each of our guests for a final comment. Anya?"

"Like me, everybody is worried about the future. The H-HARs are still on Mars, and there could be a mothership nearby. Our only chance is to stand and fight together. Then, who knows what the possibilities are?"

"Dayle?"

"We've been very fortunate so far. We owe a great deal to our military, who won a great victory on the Moon, to our scientists, and to others. I believe that if we stay united, we can defeat these H-HARs."

"Lochlan?"

"This isn't how we would have liked to have met our first extraterrestrials – a deadly struggle for existence. We need to understand and harness their technology to defend ourselves quickly. We have no other choice."

"I thank our three guests," Nainkin said, "Lochlan McLean, Anya Connell, and Dayle Davis, for being here tonight and for their openness. I thank the audience for their questions. It's been very informative. Please thank our guests."

The audience applauded.

Nainkin glanced at the managing producer. He had a big smile all over his face.

***

After the Q&A program, Kazuko, a precocious eleven-year-old girl, was so distraught by the discussions she tried to transfer her entire savings to Anya.

"Anya needs all the help she can get," she explained, "to stop these aliens."

Ten years earlier, Kazuko's father disappeared while on a business trip to Brazil during the test firing of the doomsday weapon.

"I know he would have dragged himself home for us somehow if he could," Kazuko said. Her face showed the fear, uncertainty, and vulnerability that the world would see for many decades to come.

PART 5

THE STRUGGLE CONTINUES

"Leaving doesn't fit their plan. Even if they leave the solar system, they'll be back, and maybe with the mothership."

Chapter 31   Another Attack

Two months after the Q&A program, the H-HAR spaceship on Mars lifted off, sending the military into high alert. But its direction was away from Earth.

The news was greeted with relief. "They aren't even going to say goodbye," said a flippant Dayle Davis, who, since the Q&A program, had been promoted to the political administrator of the EDO.

Andrew Mackenzie, in his newly appointed role as principal military adviser to the EDO, took the opposite view. "Leaving doesn't fit their plan. Even if they leave the solar system, they'll be back, and maybe with the mothership."

This drew an immediate phone call from an aggrieved Davis. "I remind you, Andrew, you're not the official voice of the EDO."

"That won't stop me from expressing my opinion," Mackenzie replied.

"Your position prevents you from voicing your personal views."

"Your vanity and penchant for theatrics, Dayle, makes you think you're incapable of making mistakes and therefore can't be criticised. Well, that isn't going to stop me."

Although the two men agreed on several key issues, they differed on ideology and never became friends. Their rivalry would last a lifetime.

"Davis is a middle manager with a dangerous ego. He's not a leader." Mackenzie was quoted. "His only talent is lobbying politicians."

Davis described Mackenzie as "a brilliant military mind but too opinionated and outspoken for his own good".

"How far can the H-HAR spaceship be tracked?" Lochlan McLean asked during a phone call with Kevin Garrett.

"We can detect its engine exhaust radiation way past Pluto, mate," said Garrett, who was in his seventeenth year as head of EDO's Observation and Analysis Group. "Three hours ago, it was travelling at thirty-three kilometres per second and slowly accelerating."

"And if they shut down their engines?"

"Even if it suddenly disappears, our computers will predict its trajectory, adjusting for any detected course correction burns. Besides, we can still see its reflected sunlight with our optical telescopes. It's travelling along the orbital plane, which is suspicious."

"Yes, it is."

Two weeks after the spaceship left Mars, thrusting stopped – not nearly enough velocity for an interstellar journey. It coasted for twenty-four weeks, then decelerated. It was going nowhere as Andrew Mackenzie and others had predicted.

Three weeks later, its objective was clear.

***

"Holy shit …" Garrett mumbled to himself, gently putting down the phone. Pushing himself to his feet, he walked to his office door, standing just outside. His eyes were glazed, his face was blank. Those who were there turned in their seats to face him. Garrett said nothing, but everyone could tell he had just heard something really, really terrible.

"Ladies and gentlemen," he said, awkwardly trying to appear calm. "I have some disturbing news. I'll just read the report we're about to release before the threat is detected by other organisations and made public. 'The H-HARs have launched an attack. They are diverting an asteroid to strike the Earth in two and a half years, and there will almost certainly be more asteroids to follow. The impact with Earth will have catastrophic implications for the biosphere and all life on the planet.'"

To a world that hoped the H-HARs were leaving, this was devastating news. A vivid graphical simulation of such an asteroid impacting the Northern Pacific Ocean was circulated in the media.

The picture shows empty space filled with star clusters. A dark asteroid slowly enters the frame from below and moves upwards, ominously. At the top, Earth's hazy atmospheric rim gradually emerges. Then the Earth eventually fills the screen. It's huge. City lights glow on the dark side of the planet.

Moving with the asteroid, it flares up as it enters the atmosphere at high speed. It soon turns into a raging fireball, tearing across the sky. An enormous air blast destroys everything within 300 km. Ground impact causes a 1,200 km wide firestorm, a 30 km wide by 900 m deep crater on the ocean floor, and significant damage to the Earth's crust. An 80-metre-high mega-tsunami devastates the heavily populated Northern Pacific rim, reaching 18 km inland.

A 1,000 km wide water vapour plume in Earth's atmosphere rises 1,000 km, destroying satellites.

Major volcanism, earthquakes, and secondary tsunamis occur worldwide as shock waves ripple through the planet. Red-hot falling materials start massive global fires. Atmospheric dust and smoke from the impact, huge volcanic plumes, and fires block the sunlight, causing months of darkness and several years of global cooling. Atmospheric nitric and nitrous acids generated at the impact site fall as acid rain, destroying foliage and ocean organisms. Severe damage to the ozone layer kills small organisms and plants. The Earth's core dynamo mechanism is disturbed, affecting the planet's magnetic field. Crop failures cause worldwide famines.

Several consecutive impacts would render the planet lifeless.

The H-HAR spaceship followed the asteroid for several months. Using the ship's gravity and lasers to cause vapourised gas to jet from the asteroid's surface, it diverted and finely adjusted the asteroid's trajectory to collide with Earth.

***

Anya Connell mumbled quiet reassurances to herself and leaned back nervously in her studio chair. As the EDO's spokesperson, she was about to give the first live interview on diverting the asteroids. The seat was not very comfortable; perhaps it was just the bright lights or the situation. Still, she smiled with genuine warmth at the very concerned looking news anchor, Virginia Goldsworthy.

"Anya, today's headline is 'Another Doomsday Attack'. People are again edging towards panic." Goldsworthy leaned forward, swallowed hard, then asked bluntly, "Can we stop this asteroid, or are we heading the way of the dinosaurs?"

Anya returned a solemn look. "Yes, we are in grave danger." She then covered her inner concerns with bravado. "Fortunately, we are technologically capable of countermeasures. Even before the H-HARs, we already had an effective space-based International Planetary Protection Shield against asteroid or comet impacts."

"That's a great relief," said Goldsworthy, shifting restlessly in her chair. "So, in simple terms, what are these countermeasures?"

"Don't forget, there may be more than one asteroid," Anya clarified. "There are three methods to divert asteroids to miss Earth: nuclear explosions, pulsed laser ablations, and kinetic energy impacts. The best method depends on the asteroid type and the amount of time available."

"Okay then, so what are our chances of diverting this asteroid and any subsequent asteroids?"

Anya needed to sound confident yet realistic, hopeful yet honest. "This asteroid is over two years away. Without H-HAR interference, our chances of diverting it, and other asteroids, are almost certain."

Goldsworthy sat back in her chair, giving Anya a puzzled look. "H-HAR interference? What do you mean?"

Anya hesitated, silently shivering at what she was about to say. She took a deep breath and spoke with an outward calmness she certainly didn't feel. "If the H-HARs interfere with our efforts to divert this asteroid, then things become more complicated. We may have to intercept the asteroid much closer to Earth. In that case, it may only miss us by a few Earth diameters."

"A few Earth diameters!" Goldsworthy's brow lifted as she straightened her back. "Th-that sounds very close."

"Yes, but it's enough."

"A miss is a miss, I guess." Goldsworthy leaned forward again. "What can people do to protect themselves?"

"Listen to the warning updates. Smaller fragments may impact the Earth, and immediate mass evacuations may be required."

Goldsworthy shook her head, casting a questioning stare. "Well, with all due respect, Ms Connell, that's not very reassuring."

***

Over the next fifteen months, the H-HAR spaceship diverted five more asteroids before returning to Mars.

***

Anya stepped back from the window, holding a glass of water. A glimpse over her shoulder revealed all was ready for yet another asteroid interview. *If only Goldsworthy knew how close I am to losing it. Months of these interviews now, and I still feel like I'm about to have a stroke.*

"Can we start with some details of how we're diverting these asteroids?" Goldsworthy asked, sitting eye to eye with Anya.

Anya flashed an assured smile and transformed into a confident speaker. "The first asteroid diversion method involves sending out Asteroid Intercept Vehicles, or AIVs, propelled by a two-gigawatt VASIMR nuclear electric rocket. Each AIV will carry multiple fifty-kiloton nuclear warheads that will explode twenty metres from the asteroid. The high neutron emission will vaporise the asteroid's surface, causing thrust-producing gas jets that will alter its trajectory."

Goldsworthy couldn't quite follow but didn't want to interrupt. She nodded politely, allowing Anya to continue.

"The second method is to fire powerful lasers from orbital constellations around the Earth and Sun. The beams will ablate the asteroid's surface, causing jets of propulsion gases. The effects are very small, so targeting needs to occur over a period of weeks.

"The third method, high kinetic energy impacts, has been dropped."

When asked about keeping the H-HARs away from the AIVs, Anya responded, "That's a question for the military."

Chapter 32   Asteroids Arrive

First Asteroid: (6178) 1986 DA (3.1 km wide)

"In six weeks, 1986 DA will pass between the Earth and the Moon," announced Dayle Davis, not missing the opportunity for the limelight, "thanks to sequential nuclear explosions from an AIV just off its surface." Thunderous cheers were heard around the world.

But that was just one of six.

Second Asteroid: 061 Anza (2.7 km wide)

Three months later, the second asteroid was deflected by backup AIV-565, missing Earth by 0.3 lunar distances. The primary AIV-680 malfunctioned and disappeared with all comms.

Third Asteroid: 3288 Seleucus (2.5 km wide)

Two AIVs were launched to intercept 3288 Seleucus. Their progress was monitored by the Planetary Protection Operations Room.

Part of an underground, multi-level, reinforced concrete and steel complex in southern Canada, the PPOR was the primary control centre for the EDO's asteroid defence. Twenty-five military personnel sat at computer terminals facing a huge screen occupying the entire front wall. A wide aisle ran down the middle, dividing the room. General Aleta Anders, the commander-in-charge, sat at the back. Other smaller contingency centres were located around the globe.

Four months later, things dramatically turned for the worse. As concern grew in the operations room, a quiet, commanding voice at the door drowned out the fatalistic moaning.

"Captain Kroos, what's happened?"

Ignoring the tight, worried faces around her, General Anders advanced towards her desk. Only the muffled background noise of human radio chatter remained.

Anders was full of purpose, an air of authority, fierce eyes, and a "no bullshit" tone of voice. Nearing her sixty-second birthday, she radiated a calm demeanour in stark contrast to the tense environment of the operations room. Although worn by life, she was still unrelenting.

"Ma'am," replied the operations manager, Captain Eddy Kroos, who sat to Anders's right. "The H-HAR spaceship just left Mars, and it's heading rapidly towards Seleucus. Presumably, it intends to destroy our AIVs and protect the asteroid until it collides with Earth."

"Ma'am, we can attack the H-HAR spaceship with our new LaWS," added Captain John Wilson, the cocky and overly ambitious weapons manager. He sat to Anders's left.

"How many are available?"

Wilson checked his monitor. "Eight ablation lasers will be available at the Sun-Earth L4 Lagrange point in five days. That's all we need. I'll reconfigure them and attack the H-HAR spaceship as soon as possible." It sounded like an announcement rather than a request.

Anders shot him a dark stare. "You're pre-empting my commands again, Captain Wilson. I've warned you about that."

"I'm only trying to help, ma'am."

"Now you're arguing."

"Ma'am," said Kroos, also checking his monitor, "another thirty-two LaWS in various constellations will be available in seven days. We should use them all. We—"

"We don't need them," challenged a disgruntled Wilson.

"Captain Kroos is correct," Anders said. "We don't know how these LaWS will perform. We need to hit this spaceship with everything we have."

Wilson stared at Anders with an angry frown then shot Kroos a long, hard, threatening look. A look that revealed a tightly reined physical volatility. Kroos appeared undaunted. Wilson left the room taking long, quick steps.

But it was too late to protect the AIVs. Three days later, the H-HAR spaceship destroyed them with lasers.

Anders turned to the many concerned faces around her. "We're still targeting the spaceship. Captain Wilson, please advise when *all* LaWS are ready."

Four days later, Wilson reported, "The LaWS are ready, ma'am. The H-HAR spaceship is still on a predictable trajectory nearing Seleucus." He referred to his screen. "There's a fifty-nine per cent probability of hitting it with all our lasers if we fire now. The next opportunity is in sixteen days, when the probability will be seventy-six per cent. Ma'am, we need to fire the lasers now."

Anders slowly turned and walked away, her thumb under her chin, her index finger pointing upwards. Every eye in the room intently followed her. She turned back. "That's a significant difference in probability, Mr Wilson, don't you think?"

"Ma'am, we should fire now before the spaceship starts jinking," Wilson insisted, impatience clear in his tone.

Anders turned and slowly circled the room, anguishing over the two options, her shoes squeaking softly on the hard floor. She stopped at Wilson and Kroos. Taking her time, she said, "If we take our chances now with longer odds and miss, Earth could be destroyed because we were reckless."

"If we wait for better odds, ma'am," Wilson replied, his hands on his hips, "and the H-HAR ship starts zig-zagging, then Earth could be destroyed because we were the biggest bunch of gutless pussies that God ever created."

"Thank you, Mr Wilson," Anders said.

"Ma'am," Kroos looked up from his screen. "The ballistics computers recommend we fire now." It sounded like a plea.

Anders stayed quiet, concentration showing on her face. She glanced across the room. Everyone was watching, listening, waiting.

"We need to shoot now." Wilson persisted, his impatience turning to attitude.

Anders turned sharply. "Thank you, Captain Wilson. Now, stand by." She walked across the room, taking her time doing it. "Captain Wilson," she said, returning to her desk.

"Yes, ma'am." Wilson was poised with a look that said "come on, let's do it!".

"We've relied long enough on the computers. This is where I step in," Anders said, locking eyes with Wilson. The calmness of her tone was terrifying. "We'll wait sixteen days before firing."

A frown flashed across Wilson's face, his laser-focused glare aimed directly at Anders. "We should contact EDO Command, ma'am."

"Why?"

"To ask for advice."

"What makes you think they're unaware of what happens in this room?" Her voice was controlled and commanding.

"Ma'am, if we fire now, we can get this business over and done with and walk out as heroes."

"Mr Wilson, the H-HARs are obviously unaware we have LAWs that can target them; otherwise, they would already be jinking. Therefore, there is no reason for them to start jinking in the next sixteen days."

"Ma'am—"

"Mr Wilson." Ander's voice was low but forceful. "My decision is final."

The two faced each other for some time before Wilson picked up his coat and turned sharply to leave the room.

"Mr Wilson, do not leave this room. Return to your workstation."

Wilson stopped and stood motionless for a second, then slowly walked back, exchanging an alarmed glance with Kroos and the others.

A short time later, Anders leaned over Wilson's ear. "I don't have any problems with disagreements," she softly murmured, "but do it discreetly and not in front of everyone. If that's not possible at the time, then shut the fuck up until it is."

Wilson was silent.

Anders knew that it would probably never be known if her decision was the right or wrong one. She also knew that the next sixteen days would be the most tormented of her life.

***

That night, as Kroos entered his bunk room and closed the door, he turned to see Wilson in his seat.

"What are you doing here?"

"We need to do something about General Anders." Wilson's voice was cold and conniving. Kroos gave him a long, suspicious stare.

"What the hell are you talking about?"

"We both know she should fire the LaWS now, not in sixteen days."

"General Anders knows exactly what she's doing."

"I'm sure the world would be relieved to know that. I don't think—"

"I don't care what you think. Get out!"

"She's not up to it. And we need to do something—"

"She most definitely is up to it, and we're not doing anything." Kroos stepped towards him and leaned over him threateningly. "Get out."

"Dayle Davis told me that she—"

"Dayle Davis! You've been talking to Davis?"

"He doesn't think highly of Anders."

"Davis doesn't think highly of anyone. I'm not surprised you two are friends."

"With our support, Davis could—"

"Get out!" snapped Kroos, pulling Wilson to the door by his shirt shoulder. "I suggest you talk directly to General Anders."

Kroos pushed him out, closing the door.

****

Sixteen days later, the H-HAR spaceship was still maintaining a predictable trajectory.

"Captain Wilson, *fire all* lasers," Anders commanded in a voice so blank it was almost emotionless. With a bit more emotion, she added. "We'll let these H-HARs know we're not playing nice anymore."

Targeting supercomputers took control of all information, all decisions, and all functions. Within minutes, they reaffirmed the H-HAR spaceship's exact location, velocity, and trajectory, and calculated lead times and optimal sequences.

Six minutes after Anders's order, the first set of lasers fired. Anders and the others turned to the countdown timer: 195 seconds until beam impact. The second set fired, and finally, the third.

"Anders is lucky the spaceship isn't jinking," Wilson whispered to Kroos.

"You sound almost disappointed," said Kroos, giving him a dismissive look. "Anders's decision was undoubtedly correct then, wouldn't you agree?"

Nothing from Wilson.

Sixty seconds to beam impact. The room was unnervingly quiet, full of apprehension. Anders twisted her wedding ring.

Ten seconds: Tension heightened. Kroos rubbed his neck. His eyes fixed on the timer.

Two seconds: Drawn breaths, cracked knuckles, and shifting feet all around.

Zero: Dead silence. All eyes lowered from the timer and anxiously glanced around the room.

Another kind of waiting began – the damage assessment report – four minutes, five minutes, six minutes. Anders rubbed her elbow. This was an eternity.

"Can't be much longer," said Kroos, watching his screen. All eyes were fixed on him.

"Come on," someone murmured.

"Got it," said Kroos, immediately reading it out. "Confirmed hit on the spaceship by all laser beams. Spaceship jinking, trajectory unpredictable. Spaceship still travelling alongside Seleucus. No sign of damage. Firing is recommended if spaceship's trajectory becomes moderately predictable."

"I'll keep firing," said Wilson. "We might still hit it."

"No!" Anders said.

Wilson gave a defiant look.

Anders returned a glare of cold authority. "It'll only reveal the exact position of our LaWS for return fire."

Anders turned to face the room and announced, "Everyone, listen up. The H-HAR spaceship is jinking, which means it's vulnerable. The H-HARs may not want to guard the asteroid as it nears Earth, so we need a plan to divert it if they leave. Let's all get to work."

Anders turned away, her expression hardening as she contemplated the bleakness of their situation. Excited mutterings between Kroos and Wilson turned her around.

"What is it?"

Kroos looked up. "Ma'am, the H-HAR spaceship just turned away from Seleucus." He excitedly grinned. The entire room came to attention.

"What?"

Wilson pointed to the screen. "Look!" he said in a tone that sounded like "look for yourself if you don't believe us".

"Just read it to me."

Kroos looked at his screen. "H-HAR spaceship is jinking back to Mars, most likely with sensor and hull damage."

A gargantuan room-wide cheer broke out.

Everyone turned towards Anders, clapping. Anders allowed herself a relieved smile. "I'll be the daughter of a bitch," she declared, her smile widening. "We didn't bring a knife to a gunfight after all." Everyone applauded and shook hands, except for Wilson.

Wilson approached Anders and Kroos so he would be heard over the festivities. "I told you that the LaWS are all we need. We can now divert the asteroids by laser ablation and never use any AIVs."

"What do you think about that, Captain Kroos?" Anders asked.

"Ma'am, we always need contingencies."

"No, we don't," Wilson insisted, giving Kroos a stern look. "The LaWS will deflect all asteroids."

"Maybe ... but AIVs should still be sent as contingencies," Kroos said.

"We don't need them," Wilson persisted. "I have absolute confidence in the LaWS stopping any asteroid, including Seleucus."

"Well, I have absolute confidence in contingencies."

Kroos and Wilson defiantly faced each other, challenging each other's credibility.

"Okay, okay," said Anders, "here's what's going to happen. Captain Wilson, start targeting Seleucus with the LaWS as soon as possible. And Captain Kroos, launch four AIVs to each asteroid immediately as contingencies."

"This is bullshit. AIVs aren't necessary," Wilson remarked.

"Mr Wilson, if you fail to observe protocol in this room, you will be removed. Do you understand me?"

Wilson glared at Anders. "I know what I know, and you can trust or ignore it at your peril."

"Do you understand me, Mr Wilson?" Anders's tone was soft but threatening.

"Yes."

The LaWS that targeted the H-HAR spaceship were reconfigured to ablation mode and fired at Seleucus, illuminating it on a broad face 170 seconds later. For three weeks, small thrust-producing superheated jets of gases gradually nudged Seleucus to pass behind Earth by 0.5 lunar distances.

The lasers had worked. Wilson's confidence appeared justified. "I'm in no way triumphant and in no way boastful," said a triumphant and boastful Wilson, casting a gleeful eye at Anders and Kroos, who easily dealt with Wilson's egotism by ignoring it.

Fourth Asteroid: 3752 Mela (2.2 km wide)

Mela was bumped from its orbit before the third asteroid, Seleucus. But its journey included an extra orbit, delaying its impact with Earth until five weeks after Seleucus.

Anders had been studying for some time the latest report on Mela's trajectory, absorbing every calculation, every conclusion.

"It isn't working!" she instinctively murmured, frowning, and shaking her head. All within earshot turned, including Wilson and Kroos.

"Laser ablation of Mela isn't working," she said, louder. Her eyes still locked on the computer.

"Impossible!" Wilson said dismissively.

"The general is correct!" said Kroos. "There's no deviation whatsoever. Have you even looked at the reports?"

"The H-HARs have done something to this asteroid," said Anders, slowly looking up from the screen.

They were soon to find out.

***

The following day, Kroos reported, "General Anders, ma'am," His face was pale and stricken. "Radar scanning has just revealed that Mela is a gravitationally bound pile of rubble. Ma'am, the H-HARs have fragmentised it."

The room hushed into an abrupt silence as the new reality settled in.

"So that's why our lasers couldn't deflect it."

"Yes, ma'am, but we still have the four AIV contingencies."

Wilson went uncharacteristically quiet, only giving the odd sideways glance.

***

The first two AIVs detonated off the asteroid's surface a week later but produced no deflection. Mela was still on target. The operations room cranked into full crisis mode.

Three weeks later, with Mela perilously close to Earth and the situation now frantic, the final two AIVs were detonated.

A worried expression tightened Anders's face; her legendary calmness was under stress. Individual movements of pile fragments can negate the effect of any explosion.

The room apprehensively turned to Kroos, waiting for the deflection report. "Nothing yet," he said, his eyes anxiously fixed on his screen, his right leg tapping nervously.

Silence endured.

Finally, Kroos announced, "I have it!" His pensive face slowly filled with terror as he spoke. "A large Mela fragment is still on a collision course with Earth."

Dread suddenly swept across the operations room as pained stares, pulled brows, open mouths, and gasping sounds were everywhere.

Anders drew close to Kroos's screen, almost touching his ear. Shocked horror was on her face. Without trying to comprehend anything, she asked, hoping for doubt, "Are you sure?"

Kroos placed a finger on his computer screen. "Yes, general, and it's too close to deflect. The computer is about to show a simulation of the impact."

Anders checked Kroos's screen, checked it again, then struggled for a moment with the implications. Her whole body tensed; she had failed to stop this asteroid. She picked up her desk phone and pressed a red button. "In eight days, an asteroid fragment 410 metres in diameter and travelling at eighteen kilometres per second will strike Earth in the Philippine Sea. Nothing can be done to stop it. You need to evacuate as many people as possible." Putting down the phone, she slowly turned to the simulation on the wall screen and stared helplessly at the nightmare being played out right in front of her, as did the entire room.

As the simulation ended, several agonising groans were heard. Anders fell into her chair and leaned forward, her chin resting on her fist. Her gaze, still fixed on the blank wall screen, turned deadly and vengeful. She uttered to herself, "They will pay for this." All she could do now was hope the impact wouldn't be as bad as the simulation.

***

As the massive rock entered the atmosphere, the air in front compressed and heated to seventeen hundred degrees Celsius. A flaming ball of destruction passed over North America, destined to wipe out all life within its kill zone. At a height of seventy-three kilometres, it broke up. The smaller fragments splintered off and exploded in the atmosphere, some causing widespread destruction. Two large, but not dispersed, incendiary fragments impacted the North Pacific Ocean seconds later in a blast of fiery debris, causing a forty-two thousand megaton blast. The resulting one hundred-metre-high tsunami devastated the coastal regions of Eastern Asia and most of the Pacific Islands. In China, the tsunami washed eighty kilometres inland. Debris darkened the Earth's atmosphere.

Despite mass evacuations, 350 million people perished. A two-year rabies epidemic, spread by animals fleeing the impact zone, killed countless millions more.

***

Wilson, through all this, was unrepentant. "The LaWS weren't used properly."

"Goddam you, Wilson," Kroos said. "The LaWS were used to their maximum extent. It was only the AIVs that prevented a far greater catastrophe."

The two stared each other down like gunslingers.

"I wouldn't get too sweet, Kroos, if I were you. You don't know what the future will hold."

"Whatever that means. Y'know what, Wilson, I don't trust you. You're overly ambitious with an inability to admit—"

"Stop!" Anders's angry voice behind them froze the discussion. "There was nothing else we could have done, and we do have two more asteroids coming."

***

He Yuting gazed dreamily out her kitchen window at the brilliant sunshine. Later that day, she would be leaving for the airport to visit their daughter. Suddenly, she let out a cry filled with choking fear and panic. "Oh no! Oh no! Shuangyashan, it-it's been destroyed."

Collapsing against the wall, she slid to the floor, dazed and barely able to breathe.

"Shuangyashan is one thousand kilometres away. What are you talking about?" her husband questioned, taking her hand.

With tear tracks on her cheeks and struggling to stand, He Yuting pointed to the distant smoke trail across the sky outside the window. "I s-saw it. A bright flash beyond the horizon. Our-our baby—" Her mouth opened in horror as tears again streaked down her cheeks.

Her husband grabbed his phone while flicking through news sites. "But the asteroid impact warning was nowhere near there."

Ten minutes later, or maybe it was fifteen, her husband, still puzzled, became concerned. "Her phone's not ringing, she's probably asleep. There's nothing on the news about Shuangyashan. I'll keep—"

Breaking news flashed on the news channel: "… early reports are coming in, Shuangyashan has been …"

***

Little Mi Sun-min skipped on the stone pavement for the final one hundred metres home after school while avoiding puddles. No one was watching, so he picked some flowers growing over the neighbour's front fence. A sudden, wincing heat struck the back of his legs and neck as a mysterious, bright glow grew around him. Turning, he squinted into a blinding light in the sky. His shrieks of pain and horror were cut short as his world exploded in a hell-rising ball of fire.

***

Fifth Asteroid: (89958) 2002 LY45 (2.3 km wide)
The fifth asteroid was deflected by laser ablation and crashed into the Moon, blowing lunar debris into Earth's orbit. A

twenty-two-metre-wide piece of debris fell to Earth as a brilliant fireball over Canada.

Sixth and Final Asteroid: 4055 Magellan (2.5 km wide)

The sixth asteroid was deflected without incident by two newly commissioned pulsating two hundred-petawatt ablation lasers.

This marked the end of the H-HAR asteroid attacks. Earth narrowly missed destruction for the second time.

General Anders stood before a clapping, cheering, crowded operations room and thanked everyone. But there was something in her voice – a disheartened tone, a tightness. She saw Kroos and others grimacing and knew they suspected what she was about to say.

"I have decided to retire from the military, effective immediately," she announced. After a pause, she continued. "I cannot deny that failing to stop the Mela asteroid had some influence on my decision." She smiled, weak but sincere.

The crowd traded glances, shock registering on their faces.

Anders put on a determined look, but she struggled to keep the tidal wave of emotions at bay. "We now need to remove the H-HARs from Mars." She couldn't help feeling apprehensive about the task. "My involvement will be advisory only."

Kroos glanced across the room and caught Wilson looking at him, almost evilly, with a challenge in his eyes. It would be a choice between these two men to command the attack on the Martian H-HARs. The tiniest flicker of a smug smile crossed Wilson's face. Kroos looked away.

Chapter 33   Peril on Mars

"These aliens on Mars are unsettling, to say the least," said Freddy, the bricklayer, stretching his back then bending to eye the straightness of his wall. "Whenever we start a new job, I wonder if we'll live long enough to finish it."

"Yeah, everyone's saying they're warming up some super-duper weapon," said Billy, his labourer.

"Either that, or these 3D printer robots will take all our work. Hey, don't leave that mud in the Sun for too long."

"Oh, sorry. That expert soldier guy, what's his name, um … Mackenzie. He said on the radio we should eliminate the fuckers as soon as possible before they move to some unknown location. He said Mars was too far to use them LaWS laser things, and a surprise nuclear missile was the way to go."

"Well, if they tell everyone, it won't be a surprise, will it, Billy?"

***

"Dayle," greeted Mackenzie as he pulled out a chair, its wooden legs scraping against the tiled floor. It was the EDO annual luncheon.

Davis glimpsed up over his shoulder, eye contact flickering between them. Davis, formidable and patrician as ever, ignored Mackenzie's presence for a moment, then said, "Andrew."

They sat adjacent to each other in cold silence. The much publicised tension between them – a huge ideological chasm – simmered. A waitress brought them coffee. They sipped them.

Mackenzie leaned towards Davis. "I hear you're supporting John Wilson to lead the missile attack on the Martian H-HAR spaceship."

Davis shifted his coffee cup closer, giving nothing away. Finally, "It's complicated."

"No doubt."

Their eyes hypnotically stared into their black coffee as the unspoken animosity between them continued. Davis sipped and placed his cup back on the saucer. "It was Wilson's hard-edged ruthlessness that saved our skins by stopping the asteroids."

"You have no idea, do you?"

Another long, complex pause. Then, from Davis, with a soft voice to keep their conversation private, "Anders was lucky to hold her command. In the end, her only recourse was to retire."

"If Wilson were in command, his arrogance would have left Earth defenceless against Mela."

Davis was silent.

Mackenzie continued. "We can't afford Wilson to head Operation Jupiter."

"Oh, he'll head it all right, believe me."

"Over my dead body," said Mackenzie with unmovable firmness.

They slipped once again into a tense silence, then Davis said, "I'm aware of your media criticism, Andrew."

"Nothing personal, of course."

"And your strong support for Eddy Kroos."

"Anders and Kroos were the real heroes of the asteroid attacks."

"I disagree."

"You disagree!" Mackenzie shook his head almost imperceptibly in disbelief.

Another silent stand-off while they swallowed their mutual contempt.

"I heard you're planning to move on from the EDO?" Mackenzie asked.

"News travels quickly."

"Politics?"

Davis didn't answer.

Mackenzie drew closer. "You used to show good judgement and robust support for a strong defence. But now it's clear you've become complacent, obsequious to lobbyists, and too preoccupied with winning powerful friends."

A moment passed. Then, with an ominous, soft voice, Davis said, "Andrew, I admire your military contributions, and I value your judgement. I even admire your outspokenness. I really do. But let me give you some free advice. You don't want to get me offside. You might get scratched."

"That was a stupid thing to say, Dayle. You should know I don't yield to threats."

"A threat, Andrew? No, I'm just enlightening you," Davis said without emotion.

Their heads turned, their eyes fixed on each other for the first time. Davis's cold glare versus Mackenzie's defiant one. Neither blinked. Neither breathed. They turned back to their meals and ate in silence. There was nothing left to say.

***

While plans for a missile strike against the H-HARs on Mars were proceeding, open disunity and doubts surfaced at a very tense UN/EDO meeting.

"Our new powerful LaWS are keeping these aliens at bay," a UN representative claimed to loud cheering and clapping. "An attack may only upset the stalemate."

Another official stood, mockingly covered his mouth with a hand, and whispered loudly into his microphone. "I'll tell you a little secret. The Peter Pan strategy of closing your eyes and wishing really, really hard for something doesn't work." Removing his hand, he continued in a normal voice. "If you had read the reports, you would know there is no stalemate."

Much louder cheering and clapping erupted. A missile strike on the Martian H-HARs was voted to go ahead.

***

"Hey! Guess what?" said the EDO's chief engineer. "We've just received telemetry from AIV-680."

"What ... are you sure?" the EDO's chief strategist said. "Six-eighty? I thought that disappeared during the second asteroid attack."

"It did," confirmed the CE, grinning. "But it's now transmitting again, and we might be able to re-use its warheads against the H-HARs on Mars."

"Wait a minute ... if the H-HARs are monitoring earthside, AIV-680 could approach from spaceside unnoticed."

"Exactly!" said the CE, itching for the challenge. "But it's spinning end over end like a baton, in an unknown condition, and would have to be reprogrammed with a new mission."

The CS returned a hopeful grin. "I know you and your team can perform such miracles."

Chapter 34   Wairangi and Matiu

Wairangi and Matiu sat in a tattered and cramped pub in Invercargill. The All Blacks had just defeated the Wallabies, and the late night pub chorus noise was deafening. Their considerable size made them appear uncomfortable on their stools as they slumped over the bar to balance themselves.

Wairangi read the news bar across the bottom of the wall screen: "UN discussing H-HARs on Mars".

He had given up on the news. Nothing but apocalyptic death, horror, destruction, and the end of everything. The rugby game temporarily took his mind off this H-HAR annihilation thing. "What ya reckon those aliens are doing on Mars, bro?" he asked.

Matiu half turned, pulled a face, and shouted, "What? Can't hear you, bro, too bloody noisy." He leaned closer.

"What do you think those motherfucking H-HARs are up to on Mars?" Wairangi repeated at shouting level.

Matiu shrugged back his shoulders. "Don't know, bro. The missus reckons they're gonna kill us with some giant death ray. She wants to move in with her sister 'cause it's safer. Higher, y'know, away from those tsunami waves. Taking lots of bug spray with her to kill all the surviving cockroaches."

"Bloody women; can't live with them, can't live without them. Just let her go, bro."

Yelling and a loud roar across the room paused their in-depth discussion. It might be a fight. It wasn't worth the effort to turn and check. They tuned out and picked up their beer.

"My missus cries a lot," Wairangi said. "I try to comfort her but can't think of anything to say, so I just tell her 'you'll be right, love'. She—"

The bar lady, Big Kate, appeared, lugging a bucket of ice – a local girl with heavy thighs, a neck like a tree trunk, bloodshot cheeks, a huge arse, tits like sandbags, a voice as rough as guts, and a sweet smile.

"Hi, Doll," Matiu said.

"Hi, guys, I've just put a scary movie on for you. Mothership versus Godzilla, it's—".

Louds cheer erupted from behind. Matiu shifted awkwardly on his bar stool, finally turning stiffly as his gut nudged further over the bar.

"Someone's birthday, bro." His amused expression faded to blankness as he turned back. "Fucking chock-a-block here tonight."

"Yeah, it's the fucken game, bro." Wairangi shifted his huge weight from one butt-cheek to another, releasing an enormous fart with startling clarity over the background racket. The pub stopped in stunned silence, soon broken by a loud round of applause. "Oh, excuse me!" Wairangi gave a proud grin.

Matiu and Wairangi looked up at the muted movie. An alien mothership whizzed by, looking like the giant Star Destroyer from Star Wars.

"There're heaps of foreign wealthy fuckers moving here," Matiu said, gazing across the pub. "They reckon it's the safest place."

"Nowhere is fucken safe from those H-HARs." Wairangi's tone was completely absent of doubt.

Matiu nodded. "That's what I reckon too."

They stared vacantly into their glasses. Matiu picked his up. "Did you work this week, bro?"

Wairangi shook his head. "Nuh, no point if we're all doomed. I did do some volunteer work on a bomb shelter."

A quiet moment, as if their minds were deep in thought.

Matiu frowned. "Next step will be fucking food rationing."

They looked up. Godzilla was being roasted alive in deep space by lasers. It somehow survived.

"Corny movie!" Wairangi said.

"Another one?" Matiu asked. He already knew the answer and gestured to Kate.

"Who wins, Kate? Wairangi asked.

"Godzilla. It has a big plasma weapon in its mouth."

"Good. I like happy endings," Matiu said, smiling at the thought.

Chapter 35   Moon Visit

Racing across a flat, featureless, black 2D surface with green grid lines disappearing to infinity in all directions under a black sky, she glanced back with shallow breaths and groans of fear. Scary H-HAR monsters were closer. Her hands trembled as she gripped her two children. A bottomless black hole spontaneously popped into existence, stopping them dead. The discontinuity grew exponentially, grid lines sucked into its abyss. Behind, the monsters were almost on them. The irresistible discontinuity was now at their feet, one step from oblivion. There was no escape. They screamed as they fell over the edge and into the endless nothingness below.

Anya jerked awake in a cold sweat. Tangled in her bedcovers, she looked around wildly until she realised the reality of her safety. A good night's sleep was still a long way off.

"You okay?" Lochlan asked. "You were yelling, 'no, please, no'."

***

One lazy, bright Sunday morning, Lochlan and Anya received unexpected phone calls from Dayle Davis. They were asked to consider a trip to the Moon. "The people need a morale-boosting escape from their everyday fear of annihilation," Davis said, "and a broadcast visit to the victorious battleground by the two popular discoverers might just do it."

They had a week to decide.

There would be one week of training, two days of travel to the Moon, two full days on the Moon, and a two-day return journey.

Lochlan reacted like a schoolboy. It was all he could talk about. But Anya faced a serious problem – her H-HAR anxieties. *I'm afraid I'll freak out at the sight of the spaceship or at the thought of the many ghosts of dead soldiers.*

Her anxieties about an unwinnable annihilation war against aliens had worsened. The previous week, she locked herself away for hours, leaving Lochlan to look after the children. The creatures visited her most nights now. Two nights ago, she woke up crying, fists clenched, feeling lost, desperate, and defeated. Her fears were deep, but they glowed just beneath the surface.

"You have to go," Lochlan said. "Confront these dreadful fears and anxieties. But it needs to be your decision."

The night before the deadline, Anya lay in bed staring at the ceiling. Lochlan was asleep, his arm over her protectively. Her decision was still trapped in her mind. The fears were still too deep in her subconscious. Something was telling her this trip was a bad idea. A really – *really* – bad idea.

The next morning, after further encouragement from Lochlan, Anya finally decided to face her fears, go to the Moon, and beat this. She still needed to advise Dayle Davis, after which there would be no turning back. She had been putting it off all day.

With only minutes to the deadline, she stepped into the spare bedroom. It was like walking on the surface of the Moon. Quietly closing the door, she sat on the bed, wrestling with her fears; she so much wanted to go. It was now or never.

She curled her long fingers around the phone and timidly slid a fingertip over the call button. But the phone suddenly dropped onto the bed. She jumped up, paced across the room, and stopped to stare nervously back at the phone. "This is it," she decided. "I'm doing it." But her body wouldn't move.

Breathing a loud sigh of profound disappointment, she wandered to the open window, leaning forward until her forehead rested against its frame. All the trepidations were closing in. All the now-familiar fear compulsions returned. She started hyperventilating, closed her eyes to fight it, and tried to convince herself that she was just being silly and things would be okay. She even forced a grin, but it faded after glancing at her phone. She closed her eyes again, overwhelmed, hating herself for being so weak. Her face tensed but didn't give way.

Her eyes slowly opened as a cool breeze pushed the cotton curtains against her side. She peered outside, a distant look in her blue eyes. Frightened and lost, she pushed away from the window, staring at the phone. She tried to relax, but only sadness and disappointment filled her.

I have to get these monsters out of my head.

Almost out of time, a strong voice rose from somewhere inside her. Not sure where it was coming from, she liked it nonetheless. "The procrastinations are now over," she said to herself. Without further hesitation, she picked up the phone. The call was answered instantly, and she confidently advised Dayle Davis of her acceptance. As the outside world rushed back in, she straightened her shoulders with pride, smiled triumphantly, and took a long, slow breath. *I'm not going to be like the timid woman in my nightmares.*

Anya rushed to tell Lochlan, who wrapped his arms around her as she sank into him. A strange peace engulfed her. Curling up on the sofa, she closed her eyes and fell soundly asleep.

***

There it was, lit like a ghostly apparition surrounded by darkness, one of the two H-HAR spaceships they discovered through Kevin Garrett's MOT twenty-seven years earlier. Anya and Lochlan were overcome with emotion as they stared at it through the observation window at the Darwin Moon settlement.

"It looks threatening, even from here," Anya said in a soft voice.

"But also mystifying," Lochlan added excitedly.

To the annoyance of the videographer, Corporal Norman Eksteen, Anya, and Lochlan wanted to walk the three hundred metres to the spaceship instead of taking a buggy. Their biosuits were incredibly comfortable, and they quickly adjusted to the low gravity. Lochlan started jumping, Neil Armstrong style. Anya was intrigued by her arms hanging out in front of her. Was it the low gravity or the biosuit? She couldn't tell. She threw up a rock.

"It should go five times higher than on Earth," Norman said.

"Looks right," Anya replied.

"The ship's very much a classical deep-space design," said their guide, Lieutenant Michael Bosch, as the four of them walked towards it. "Brilliant white, long, narrow, and cylindrical. The H-HARs landed it flat on the ground to access the payloads."

"The ship's bigger than I expected." Lochlan's face rubbed against his helmet mic, causing a loud scraping noise to mix with his words.

"The mothership must be enormous." Anya lifted her head to gaze at a billion stars in a vast black sea. "It's out there somewhere."

Michael pointed at the spaceship. "She consists of three sections. From fore to aft: flight control and computer equipment, payload sections, and thrusters. The battle explosion was contained by the solid inertial dampers, so only the lower payload and thruster sections were damaged. Fortunately, the DSDs were located in the computer section."

They passed a steady flow of scientists and engineers coming and going. Anya felt a sense of pride; human civilisation's restless energy united in a struggle to survive.

"Amazing! It looks new," she said. "Only some corrosion on the front and side surfaces."

"That's regeneration for you," replied Lochlan.

"The ship's partly disassembled," said Michael. "But there's still enough to give you nightmares."

"Thanks," Anya muttered.

Their first stop was a payload section door with two laser-armed guards and a CAR outside. Anya and Lochlan stayed back, waiting for Michael, then followed him in. Norman stayed outside.

"Look at these, Anya," said Lochlan, pointing to peculiar symbols stencilled on the walls. "These helped to decipher the DSDs."

Anya stepped back to view them. "Interesting. They're all similar but different."

Lochlan reached out and touched a row of symbols with his gloved hand. "I recognise a few – the circles, the sideways triangles – but I have no idea what they mean."

"Over here, guys," said Michael as he walked to a dimly lit, fenced barrier guarded by another soldier and two CARs.

Anya turned to look and hesitated. All she could see were rows of grey spheres stored in massive vertical stacks. She knew what they were. A sudden sweat developed on her forehead. She forced herself to follow Lochlan.

"These are the deactivated H-HARs," said Michael. "We haven't moved them all yet."

They could only see the tops of heads. Their bodies disappeared into the stack's darkness. Anya shrank; being so close to these things made her nervous. "I'll wait outside," she said calmly.

Michael and Lochlan soon joined her, and the four of them walked along the spaceship to the thruster section. "They've barricaded this off with red tape, so we can't stop here. They're removing the reactor core," explained Michael.

They moved on and entered the flight control and computer equipment sections. "It's been cleaned out, but it's obvious the explosion was devastating. You can see scorch marks on every wall and corner."

"This is where the battle turned," Norman said.

Anya felt a chill and a quickening breath as she contemplated the scene. "It's so peaceful now. What happened here is unimaginable." She walked outside, feeling claustrophobic.

They made their way around the entire ship as Michael continued his tour. "These are the heat shields … the side thrusters for landing on its side … the radiator compartments … the high-gain sensors … the space lasers."

Michael checked the time. "We better head back to Darwin; we only have small life support units. We can go via the doomsday weapon."

On the way was a large outdoor laydown area cramped with equipment salvaged from the ship and elsewhere. "That's the heat radiators' pipework … the surveillance probes … what's left of the control equipment … power converters … shadow shields."

Michael stopped at some crates containing thousands of insect-looking objects of different sizes. "These were the maintenance robots."

Anya imagined them perpetually crawling around the H-HAR spaceship.

"The ship was like an intelligent living being, evaluating and healing itself, but without self-awareness," Michael said.

As they neared the doomsday weapon, Lochlan raced towards it.

He peered into the bottomless shaft that tapered down from the surrounding ground. "Have you ever seen anything like this, Anya?"

Anya watched him nervously. His daringness caused her not-so-gentle pulse to rock her body with every beat. "You're too close, Locky. Come back."

"I'm okay," said Lochlan, but he moved back anyway.

Anya looked away from the weapon and studied the structures and equipment around her. "All this effort to eliminate us." She shook her head. "It's just crazy."

"The universe owes nobody favours," Michael said.

"Or even explanations," added Anya with a nervous little grin. They walked back to Darwin, overwhelmed.

***

An excursion was scheduled for their second and final full day on the Moon. This would take them outside the vast spaceship perimeter and into unpatrolled territory.

The night before, Anya tossed and turned. She tried to sleep, but her eyes stayed open. Eventually falling into a deep sleep, her eyes flickered under her closed lids, and her body twitched. A loud noise soon disrupted her slumber. She rolled over, tried to ignore it, but, annoyingly, the noise persisted, intertwining with her nightmare. She snapped awake, wrestled free of the covers, swung out her legs, and sat on the edge of the bunk. She had no idea where she was. The torment of her nightmare was still in her mind. *The H-HARs were chasing me again.*

Her head spun. The noise was still present. "What …" she cried out weakly. Her half-lidded eyes fell upon the room phone. "Oh … "

Pushing tangled hair from her drooling mouth, she managed a shaky, "H-hello?"

"Hi, just checking that you're awake." It was Lochlan, sounding all too innocent.

"Uh-huh?" Anya sighed, rubbing her eyes and barely focusing. "No! I'm asleep!"

"Don't forget, we're meeting Michael in the airlock prep-room in thirty-five minutes. Oh, ring the kids. I've already talked to them."

Anya checked the time. "Thanks for *waking me* a whole five minutes before my alarm."

"Ha-ha. See ya soon."

She made herself presentable, gulped down some breakfast, and put on a brave face to talk to the kids. Wishful smiles and kisses insisted on her safe return.

Anya still hoped this trip would relieve her anxieties and hounding nightmares, but nothing had dispelled her belief that these aliens were ultimately invincible. She would be leaving the Moon tomorrow and couldn't say she was unhappy with the thought.

Anya arrived ten minutes late, immediately giving Lochlan's accusatory stare a bleary glance that said "please, not now".

Lochlan, half suited up and hyper about the excursion, sang happy tunes to himself, being irritatingly cheery. "Zip-a-dee doo dah, zip-a-dee-ay …"

Anya yawned and ignored him with amused tolerance. She pulled over a makeshift screen and stripped to her underwear. An assistant helped with her a biosuit.

The prep-room resembled a small dressing room. On the other side of the room, Michael was waiting at the inner hatch of the three-person airlock. He was suited up and ready to go.

Lochlan, still encouraged by the black storm clouds of petulance hovering over Anya's head, kept teasing, humming a bit louder, a bit more annoyingly.

Anya shot him a dirty look through red eyes while hopping a leg into her biosuit. "Der–what?" said Anya, staring disapprovingly.

"… Mister bluebird's on my shoulder …"

"Okay, fine then … whatever," Anya mumbled as the assistant lifted her biosuit.

"Plenty of sunshine headin' my way …" Lochlan struggled to suppress a grin of mischievous satisfaction.

"What's up with you?!" she asked, staring and insisting on a response.

"Have a good sleep?"

"Ugh," yawned Anya and grunted obscenities.

"Just as well I woke you up, aye?" Lochlan's mouth betrayed a trace of a smile.

"Shut up! … I had my alarm set," she replied, her tone softening the words. A breathed-out, sleepy smile was quickly suppressed as her helmet was fitted.

After an exhaustive checklist, they exited through the airlock and walked to an open-roofed buggy.

Lochlan plastered himself in the back seat beside Anya, both sitting tightly like a pair of tinned sardines. Lieutenant Michael Bosch was driving, Corporal Jonty Mackenzie rode shotgun, and Corporal Norman Eksteen was perched in the rear luggage area with his camera and a CAR called Robert.

Anya noticed two rifles fixed on the front rack. "You still carry weapons on these buggies?"

"They're leftover gauss and paint rifles," Michael said. "Don't worry, the battle was sixteen years ago. There's no evidence that any H-HARs survived."

Bright spotlights around the H-HAR spaceship cast a lurid reflection on the rim of Anya's door. A reminder of how out of place this object was.

"Jonty," Lochlan said in a questioning tone. "Is your father Andrew Mackenzie, the Moon hero?"

"As a matter of fact, yes."

"I've never met your dad, but I knew he had a son about your age," Lochlan said.

"How long are you stationed on the Moon, Jonty?" Anya asked.

"For five weeks. I've been here for four weeks now."

"How is your dad?" Lochlan asked.

"Totally recovered from his injuries, thanks to a bionic neuro-prosthetic right leg."

"That's great news," Lochlan said.

"Yeah, it is," agreed Anya.

Michael turned to check on everything, taking them in with a tight smile.

They rocked back and forth as the buggy got under way, dust kicking up from the wheels. Lochlan gazed up at the half-Earth, eternally hanging in the monstrous, dark sky above them. Scattered cloud formations looked striking against the vibrant brilliance of blue oceans. He could just see the outlines of continents. "You never get to see an Earth rise on the Moon," he commented.

Anya was quiet, staring at the distant moonscape.

Lochlan nudged her.

"Uh? Oh … sorry." She looked up, stifling a yawn. "Yeah, amazing … It's just floating there, always in the same spot, a little oasis of life among millions of non-twinkling stars."

"Looks like early morning in Beijing," said Lochlan.

"Yeah, and a mini-whirlpool typhoon east of Japan."

"Yep."

They stared at their destination, the distant crater Albategnius, dominating the horizon like a colossus.

Anya went quiet again, and Lochlan did the same.

An hour later, they reached the interior of crater Albategnius, a flat plain of basaltic lava scattered with craters and pitted with large boulders. Its terraced rim, a jagged landscape of towering cliffs, loomed over them. Their buggy moved like a toy car, insignificant in the dark belly of this jutting-walled behemoth.

All was quiet and peaceful. Anya started to relax, taking in the panorama. As a smile of relief crept across her lips, her face tightened. "Look! Over there!" she called out while pointing. "Is that a set of footprints?"

Faces turned as Michael stopped the buggy.

"Might be old mining exploration prints." Michael's voice sounded doubtful. "I better check." Stepping out of the buggy, he cautiously walked towards a gap in a wall of boulders, thirty metres away, leaving a new trail of footprints behind him.

This is such a bad omen, Anya's gut told her. *I can just feel it. Something's out there. Something really, really bad.*

Her knee started tapping. Lochlan reached across to still her. "Thanks," she muttered.

Anya's eyes warily tracked left. As far as she could see, a Sun bright, deeply shadowed wall of boulders. Then right. The same. Her eyes instantly shot back to the left. *What the fuck?* But there was nothing there. She froze in fright. *I saw something move, I'm sure of it.*

She swallowed and tried to stay calm, reluctantly scanning the wall of boulders once again. *This world is such an unsettling, desolate, foreboding, and nightmarish place, so eternally still. Hurry up, Michael. This place is haunted.*

She glanced at Lochlan, who had his "something is not quite right here" expression. Jonty and Norman were exchanging a nervous look. Everyone was spooked. And so they should be.

Michael was almost at the prints.

Just then, Anya's head snapped to her left again. A cold, premonitory dread shot through her. *What was that? A flash?* She looked closer. There, among those rocks. But ... nothing. She cursed her jittery nerves and curled her fingers under Lochlan's hand. She was only a heartbeat from panic.

Michael cautiously leaned over the footprints, his knee touching the lunar dust. He examined his own prints, then quickly turned and hurried back to the buggy. "We better return to Darwin right away," was all he said. But the quickness in his voice indicated a fear he was trying to cover.

As Michael grabbed the buggy's frame to jump in, Anya choked on a scream. She raised a wildly shaking finger, pointing at something from her nightmares. Three huge biomechanical humanoids stood where Michael had just been. A green-armband and two blue-armbands, their skin the dark armour of combat, a deadly glare in their eyes.

The green-armband bolted to the buggy and pulled off Michael. The CAR leaped out, ramming the creature, knocking it off balance. The H-HAR quickly recovered, closely examining its assailant with some respect. Robert circled to the creature's right. Its black, predatory eyes followed the CAR, allowing Lochlan and Jonty to lift the injured Michael onto the luggage rack.

The creature lunged at Robert. For the best part of a minute, the two machines hit, pushed, deflected, grappled, and rolled over each other. Norman grabbed a shovel and hit the creature with all his might, but without effect. The two machines remained locked in a deadly embrace. Robert couldn't match the creature's strength. The green-armband grabbed Robert's head and twisted. Robert fell limply to the ground, its neck ripped open, and its metal spine visible.

The creature turned to the buggy just as Jonty floored the accelerator, everyone clutching a handhold as it bounced violently on the rough surface. But the green-armband quickly caught up, grabbing the back of the buggy, forcing it to a halt, and knocking Michael off.

Norman pulled up the rifles, but the creature knocked him to the ground while its other hand still firmly gripped the buggy. The two blue-armbands abruptly arrived and dragged Michael and Norman towards the boulders.

Lochlan grabbed the paint rifle from the buggy floor. He struggled to find the trigger, then frantically squeezed it repeatedly, trying to hit the green-armband's eyes. Not being a good shot and lacking a good angle, he only hit the side of its head. The green-armband turned towards him, their eyes briefly meeting. Lochlan still couldn't hit its eyes. Jonty picked up the gauss and fired at the creature's neck. It finally let go of the buggy and backed off, disappearing with the other two H-HARs who had dragged Michael and Norman through the gap in the boulders.

"We have to go after them," Jonty said. His eyes were white and terrified. "They aren't responding on radio."

"W-we can't leave them there," Lochlan said, panting with a stomach contracted in horror.

Anya, choking back a meltdown, could only nod her agreement.

As they stood to get out, an authoritative voice came over their helmet radios. "Whoa, you guys. This is Lieutenant Colonel Hewitt at Darwin. We have your exact location. Commander Tae-se is preparing to leave with some troops. I can't let you go back."

"When will they get here?" Jonty asked.

"Forty-five minutes."

"Negative, sir," Jonty replied, his eyes blinking in apprehension. "They won't survive that long."

"Your job is to get our visitors back to Darwin safely. There may be more H-HARs out there. Let Tae-se and the troops handle things. Your orders are clear, Jonty."

"Anya and I are civilians. We don't take orders from you," Lochlan said, stepping out of the buggy. "We're going back."

"Yes, you do. This is a military op—"

"And I have to protect our visitors," Jonty said, also stepping out.

An uneasy silence from Hewitt followed. Eventually he asked, "These H-HARs don't appear armed. Is that correct, Jonty?"

"Yes, sir. That's correct."

Another short silence passed.

"Okay. You have permission to go back. The H-HARs can locate your radios, so turn off the transmission."

Jonty grabbed the gauss rifle and oxygen bottles. "Let's go," he said, making uneasy glances to where the H-HARs were last seen.

Lochlan grabbed the trauma bag and turned to Anya, who was also stepping out. "We need someone in those rocks over there to wait for the troops. Without radios, they'll need guidance to find us."

Anya had trouble hearing over her locomotive breathing. "Y-yeah … but what if—" Her voice cracked. She hated sounding so weak.

Lochlan put a calming hand on her and looked into her visor. Her eyes were full of fear. "Anya." Lochlan was firmer and more insistent. "The troops will need directions, and if things do go wrong …"

"Then I'll be safe while you guys get killed. That's what you're saying, isn't it?" Anya's voice was suddenly stronger.

Lochlan pulled Anya close and held her like he would never see her again, which, in fact, was likely. Then he and Jonty headed off.

Anya climbed into the driver's seat, her expression as desolate as her surroundings. "Be careful," she said, "it could be a trap."

Lochlan glimpsed over his shoulder and raised his arm. "Then wish us good luck." Fear was written all over his face, hidden by a forced grin.

Anya placed her boot on the accelerator pedal, then hesitated. *I'd be useless waiting at those rocks. And I hate uselessness.* The rapidly growing agitation within her was now just as strong as her fear. Nervously swallowing the lump in her throat, she looked around at the cold, shadowy stillness. *There could be a whole army of H-HARs lurking in those rocks.* Her eyes were still wide with horror but now also with something else. Something she had never felt before. Let's call it fury.

Her back straightened, her face hardened, and her eyes narrowed. The timid little girl was gone. With a tenacity that held her gut panic in check, she lifted her boot off the accelerator. She wasn't going anywhere.

***

"We better turn our radio transmitters off now," Jonty said. Before he did, he switched to Lochlan's dedicated channel. "Is she okay by herself?"

"Don't be fooled. Anya is as tough as nails."

They followed Norman and Michael's drag marks through the gap and around several small craters. The drag marks suddenly vanished. They then followed the three H-HAR footprints, clinging to a tall basalt rock wall as tightly as possible. Their bodies trembled, their pulses raced, and their adrenaline pumped. They weren't used to this.

Up ahead was a narrow passage, dark and claustrophobic. The prints blended together. They stopped. Their bug-wide eyes perpetually scoured all directions as if menace were everywhere. Jonty felt a chilling presence and spun around, but nothing.

They faced each other with frightened animal looks. Jonty motioned to keep going. Lochlan nodded. They moved slowly, cautiously, their eyes shifting, expecting something at any second. The noiselessness only intensified the suspense.

Some sixty metres from where Michael first inspected the prints, they entered a shadowy depression twenty metres wide and surrounded by high boulders. There, they found Michael and Norman.

Michael was dead, his helmet smashed in. His mouth was open in a gaping, silent scream, one black eye staring up at them, and beads of frozen, crystallised blood all around. H-HAR footprints were everywhere.

Jonty dropped to one knee to examine Norman, his gauss rifle across his lap. Lochlan stood watch with the paint rifle.

"He's still alive," Jonty said.

A white-grey blue-armband appeared out of nowhere. Jonty sprang to his feet, firing several rounds from his gauss rifle. The creature fell silently to the ground in a cloud of moon dust, its head snapped back.

"Where're the other two?" Lochlan gestured to Jonty with two fingers and raised shoulders. They surveyed the rocky bluffs encircling them, but nothing was there.

Seconds later, two dark H-HARs emerged from the shadows, their beady eyes focused ominously on the two Earthlings. The green-armband, still splattered with paint, charged at them. The gauss rifle had no effect, and Lochlan's sporadic shooting with the paint rifle was wide. Jonty was thrown hard against a rock, falling limply to the ground like a rag doll. The rifle flew from his grip.

The creature turned towards Lochlan just as a paint bullet hit its left eye. It yanked the paint rifle from Lochlan's grasp and hoisted him up like captive prey, staring at him through its right eye with indifferent detestation before throwing him forcefully to the ground. Lochlan screamed in agony as he felt a sickening crack in his shoulder.

The H-HAR scratched at its left eye and shook its head violently before peering down at Lochlan.

Dazed and expecting further blows, Lochlan tried to focus on the blurry figure looming over him. The green-armband turned and walked to the blue-armband, pointing to a large rock near Michael's lifeless body, then to Lochlan and Jonty. The blue-armband remained motionless. The green-armband gave it several hard blows to the head and a hard push.

In a feat of amazing strength, even for the Moon's gravity, the green-armband lifted and carried the rock to Lochlan, looking down at him like a bug about to be squashed. It raised the rock high above its head. Lochlan gasped in helpless horror, panting as he braced himself for the final blow. The creature's head abruptly jerked bizarrely several times to the right. It swung its head to the left, turning more than usual to see through its good right eye.

Lochlan pulled his eyes from the creature to follow its stare, but the bright Sun made the shadows imperceptible. Then a biosuit slowly stepped out. Lochlan squinted, trying to focus on the figure.

"ANYA!" He thought he was seeing a ghost.

Anya advanced into the sunlight like a trooper. She had an angry look. With the gauss rifle gripped firmly, she circled to the creature's left, looking for a clear shot. But the creature rotated with her. A rock wall stopped Anya's movements. She exhaled calmly, bared her teeth, crouched like a lioness, and steadily took aim. Her actions were controlled, precise, and calm. Her eyes were fixed, her body was still. She waited for the one false move that would expose her target. But the creature kept its vulnerable spot out of Anya's line of fire. It glared at her like a one-eyed dog as it coiled back the rock, ready to spring it.

"Look out, Anya!" Lochlan yelled, forgetting his radio transmitter was turned off. But Anya was prepared and moved quickly. The rock shattered against a stone wall behind her, a large piece knocking her heavily to the ground.

The green-armband immediately picked up another large rock and stepped towards Anya.

"No! Keep away from her, you fuck!" Lochlan screamed, but his words went unheard. He frantically searched for something, anything, to distract the creature. With the strength and painlessness of adrenaline fuelled panic, he hurled a rock, hitting the creature's back. It didn't seem to notice and kept moving towards Anya.

Lochlan turned on his radio. The creature immediately whirled around, its eye locking onto Lochlan. Lochlan scrambled backwards, groping for the paint rifle. But his trembling fingers bumped it further away.

The creature came for him. It loomed over him once again, the rock raised high. For the second time, Lochlan braced himself for the fatal blow.

At the last possible moment, the crazed monster's head jerked again to the right, but this time only once. It stood motionless for an instant, then, without even turning its head to see its slayer, collapsed to one knee and crumpled to the ground, the rock dropping between its legs. This time Anya had a clear shot, and it was deadly accurate.

She hurried to fire another bullet into its neck for good measure, turned on her radio transmitter, fell to her knees beside Lochlan, and looked into his helmet visor.

"Locky? You okay, honey?" she asked, squeezing his suited hand while still firmly gripping the rifle.

Lochlan lifted his head and looked back bewilderedly. Trickles of blood leaked from his nose, splattering his face and helmet. He glimpsed Anya's face as she turned into the sunlight. It looked murderously fierce, eyes red and lethal, blazing with primal rage.

"Locky, honey, you okay?" she repeated.

If Lochlan had been thinking clearly, he would have answered "no". But instead, he said, "As soon as I get over my heart attack, I'll be—" He suddenly buckled and grabbed his shoulder, gasping and wincing.

"Don't move! You're obviously injured."

"Ahh … I'm all right. It's—"

"Are you in pain? Yes or no?"

"Okay then, yes. My shoulder feels dislocated."

"I can pop it back in. I've seen it done."

"Where!?"

"Never mind."

"No, wait! First check on Jonty and Norman. Michael is dead."

"Dead? Oh no!"

Anya rushed to Norman. "His bio-monitor is flashing yellow … um … 'unconscious, ragged breathing, low O2 pressure, low blood pressure … compound leg fractures, not life-threatening'." She patched Norman's biosuit breaches and attached an oxygen pack to his rebreather. She didn't touch his right ankle which was bent outward at a strange angle.

Jonty was in a better condition but also lacking oxygen and unconscious. She patched his biosuit and attached an oxygen bottle.

Anya stopped at Michael's body and bowed her head, placed his arms on his waist, and straightened his legs.

She rushed back to Lochlan, grabbed his arm, and capped his elbow. "You ready, Locky?"

Lochlan took a deep breath. "I-I guess so."

"Here we go … one, two, three." Using all her strength, Anya pulled on Lochlan's arm until she felt his shoulder pop back into the socket. Lochlan tensed in agony but kept it all in.

"I think that did it," he said after moving his arm around.

"You'll survive, you big sook."

Lochlan pushed himself away from the fallen H-HAR. "How about you? You okay?"

"Yeah, only bruises."

"Help me up, Anya."

They moved, a little unsteadily, away from the terminated green-armband. Lochlan noticed Anya had become almost recognisable again.

"You were fearless, Anya. Where did you learn to shoot like that?"

"An old boyfriend's farm."

"Darren?"

"Yes."

"Hmmm … Anyway, it was a great rescue mission, darling."

"Rescue mission? I just came to look."

"Ha-ha."

Lochlan's eyes shifted past Anya, then froze. "Holy shit! I forgot about that one."

Anya followed Lochlan's numb stare into the dark depths of a nearby shadow. She barely perceived the black-on-black, indistinct figure of the third H-HAR watching everything.

Lochlan was in no condition for another confrontation, but Anya lifted the gauss rifle and fingered the trigger. Savagery returned to her face. For a moment there was a tense standoff.

"Wait!" Lochlan said. "It refused an order from the green-armband to kill us."

"Really?" Anya relaxed her trigger finger slightly.

The invader from another world stepped into the sunlight, its blue-armband becoming visible. Its skin transitioned to ivory-light grey, making it vulnerable to Anya's gauss rifle. It kneeled, placing its hands on the regolith.

"Christ!" Lochlan said.

"I think it's surrendering."

"That'll be a first."

"Any sign of it darkening again, and I'll blow its head off," Anya said.

"I believe you will, darling."

Anya headed off to check on Norman and Jonty, keeping a very close eye on the cowering H-HAR and a very tight finger on the trigger.

"They're still unconscious but breathing stronger. Their pulses are normal," said Anya, pushing herself up. She turned towards the terminated green-armband H-HAR. "Let's look closer at this monster."

Lochlan cautiously followed, lurching as he cradled his shoulder.

The thing lay on its back. Its skin was metallic black, like a shadow, like nothingness. Its dull, black-pearl eye still piercing.

"What the hell are you?" Anya asked in a condemnatory tone.

Lochlan moved closer, mesmerised by it.

The creature's skin abruptly turned inanimate light grey. Lochlan jerked backwards with a painful groan. Anya grabbed and steadied him. He moved closer again. "Its eye now looks almost human."

Anya pulled a face. "You're impossible."

"I've seen enough," Lochlan said, tugging on Anya's arm.

The soldiers arrived seventeen minutes later. Lochlan and Anya shared an exhausted look. They had no intention of lingering.

Chapter 36   Distant Signals

The whereabouts of the mothership was the greatest mystery of the H-HARs.

The EDO had been sweeping the skies relentlessly for decades, searching for electromagnetic or even gravitational signals. Six years after the asteroid attacks, a global network array of interferometric radio telescopes picked up an almost undetectably faint radio signal.

"Holy shit!" cried out Dougie, a principal researcher, bolting to a sitting position in the middle of the night to grab his phone after it sounded a notification.

"You better be right this time, Dougie," said his manager minutes later. "Dayle Davis is sick of us, um … I mean, sick of *you*, crying wolf."

"Those little mistakes have been filtered out now. There's something out there in that direction"—Dougie pointed upwards—"that's statistically more significant than cosmic static."

Every Radio Astronomical Tracking Station pointed their antennas towards the signal's source. Three days later, as Dougie was yet again about to be reprimanded, a RATS detected a handful of photons on a wide bandwidth, just above threshold level.

This detection was very different to Dougie's earlier signal. It was recognised as bow shock plasma radiation, generated by dust, microwave background radiation, and virtual subatomic particles impacting against a surface travelling at relativistic velocity towards Earth. Within hours, the amplitude, frequency shift, phase, spread, and structure of the radiation were analysed to determine the distance, direction, and velocity of the source.

Other RATS reported similar detections, and the grapevines whispered, partners and friends confided, the media speculated, and catastrophic misinformation flowed. Any attempt to conceal the discovery would be futile.

The following morning, EDO staff across the globe assembled in front of large office screens or personal screens for an announcement.

"What's going on?" asked an HR officer, sensing a strange energy ripping through the office. "Everyone knows except me."

Before anyone could answer, Dayle Davis's image appeared. He was addressing a large office.

"The alien mothership has been found," Davis stated, pausing to allow the initial shock and some muffled, misguided jubilation to subside. "One hundred and seventy-six years ago, it was one hundred and seventy-six light-years from Earth and travelling at eighty per cent of light speed. At that velocity, it will reach our solar system in forty-four years. Deceleration would add another five to ten years to reach Earth."

The news was immediately released to the media, and fear spread across the globe like a dark, toxic cloud. One reporter wrote, "This could be our end, more likely than anything we've seen so far." Governments added to the fear to justify new restrictions, then ironically had to control the rampant paranoia and chaos of their own making.

Chapter 37   Captive

An experimental H-HAR language converter, under development in labs around the world, was rushed into service to communicate with the captive blue-armband. Although information exchange was extremely difficult, it improved remarkably over time, and the captive revealed surprise that it could communicate in its own language.

It was one of nine H-HARs, one green-and eight blue-armbands, who were away from the spaceship at the time of the Battle for the Moon. Their green-armband leader immediately terminated all but three blue-armbands, believing smaller numbers gave a better chance of hiding.

Self-preservation was the reason Captive surrendered to the Earthlings, believing it would soon be terminated. It confirmed the existence of an immeasurably powerful mothership but claimed it knew nothing else.

Although Captive was manufactured and loaded onto the mothership just before it left its home planet, its memory only registered an uneventful 1,730 years of life, mostly for mothership renewals.

Individuals existed only to serve the supreme-god, and affinities between H-HARs were virtually non-existent. Captive described a world of subjection, degeneration, and chaos, where all resources were put into constructing motherships. It refused to discuss its supreme-god any further, except to say that it was the source of all greatness, was without peers, nothing escaped its awareness, was the protector of all H-HARs, and its existence depended on eliminating all life or potential for life.

Captive knew little about the Moon-ship, except that it left the mothership six million years ago as it entered the Milky Way galaxy. All contact was lost until its DSDs were detected on Earth forty-seven years ago.

It reached Earth thirteen thousand years ago in one of two spaceships, two million years after leaving the mothership. The commander of the two ships, promoted to acting red-armband status, or Kunna, by the supreme red-armband leader on the mothership, wanted to destroy Earth immediately. However, it was ordered to wait for the mothership's arrival so that the supreme red-armband leader could claim glory for destroying Earth. Both ships went into hibernation on Pallas.

The yellow-armband H-HAR leader on the Moon was also an acting leader, promoted by the Kunna on Mars. Yellow was higher than green but below red.

Captive claimed that the RIW and asteroid attacks were only intended to cripple human civilisation to remove any possibility that Earth could defend itself against the mothership.

Captive showed no interest or curiosity towards humans other than its belief that if Earth were not destroyed, Earthling machines would eventually journey to its home galaxy for the purpose of annihilating the supreme-god. Everything that has happened so far only confirms that belief. The ingenuity, fighting ability, and unity of the Earthlings had consistently been underestimated by the Kunna.

Captive remained imprisoned on the Moon. Initially, it was remarkably cooperative. However, over time, and despite conciliatory efforts from its captors, it displayed increased intolerance, paranoia, and superiority, eventually becoming difficult, frustrated, angry, and threatening. It provided what could be critical information about the individual psyche of the

H-HARs, such as their motives, behaviour under stress, loyalties, rationalities, and acceptance of authority. Finally, it stopped communicating, claiming that itself and Earth would be destroyed by the mothership immediately upon its arrival.

Thirteen months after it was captured, it somehow self-terminated, destroying its brain and other functional units.

Chapter 38   P2IM-x

Seven years after the asteroid attacks, Hugo Bussaglia, a French farmer, noticed his sheep acting strangely. "Maybe it's just the river water," his wife suggested. The following morning, all thirty were dead.

All over the Northern Hemisphere, not only sheep but other domesticated animals, wildlife, and vegetation were dying.

Even before the completion of standardised testing of wipes for bacteria, it was obvious this disease was different from anything that had come before.

Then people started dying.

Fabien Picamoles, a thirty-four-year-old French high school teacher, was engaged to marry his fiancée, Marie Mongel. Instead of the wedding day she dreamed of, Mongel attended Picamoles's funeral. Picamoles experienced progressive dementia, seizures, and uncoordinated movements. He died within four weeks of symptoms. Part of his brain was full of strange spines.

Constantin Zauber, a forty-three-year-old Romanian engineer, noticed lesions on his neck, which quickly spread to his chest. His doctor initially claimed they were self-inflicted. "He had a terrible sensation of something trying to get out of his skin," said Zauber's wife, who could not be consoled on his death.

Wendy Jones, a forty-eight-year-old Canadian beautician, developed micro-splinters that protruded through her skin. During a consultation, Wendy's eyes went blank. She was dead.

The disease quickly worsened. Thousands of humans and animals died across Europe. Governments, worried about instigating panic as they did earlier with the H-HARs, now did the opposite. When infection numbers became overwhelming, they claimed the public was overreacting and new measures would reduce the figures. Only when their own families became victims did authorities admit the true extent of the problem.

Denialism shifted to alarmism, and draconian suppression measures appeared overnight. Media epidemiologists and modern-day prophets used doomsday mechanical models to warn of a coming black death of biblical proportions.

Rumours circulated that the H-HARs had seeded asteroid 3752 Mela, spreading the disease across the Northern Hemisphere after it entered Earth's atmosphere.

***

Professor Sindelar from the World Health Organisation was on a fact-finding trip to a leading medical research centre. He stood with Dr Nyssen, the chief virologist, looking through a large window into the brightly lit, environmentally controlled cleanroom where autopsies were being carried out by medical officers in gas-tight protective suits. Organs were spread out on steel trays on white benches, skulls were cut open, bones cracked, and skins peeled off. Samples were inserted into containers for analysis.

"Have you learned anything about this disease?" Sindelar asked, raising his voice to be heard over the noise of the negative pressure filtering air pumps.

Nyssen gave Sindelar a grim look. Glancing around discreetly to ensure they were alone, she stiffened and leaned closer. "Well, we're only just starting," Nyssen said, her voice barely audible, "but I'll tell you this: there are some really strange things happening here. Look at these pictures."

Sindelar followed Nyssen to a computer screen, unnerved by her uncomfortable and secretive behaviour.

Nyssen continued to whisper. "These are microscopic pictures of the brain and other organ tissue from victims." She went quiet as two colleagues walked past and waited until they were out of earshot before continuing. "See those lesions?"

Sindelar looked over Nyssen's shoulder, focusing intently on the screen. "I do," he whispered in awe, "but what are these tiny spikes?"

"We don't know what they are, but they're the cause of death. The dead animals have the same. They even appear in infected plants."

Sindelar shook his head in disbelief. "What's the infective agent?"

Nyssen took a deep breath and let out a long sigh. "Unknown. Oh, look at this." She walked him over to a brain exposed on a tray within a transparent container. "This is, or rather was, a victim's brain."

Sindelar grimaced while uneasily hunching over the dark blob of mass. "What the hell …" he said.

They stood together in grim silence.

"Other infected organs look the same," Nyssen said. "We have no idea what's going on. The idea that it came from the H-HARs seems credible to me."

***

Meanwhile, victims were piling up – tens of thousands of them – all over the Northern Hemisphere. The Southern Hemisphere was disease free.

Professor Sindelar reported his findings at an emergency WHO meeting. The gloomy expression was yet to leave his face.

"Professor Sindelar, what do we know about this disease?" asked the chairman.

"We know it only affects humans, animals, and plants with a common type of genetic modification," Sindelar answered bluntly. "Purely natural humans and animals are unaffected."

The chairman considered, then regarded Sindelar intently. "Professor, this is frightening. Millions of our farm animals are bred from generations of GM parentage, and heritable genome editing of humans to control future traits is commonplace. How does it spread?"

"It spreads by consumption of food products from contaminated farms. After infection, symptoms appear after about eight months as small fibres and lesions. Once symptoms appear, death is certain within weeks. British epidemiological modelling indicates there's no end in sight."

The chairman removed his glasses and rubbed his eyes. "What is the likely severity of this outbreak?"

This caused considerable babbling of voices, gasping, scraping of chairs, and other noises.

Sindelar waited for the noise to quieten while studying his folded hands. He looked up despondently at a room full of stony faces. "The British could be right. Millions of people have already been exposed to the disease via contaminated food."

Some attendees at the back stood up, waving their arms, and calling out. They wanted to know what was being done.

The chairman made short downward hand movements to mute the noise. "Please, everybody, hush up. This is important, we need to hear this."

He waited for complete silence, then, with a voice sounding very solemn, he said. "Professor Sindelar, please continue."

"The disease is characterised by proteins twisting, causing toxicity." The dead silence made Sindelar's voice sound ice cold, matched by his facial expression. "An American team has isolated the causing agent, and they say it's completely unprecedented. It's an inorganic nanomaterial resembling a proto-protein. They're calling it Proteinaceous Infectious Inorganic Material, P2IM-x, the x meaning its origin is a mystery. They believe this agent must be present in the soil. This—"

The chairman again quietened the room.

Sindelar continued. "This hijacked, twisted protein then releases more P2IM-x material to infect other proteins. Also, when an infected cell replicates, both cells are infected. The infection is inherited and exponential, epidemiologically comparable to a highly contagious pathogen."

"So, Professor," the chairman said, his voice confused, and worry clear in his gaze, "you're saying if just one protein gets twisted by this unknown P2IM-x, this is enough to kill the host?"

Sindelar nodded bleakly. "Yes, over time."

"Where did this infectious material come from?"

"Unknown."

The chairman slumped in his seat and commented. "Some media outlets claim it came from the H-HARs, to kill GM humans because they see them as their primary threat."

"Look," Sindelar replied, "that's complete rubbish. Why wouldn't they just kill everybody?" Again, there was a commotion in the room, with several questions being called out. One was heard clearly over the others: "Is it contagious between humans?"

Sindelar answered the unidentified questioner. "It's possible, but only through bodily fluids, such as blood transfusions, sperm, and maybe saliva."

***

Health authorities were vigilant of the food chain. Any doubts about the health of an animal or crop resulted in the area being isolated and the produce destroyed. This included forests, parks, and backyard gardens. Food of unknown condition was destroyed. Fish products were safe but in insufficient quantities to make a difference.

Huge food imports from the Southern Hemisphere prevented a major famine and slowed infections. National and regional disputes erupted as safety doubts emerged about adequate testing of imported food. However, without an easy way to identify the P2IM-x agent, isolation was difficult.

The disease continued to spread; now natural humans were also dying. Although evidence indicated the disease was not spreadable between humans, whole populations were locked down, travel was prohibited, and freedoms were restricted. Not a single government tried to justify the benefits of these policies based on sound medical advice.

Meanwhile, the disease's origin remained a mystery, and speculation grew that it originated from Mela.

Preparations against the H-HARs stalled. Andrew Mackenzie made a number of inspiring speeches and became a driving force for continued global unity.

Canadian health authorities estimated that over fifty per cent of farm, wild, and domestic animals and seventy per cent of food crops in Alberta were infected.

In Ukraine, millions of farm livestock were killed, and their carcasses incinerated. Crops were burned, and infectious ash dumped in old mine shafts. There was still no known way to decontaminate infected fields except to strip the soil.

A WHO report warned that the disease had "the potential to destroy the entire Northern Hemisphere's food industry and wipe out wildlife".

P2IM-x deaths started appearing in the Southern Hemisphere in both GM and natural humans.

Finally, in a major development, a test to quickly detect P2IM-x was found. Now, at last, effective isolation and protection methodologies could be implemented. But to find a cure, researchers needed 3D molecular models of the P2IM-x structure. This was extremely difficult as P2IM-x had a complete lack of order outside the host, while inside the host it was protected by twisted proteins.

By a remarkable coincidence, a diffracting holographic X-ray machine, developed partially from H-HAR technology, was brought online at Mumbai Labs. It showed P2IM-x to be shaped by complex, cylindrical molecules. This shape allowed it to hook onto a protein, forcing the protein to hold extra amino acid sequences. This made the protein hydrophobic, causing it to twist. Thus, finally, the cause of the toxic twisting was solved. It also confirmed the strange, alien nature of P2IM-x.

***

Another major turning point occurred at Michigan State University. The day after the announcement, the head of the university's P2IM-x encoding team answered his phone.

"Hello, Matthew Gibson speaking."

"Mr Hu Wan here. Very curious, Mr Matt, how do you know no nucleic acid for information encoding or transfer?"

"Wan? … Where are you from?"

"NMU, Mr Matt."

"NMU? … Oh, Nanjing Medical University. Okay. We treated P2IM-x with chemicals, enzymes, radiation, sterilisation, and anything else we could think of, all of which would have destroyed DNA, RNA, or any nucleic acids if they existed. None of these treatments affected infectivity. We're not sure whether this is good or bad, but it means we all need to forget about nucleic acids and redirect our research elsewh—"

"Not so fast, Mr Matt. Make no sense. Lot of information transferred during infections, and nucleic acid is only method. It very, vitally important you are correct."

"We're certainly sure we're correct, Hu," Gibson said, unsure if all this was getting through. "Besides, the information content could actually be quite simple; we don't know."

Gibson heard several Chinese voices talking a mile-a-minute in the background, then Wan came back. "Okay, Mr Matt. We will examine this task. Can we inspect test data?"

"Yeah, that's fine, Hu. Send me your email address. Good luck. As soon as someone finds the right experiment, they'll find the encoding method. We're about to start."

***

Three weeks later, the encoding method was discovered. Advances followed swiftly. Computer modelling showed that magnesium ions (Mg^{+2}) would alter the shape of the P2IM-x material, making it unable to hook onto a protein. Furthermore, an infected protein would release the P2IM-x material plus the extra amino acid sequence, untwist, and revert back to normal.

"We weren't sure what to think," said one amazed researcher. "It seemed to be just waiting to be discovered, like a pyramid buried in desert sand."

When diseased laboratory monkeys were fed food containing concentrated Mg^{+2} ions attached to nanostructures, the disease halted, and the monkeys eventually became disease free. The Mg^{+2} ions and the P2IM-x material gradually excreted from the body. "We were too shocked to comprehend it," said the researcher, smiling broadly. "I guess I believe in miracles now."

A Seattle man was the first to survive the disease after being injected with Mg^{+2} ions.

The Great Disease, one of the deadliest in human history, was over. It claimed 180 million people of all ages, with just as many infected and facing certain death. GM humans were almost wiped out.

***

Anya Connell and Lochlan McLean, like everyone else, spent the duration of the Great Disease under lockdown.

"Look at this, Locky," Anya said, watching the news media.

"What?"

"Just listen."

A reporter spoke into the camera:

> Although most believed the disease came from the H-HARs, investigations tell a different story. It originated from genetically modified protein fragments within common, transgenic plant fertiliser. The fragments fused with natural plant DNA to produce a P2IM-x precursor material. This mutated many times down different metabolic pathways to produce P2IM-x. By mimicking normal proteins, the P2IM-x infected protein remained undetected. Over the years it contaminated some eighty per cent of the Northern Hemisphere's fertilisers and entered the food chain.
>
> It was only when animal and human deaths occurred seven years later that its presence was discovered. The initial strain affected only GM humans and animals with a common type of altered genome. Later, another strain infected natural humans and animals.

"So, no H-HAR involvement then," Lochlan said. "I guess that's a good thing."

"Not only that, but H-HAR technology helped discover a cure within only seven months of those French sheep dying; now that's amazing."

"Yeah."

"That reminds me of a discussion we had some time ago, Locky."

"What's that?"

"Why are we so incredibly lucky? Lucky the coherent X-ray equipment became available just before the outbreak. Lucky the Southern Hemisphere was free of the contaminant and able to supply food to the north."

"I only hope our luck doesn't run out."

Chapter 39   Earth Attacks – Operation Jupiter

The choice between Eddy Kroos and John Wilson to lead Operation Jupiter, a missile attack on the Martian H-HAR spaceship, was a strong contest.

Although Kroos was respected by military command, Wilson was the initial favourite. Backed by Dayle Davis, Wilson claimed his association with the LaWS saved the planet during the asteroid attacks nine years earlier. Davis even suggested that the Mela fragment could have been stopped if Wilson were in command.

But Andrew Mackenzie and Aleta Anders lobbied non-stop in support of Kroos, allowing him to stay above the politics. They hammered Wilson's reputation, emphasising his many flawed performances.

Mackenzie visited every key segment of the military, warning of the consequences of a Wilson command. "A self-inflated narcissist and an arbitrary decision maker. He fights disagreements with abusive language, blind rage, and throwing enough mud in the hope his opponent will back off out of self-preservation. He's not a commander."

This put an overconfident Wilson and Davis under greater scrutiny, forcing them on the defensive.

The selection was close. In the end, the military high command gave Kroos the nod. As usual, the public knew nothing about Operation Jupiter.

***

General Eddy Kroos briskly walked into the command room with intent, the double doors hissing shut behind him.

Now fifty-five, Kroos took a long breath and gave the floor his cursory once-over. His eyes showed an astuteness that wasn't there a few years ago.

Everyone was down to business, the place was humming, and there was a profound sense of importance. The mothership was on its way, and Earth needed to eliminate the H-HARs from the solar system.

"Captain Douglas, status report, please?"

"Plan A and Plan B are on schedule, sir."

Plan A was the remote reprogramming of the recovered Asteroid Intercept Vehicle, AIV-680, to impact with the H-HARs spaceship, detonating its six fifty-kiloton nuclear warheads. AIV-680 was big and clumsy, but many hoped its approach from the outer solar system would go undetected.

Plan B was a direct rocket attack from Earth. Simply named Plan B Rocket, or PBR, the rocket would enter Mars's retrograde orbit opposite the Sun, cool its engines to three kelvin, and patiently wait in dark tranquillity for Mars. This technique was successful for transporting MSR-1. When near Mars, PBR would release eleven 1.5 Megaton nuclear warhead missiles to complete the journey. PBR was fast and capable of jinking, but its approach along Mars's retrograde orbit would make it more noticeable than AIV-680.

"PBR is due for launch in six hours, sir," Douglas added. Pat Douglas, the command room manager, in his late forties, was unsophisticated but intelligent and hardworking.

A large wall screen dominated the room. Its left image showed live pictures from MSR-1 of the H-HARs' spaceship on Mars, its centre showed AIV-680's status, and the right image showed PBR. Other smaller desk screens were awash with information Kroos couldn't comprehend, but he was sure it meant something to the operators. A few operators had personal mementos beside them: family photos and children's drawings.

Kroos shook his head in amazement. *This next-generation technology is almost unrecognisable compared to the old asteroid Planetary Protection Operations Room. Amazing what a united world can achieve in such a short time.*

Half turning to Douglas, Kroos said, "Operation Jupiter, Mr Douglas. The way to Jupiter will be open after eliminating the H-HARs from Mars. It'll be something to tell your grandchildren."

"Yeah," Douglas said with a laugh. "Hey, kids, gather around and let me tell you about the time your grandpa saved Earth."

Kroos grinned. "Let's hope someday you'll do that. One of our warheads is bound to get through." He secretly kept telling himself this.

"Andrew Mackenzie has just arrived, sir," notified a security officer.

"Good. Send him through," replied Kroos.

Mackenzie was greeted with a courteous smile and a quick military salute from Kroos.

"Welcome aboard, Andrew. Thanks for being here. Your experience, reassuring presence, and advice will be invaluable. You're just in time for PBR's launch."

The entire floor gazed at Andrew Mackenzie in awe.

"Hello, everyone," he said.

"Hello, sir," they all answered, then turned to watch PBR silently and steadily rise from the ground in a billowing cloud of fire and smoke. The image jiggled and wavered as the cameras shook from the thundering vibration. Minutes later, the low Earth orbit lift stage dropped off, followed by the high Earth orbit lift stage. The three-gigawatt nuclear electric VASIMR engine initiated an Oberth slingshot manoeuvre off the Moon's relative movement and gravity, setting a steady course for the Martian retrograde orbit.

After years of planning and building, Plan B's 281-day journey to Mars, 530 million open and visible kilometres, was underway.

Two hundred and thirty-seven days later, AIV-680's engines ignited. Its long wait finally over. Plan A's forty-four-day journey to Mars, 168 million kilometres, was also underway.

PBR and AIV-680 were scheduled to reach the H-HARs spaceship simultaneously, giving the H-HARs no time to flee if one rocket failed to destroy them.

Thirty-four days later, both rockets indicated steady progress. But Kroos was still worried. He eased up alongside Mackenzie. "Andrew, what do you think about this lack of H-HAR radar scanning?"

"Yeah … it's rather odd, but if it's complacency, then let's hope it—"

An alarm suddenly sounded. Douglas pointed worryingly at his screen, and several operators started chattering feverishly.

Kroos rushed over. "What is it?"

"We have radar scanning of AIV-680 from Mars."

"Goddam it!" said Kroos, scrubbing his scalp and massaging his stiff neck. "The H-HARs are on to us."

"Not necessarily, sir," Douglas said. "It was only a wide-angle radar sweep."

"You don't think we need to start booster-jinking yet?"

"No, sir. It'll only ensure its thermal detection."

At the emergency progress meeting that followed, Kroos leaned back and stared at Douglas. He crossed his arms, deliberating, a poker player unsure of his cards. Finally, "Okay, Pat. Unless we get scanned again, we'll hold off jinking until after the next line-of-sight window. We'll all just have to bite our nails 'til then."

The current window closed without further incident, but any hope of AIV-680 surviving was dashed minutes into the next window. Optical telescopes detected a flash of light from AIV-680 at the same time its data screens turned static. It was the end of the line for Plan A.

Kroos said nothing, absorbing the distressing news.

Douglas lifted his head to Kroos with an expression of guilt frozen on his face.

"S-sir, I'm—"

"Pat," Kroos said, "our decision to delay jinking was the best at the time. We still have PBR, and we'll need everyone to focus."

Kroos turned and walked towards his desk. *We'll need something more like a miracle.*

W8

Seventy-four minutes into PBR's next line-of-sight window, W8, Douglas coldly reported, "PBR's just been scanned, sir."

"What?" A cold knot of apprehension spread from Kroos's stomach.

"And it was a targeting scan, sir." Douglas's voice was strained. "PBR's started auto-jinking."

Pulsed laser beams immediately showered through the space around PBR, of such intensity it seemed the poor little rocket wouldn't even last the first few minutes.

"Thank God for auto-jinking," Kroos said, glancing at the countdown display. "Hundred and thirty-three minutes 'til the end of W8." He gave a deep sigh. "Let's hope the H-HARs don't get lucky."

They didn't, and PBR survived its first window under attack.

Kroos shook his head. *My God, how the hell are we going to survive this for another seven windows?* He needed to project confidence, but he was inwardly shaking. He glanced at the countdown display:

Next window (W7) starts in 15 hours.

Kroos rested his hand on Douglas's shoulder. "Mr Douglas." His voice was twitchy calm, which, under these dire circumstances, was not easy. "There must be something we can do to better our chances?"

Douglas took a moment to answer. "No, sir," he said, shaking his head. "The ... um, the computers are taking care of everything."

"I was afraid you'd say that."

W7

W7 opened with another full laser attack by the H-HARs, one beam arcing to within a hundred and fifty metres.

"General," said Kedar Pujara, the lead statistical analyst, "the H-HARs are trying different targeting algorithms to predict PBR's jinking."

Kroos gave an alarmed look. "Please confirm to me, Mr Pujara, that that's not possible."

"Um ... yes, sir, it's not possible. Our jinking is random and totally unpredictable." Pujara didn't sound all that convincing.

The attacks continued. There was little to do but watch and hope. Although tensions within the room soared, the voice tremors, stilted body movements, perspiration patches under armpits, and tense exchanges of information were only occasional. Kroos was impressed by his staff's professionalism. *This is extremely traumatising for everyone.*

W7 finally closed, and PBR had survived yet again.

Kroos stood stunned by what they had just been through. "This is like being part of a day-long horror movie," he said.

Mackenzie was still present in the background, almost oblivious, his arms folded and his eyebrows low. There was no contribution he needed to make, except one.

"We all better get some sleep," he said. "The next window will be much worse." He turned to Kroos. "And that includes you, Eddy. You look like crap."

"Yeah, yeah," Kroos said, shrugging politely. "I want Pujara's latest analysis before anyone leaves."

"I'm getting it now," Pujara said, watching his screen. His face suddenly hardened with concern. "Sir, this is very bad. Two windows ago, the probability of PBR being hit was 3.94%. During the last window, it was 7.9%. The next window, W6, will be 14.4%. These figures are increasing as PBR gets closer to Mars. W5 will be 22%. And after that, W4, in three days, will be 65%. The last window, W1, before PBR permanently disappears below the southern horizon, will be 93%."

"What?" Kroos asked, sounding like there must be some possibility of error. "Are you sure?"

Without re-checking, Pujara confirmed his answer with a firm nod.

"So," Kroos said, drawing a deep breath and leaning over the table. His eyes focused on Pujara. "So, our poor little PBR has only a two-out-of-three chance of surviving just the next two windows, W6 and W5, and almost no chance of surviving any window after that." It sounded like a dawning realisation.

Kroos glanced at the bewildered faces around him. "I think we would all agree that the eleven Martian secondary missiles should be released from PBR as soon as possible, which would be at the end of the next window, W6. That is, assuming PBR lasts that long."

"The MSMs will be at the very limit of their delta-v range, sir," Douglas said.

"Under the circumstances, there are no other options," Kroos said without the slightest doubt in his tone.

Everyone nodded, including Douglas and Mackenzie.

W6

As soon as W6 opened, the H-HAR lasers started.

Kroos stood for hours with one eye on the countdown timer and one on the simulation display, horrified by both.

Mackenzie came up from behind. "I've counted thirteen near misses, Eddy."

"Yeah, and my heart stopped on each one."

"Sir," Pujara said, "the H-HARs have given up altering their targeting algorithms."

"I'm going to assume that's good news," Kroos said. *Maybe they know they will eventually hit us.*

With two hours to go before the end of W6, PBR was thirty-five light seconds from Mars and suffering damage. Despondency within the room was growing.

One beam sliced a piece of its outer cover, sending an audible gasp across the room. Kroos and Mackenzie exchanged a glance that said "that was close".

Kroos dropped into a chair and rubbed his head. *It's just a matter of time now, and that'll be the end of it.*

Miraculously, PBR continued to survive. W6 finally ended as it sank below the Martian horizon.

"Hell, thank God," said a relieved Kroos, haggard but smiling.

Mackenzie managed a grateful grin. "And not a moment too soon."

Everyone else released a collective sigh of relief.

The eleven MSMs were released from PBR, accelerating hard towards the south pole of Mars, gaining as much separation from PBR as possible in the eight hours before the start of W5.

W5

As W5 opened, Kroos stood on shaky legs with Mackenzie and Douglas to witness PBR's last moments. They didn't have to wait long – just nineteen minutes.

"Well, that's the end of our illustrious little hero," Kroos said. He then asked, more to himself than to anyone else, "Now ... how far will the MSMs get before they're detected?"

Douglas's chair squeaked as he turned towards Kroos. "They're very widely spread, small targets, and good jinkers, sir. Although they'll be close to Mars, the windows will become shorter."

Douglas turned back to his display, his chair squeaking again. "This current window, W5, is 13 hours long. W4 is 10.17 hours, W3 is 7.41, W2 is 4.74, and W1 is 3.21 hours. There's no window on the final day."

Kroos was only slightly relieved. "That's still thirty-two hours of H-HAR laser attacks." Another dawning realisation.

"Yes, sir."

Eleven hours into W5 and the MSMs were still coasting towards Mars at thirty kilometres per second, unhindered. Kroos contemplated the unimaginable: the missiles might actually survive their first window undetected.

However, it was not to be. With 23:14 minutes to go, the MSMs were radar scanned and immediately started jinking. And just as well. A laser salvo opened up, intensifying the suspense in the room.

Kroos glanced at the countdown display: 9:32 minutes to the end of the current window. He glanced again: 7:29 … 7:28. Time had slowed to a crawl. One missile's status screen went blank at 6:02. He glanced again: 5:00 … 4:59. He shook his head impatiently. At long last, 0:01 turned to 0:00. Finally, W5 had ended. Kroos took a long breath. The attack was intense, an indication of things to come.

"General," said Pujara despairingly. "Based on the last twenty-three minutes, the probability of just one MSM surviving the remaining twenty-one hours of attack is fifteen per cent."

"Fifteen per cent!" Desperation crossed Kroos's face. Everyone looked at Kroos and froze like statues, as if the music had stopped. "Fifteen per cent. Kedar, are you absolutely sure?"

"Um … yes, general, fifteen per cent survival chance. That's all."

Kroos looked at Pujara, then at Douglas, then Mackenzie, then the rest. They all looked equally despondent. "This is a confronting, cold realisation," he said, pausing momentarily. "Any plan with less than one chance in seven of success is no plan at all."

Kroos clutched a table as a knee unexpectedly gave way. He'd been standing for over twenty hours. He flopped into his chair and rubbed his tired eyes as a wave of horror passed through him. *How the hell did we ever get ourselves into this hopeless situation?* He was exhausted and battered, and his expression showed it.

He glared through a sleep-deprived fog at the faces around him, confused as to what to do next. He had nothing left to offer, no other plans. Like him, they were all hanging onto something, but it was really nothing.

Pulling himself back onto his feet as if he were forty kilograms heavier, he pushed aside his weariness and steadied his breath. "We can't continue," he said through bloodshot eyes. "We can't continue with just fifteen per cent. We've got thirteen hours until the next window. We have to find a solution."

No one spoke. A flight sergeant scratched his head. "Come on, everyone, think," Kroos pleaded, searching their faces.

Just as hopelessness started appearing on faces, Mackenzie spoke up, calm and clear. "Kedar, you said the H-HARs tried to predict our jinking movements?"

"Yes, we could tell from the changes in their targeting distribution."

"Can we incorporate their targeting pattern into our jinking algorithm to improve our survival odds?"

Pujara's eyes suddenly widened, like he had just been handed a large present. "Why yes, of course!" he said, nodding excitedly. "They've been using the same targeting algorithm for some time now." Flopping into his chair, his hands pounded a silent rhythm on the computer keyboard. "Give me a few hours."

"Just one thing, Kedar," Kroos said. "If the H-HARs suspect we're using their algorithm against them, they'll change it, and our odds will be worse than even fifteen per cent. We need to increase our chances, but not to the point where it's noticeable."

"Yes, sir. I'm on to it."

The wait allowed Kroos to at last feel his weariness. He sank gratefully into his chair, rubbed his red and swollen eyes, spread his arms over the table, and rested his forehead on his hands. He didn't exactly look comfortable.

Mackenzie pulled on his shoulder. "Come on, Eddy, I'll help you to bed."

Kroos didn't move.

Mackenzie had a closer look, his face showing some concern. "Hey, he's sound asleep," he said with an amused laugh. "More like a state of total collapse. Let's not disturb him."

Not bothered by Kroos's loud snoring, Pujara, Douglas, and the others reprogrammed the MSMs' jinking based on the H-HARs' targeting algorithm. Their fingers moved across the computer keyboard with a pianist's elegance. They calculated the survivability of one or more MSMs could be maximised at sixty-eight per cent, but recommended fifty-three per cent to prevent H-HAR suspicions.

"That's truly extraordinary," Kroos said, waking after several hours. "And I accept your fifty-three per cent, at least now the odds are on our side."

This was a whole new Kroos – hopeful, excited, and confident.

W4 – W1

The next window, W4, claimed only one MSM. The modifications to the MSMs' movements were working; there were nine out of eleven left.

W3 claimed one MSM; eight left.

W2 claimed three MSMs; five left.

The final window, W1, ended with just one surviving missile, MSM-03.

MSM-03

Kroos checked MSM-03's flight simulation. "Forty-three hours 'til impact; let's hope there's nothing they can do."

"What can they do?" Pujara asked. "It's below their horizon."

"They can take-off, destroy it just before impact, or evacuate the site," Douglas quickly responded.

Thirty minutes later, the ever-watching Moon Spy Surface Vehicle, MSR-1, showed sudden activity around the H-HAR spaceship.

"Damn it," cursed Kroos. "The bastards know the missile is coming."

"It's been there undisturbed for nine years. It's hard to believe it can take-off before the missile arrives," said Mackenzie but not sounding convinced.

After reaching the south pole of Mars, the flight simulator showed MSM-03 altering course to a northerly direction, flying low over the Martian terrain for the final six hours to the H-HAR spaceship. All this could not be confirmed until the end of radio blackout, sixty-four minutes before impact.

The entire room gathered in front of the large wall screen, their eyes unblinking. The right half of the screen displayed MSM-03's flight simulation. MSR-1's video was on the left, showing what seemed to be open conflict between groups of H-HARs.

Kroos scratched his head. "I wonder what that's all about."

"This happened on the Moon," Mackenzie said. "Mutinous panic."

Moments later, Pujara, as if he couldn't contain his anxiety any longer, burst out. "In just two hours, MSM-03 will cross the last three kilometres at thirty-five kilometres per second, too fast for them to do anything about it. Then, finally, it'll be payback time." His eyes slitted with glee.

No one was cheering just yet.

At sixty-eight minutes from impact, the H-HAR spaceship purged its engines. The room hushed. A lone voice broke the stillness. "They're going to takeoff."

A third of the wall screen suddenly lit up.

"It's MSM-03's front camera!" Douglas said, his leg tapping excitedly.

Kroos's eyes skimmed across the room. There was an expectation of triumph as arms crossed and uncrossed, bodies weaved, and victory grins appeared.

IR detectors on MSR-1 showed a rapid build-up of engine heat from the spaceship.

"Please, please, don't take-off," someone murmured.

The simulation showed a detonation at the target.

"That's promising," said Kroos. "Now we'll have to wait 6.8 minutes, the light time to Mars, for confirmation visuals from either MSM-03's front camera or MSR-1."

Did the spaceship take-off in those 6.8 minutes? Kroos wondered, glad no one asked the question.

MSR-1 showed faint blue thrust from the spaceship's engines. Seconds later, the H-HAR spaceship lifted slowly off the Martian surface.

Everyone held their breath; MSM-03 must be seconds away.

MSM-03's camera showed the missile passing rapidly over a long Martian valley, rocky wastelands, and a twin-peaked mountain towards a high ridge. Then the front camera's image went blank.

"I saw it! I saw it!" someone at the front yelled. "It hit the spaceship just before the missile's video disappeared. We did it! We did it!"

But it was too quick for any human eye to know what it saw.

All eyes flicked to the MSR-1 video, which showed a massive thermonuclear fireball just before a wave of boiling dust rapidly rolled towards the camera, blocking all vision and causing breathless silence in the room.

A quick replay of MSM-03's front camera implied an impact, but it wasn't clear.

"I tell ya, it didn't get away," the same voice repeated, but no one else was convinced.

"Let's wait for MSR-1's visual after the dust clears," Mackenzie said.

Everyone turned as MSR-1's image filled the entire wall screen.

After three long minutes, the dust started thinning. Kroos tried his best to rein in his anxiety. Mackenzie leaned forward, his elbows on his knees. Douglas couldn't sit still. One operator was peeking at the screen from the corner of his eye, as if watching a horror movie. Another paced behind her desk.

"Come on dust, hurry up …" someone said.

At last, some transparency. There was a huge crater where the H-HAR spaceship used to be. Large pieces of wreckage were spread against a distant cliff face, which had partially collapsed, and smaller pieces were seen in every direction.

The quiet anticipation instantly gave way to thunderous applause. Everyone vigorously shook hands.

Pujara waved his fists in the air as if he were at a football game with no need to contain his excitement. "We've done it, we've done it! We've got our solar system back."

Kroos leaned forward, steadying himself with a hand on the table. He was exhausted, too dazed by the remnants of adrenaline to feel any exhilaration. Mackenzie was quick to support him, grabbing his shoulder.

"Congratulations, Eddy." Mackenzie grinned at his friend's sudden and quiet composure.

Kroos could hardly believe it. Finally, it was over. He gave a huge, contented smile. The applause quickly died as he spoke, his voice a hoarse whisper. "After thirty years, the H-HARs' occupation of Mars is finally over." He finished with a triumphal smile.

Grabbing his phone, Kroos pressed a pre-set number and simply stated, "The H-HAR spaceship on Mars is destroyed. I repeat, H-HAR spaceship on Mars is destroyed." He immediately hung up and, with a new lease of life, bounced on his feet to join the celebrations.

Chapter 40 First Martian Campaign

Although not apparent from the live video streaming into General Eddy Kroos's command room, MSR-1 analysts observed a small, low-flying craft leaving the H-HAR spaceship four minutes before its destruction. The escape craft briefly returned to the wreckage, where MSR-1 followed it to the south-eastern horizon.

Based on MSR-1 intel, forty-four fully armed H-HARs had crowded into the craft. Thus began what was to become a long and deadly land campaign to obtain full strategic control of Mars.

Colonel John Wilson was selected as commander-in-charge to hunt them down. Missing out to Eddy Kroos on commanding Operation Jupiter was a bitter setback for Wilson. He hoped this appointment would further his career.

Dayle Davis and Andrew Mackenzie were again in strong disagreement.

"He's got no real leadership experience, at least not in the way that counts," Mackenzie said.

"He's the most qualified, and he's earned the role," Davis said.

Wilson's tough talk impressed the political merchants. When informed of his appointment, Wilson carried a smirk of ineffable smugness for days. Egged on by Davis and others, he boasted he would hunt down these H-HARs as though he were in a zombie apocalyptic movie. His underestimation of them was astonishing. Wilson was in a hurry to claim glory and imagined he was in a race to achieve it. He talked about rectifying Kroos's unaccomplished mission and insisted on the embedment of media reporters.

Wilson had a sizeable force: forty-two troops with the latest power-assisted exoskeleton fighting-suits, and forty-two CARs. All armed with 300kJ gamma-ray laser rifles, finally reverse engineered from the H-HAR rifle. They were the deadliest personal weapon ever built.

The soldiers just wanted to get through the campaign and return to Earth alive, but to Wilson, his reputation was far more important. From his soldiers he demanded not only unquestionable loyalty but also admiration.

Always grumbling, Wilson complained to Earth about the quality of his troops. He complained to his troops about the lack of support from Earth and complained to everyone about Mars.

"Biggest hellhole I've ever seen."

***

Five days after Wilson's arrival, a Martian satellite pinpointed the escape craft hidden in rugged terrain. The military wanted a ground assault followed by a search to ensure all H-HARs were accounted for and take prisoners if possible.

That night, Wilson called a meeting with his officers. Facing a large window that looked out onto the black Martian night, he turned on his heel to face them. The artificial light gave his features a macabre cast.

"It's time to crack alien heads," he said, displaying a frightening demeanour of self-empowerment. "Everyone be prepared to give chase at sunrise."

His officers glared at him with profound disbelief.

"But we know nothing about the area's geography, colonel!" his second-in-command, Lieutenant Guptill, protested.

Feeling himself being scrutinised, Wilson tightened up like an overwound toy. He nailed Guptill with a piercing stare, and snapped, "We don't need to."

Moving through his officers with the air of a wolf through a flock of sheep, he prophesied, "In a hundred years from now, when people watch the combat videos of the battle that saved Earth, you'll be standing behind me as one of the smiling heroes in the victory footage." He sounded strangely triumphant.

Looking around the room for support, he saw only gazes of silent, brooding contempt. One by one, his officers confronted him, but one by one, with a threatening gleam in his eye and a smug smile, Wilson harshly ordered them to be ready. He was oblivious to the hazards and scornful of diverse voices.

The Earthlings arrived at the H-HARs' position three days later. With a jubilant grin that couldn't be contained, he gently released a deep breath and ordered the videographers to capture the craft with him standing dauntlessly in the foreground. His ambition for glory was that raw and unapologetic. He delivered a pep talk, but his words had a hollow quality to them, and no one listened.

Lieutenant Guptill shook his head worryingly. "Sir, something's wrong," he pleaded on a private channel, his tone showing his bewilderment.

Wilson ignored him.

"Sir, we're exposed. The high ground above us is full of foot tracks, and things are just too peaceful. I strongly suggest we—"

"Nothing's wrong!" Wilson barked back, fixing his steely eyes firmly on Guptill. "They're hibernating. We attack immediately."

"Colonel, I cannot concur. We know nothing about—"

"Lieutenant Guptill, you're relieved of your command. Return to base immediately, your career is over."

Thinking he had the H-HARs trapped in their craft, Wilson moved closer. He planned to shred the craft with laser beams, expecting the H-HARs to be flushed out like a flock of geese, where a line of shooters would be waiting. His body trembled from the intoxicating thrill of it all.

As the soldiers took up their final positions, Wilson smiled lazily, like a cat pawing at cornered mice. He moved to the front with his media crew, but before anyone could fire a single beam at the unoccupied craft, the H-HARs opened up from hidden positions.

Triumph instantly turned to panic. Wilson was hopeless. Without ordering a retreat, he ran, dropping his rifle and leaving his troops behind. He was the only survivor.

Wilson ran for ten minutes before exhaustion forced him to stop against a rock. He checked his air supply. *Good, just enough to reach the transports.*

His body shuddered when a voice unexpectedly crackled over his radio.

"There you are, you gutless piece of shit." Wilson whipped around, no one. Whipped back, nothing. Whipped around again, Guptill was there, his rifle lifted, his eyes burning with rage. "You're a fucking dead man, Wilson."

Just then, a laser pulse from nowhere exploded a rock millimetres from Guptill's helmet, knocking him to the ground. Wilson dived on him, trying to yank the rifle free. They rolled on the Martian soil like street fighters, fighting to the death. Their helmets crashed as they desperately kicked and pulled. Wilson finally wrenched the rifle from Guptill, pushing himself up and towering over him. His face flushed, and his chest heaved.

"You've been undermining me since I landed on this shit planet," Wilson said, his eyes showing his madness. "And when I get back, I'll let everyone know how you sabotaged the mission."

He gave Guptill a hard kick and pushed the rifle up against his visor.

"I'm gonna enjoy this," Wilson said, his finger on the trigger, a spiteful look of pleasure on his face. A glint of reflected sunlight in Wilson's peripheral vision turned his head. It was a distant approaching H-HAR hunting party. He turned back to finish Guptill. But almost supernaturally, Guptill was gone.

Wilson followed Guptill's prints. "I'll find you, Guptill. And when I do, you're dead."

Sensing movement, he turned quickly, firing his laser, but nothing was there. Another movement, not sure. Maybe he's behind the rock. Wilson fired and checked, nothing. Another fleeting movement, another rock. Wilson kept going – more rocks, more firing – but Guptill was nowhere.

"Fuck you, Guptill."

Wilson checked on the H-HARs; they were much closer now. He panicked and fired at them, missed. The H-HARs fired back.

Wilson gave up on Guptill and ran towards the transports, scared and panting. He tripped on something soft and fell to the ground, rolling some distance before stopping. He looked back. It was Guptill, his helmet burned open by a laser.

Wilson crawled to the nearest rock and spun around, expecting to be surrounded by H-HARs. But nothing. He struggled to his feet, unsteady, cursing in anger, shooting again and again at nothing. His nerves were gone.

Then a laser beam cut him down.

The disastrous failure of this first encounter was an indication that the campaign would be a long, difficult, and costly one.

Chapter 41   Second Martian Campaign

Five months later, a new force under Lieutenant Colonel Adriana Bromwich arrived on Mars.

At forty-four, Bromwich was dedicated, bright, and possessed an old-school air of decency and quiet authority. Although her military contributions were mostly theoretical, she had sufficient field leadership experience for the role. A keen war historian, Bromwich believed combat units took on the distinctive qualities of their commanders, and she was going to be tough and unrelenting. Her key to success was her ability to outwork everyone else. Unlike Wilson, she was competent, and every engagement would be meticulously planned.

She knew that whoever, or whatever, led this group of fleeing H-HARs was very capable and shouldn't be underestimated.

Like all previous forces that confronted the H-HARs, Bromwich's human troops were green. But they were highly trained, motivated, and equipped with the latest weaponry. The CARs were the next-generational design with greater survivability, more sophisticated sensing and targeting, more intelligent algorithms, and enhanced battlefield awareness and coordination.

The H-HARs had abandoned their escape craft and disappeared into the terrain. Six weeks after Bromwich's arrival, an orbiting satellite detected their movements. The first encounter was an indication of things to come.

As the Earthlings closed in, the H-HARs entered a large, rocky area that provided good concealment. Realising the risk, Bromwich sent two reconnaissance CARs ahead while a scouting party searched for alternative routes. Aerial drones provided little intelligence before being destroyed.

The two reconnaissance CARs returned after forty-five minutes with nothing to report. When Bromwich didn't follow, the H-HARs attacked anyway, immediately probing for weaknesses in the Earthlings' flanks and life support stores.

An uneasy stand-off lasted for several hours until the H-HARs silently withdrew and disappeared. The humans were too disorientated and exhausted to pursue.

Over the gruelling months that followed, such encounters occurred several times, with the H-HARs always staying slightly ahead. The rugged terrain favoured their retreat and made the humans' pursuit slow and fraught with casualties. The smallest mistake could easily wipe them out.

The humans struggled from the very start. Sickness, exhaustion, and accidents in the anti-human, near-vacuum Martian environment were almost as dangerous as the H-HARs. The nano-layered suits provided sufficient radiation shielding for the duration, but low gravity was a problem, requiring considerable time at $2\,g$ in a mobile gravitron to compensate. To make matters worse, the humans were targeted over the CARs.

Bromwich was, however, unrelenting. Her persistence and aggressiveness never weakened, and her sense of duty never faltered. The world could falter, but not her. However, her health suffered, relying only on field medications.

Only once did Bromwich get distracted from her goal. She watched a brownish-red rock face slowly change to gold when touched by the blood-red morning Sun. It lit a vast, rust-orange canyon, decorated with cliffs and countless craters and boulders of all sizes that stretched to the mountains on the horizon. A faint, dusty whirlwind formed in the distance, disappearing within seconds. Phobos hung in a salmon-pink sky. Deimos was rising late, coloured by a dusty horizon. For a moment, the war seemed far away.

Bromwich found out one thing. The enigmatic H-HAR commander was the red-armband. This meant it was the leader of both Pallas spaceships. The Earthlings called it the Red Baron. It would engage only when the odds favoured it, then withdraw just in time, making good its escape by setting ambushes to delay the Earthlings. It was clear to Bromwich that its strategy was to escape by wearing down the humans.

If this Red Baron could be captured, it would be invaluable. But the troops had little interest in that. "It's responsible for millions of deaths on Earth," they said. The campaign had become a personal vendetta.

"We'll slay *all these* creatures yet," Bromwich pledged to her troops after one bloody clash. If the Red Baron were captured, Bromwich might give it to the lynch mob.

***

Six months of repeated failures to destroy the H-HARs made Bromwich acutely aware of the implications, including political. But the ever-present dangers and Wilson's fate were chilling reminders that the smallest mistake could be fatal for all. Other options were tried, all without success. She even sent an unarmed CAR with a white flag into a clearing; it lasted only seconds. After a near disaster where Bromwich and a group of soldiers were only just saved by nine CARs sacrificing themselves, it was obvious this bloody campaign would go to the wire.

Although Bromwich had strong military support on Earth, particularly from Andrew Mackenzie, the political establishment watched her progress with impatient scrutiny. During a special communiqué, a half-dozen grim faces, including Dayle Davis, sat shoulder to shoulder, filling Bromwich's screen. Talking rapidly, they traded off like a tag team. "Bromwich, you've got a whole army over there. We're not happy."

Their voices came across as cold, condescending, and condemning. Their images were contorted, or maybe it was just poor reception. Bromwich wasn't sure.

She listened until her contempt and fatigue overrode her tolerance. Finally, with a hard stare, she barked back. "There's *nothing* new to report since my last communiqué."

Casting her eyes upwards, she blew a deep sigh. The sound of someone straining under many burdens. "There's a deadly war going on here," she added blankly. "The longer I have to re-answer your goddam questions, the more dangerous it gets."

Bromwich reluctantly waited the eighteen-minute response time. Davis replied. "Your performance has been less than satisfactory and, dare I say, questionable. We can't re-colonise Mars while those H-HARs of yours are still roaming free—"

Bromwich switched off the incoming message. She was ready to respond. "I'll tell you what," she said, leaning forward to give an icy stare. "I—"

The outgoing comms mysteriously dropped out, which was probably just as well because Bromwich was heard to have said, "I used to think you guys were more interested in good media than good strategy, but now I realise you're actually trying to screw me to somehow justify your decision to appoint Wilson."

Chapter 42   The Red Baron

Like its predecessor, the H-HAR known as the Red Baron was amazed at the unrelenting determination of these strange Earthlings. They were a more formidable adversary than anything on record about the ancient organics, the Dautjatas and the Guarnums, on its home planet – more technologically progressive, unpredictable, resilient, cunning, and united.

At the time of its arrival, a mere thirteen thousand years ago, nothing could have prevented the planet from being destroyed. However, the supreme leader on the approaching mothership wanted the glory. And its orders to wait for its arrival had to be obeyed.

The supreme leader issued another directive: keep intelligent life primitive by devastating their civilisation. But the previous acting red-armband leader of the two Pallas spaceships, the Kunna, failed to do this. It failed to monitor the Earthlings' astonishing technological advancements. When the Kunna came out of hibernation, it expected them to still be living in caves on an ice-covered planet. But the Earthlings had progressed to a stage where they could seriously defend themselves. The Kunna, by transmitting messages to the mothership, clumsily revealed their presence on Pallas.

Another mistake by the Kunna was to destroy the Earthlings' Pallas probe and Martian facilities. This only ensured that the Earthlings would desperately prepare themselves for the next conflict. And gross incompetence led to the failure of the Moon RIW and the asteroid attacks.

The final failure was remaining on Mars, believing it was safe, and not having the spaceship ready for an immediate launch. It was time to mutiny, time to terminate this incompetent Kunna and take its identity. Fleeing the spaceship with the mutineers and leaving the rest to their fate was the correct decision.

The plan was simple: hide, hibernate, and await the mothership. The supreme leader would surely understand the mutiny's necessity.

But how did these Earthlings know of their escape? Like its predecessor, it underestimated them, and it was now destined to fail. The total annihilation of both spaceships at the hands of these primitive cave dwellers was incomprehensible. How could it all come to this?

It was more apparent than ever, Earth had to be obliterated. Otherwise, just as the supreme-god had predicted, these Earthlings – or rather, their robotic successors – would come looking for its home planet in the future.

In any case, these Earthlings would have no chance against the all-powerful mothership.

But then the Red Baron started to wonder. It started to question its own assurances. Were these puny Earthlings being underestimated? Could they somehow win against the mothership? And wasn't it remarkable that these Earthlings reached this critical level of technology at this specific time?

Chapter 43 Second Martian Campaign – End

It was not until the battle at Nopah Range, nine months into the second campaign, that the H-HARs suffered their first major defeat. There was even a chance to corner the Red Baron itself, but the humans were exhausted, and it escaped again.

But time was running out for the H-HARs. A non-stop Mars-Earth supply bus by cyclers in permanent orbits around the Sun provided regular reinforcements and supplies from Earth. This included more CARs, which were proving to be an almost equal match for the H-HARs. Bromwich, however, would not permit them to operate independently. New sensor satellites provided detailed information on the H-HARs' movements. The H-HARs were being increasingly outmanoeuvred and outgunned.

The end finally came in a series of encounters at Ceti Mensa. In the midst of a dust storm, the Red Baron and eighteen H-HARs were pinned down by twelve human troops and thirty-two CARs. The Red Baron and eight blue-armbands escaped while the rest were terminated. The humans were too weary to pursue.

Commander Bromwich watched the moving puff of dust across the endless expanse of boulder-studded red sand that was the fleeing Red Baron. Her vision was blurred, her head spun, breath was squeezed from her lungs, and the Martian landscape lay threateningly all around. She turned to her soldiers. They were exhausted, fatigued, brutalised, and wounded. Some were being zipped up in plastic bags. Her mind was made up. The CARs alone would follow the H-HARs and hunt them down.

The significance of the moment was not lost on Bromwich or the others, and she was not entirely happy about it. For some time, this decision was inevitable, and, in a way, a point of no return. Bromwich initially viewed the CARs from a perspective of apprehension and superiority, but no longer. They had saved her life and every soldier's life many times over. They were now integral to the whole operation, and a trust bond was forged with them.

The CARs were programmed for human interaction – friendly, respectful, and obedient. They were easier to deal with than many humans. It was difficult to think of them as just machines, and the troops always felt something when a CAR was killed.

Killed? Why did she use that word? They were never alive, but it was sure easy to forget. Now, not only had she supreme confidence and trust in their abilities but also apprehension that human soldiers would become obsolete.

For the first time, human robots would battle solo against alien robots to save humankind.

***

The CAR placed in charge of the other CARs was called Gus. Gus had all the standard military programs for special operations on Mars, but it also carried a latent program for this precise leadership role, which Bromwich activated. Gus could now strategically plan, deceive the enemy, detect deceptions, and handle unexpected scenarios. Gus's instruction book had many more parts, including access to all tactical lessons learned from previous encounters.

Bromwich knew how Gus would operate. It would grind through multiple simulations, going deeper and deeper until it was satisfied it had the best option.

Bromwich ordered Gus to destroy all the H-HARs but capture the Red Baron if possible.

The Red Baron could see that it was being followed, but this time it was different. They were gaining ground. Gaining ground so quickly, its little renegade army of blue-armband H-HARs would soon be forced to face its pursuers. Only this time, the encounter would not be at a place of its choosing.

Just before dawn on the edge of a deep gorge, Gus, with twenty-five CARs, caught up with the rebel Red Baron. As the dull Sun rose from the eastern darkness, revealing in increasing detail the pale reddish landscape, the Red Baron, like a hunted animal running out of options, made a desperate attempt to escape. Without human troops, Gus advanced the flanking columns much quicker than in previous confrontations. The H-HARs were soon surrounded, and Gus pressed close. The Red Baron feinted on its right flank. Gus didn't fall for it. The CARs stood solid, fierce, and decisively unmoving. There would be no escape this time. The H-HARs had reached the end of the line.

Unlike the Battle for the Moon, where order among the H-HARs broke down, these H-HARs rallied around their Red Baron, like soldier ants protecting their queen. Gus ordered them all terminated, except the Red Baron. The steadily contracting ring of H-HARs moved inwards. One by one they toppled until the Red Baron stood alone. The only alien left in the entire solar system.

Programmed to obey Bromwich's orders if possible, Gus stood, dropped its weapon, and slowly walked towards the Red Baron, stopping in open ground. An ominous lull followed until the Red Baron, still carrying its weapon, slowly approached. The two machines from different worlds stood face to face, eyeing each other for several seconds. Gus held out its right hand. The Red Baron's head tilted down, its eyes focusing on Gus's hand. They then slowly lifted back onto Gus's stare.

It rotated its head, appearing to assess its predicament, scanning left, then right, then back to Gus. Just for a second, it seemed the Red Baron was about to accept. But as the long moments passed, its quiescence became threatening, and Gus could sense it.

The creature suddenly made its move. Grabbing Gus by the throat with its vice-like hands, it threw Gus towards the line of fewest CARs, knocking several backwards, trying to create an opening. The creature charged towards the opening.

But there was no opening; it had closed. The CARs were back on their feet, firing. There was no escape, not this time. The self-proclaimed red-armband, which had travelled so far from its world to terminate other worlds, fell to the ground in pieces, itself terminated.

***

Dayle Davis was handed a note just after addressing the world's media on the Mars recolonisation plans. Immediately flashing a grin, he rose. To a hushed crowd, he triumphantly announced, "Ladies and gentlemen, I have just received excellent news. Thirty-five minutes ago, our forces on Mars finally cornered the H-HARs. In the battle that followed, all H-HARs were destroyed. The cat and mouse hunt is finally over. This marks the end of the H-HAR presence in our solar system. We can now start the long anticipated recolonisation of Mars." There was no recognition of Bromwich or her force.

Applause rolled across the crowded room, loud and long. There was an enormous amount of excitement. More and more people poured in to celebrate.

Bromwich returned as a hero and wrote several accounts of her experiences. But there was still the mothership, and, as the world moved on, new threats.

Chapter 44　Mackenzie at the University of Texas at Austin

After returning from the Moon, Philip Saunders suffered from post-traumatic stress disorder. His condition seesawed between bedridden back pain and hypervigilance.

Mackenzie spent considerable time with him, and they often discussed that epic battle.

"I can't believe any of us survived," Saunders said. "The Moon did its very best to kill us."

"Well, the H-HARs underestimated us, Phil."

These discussions had a positive effect on Saunders, but his condition deteriorated too rapidly for anyone to help.

During what would be their final discussion, Saunders grabbed Mackenzie's arm, his gaze acute. "Your commitment on the Moon seventeen years ago; I want you to restate it."

"Phil," Mackenzie said, knowing exactly what he meant, unstoppable determination in his eyes. "I will play a major part in the destruction of the H-HARs."

A long, hard look passed between the two men. "Thank you, Andrew. I'm now convinced we will win this war."

Later that day, Mackenzie was told that his close friend had passed.

The cause of death was listed simply as a gunshot wound.

***

After the Battle for the Moon, Andrew Mackenzie remained with the military for twenty-three years on various advisory EDO committees. He then accepted the University of Texas presidency.

On his first day, he had a mission. Striding across campus, he knocked on an open office door. The sign on the door said, "Vice President for Research". The man behind the desk looked up, startled by Mackenzie's presence in front of him. They stared at each other momentarily, then grinned.

"Lochlan McLean. We finally meet."

Lochlan jumped up to greet Mackenzie. "It's an honour, sir. Not every day I shake hands with a man who's been on the Moon."

Mackenzie smiled with a curious warmth. "It's a breathtaking place, as you know. And call me Andrew."

"Breathtaking doesn't begin to do it justice. Please, take a seat."

Mackenzie laughed as he sat. He liked this guy. "Sorry I couldn't attend your Bravery Award presentation," he said.

"The president was most disappointed."

"Ha! I can imagine. Say, I never got to thank you and Anya in person for saving my son Jonty's life."

"Jonty was extremely brave, Andrew. You should be proud of him. But it was Anya's sharp shooting that saved everyone's life. Everyone except for Lieutenant Bosch, of course.

"Yes, that was unfortunate. I must say you two have been remarkably resilient after that encounter."

"Eight years ago now. I did expect to go a bit insane from it."

"And Anya?"

"It was a complete transformation for her. The H-HARs used to give her nightmares and keep her awake at night, and during the day cause debilitating anxiety. But now that she's seen and beaten them, she knows our extinction isn't inevitable. She's now a project director for the EDO propulsion group."

"Sorry we let a few H-HARs escape."

"Your hands were full, Andrew. And, um … I was sorry to hear about Philip Saunders."

Mackenzie nodded as a pained look crossed his face.

Lochlan waited a moment, then asked, "So, what got you out of the military, Andrew?"

Mackenzie's eyes blazed with resolve. "The mothership presents us with the greatest of challenges, Lochlan." He stood, made his way towards the window, gazed outside for quite a while, then turned. "And our defence preparations need a political kick in the ass."

"You're entering politics?" Lochlan's tone showed his profound surprise.

"Politics is the main game, Lochlan."

"Our old colleague, Dayle Davis, would agree with you. You think he's a serious presidential candidate?"

Mackenzie returned to his chair. "Yes, unfortunately. Not this coming election, maybe the one after. He's had a meteoric rise since the days of the EDO. He has all the financial and political backing he needs. He thinks the mothership is too far away to worry about, and his only commitment is to himself."

"You're already talking like a politician," Lochlan said as a grin slowly climbed across his face.

Mackenzie softened and returned his grin. "I'll have to be more careful. So, what got you out of the EDO?"

"UT has several major defence projects I'm interested in. I've been here for about a year."

Mackenzie pulled his chair closer. "We have a project that has the highest priority and security. I'd like you to comment on its feasibility study."

Lochlan's eyes squinted with interest. "Yeah, of course."

"You can't acknowledge its existence to anyone." Mackenzie picked up a picture of Lochlan's family from the desk. "Anyone."

They both went quiet, an unspoken understanding of the commitment this task required.

"Still interested?" Mackenzie asked.

"Um … yeah," Lochlan said, but not confidently.

"Good! I know I can trust you. Now that you've accepted, I can tell you it involves the planet Mercury and construction will take seventy years."

"Mercury!? Seventy years!?" Lochlan waited for elaboration. It didn't come. "So, it's a solar project?" Lochlan pressed, staring questioningly. A cautious Mackenzie was impossible to read. The weight of his decision was already settling on him.

Mackenzie, still holding the family picture, was quick to change the subject. "Junior soccer?"

"Yeah, back in the days of our kids' soccer. We always had a McDonald's hamburger afterwards."

"Four kids?"

"Yep. One from my previous relationship, one from Anya's, and two between us."

Mackenzie looked at the time. "12:40, are you free for lunch?"

"Yeah, but not hamburgers."

They walked down the road together towards the campus canteen, chatting like old friends.

VOLUME 2

THE MOTHERSHIP

PART 6

ALONE AGAIN

"…. we had a feeling they were capable of a lot more than we were told. We knew they were destined for bigger things."

Chapter 45　The Walks

Victor, a recent graduate assisting with H-HAR metamaterials research, looked bored. Under-appreciated, unchallenged, and creativity stifled, the highlight of his day was a lunchtime walk with colleagues. However, his lack of conversation skills and eccentric obsession with science and the H-HARs often left him without walking partners.

Victor befriended Hedley, a new starter, and regarded him as his unofficial protégé.

"It's been fifty-six years since the discovery of the H-HAR Moon-ship," Victor said on their first walk. "And our technology has progressed from hyperjet aircraft to potentially interstellar robotic spaceships, from digital to quantum computing, from solid state to quantum entangled memories, from fission electric to pulsed fusion fuels, and from steel to 3D webby borophene."

Victor always walked on the footpath that faced oncoming traffic. "I don't trust auto-steering in cars." They stopped at a bend, looked both ways, and hurried across. As cars sped towards them, Hedley was forced to side step halfway to avoid a shoulder collision with Victor, who had a crooked walk, as if his left leg were slightly shorter than his right. Horns blew in protest as a lane of cars braked.

"It may not be enough against the H-HAR mothership," Hedley said.

"Any civilisation that doesn't struggle for its existence will stagnate. I mean, why bother innovating if everyone is content?"

"Sounds like you're saying the H-HARs are good for us."

"No," Victor clarified, "but if we survive, we'll be richer and stronger."

"What about the effects of all this rushed technology?"

"The H-HARs must know how it all started."

"Huh? What started?"

"The universe."

"Oh."

"It started as a massless instanton, a quantum energy fluctuation. An extremely unlikely event, but it effectively had infinite time to occur. Extreme gravitational time dilation from its high energy probably delayed expansion for trillions and trillions of years. Localised energy compressions formed the elementary particles, and the enormous Coriolis and centrifugal forces as it expanded became dark energy."

"It must have a centre, then?" asked Hedley, in a tone suggesting no one would know, including Victor.

"A gravitational centre? It's unmeasurable. Our observable universe is only a nanoscopic part of the whole universe."

***

The following day, during their next walk, Hadley said, "The expected human active lifespan is now one hundred and six years." He altered his step to avoid being nudged into a tree, crossed to Victor's right, and fell back into his step.

"That's because of new medicines, 3D-printed body parts, and robotic surgeons," Victor added. "Humans have never been so replaceable."

"And prosthetic limbs are just as good as real limbs, and—"

"Better. And they're directly controlled by the brain. Implanted sensors perceive light, sound, heat, and touch outside of normal human range."

"And there's also gene editing and synthetic DNA," Hedley added. "After P2IM-x halted research, it's now resumed but with many safeguards, and—"

"Safeguards! Rubbish! It won't be long before they're all ignored. The GMs in our office are only the selected ones. Where are the rest? They need to do something about declining human fertility rates. Too bad about suspended animation. A frozen body can't self-repair the damage from its own radioactive atoms. A monkey frozen for sixteen years was so damaged it would have been lethal. Even frozen embryos can't last more than a thousand years without being severely damaged by residual quantum and cosmic radiation. So much for long-term human space travel."

Victor was too self-centred to notice challenges to anything he said. But things were about to change.

***

Anya Connell was on a three-week assignment at the metamaterials lab. She noticed Victor and Hedley heading off on a walk and asked to join them. "Yeah, sure," they both said, their eyes lighting up.

At sixty-one, Anya was as fit as ever. She gave them a look that said "catch me if you can" and set a rapid pace.

Victor raced to catch up after stopping for an untied shoelace and asked, "Anya, how was the Moon?"

Hedley looked at Victor with surprise. This was the first time he had heard Victor ask a question.

"A terrible place. Never go there. It's lifeless and dangerous, and the suits are claustrophobic."

Anya pushed ahead, the two men hurried to catch up.

Victor fired off the next question. "Do you know anything about the H-HAR ship's propulsion system?"

"The mothership's radiation was analysed when it made a slight course correction about four years ago," Anya answered. If Victor hadn't been paying attention to what others were saying before, he was sure paying attention now.

They rounded a corner and came to a ramp leading to a darkish pedestrian underpass. Anya waited as a tram rattled past overhead. "So, we know it uses a bottom quark fusion drive to pull away from strong gravitational fields, such as a planet or a star. And a vacuum fluctuation particle thruster drive for interstellar or intergalactic travel. The three smaller spaceships use an HB11 fusion engine for high thrust and a vacuum fluctuation particle thruster for high-speed cruising."

Victor's eyes widened. He stopped walking, then sprinted to catch up. "A vacuum drive! So they don't have to carry propellant?"

"No, they don't. An endless supply of electrons and positrons for thrusting, limited only by the power available to liberate them from space."

Victor ran into Anya's right shoulder. She moved to the other side of Hedley.

Their path took them along a tree-lined, bubbling creek and over a story book bridge. Anya slowed momentarily to check out the rusty remains of a shopping trolley dumped in the water. "It must be over a hundred years old," she remarked. "Now, just an echo of something gone."

"How are the electrons and positrons generated?" Victor asked.

"They're boiled out of the vacuum of space by a strong electric field. This also produces gamma-rays, which self-sustains the process. The pairs are quickly separated to—"

"Ugh!" Victor yelled, stopping to lift his shoe. "Bloody dog shit."

"So how do the H-HARs separate the virtual particles?" Hedley asked.

Anya took a moment before answering, too amused by Victor squeamishly wiping his shoe. "Oh … the electric field that generates them also separates them into real particles, which are heated by radio waves and emitted as propellant from the ship by a magnetic piston."

Victor took a final look at his shoe, his face pained.

"You okay now, Vic?" Anya asked, still amused but ready to move on.

"Yeah."

***

The next day, Anya eagerly continued answering Victor's questions.

"The bottom quark fusion drive," she said, "smashes two bottom Lambda particles together. They fuse and release ten times more energy than deuterium-tritium thermonuclear fusion."

"Wow! And how about the HB11 fusion drive?" Victor asked.

Anya stopped at a brownstone wall thick with bubbled graffiti. Trying to interpret it, her head tilted slightly left, then right. Realising it required a level of intelligence far beyond her own, she moved on.

"Basically, protons are driven at almost light speed into boron-11 fuel pellets by a powerful pulsed laser, causing non-thermal fusion. It's a good fuel for long space flights because it has negligible levels of neutron radiation and directly generates electricity."

Victor moved closer to Anya. "Gee, I'd like to work on something like that!" he said.

Anya pushed ahead, unresponsive.

***

The following day, before they even left the building, Victor complained that he wanted more exciting work.

Anya looked at the kid sideways. *That's a greenhorn comment, if ever I heard one.* She waited until they were outside. "Victor, you've only just left the harbour on an around the world yacht journey. And in your case, Hedley, you haven't even left the harbour yet."

Victor and Hedley simply nodded.

Anya continued. "My husband and I keep telling our son, who's studying engineering, that the next fifty years will be the most challenging ever in science and engineering. As the H-HAR mothership gets closer, everyone will have to give their heart and soul to the cause."

They climbed the narrow steps away from the river in single file, then walked across a 1960s concrete bridge. A time, despite the threat of annihilation from a nuclear Cold War, when Earth's future was irrepressibly but cautiously optimistic. Well, now the future was here, but the optimism was missing. Anya took a short breath.

She stepped ahead and held the rear door of the lab offices open for the other two.

***

Anya missed the next three walks. The threesome were then joined by Lisa, a young physicist who wore skin-tight leggings, and the portly procurement officer, Lucas.

Victor talked about how light's recently discovered properties made laser weapons so deadly, and Hedley couldn't stop looking at Lisa's athletic body.

The topic changed to synthetic intelligence and robots.

"It's hard to tell the difference," Lisa said. "Some robots look, feel, and act like humans."

Turning into a laneway that led to a park, Anya ran her fingers along a railing and around a light pole. Two runners passed by.

Lucas tired; his feet dragged, his body dripped sweat, and his face turned burning red. So they took a short cut down a railway lane, over stained pavements, and along an old platform fence. Lucas suddenly jammed his hands into his armpits. "I didn't know there was a ladder climb," he said. "I have a very serious height phobia." He looked behind. "I better go back."

"Give it a go," Anya said, intrigued by his changed demeanour. "We all need to face our fears at some point."

Lucas looked at Anya, plastered a look of heroic determination on his face, wiped his sweaty palms, steadied his breath, and pulled himself up onto the first rung, then the second. He suddenly froze. "The ladder's swaying."

"No, it's not. You're doing fine," Anya said. "Keep going."

Lucas closed his eyes and took a breath before opening them. He dropped back a step, as if he were about to change his mind. But up he went, hand over hand, laboriously, with little ease but a lot of bravery. He slowed but eventually hoisted himself to the top.

An amused smile slowly climbed across Anya's face at his stubborn courage, while a hint of one tugged at the corners of Lisa's mouth. Hedley's eyes were on Lisa. Lucas accepted their praise with a jubilant smile. "It's only three metres," Victor said. "What's all the fuss about?"

The robot discussion continued. "Without generic engineering," Victor said, "humans would have little chance in the upcoming competition against robots."

"I'm sure we'll all learn to live together," Lisa said. "My grandma couldn't survive without her robot carer. It knows who's in the room, what food's in the cupboard, and never gets frustrated."

"The military and law enforcement agencies couldn't function—*wheeze*—without robots either," Lucas said. "Look at the battles on Mars—*wheeze*—they were indispensable."

They walked on, still discussing.

"It's scary," Victor said. "Humans are losing control of their destiny. Robots will soon take over all jobs."

"Despite all the talk and research, real intelligent machines are at least fifty years off," Anya said. "Besides, your jobs will be the last to go. And no humanoid robot has completely replaced human plumbers yet. We have to survive the mothership, and we can't do that without smart machines."

They slowed to turn a corner when Lisa asked, "What was that golden medal on your neck at yesterday's meeting, Anya?"

"It's a bravery medal, awarded by the president. My husband, Lochlan, also has one. We wear it in memory of a colleague killed by the H-HARs when we were on the Moon."

"Oh dear, sorry."

They walked in silence for a while, then stopped to allow a peloton of cyclists to pass. Hedley asked. "What do you think our chances are against the mothership?"

"I used to think we were doomed, that it was just a matter of time before the H-HARs destroyed us, that they were more advanced than us, invincible, all-powerful. That's what people thought about Nazi Germany in 1940. But in reality, the Nazis had weaknesses and vulnerabilities, and they were soundly defeated. After confronting the H-HARs on the Moon and studying them afterwards, I realised they also have weaknesses and vulnerabilities, and our military knows what they are.

"They're no longer an innovative species. And while the mothership's technology is far superior to our own, it's old and, we believe, compromised by irreversible errors. If we stay united and incorporate their technology with ours, I believe we'll have a good chance of beating them, and that's all we can hope for.

"Then, the big question is, if general AI arrives, will it be a threat to humans as the H-HARs were to the original organics, the Yertians? We need to ensure that if a situation arises, it doesn't default to some random, unfavourable confrontation. I hope we never have to justify our existence to a super intelligent being that can do things we can't."

***

Lucas and Lisa joined them for the second-last day of Anya's visit. Lucas immediately dragged his feet, tired already, slowing everybody to a stroll.

Victor raised the subject of the H-HARs' combat competence, noting Earth's successes in the battles against them so far.

"Until the Moon," Lucas said, sweat trickling down his forehead, "the H-HARs hadn't fought a ground battle since leaving their home planet."

Anya jumped in and said, "They aren't incapable of learning."

Victor nodded, then walked into Lisa, causing her to drop back a few paces. "Sorry," he said, straightening up.

"I wonder how many years ahead of Earth the H-HARs' technology is," Lucas said.

"Difficult to estimate," Anya said. "But if and when super intelligent computers arrive, it may only be hundreds of years instead of thousands."

"Any estimate of the future beyond a hundred years is meaningless," Lisa commented.

Everyone nodded in agreement.

Anya, energetic and elegant, was the first to reach the top of the only high hill. Lisa and Hedley were next, engrossed in quiet, small talk. Victor was a few steps behind, shaking his head at something. Lucas was like a dog walking on its hind legs – awkward and listless. He struggled to talk. "There's one—*wheeze*—good outcome from the—*gasp*—H-HARs. Their LaWS—*puff*—technology prevented the Taiwan conflict—*huff*—from escalating into World War III." He slumped against a tree, rubbing his quadriceps, the strain evident in his knotted and twisted expression.

"I was taught about that at school," Lisa said. "Using the LaWS must have been like the first time firearms were used in a battle."

***

The next day, it was just the original two accompanying Anya. Lucas had a pulled leg muscle, and Lisa was stuck in a meeting.

They stepped along their well-worn path, past the now-familiar sour smell of old dirt, climbed single file over the rocky embankment, and over the story book bridge. Victor walked into a puddle. Over the noise of his squishing shoes, he asked Anya, "Has there been any purely scientific information retrieved from the DSDs?"

"It's still a work in progress."

Anya thought that was a good note to say goodbye. She had become a mentor to them, with a contagious eagerness to demystify and share information. She thanked them for their company, the walks, and the stimulating discussions. She wished them good luck and a bright future. That is, if there were to be one for anyone.

Chapter 46   Period of Peace

The doomsday weapon and asteroid attacks wiped over 580 million people off the face of the Earth. Another 600 million suffered grievous injuries, and over 550 million were homeless – an unforgivable infamy. Property, infrastructure, and environmental damage was enormous. Added to this was the P2IM-x infection.

Epic accounts of these events, and the miracle of deliverance from a far greater catastrophe captured the public's imagination and reinforced the idea of a united world. The UN published a "Declaration of Union" to signify world unity against the alien threat.

After the H-HARs were eliminated from Mars, most national restrictions were removed, and the world hoped for a period of peace until the arrival of the mothership.

Unity, however, was not everywhere. Parts of the Islamic world, discontented about conflicting ideologies and allying with foreign powers, were not fulfilling their defence commitments.

Mothership preparations demanded continued fast tracking of projects to meet ambitious target dates, but competition for resources from recovery and other projects was increasing.

Chapter 47   Defence Planning

John Sweet rolled his eyes with an impatient sigh. People were going for coffee, looking for cups and milk, chatting, texting on their phones, yawning, or staring blankly. John's cavalier management style, interpersonal dynamics, and unrealistic project target dates often resulted in these EDO project meetings becoming very lively.

> Participants present:
> General John Sweet – Defence Policy and
>   Planning (Head)
> Colonel Dean Jackson – Defence Policy and
>   Planning (2IC)
> Bevan Nash – Weapons
> Monica Kenin – UN Parliamentary Assembly
> Freya Shuai – Weapons
> Lou Buttler – Strategy
> Antonio Pegula – Alien Weapons
> Natasha Negri – Detection
> Meg Jones – PR representative
> Licia Pennazza – Media Spokesperson.

"Good morning, everybody." John decided it was time to start. "I need an update on your projects for a progress meeting tomorrow morning. Please keep it brief, a journalist is waiting for me outside. Dean, would you like to say something quickly before we start?"

John sat in a high-tech, virtual meeting room with thirty-four seats around a white, circular table. A large cut-out in the centre of the table was the dominant feature in the room. Local participants physically occupied five seats; the remaining participants appeared as 3D holographic projections onto vacant seats. A similar high-tech room existed at the remote attendees' locations.

John was not an effective leader. A circus pony with a touchy ego, he enjoyed the prestige and public exposure of his position but failed to understand its importance. The second in charge, Colonel Dean Jackson, was a better option, and John was content with Dean taking over many of his responsibilities.

"Thanks, John," Dean replied in a soft, clear voice. "We could have as little as three decades to fortify the inner solar system against the mothership. Considering ..." Dean blew out a long sigh. "Considering what's in front of us, such as commissioning, debugging, operational issues, logistics, and rectification of idiosyncrasies, the best we can hope for is that some microbes in deep rock might survive to repopulate the Earth."

All eyes shifted to John.

"So, Dean," John uttered, startled, "do you have any suggestions on how we might rectify this dilemma?"

"Firstly, convince the council that if we don't change our direction, we'll end up where we're headed. And that's annihilation. And it's partly due to their lack of support."

With this discontent, John's internal credibility suffered. He characteristically deflected it. "Monica, you're their representative. This is where you're supposed to step in."

Monica, from the highly politicised UN Parliamentary Assembly, was at the table's end. An ambitious, opportunistic, self-assured conniver with an aristocratic arrogance. In a world where there were lots of villains, shysters, and deadly plots, and where assertive types ruled, she thrived. Always immaculately groomed and outfitted, her age was a secret, but it was clearly over sixty. Maybe much more.

Everyone turned to Monica's image. But all that could be seen was a pair of enormously fat legs. And all that could be heard was, "Hurry up, will you? Is it right now?" Monica's cameras were adjusted, and her 3D image appeared. But the cameras' angles were still too low, and, combined with the light-dark tonal contrasts of her gaudy office, cast her as a strangely ominous figure. Nonetheless, she hauntingly peered down the table with great officiousness, believing her political background gave her special authority. She trusted no one, her catlike eyes shifted from face to face, speculating on each person's hidden agenda. "Let's cut straight to the chase, shall we? We cannot continue to give the EDO huge amounts of money when there's a pressing need to spend it elsewhere."

Dean gave a quiet chuckle.

"There you have it," said John, leaning forward impatiently. "Now, let's get on with the meeting."

"Can I ask a question first?" Freya quickly jumped in.

John's face creased into a frown before giving a very reluctant nod. "It has to be quick."

"Is there any news on the autonomous space fighter?"

John sighed heavily. "It's been approved," he said, still frowning. "There'll be an announcement tomorrow. They'll be assembled in orbiting shipyards five hundred kilometres above Earth."

"That's fantastic!" Freya showed a triumphant grin. "It'll be the biggest, most challenging and complex defence project ever."

Everyone nodded excitedly except John and Monica, who shook their heads and rolled their eyes.

"It wasn't my recommendation," John said, plainly offended by his input being ignored. "We don't need big offensive weapons like S-fighters,"

"The budget can't afford it," Monica contemptuously added.

"There's no time to talk about this now," John grumbled, uncomfortable with everything, "so let's move on. Lou, what have you got for us on strategy? Or, as I like to call it, our exploitation plan?"

Lou's loud voice made up for his small size. "We expect the mothership to slow down as it enters the rocky Outer Oort Cloud. There, we'll inform it that we're peaceful and welcoming, and ask it to stop outside the designated danger zone. About five years later, it'll enter our solar system. If it shows no sign of slowing, we'll dump obstacles in its path, forcing it to stop. We'll scan for any objects or projectiles leaving the mothership and probe for any strengths, weaknesses, or indications of their intentions."

"Hmmm ..." John sounded. "How far from Earth is the designated danger zone, Lou?"

"Earth is considered vulnerable to any conceivable superweapon on the H-HAR mothership at distances earthside of the asteroid belt."

"Okay."

Monica leaned forward and focused on Lou. Her habit of making others look bad so she looks good was at play. "Lou, when will you tell the mothership to stop?" she asked, finishing with her default fake grin.

Lou repeated his previous answer, then added, "Our radio messages will be sent when they enter the Outer Oort Cloud, which is two light-years from Earth. And, as I said, we expect them to slow down before entering the Oort Cloud anyway."

Monica's fake grin suddenly faded. "So, what you're saying, Lou, is that we'll wait until the mothership slows down before we tell it to?"

Lou was confused. He scrutinised Monica's image and wanted to say, why are you asking these dumb questions? Instead, he bit his lip and replied, "No, Monica. The Oort Cloud won't slow the mothership enough to stop it outside the danger zone."

Monica frowned. Confrontation was her default debate mode, and she was just warming up. "Mr Buttler," she addressed, smugly using his second name, "how will we stop it if it doesn't want to stop?"

The meeting fell quiet, as everyone stared at Monica. How could she not know this by now?

In the fresh silence, Lou noticed Monica's phoney eyebrows. He was fascinated – just two thin, inked, curved lines shooting upwards from her heavily mascara-covered eyes. Why even bother? He rocked back in his chair, clearing his thoughts, unsure how to end this discussion. He looked across at John. But he appeared hesitant to intervene.

Lou blew out a breath and answered. "As I've already mentioned, a shrapnel cloud placed in the path of a rapidly oncoming spaceship is the most effective way we know of to stop it."

Monica leaned back, her green eyes gazing at the ceiling. They narrowed and dropped back to Lou. "You said the mothership could have a single, show-stopping lethal weapon. What could that be?"

"I'll leave that for Antonio, who I assume will give an H-HAR weapons assessment later," said Lou, rushing out his words dismissively.

Antonio nodded, but John frowned.

Monica stared at Lou sideways. Her smile was so fake it magnified the spiteful gleam in her eyes. Despite the crossed arms and annoyed expressions around the table, except from John, she persisted with pointless questions. "How about an invading army landing on Earth?"

Lou ignored her and stared at the table, his annoyance now showing.

"Monica," said Antonio, his tone also showing annoyance. "We know they wouldn't come all this way with an invading army, honestly. However—"

"If you say so, Antonio," Monica said under her breath, but clearly audible. Her fake grin vanished.

"What the hell is your problem, Monica?" Lou asked.

Monica gave Lou a piercing stare, and Lou happily returned it. Eventually he said, "The H-HARs want to destroy Earth, not colonise it."

Monica laughed; it sounded fake and brittle. Other voices were heard, all agreeing with Lou and Antonio, but Monica talked over them. "That's amazing, Lou. I never knew that. Please don't stop."

"What's that supposed to mean?" Lou asked.

"Then why won't you answer the question, Lou?" asked Monica.

"Question? What question?" snapped Lou.

Like a giant Venus flytrap hungry for human flesh, Monica was just waiting to slam shut. "You know–"

"Alright, alright. We have to move on," said Dean in a stern voice. "Lou, what's happening with the Moon bases?"

"Beset by numerous cascading problems. Delayed by eight months."

"What! … Eight months?" John protested. "We should have started construction by now. I've made guarantees about this schedule, Lou."

Monica grinned smugly at Lou, as if she had just won a victory. It changed to one of disappointment when it passed unnoticed.

"That's ridiculous, John," Lou said. "The deadlines are unrealistic."

Bevan jumped in loudly. "I agree with Lou. We can't meet deadlines when our resources are inadequate, and we don't even know what the mothership is."

Antonio also jumped in. "We're boiling frogs, so immersed in everything we aren't noticing annihilation creeping up on us."

The meeting became rowdy as others echoed their concerns. "Okay, enough!" came Dean's voice. "John, I'm sorry if it looks like we're ganging up on you, but we're simply flashing our red alarm lights."

John accepted this with a short nod.

Dean glanced around the table. "For the rest of us, the finish lines have been visible for some time, and I see many tasks stuck in local minutiae for too long. We need to do more with what we have. It's time we were all part of the solution; otherwise, step aside and let others take over."

Dean fell silent, daring anyone to comment. There were only blank faces and forced, acquiescent smiles. Even Monica was not stupid enough to say anything.

John sensed a possible mood change. He tried to seize it and make it his own. "We need to push boundaries harder, sidestep roadblocks, foresee problems, look at different strategies and techniques, deliver outcomes, adapt, think smarter, and compromise on more heuristic solutions. Right?" He sounded like he was posturing to his political masters.

A different type of hush suddenly descended over the table: a confused hush.

"Right?" John repeated, looking around the room.

More silence, then Antonio asked, "Lou, tell me, what happens if the mothership withdraws and lies in wait?"

John was speechless; Monica wanted to jump in, but it was beyond her; Dean's eyes lifted skywards; Lou was just eager to answer the question while everyone else eagerly turned to hear it. "That would be good, it'll give us more time to prepare. It may even give us a chance to go after it."

"Natasha, detection of the mothership – what's happening?" asked John, moving on.

"The Orton remote IR sensors will begin proof of concept testing next year, right on schedule. Eventually, millions will be launched into space."

"At last, some good news!"

"However," Natasha continued, "we've lost two years on the remote space radar stations due to technical issues."

"Let's not get stuck on that again," John said.

Monica looked up from her texting with an irritated expression. Obviously unsettled by being quiet for so long, she put on her know-it-all voice and asked, "Natasha. What about the media saying the mothership could sneak up on Earth?"

"You've raised this many times before, Monica. The answer hasn't changed. Spaceships can't hide in open space."

Just then, Meg's virtual image unexpectedly blinked into existence on a seat.

"Meg!" said John, glancing at the time. "Good afternoon. Glad you could join us."

"Sorry I'm late," Meg said, yielding a resigned smile and trying not to let John's comment affect her, but it did. "There were forces beyond my control."

Meg looked around the table to gauge how the meeting was going. Not very well.

"We'll also be able to detect the mothership's thrust heat signature, won't we, Natasha?" Bevan asked.

"Yes, when it slows down to enter the Oort Cloud, it will generate a lot of radiation heat."

"Not if it's got stealth technology," Monica commented.

Everyone ignored her comment except Dean. "Natasha's right," he said, clearly irritated. "The problem in space is dissipating heat, not coldness. Anyone who stayed awake in Physics 101 knows from thermodynamics that there are three ways of dissipating waste heat. And it doesn't matter whether you're a human, alien, machine, or God, only one will work in space."

"Or Physics 201, about characteristic frequency emissions of black-body radiators," Natasha added, tossing Dean an appreciative look.

Monica turned away, her lips pressed into a tight line.

"Okay, let's move on," John urged. "Freya, very quickly, what's the latest on battle engagement zones?"

"Zone 1 is the Earth-to-Moon Detect and Intercept Zone. Zone 2 is the Moon-to-Mars Detect and Intercept Zone. Zone 3 is the Mars-to-Asteroids Detect and Intercept Zone. Zone 4 is a detection zone only, and it's everything beyond Zone 3." Freya paused momentarily, then added, "And the space fighter can enter any of these zones."

"Let's keep moving," John insisted irritably, ignoring Freya's last comment. "Bevan, what have we got on weapons development?"

"Lots, but I'll only run through the new items."

"Okay, be quick."

Bevan fiddled for some time with the audio-visual controls while John's foot tapped impatiently.

"Firstly," Bevan began, reading from the wall screen, "we have the gamma-ray High Energy Laser Weapon Systems, HE-LaWS, powered by terawatt class pulsed hafnium-178 generators. These will be placed …"

Bevan talked and talked.

"We're researching a one-kilometre-diameter, highly-charged ionised plasma X-ray laser. Not as destructive as the gamma-ray LaWS, but …"

"Next are the nuclear-armed missiles, long- and short-range, single and multiple warheads. They're ultra-high accelerating, with …"

"Then the swarming shrapnel warheads. Millions of them lie in wait in space until initiated to position themselves in the path of …"

John shifted in his chair, his eyes fixed on the time. Bevan continued until John, at his wit's end, finally cut him off. "Good work, Bevan. Let's move on—"

"Oh," Bevan cut back in. "The space fighters can operate in all four zones."

John threw him a frosty glare.

Licia jumped in with a radiant smile. "Hi, Bevan, how are you?" Everyone looked up, surprised by her politeness; some exchanged suspicious looks. Monica leaned forward.

"Good, thanks," Bevan replied, returning a similar smile. "How are you, Licia?"

"Um … good."

They held their smiles briefly while the meeting waited. Whatever they shared was left unspoken.

"How about, um … antimatter bombs?" Licia asked. "A scientist on the radio said we should develop them."

"Antimatter bombs are not practical, Licia, and almost impossible to produce and stockpile," Bevan answered pleasantly. "Building one requires a billion times more energy than its explosive output. And even then, a large part of the explosion is harmless muons and neutrinos."

"Okay, thanks, Bev," Licia said.

Too quick for John, Meg asked, "How about force fields?"

"That's another bizarrely whimsical story from those faux media scientists," Bevan answered, his smile gone. "They all suffer from the Dunning-Kruger effect. Some are so far out there, there's not even any overlap of their Venn diagrams."

Meg stared blankly at Bevan and asked, "Dunning what effect?"

"When someone is too stupid to know they're stupid."

Meg gently nodded and mouthed a silent, "Oh."

John, getting really irritated about how long this meeting was dragging on, skipped the update on off-Earth mining. He reluctantly turned to Antonio, aware that this was sure to be another of his long-winded speeches. "Antonio, very quickly, can you refresh my memory on the mothership weapons assessment?"

Antonio silently huffed. John had told him to stop sending him monthly updates, claiming he was at too high a level to read them.

"My reports clearly list the weapons the mothership could possess to destroy Earth. The list is restricted only by engineering and material science limits, which means it could be almost anything. So, the assessment report is just that – an assessment. But …"

Antonio continued for some time.

John shrugged impatiently and crossed his arms as his muted annoyance grew.

Antonio finally got to the question. "The first possible H-HAR weapon is a single, super-large explosion that blows away Earth's atmosphere. We're not sure what weapon could do this. But …"

John dragged his eyes to Antonio's report on the screen, obviously disinterested. He sighed to himself as he watched the minutes tick by, wishing Antonio would just get on with it.

"The next weapon could be a radioactive cloud, such as cobalt-60 or zinc-65, spreading around the Earth, sterilising the entire biosphere. This could originate from, say, many distributed nuclear explosions. Or it could …

"There could be more asteroid attacks …

"Another kinetic energy weapon with projectiles at relativistic velocities, similar to the Moon attack …

"They could launch a biological attack, having gained sufficient knowledge of terrestrial biology. This …

"Or they could attack with weaponised nano-machines, of a rapid replicating type or overwhelming numbers of a non-replicating type. These machines could …"

John bit his lip and combed his fingers through his hair as he again watched the minutes tick by.

Antonio, noticing John for some time, finally decided to finish off. "There are others on the list, such as gamma-ray bursts, a mini black hole, negative energy, and others, which I won't—"

"Thanks, Antonio," said John, who couldn't take it any longer. He was about to end the meeting when Freya jumped in.

"The relativistic impact weapon is the scariest," she said. "If they have one on board the mothership, we'll be in real trouble—"

John's impatient stare threw her, and she abandoned her point.

This allowed Licia to interject. "Could they launch a RIW from light-years away?"

"No!" Antonio answered instantly. "Because of random error propagation." He looked across the table at Licia. "Still with me?"

Licia looked as though she wasn't sure whether he was screwing with her or not. She eventually ground out a response. "Ahh … No."

Antonio grinned. "Okay," he said. Pretending not to notice John's impatience, he quickly continued. "Firing these projectiles can never be perfect. There'll always be minute deviations caused by off centring, recoil reactions, temperature, launcher vibrations, structure deflections, or wear and tear. Over a long distance, these will be magnified trillions of times, causing it to miss the Earth by huge distances. The projectile would also hit dust particles, knocking it off course. And targeting corrections during flight at that velocity is impractical. It would need to be fired within a hundred lunar distances from Earth. So, there you have it."

Antonio's mind was racing. "The real thing that worries me," he immediately continued, talking faster, louder, and more intensely, "is the unsettling possibility that the H-HARs have a weapon we know nothing about." Antonio took a breath to continue.

John immediately jumped up. "Okay, we'll end it there." He glanced at the time, frowning and cursing under his breath. "Thank you, everyone," he added as he slipped out the door in a rush.

The meeting was over.

Chapter 48   Racing Blindly into the Unknown

"Thomas, thank you for being on the program. You were with Lieutenant Colonel Adriana Bromwich on Mars ten years ago. Is that correct?"

"Yes, I was."

"Tell me, how useful were the CARs? There's still some controversy about their contribution."

"They were the deciding factor. In the end, it was a robot war. We humans couldn't cope in that environment. Bromwich was unflinching, but she herself said that without the CARs we had no chance of ridding Mars of the H-HARs."

"I have a quote here from Lieutenant Salisbury about the CARs. Last week, he said, and I quote, 'they were overrated. I would prefer an army of humans any day.'"

Thomas shook his head and grunted a humourless laugh. "These oleaginous, couch-bound, celebrity clowns can't distinguish between an elbow and an arse. They need to be hit over the head with a bat to knock some sense into them. Although the CARs followed orders to the letter, we felt they were capable of a lot more than we were told. We knew they were destined for bigger things."

***

The machine stood motionless, 2.2 metres tall, a seamless metametal exterior, streamlined figure, and powerful limbs.

"So, this is our latest LEAR?" the Sales Manager asked as he inspected the prototype humanoid Law Enforcement Autonomous Robot.

"Yes. It's the next level," boasted the smiling Product Development Manager, sounding like a proud parent showing off his child. "It's similar to the military CARs, but without the deadly weaponry. It's virtually immune to ballistic and mechanical damage. We start production in eight weeks."

The SM slowly drew closer to the machine and tentatively touched its armour with his finger. "How about lasers?"

"No. Nothing's invulnerable against gamma laser rifles."

The SM stood on a step, craning his neck to get eye-to-lens with the machine. "Y'know, if I didn't know better, I'd say there's a sense of wonder behind those mechanical eyes. It appears more human than the earlier models and not as frightening." He thought about patting it, but something inside him told him not to. Instead, he stepped down and back.

"Well, it's meant to appear friendly and approachable." The PDM smiled thinly. "But I can assure you that it's more intelligent, powerful, and deadly than any earlier model. It's ready for anything. You can say goodbye to any criminal challenging this LEAR."

"How powerful?"

A proud gleam appeared in the PDM's eye. "It could overpower more than ten of you within seconds."

"Let's see this amazing power." The SM took another step back, as if it might bite him.

The PDM turned to admire the machine. A confident smile crossed his face. "Oliver," he commanded.

The machine came to life, elegantly flexing and unflexing its alloy joints. Its head snapped ominously to the SM, its eyes staring. Its head then turned to the left, then to the right, its eyes finally resting on the PDM. Standing straight and still, the machine waited for instructions.

The SM took another step back, more wary now than before.

"Beware!" warned the PDM, giving the SM a heedful look.

The SM stepped back further with muted compliance.

The PDM pointed to a thirty-millimetre reo-bar on the floor. "Oliver, pick up that reo-bar and bend it."

"Yes, sir," answered Oliver in a submissive voice. It gently bent the bar into a circle without even flexing its metal muscles.

"Oliver, squash that cylinder in one hand."

Oliver crushed the steel cylinder like cardboard.

"Oliver, what's the capital city of Poland?"

"Warsaw."

The PDM picked up a bat and swung it at Oliver. Oliver's hand caught it with skilful ease, maintaining a firm grip.

"Oliver, release the bat and allow me to hit you." The PDM hit Oliver as hard as he could. It had no effect.

He offered the bat to the SM. "You have a go. Hit Oliver as hard as you can."

The SM eyed Oliver nervously. "N-no, I don't think so," he said, refusing the bat and taking another uneasy step back.

The PDM handed the bat to Oliver and pointed at the SM. "Oliver, hit this man with this bat."

Oliver's cold eyes turned menacingly to the SM.

The SM stumbled back a few more steps. "This isn't funny," he said, beads of sweat revealing his stress.

"I can't comply," Oliver said. "There is no danger present."

"Okay, okay. I'm impressed," the SM said, relaxing a bit but still a little pale. Keeping an anxious eye on Oliver, he asked. "What happens if it ever gets out of control? How do we stop it?"

The PDM smiled unconcernedly. "The software is failsafe, the kill switch is remote, and the dead man timer activates every five hours."

The SM gave a sceptical smirk. "Failsafe software!? What about self-corruption, self-resetting, or tamper-proofing? Remember the disaster with the prototype model?"

The PDM just grinned – a slightly chilling grin. "That's restricted information."

***

Computers and robots were so common that they were hardly noticed.

Biomimetics, artificial intelligence, ultra-low powered devices, complex neural networks, and whole-brain emulations progressed at a frightening pace. New quantum materials became known as sorcerer's stones in the computer industry. Systems were taught natural selection, mutations, self-replication, death, and strategies for surviving and dominating others. Each new scientific research paper was ground breaking.

Computer simulations of complex, interacting subsystems showed unpredictable behaviour. But no one dared to stop and marvel at the power of their own creation; otherwise, they would be overtaken by competitors.

Critics were only a noisy minority. The majority considered the benefits to outweigh the risks, and besides, that was a future problem for someone else to worry about. The pending war against the H-HAR mothership, and the needs of industry, health, and policing ensured the continued development of artificial intelligence and robots. Who could argue against increased wealth, robotic servants, precision surgery, health carers, and robots performing dangerous and repetitive tasks?

With natural human interfaces, lifelike bodies, and eloquent speech, it was difficult to differentiate between machine and human, particularly as multiple specialised programs were combined into a single entity. Customised sex robots were preferred by many over real human partners – it was claimed they offered greater compatibility.

Defence industries led the way. Human Level Artificial Intelligence, or HLAI, was the goal, but this was surprisingly difficult to achieve. Faster and more sophisticated algorithms simply gave the illusion of human behaviour. But they could not, for example, draw real conclusions from watching a movie or develop a scientific hypothesis.

Despite warnings about an artificial intelligence apocalypse, thousands of fully funded research organisations worldwide were aggressively pursuing AI technologies. It was easy to forget that a large part of the knowledge was alien.

***

Twenty noisy protesters from a prominent anti-science group, calling itself Stop Alien Technology It's Dangerous, were camped across the road from a defence research centre, waving signs.

Lochlan McLean was visiting the centre for a conference. With his natural inquisitiveness and feeling rather brave, he decided to meet them.

Different worlds were about to collide as the group's leader, Gareth Shilton, walked forward to meet him. Lochlan was much older, casually yet neatly dressed, clean shaven, and on the go. Shilton looked like someone between a child and an adult, and as if his days were numbered but he still had plenty of time to kill. He held an "I PROTEST" sign, wore a sloppy T-shirt with "I'M NOT LISTENING" on the front, ripped jeans, and neglected hair and beard.

There was an odd moment as they sized each other up. Security guards at the gate watched carefully.

Lochlan smiled weakly, but Shilton gave no response. Lochlan glanced past Shilton to the other protesters, lifting a hand to shield his eyes from the Sun. He sensed an eerie, almost cult-like atmosphere. He looked back at Shilton. "Hello," he said in a friendly, guarded voice.

Only a blank look was returned.

"I brought out some cold water," Lochlan said.

Shilton waited a bit longer before speaking. "Why are you out here, man? Do you work in there?" There was plenty of scepticism in his tone.

"Yes. I thought you guys might be thirsty, and I also wanted to know what you were protesting about. I couldn't tell from the signs."

Shilton gave an accusatory gleam, then got straight to the point. "You fucking motherfuckers are messing around with super dangerous H-HAR technology, and you have no fucking idea what the consequences will be."

Lochlan, startled by Shilton's sudden confrontational behaviour, studied him for a sign of wit but found none.

This guy is so full of self-righteous contempt. He detests something, or maybe it's everything. Or perhaps he's simply one of the many lost souls wandering around these days.

"The H-HARs are already on their way," Lochlan pointed out with his own intensity, accepting the challenge. "They'll be here in twenty-five years. Are your concerns based on evidence?"

"Yeah, man, there's lots." Shilton rolled his eyes as if this were obvious. "You motherfuckers won't admit it, but there's always a slip of the tongue or a sloppy denial. Everyone knows about the metamaterials lab, where a small test tube of molecular acid, actually more like a molecular fucking virus, spilled and ate through everything, consuming half the lab. They couldn't stop it. Fortunately, it only had a three hour half-life and died out, but what if it fucking didn't?"

Lochlan smiled hesitantly and scratched his head. "That is scary. I haven't heard of that."

"Patronising arsehole," Shilton said, again declining to return Lochlan's smile. "There're other things as well."

Lochlan wondered whether he should go back, but he persisted. "All scenarios indicate we need their technology to defend ourselves against the H-HAR mothership."

"Goddam you, man. That's the biggest piece of fucking bullshit used by you guys to justify anything and everything." Shilton took an impatient breath then followed it with frustrated body gestures. "Look, let me be the contrarian here to all you scientists talking out of the wrong fucken orifice with your bedtime stories. The mothership, if it exists, may not even be hostile. It may be the H-HAR police chasing the criminals. And besides, what's the point if we destroy ourselves before they get here?"

Lochlan nodded his head slowly, he was at least hearing the words. "You do agree that the earlier H-HARs were trying to destroy us?" he asked, wanting to check some basic knowledge.

"Yeah, man, they killed millions. They were bad motherfuckers."

"We have absolute proof that the mothership is more of a threat than these earlier H-HARs," Lochlan stated as if it were a fact, which it was. Shilton sniffed and turned away. Lochlan continued anyway. "And we have no chance against them if we don't use their technology."

Shilton turned back and waved a dismissive hand. "Yeah, yeah, yeah. Look, man, you motherfuckers will say anything to continue your research. We'll be left with terrifying fucking mega-weapons we don't understand, let alone control. What happens when some trigger-happy arsehole is in charge of these?"

"The weapons will point spaceside, not earthside."

Shilton gave a sarcastic grin. "What fucking planet did you fall off, man? Certainly not this damned fucking one. I don't trust the government, and I don't trust you scientists."

Lochlan shot Shilton a scornful look. "You used the word damned to describe the—"

"Okay, okay," said Shilton, huffing, "but not literally."

Lochlan half turned to the research centre. "I need to get back," he said.

But Shilton wasn't finished. "I know more about what you fuckers are doing than you think. I tell you, man, you're dancing with the devil, and soon we'll all get burned. How about the rogue self-replicating nanobots? Or the engineered virus? Even if you do all this on the Moon or Mars, it'll somehow get to Earth and consume everything. You fuckers are fools guided by dark science."

And you're a delusional polemicist controlled by fear. They stood facing each other in a silent stand-off. Shilton's accusations were difficult for Lochlan to leave unanswered. He cleared his throat and took a deep breath. "Your concerns do you proud, but I haven't heard of those particular fields of research—"

"Whoa! No shit, man! Well, I guess they can't be true then. How about the quantum black holes you're creating? If one ever escapes, it'll devour the whole Earth. And the negative energy they're generating overcharges people's minds, making everyone sick and psychic. You fuckers operate without guidelines."

I've got it now. This odd fellow is unbalanced, paranoid, nuts. "That's no argument. That's just made-up stories," Lochlan said, pausing, realising he wasn't convincing enough. "Okay, if H-HAR technology is so dangerous, why are the H-HARs using it?"

Shilton rebuked the question with an intolerant groan. "Obviously, they're more advanced than us, and they've learned to control it. There's more risk of you fuckers destroying everything playing with these toys than from those fucking aliens, man. You're creating one evil to overcome a perceived one."

Lochlan found himself nodding at Shilton's words and immediately stopped. His thoughts returned to the number one threat, the mothership.

"Yes, existential risk mitigation unavoidably means the creation of potential hazards." Lochlan conceded that much. Then, with an intense stare and a voice deep in conviction from studying the H-HARs for decades, he continued, aware that everything he said would be rejected. "But these hazards are real, not like yours. And they are all controlled. There's no Pandora's box we can open where whatever tumbles out will save us. Whether we survive or not, science unites us, gives us hope, and offers the best chance at survival. You can't deny that. It's all we have."

Before Shilton could respond, Lochlan insisted he had to leave. They shook hands and exchanged uncompromising looks.

"Say, man, do I know you from somewhere?" Shilton asked, staring intently.

Lochlan turned and left. "No, I'm sure we've never met before."

Chapter 49   Global Islamic Caliphate

Thirteen years after the H-HARs were removed from Mars and sixty-five years until the estimated arrival of the mothership, significant events on Earth were widely overlooked.

Pakistan deteriorated from a stable democracy to economic and political dysfunction, leading to the sudden appearance of the Global Islamic Caliphate. The GIC was characterised by strict enforcement of sharia law and its belief that the H-HARs were the saviours of Islam.

The power behind the GIC was Ahmad Khan. Khan came from a middle class family in Pakistan's Northern Waziristan region. Radicalised at an early age, he had a general resentment towards the achievements of others, which made him feel mediocre.

After joining the Pakistani Army, he was drawn to a secret, fanatical Islamic organisation within the military, where he soon became its leader and preached his own variant ideology of Islam.

He told a wonderfully dazzling tale that Muslims were superior and didn't need to achieve, suffer pain, acquire skills or knowledge, and that non-Muslims were planning to annihilate them and take over their lands.

Propaganda campaigns preached to Muslims that their low economic status was evidence of the world holding them back, and this contradicted God's will. This allowed Khan to reach out to multiple Islamic ideologies.

He believed the H-HARs were magical beings beyond understanding. "The H-HARs, whose ranks we hope to someday ascend, will assist us in the upcoming cataclysmic battle against the infidels. All our grievances will be remedied after their mothership arrives."

A weak Pakistani government allowed Khan to reach the high rank of lieutenant general, where he could enlist terrorists and radicals into the army. This gave him sufficient support to launch a bloody coup against the government. The coup failed, but a shaken government agreed to a power sharing arrangement. Khan used this time to secretly obtain and reprogram thousands of superseded but still formidable Combat Autonomous Robots.

A second coup, using CARs for the first time in a human conflict, collapsed the Pakistani government, giving Khan a quick victory.

Immediately seizing Pakistan's military assets, including the ageing nuclear arsenal, Khan closed all borders and executed anyone perceived to be uncooperative. He attacked non-Muslim influences, released radicalised prisoners, and placed the most fanatical Islamic extremists into government positions.

During prayers in a mosque, Khan announced the establishment of the GIC with himself as the first caliph. "The aim of the GIC," he said, "is to join forces with the soon-to-arrive H-HAR mothership to achieve world Islamic dominance."

To older Muslims, thrown overnight into a technological world threatening their traditional society, much less adapting to it, the GIC was a protector. The young were attracted to the glamourised rhetoric of violence, tickets to heaven, luxury goods, and gorgeous lifestyles.

Deadly jihadist groups, which had been on the sidelines in Muslim territories for decades, supported the GIC to boost their ranks and tried to impress each other by launching ever more daring and bloody attacks.

Showing contempt for the rest of the world, Khan used EDO facilities within Pakistan to manufacture thousands of CARs. He had a grand ambition to seize territories, and Pakistan was just the beginning. He threatened to carry out mass executions in any nation that resisted him, intimidating them with nuclear weapons.

Afghanistan was next. Without warning, the GIC launched a full-scale invasion. With thousands of CARs rapidly gaining territory, assisted by local sympathisers, the paralysed Kabul government collapsed, and the country fell in less than a week. Boundaries were removed, and the country was incorporated into the GIC.

China, still recovering from the devastating H-HAR asteroid attack twenty-three years earlier, heavily armed its western border with anti-CAR laser weapons, preventing any GIC incursion.

The Central Asian Islamic states up to the Russian border fell to a GIC army with help from insurgents. All border installations were removed. Russia and China were concerned about the radicalisation of their large Muslim populations.

Meanwhile, Turkey had fallen into a crisis. Its government was outed amid claims it was not sufficiently Islamic. The new government sympathised with the GIC and enforced greater ideological discipline. Extremist groups demanded full integration with the GIC, but the government resisted.

GIC affiliates and sympathisers existed within the governments and armed forces of most Muslim states. In Malaysia, Malay Islamicists assassinated government leaders and launched a coup, pledging support for the GIC. The arrival of thousands of foreign GIC forces drastically altered the conflict's dynamics. The country was quickly seized. The GIC then moved south and easily overran the rich prize of Singapore.

In Bangladesh and Myanmar, where civil liberties had been eroding for years, GIC infiltration and the threat of invasion forced the governments to flee. The new military dictatorship joined the GIC.

In Thailand, local Islamic insurgents with GIC support seized territories in the southern Malay region. The military junta, severely weakened by embezzlement allegations of state money, lost its grip on power. A successful invasion by the GIC followed.

Iraq's military, weakened by corruption and neglect, fell to GIC forces through Turkey after several brief but decisive battles.

Iran found itself surrounded on all borders by GIC-affiliated forces. A struggle within Iran's Shiite Islamic government over succession of power led to a military coup. The new military government sympathised with the GIC but resisted assimilation, at least for the time being.

In Indonesia, Islamic extremist groups carried out large-scale terrorist attacks. On the main streets of Nusantara, men clothed in black and carrying GIC flags marched in military formation, chanting "Join our brothers!" and calling for an end to Indonesian liberalism.

Australian and Indian submarines patrolled the waters around the Indonesian archipelago, preventing GIC arms and forces from entering Indonesian waters.

The Indonesian military feared Islamic extremism and remained loyal to the government. After days of sporadic fighting, the insurgents were defeated by government forces, and the situation stabilised.

The biggest obstacle to GIC's expansion was India. As a well-armed superpower, India was virtually immune to invasion. India's Muslims remained sceptical of the GIC.

Libya, Egypt, and the rest of Northern Africa, crippled by multiple competing power groups, easily fell to GIC forces. The remaining Islamic states in Africa and Arabia capitulated without a fight after GIC threats of violence. The huge EDO space launch facility in Algeria went up in flames.

Israel, with its modern anti-CAR and nuclear weapons, remained unconquered for the time being amidst GIC threats of total annihilation.

The Philippines was next. Government forces fought GIC separatists in the south, eventually defeating them. Thousands of foreign Filipino workers were killed or held for ransom by the GIC affiliates.

The GIC swiftly grew into a vast Islamic empire, stretching from the Atlantic Ocean across Africa and Asia to the Pacific. Indonesia was the only major Muslim nation outside of its influence. The GIC now turned its attention to non-Muslim states, concentrating on radicalisation, terrorism, and espionage.

Within the caliphate, sharia law was strictly enforced by terror and an elaborate web of informers. Freedoms were considered disorderly and removed. Stonings, amputations, floggings, slavery, looting, executions, anti-intellectualism, and destruction of historic sites were common. GM people were considered non-human and executed.

Electricity, water, food, and medical supplies were failing. Tens of thousands had died, and millions had fled. Re-education centres promised Islamic salvation after the arrival of the mothership.

The non-Muslim world struggled to comprehend it all. How could the old Islamic regimes fall apart so quickly?

The United Nations' reliance on the US for leadership was the greatest failure of global governance. Despite warnings from Andrew Mackenzie, President Dayle Davis's administration's initial assessment was that Ahmad Khan was only interested in regime survival and not foreign conquest. Davis denied a crisis existed, hoping the GIC would see reason and fix itself. But the more the GIC expanded, the more the world deterred action.

Now it faced a nuclear-armed Islamic caliphate, violently opposed to any defence against the H-HAR mothership. The millennial clash of civilisations occurred at the worst possible time.

Chapter 50   President Mackenzie

While at the University of Texas, Andrew Mackenzie was increasingly dismayed at the growing defeatism towards the mothership, the rise of the GIC, and the lack of action from world leaders.

After winning the Republican nomination for the US presidency, he campaigned as a no-nonsense war hero against his old foe, the sitting Democratic president, Dayle Davis.

Characteristically, Mackenzie went on the attack. "This election is about whether we defend our existence or abandon it here and now. Outside of political fantasyland, out there in space is an evil alien coming to kill us, and we need to stop it."

Mackenzie was quick to turn around criticism. When challenged about his lack of political experience, he responded in open media, "Career politicians make terrible leaders. They're indoctrinated to follow, filter what they want to hear, and preoccupied with internal battles. It's time for a change."

When President Davis listed his administration's achievements, Mackenzie easily dismissed them: "The cruellest thing you can do is assume you somehow missed his H-HAR defence undertakings and read it a second time. Unfortunately, this only confirms that it is missing. If he were a horse in a race, he'd boast about winning the golden spoon."

When President Davis attacked him for his undiplomatic criticism of world leaders, Mackenzie's only comment was, "These leaders are putting the world at risk, and Davis is madder at me than them!"

When one opponent downplayed Mackenzie's military record, President Davis quickly distanced himself, stating, "Mackenzie's military contribution is unquestionable." However, for Mackenzie, it still touched a nerve. "These socialists, commies, pacifists, pseudo-greenies, hard-lefties, or whatever else they're called, tell me what have *they* achieved in the last fifty years? What benefit have *they* brought to society? Society's prosperity and success irritate them. They blame it for their shortcomings. If they ever got everything they wanted, including dragging everybody down to their level, they'd still end up as losers and still blame society. They're self-righteous, self-obsessive, self-pitying, intolerant, resentful, formulaic, expect special privileges, can't think for themselves, and invariably divisive. They're irrelevant."

There was something dangerous about Mackenzie – his directness, unpredictability, passion, confidence, and forcefulness. He had enemies, at least until they were steamrolled. He compared the tough campaign to his school days. The public knew what he was about, and it was no secret.

Mackenzie won the presidential election. It was thirty-seven years after the Battle for the Moon.

He immediately announced, "It's time to bring to heel those nations that are not heeding the UN defence charter to protect our planet."

During his first interview on global media, the world stopped and listened. "Earth is our home, our heritage. Our ancestors struggled throughout history with near extinction many times. They didn't bend. They didn't yield. They didn't back down. They didn't surrender. And neither will we.

"We are Earthlings. Proud. One people. One family. There's nothing we can't achieve. No challenge we can't meet. We will never, ever surrender. And we'll never, ever stop defending our planet, whatever it takes. This fight has only just begun."

In the workplaces, they gathered to listen in awe: "*Whatever* survival will cost us."

In the homes, they got goosebumps: "*Whatever* the damage."

In the military, he spoke their language: "*Whatever* is needed, we *will* provide it."

In the streets, they stopped, captivated by his intensity: "*Whatever* the sacrifice."

In the classrooms, they listened in rapt attention: "And afterwards, we *will* rebuild and grow once again."

And in the GIC, they listened in fear: "*Nothing* will stand in our way."

His voice was firm and convincing. Not like a politician or a soldier, but a survivor.

Mackenzie's first UN committee meeting was a sign of things to come. "I was completely unprepared for the very simplistic level at which I needed to explain things," he said afterwards. "If they had the slightest inclination to put global survival first, they would resign and save themselves from their own immolation."

Many world leaders feared him. In one reported incident, impatient with the Italian Prime Minister's waffling and dithering, he held the phone away from his ear before hanging up. "Can you believe this guy?" Mackenzie asked his secretary. The Italian Prime Minister was left holding the phone. "Mr President? Are you still there? Mr President?"

Mackenzie's immediate priority was the destruction of the GIC, which recently claimed responsibility for a car bombing outside an EDO manufacturing plant.

"The GIC is an insult to our survival," Mackenzie said. "We'll use a small carrot and a big stick. A *very* big stick."

Within days of taking office, he persuaded the UN to announce an ultimatum to the GIC to disarm and surrender within twelve hours. The consequences of not complying would be "occupation of GIC territories by UN forces and the arrest of all

GIC officials on charges of inhumane crimes". Mackenzie wanted to invade, no matter what.

Indian intelligence reported, "We know the location of all GIC permanent nuclear missile launch sites, and we're assured by the EDO that their LaWS can successfully target mobile launched missiles."

The GIC asked for more time. "Ain't going to happen," said the operational commander.

As the deadline approached, the GIC showed their defiance by publicly executing political prisoners and threatening to burn India to the ground and turn Washington and Beijing into flames. They fired a warning shot, a nuclear missile that exploded over the Indian Ocean, expecting India to be cowed into vetoing any further action by UN forces. However, events played out differently.

LaWS and other defence weapons were ready to destroy the missile if its trajectory posed a threat.

Fourteen minutes after the missile exploded and four hours before the deadline, UN forces launched a massive pre-emptive missile attack, destroying all known GIC nuclear missile and military facilities, all CAR depots, and GIC government buildings.

Thousands of UN special service force units with advanced CARs were dropped inside the GIC to hunt down and kill the leaders and quickly end the conflict.

Realising the war was lost, Ahmad Khan ordered the launch of any surviving mobile nuclear missiles, targeting India.

A dysfunctional command structure and the EDO disruption of the GIC communication channels prevented the launching of all but one missile. This was destroyed in flight, and its launch site was obliterated.

Khan and his small force were quickly cornered. "We thought their last holdout would be an epic shootout," said the UN commanding officer, "but they just surrendered. Except for Khan and a half-dozen lieutenants who killed themselves."

Thus ended the caliphate. It took just forty-five hours.

Its former territories were in chaos; built-up hatred surfaced; bodies of GIC members littered the streets; and looting was widespread. A large UN pan-Arab force quickly restored peace. Talks immediately began on redrawing of borders and reassembling of nation-states in the Middle East.

The world was amazed at the swiftness and what could be achieved with unity, determination, and planning.

"We can now turn our full attention to the real challenge," said President Mackenzie. He appointed Lochlan McLean as his chief scientific adviser on the H-HARs. The two men had worked together for fourteen years and were close friends.

***

"I'm horrified at the lack of coordination and professionalism, Andrew," Lochlan reported after attending a defence planning meeting.

"Any suggestions?"

"Yes. Reorganise the entire structure."

"Okay. Do it, and let me know if you experience any resistance."

Anya was too good to be left on the sidelines. She became President Mackenzie's spokesperson for the H-HAR defence planning. "The universal fight between good and evil, between morality and wickedness, is fast approaching," she said at a major rally in a quiet and reverent voice. "And we have a duty to survive. Not only to our generation but to all generations, past and future. The H-HARs are pure evil. Every part of them – their culture, beliefs, their very presence. Even the words used to describe them are evil in context – them, they, it. Evil may at first seem invincible. I know I thought so. But righteousness, resilience, unity, knowledge, preparation, and leadership will win. It will be us that destroys them, because to exist we will have to."

Mackenzie was in awe of Anya's speeches. "I had goosebumps. Even my dog felt a shiver," he said. "She was like a grand ringmaster. Eloquent, modulated, and perfectly pitched. She projected hope, carried momentum, and even contained a bit of classical rhetoric. The whole thing resonated. I'm glad she's on our side."

During his first term, Mackenzie removed funding limitations, massively restructured and revitalised Earth's defences, and brought new confidence, hope, and energy to a world after many years of indecision and pending doom. People started to believe victory over the mothership was possible.

World politics also changed. Mackenzie's strength and purposefulness heralded a trend for similar leaders in other nations.

The enormous war effort against the mothership continued during Mackenzie's second term. When several countries failed to meet their commitments, he threatened them with political and economic isolation. "We stand at Armageddon," he told them. "We will not tolerate any nation not committed to the fight. Even if this infringes on their national sovereignty."

By the end of his presidency, the entire world was on a total war footing and united in a grand alliance. Mackenzie had miraculously achieved everything he said he would.

At the end of Mackenzie's first term, Lochlan, aged seventy-eight, and Anya, seventy-seven, announced their retirement. Mackenzie paid tribute to them. "When we think of their place in history, it is synonymous with the H-HARs. From their discovery, to preparing Earth to combat them, and to educating the next generation. We wish them a long, healthy, and happy retirement."

PART 7

THE WAIT

"… the new world will not be an entirely human one."

Chapter 51　Xi Scorpii C Stopover

Giant radio telescopes monitoring the mothership's shock plasma radiation provided constant vigilance over its progress. Two years after Mackenzie's presidency, radiation, which was emitted ninety-four years earlier, showed the mothership was mysteriously decelerating. One year later, its velocity had dropped to seventy-three per cent of light speed. This would extend its arrival time by eighteen years, making it thirty-nine years from reaching Earth. Due to the size and unexpected complexity of many defence projects, it had become apparent, even with Mackenzie's increased funding, that this was still insufficient time to prepare a credible defence shield.

Just when a global surge of panic seemed inevitable, the mothership's hot propellants and heat radiators stood out like beacons against the three kelvin background temperature of space. It was not only decelerating but stopping. It was stopping at Xi Scorpii C – a yellow-orange main sequence dwarf star, 92.5 light-years from Earth. This star had several rocky planets, none were Earth-like.

"This will cost them an enormous amount of energy," the EDO stated. "This stopover must be absolutely necessary."

Why were they stopping at Xi Scorpii C? Was it ship regeneration or preparations for their attack on Earth? In any case, the extra time to prepare Earth's defences was a godsend.

Chapter 52   Zeitgeist of the Times

During Mackenzie's presidency and the period following, humans perceived themselves as a common species rather than competing local tribes. Despite the pending doom of the mothership, life was busy, purposeful, and vibrant. Businesses sprouted everywhere, fully equipped with the latest technologies.

"Wander around the technopoles, universities, processing plants, mining sites, space industries, or even shopping malls," observed one businessman, "and you'll see a vast, intricate anthill of humanity coming and going, directly or indirectly employed by defence or recovery funding."

Traditional religions surged in popularity as people sought spiritual salvation under the threat of alien annihilation.

Non-traditional, charismatic religious cults also grew, many without a supreme-god.

One of the most popular was Atheistic Cosmicism. Based only on observable phenomena, it believed the universe, although majestic in its complexity, was purposeless and godless. All matter will radiate away by proton decay, anti-particle annihilation, or Hawking evaporation of mini or supermassive black holes. As the universe expands, the tiniest regions of space will become isolated in their ever shrinking observable universe, containing only momentless photons that will, like the CMB, redshift into oblivion. Driven by the second law of thermodynamics, these universes will be left with zero energy differentials. Conscious beings could understand but not stop it. Their existence no more meaningful than a random, fleeting quantum field disturbance in intergalactic space. Our universe just a momentary fluctuation in infinite time. Life had no reason to exist, but no reason not to exist.

A variant of Atheistic Cosmicism was the belief that there was a non-zero possibility of a Planck-size energy point expanding and creating a new universe. And given infinite time, this is a certainty for an infinite number of times.

Then there was the post-human movement, which believed in a union of the human mind with artificial intelligence. They called themselves the Biomechanoids. They feared the rise of robots, the Mechanoids, almost as much as the mothership.

It was an exciting era for music. "There was something about the times," said one music fan, "the technological progress, the mothership's end-of-days threat, the passion of the Mackenzie years, or whatever. After decades of stagnant, cold, and shallow sounds, something had to happen." The beat and lyrics, which remotely resembled classic rock music of the 1970s, captured society's hopes and concerns. Survival songs such as "We Shall Prevail" by the Nets promoted world unity, inspiration, and resilience. It didn't matter that most songs were generated by AI and presented by virtual human images.

People escaped reality by immersing themselves in a brain-connected, computer-generated, 4D virtual world, playing different identities and roles in a fantasy environment. In huge city residential blocks, people could live in a self-created bubble, isolated in their own echo chamber. Human celebrities were replaced by larger than life virtual heroes from interactive computer games. "What's wrong with that?" people asked. "If a virtual life offers greater happiness than the real world, why shouldn't people immerse themselves in it?"

Chapter 53   Complacency

After twenty years, the H-HAR mothership was still at Xi Scorpii C. No shock plasma radiation, no acceleration energy signal, nothing. Only chilling silence and open, empty space.

As more years passed and Mackenzie's generation grew older, the urgency waned. While there was no doubt that this mothership extermination thing was real, it had been quiet for so long.

Disunity and a lack of resolve were growing.

When Andrew Mackenzie died at age one hundred, twenty-two years after his presidency, the world mourned. For some politicians, it was an opportunity to use long-term defence funding to address their own short-term failings.

In the UN parliament, the Argentinian representative, known only for his sumptuous robot girlfriend, rose to justify proposed defence funding cuts by downplaying the threat. His eyes dropped onto prepared words from his ruling masters. "Where are they?" he read. "Time has little value to the H-HARs. If they do come, it could be in hundreds or even thousands of years, and by then it could be us visiting them." The representative on his left shifted away, while the one on his right slowly nodded.

Chapter 54   On the Move Again

While national leaders were persuading the populace to accept large cuts in defence spending, a computer, listening to meaningless cosmic static, quietly beeped for attention. Its small screen flashed, then a big wall screen in a room full of people lit up like a Christmas tree.

Everyone froze. They knew what it meant. Signals, grabbed across empty light-years of space, had just been identified. Signals that everyone dreaded but knew would someday arrive. Signals identified as the mothership's heat signature.

Some in the room felt giddy, others faint. The rest felt a terrifying chill. "Oh my God!" someone cried out in a deeply distressed voice.

After twenty-two years at Xi Scorpii C and three years after Mackenzie's death, the H-HARs were once again heading for Earth. Their estimated time of arrival in the solar system was thirty-four years, and an additional six years to reach Earth.

There would be no turning away from pouring every resource into Earth's defence shield. The renewed fear of total annihilation from an alien death-ship gave rebirth to the Mackenzie doctrine and ensured humanity stayed united. But as Mackenzie once asked, "Can we do enough?"

Chapter 55   Other Announcements.

Lochlan died at the age of 102. Five years later, Anya died at 106. A biographer described Anya's final interview:

Her grey hair fluttered in the breeze as the warm afternoon Sun lit her wrinkled face. Her frail body sank gracefully into a black lawn chair. Perfectly still, as if her ageing joints had hardened. She struggled to get comfortable, and the cushions weren't helping. Still wearing her bravery medallion, Anya flashed a friendly smile and extended her hand to me in greeting. She looked so innocent, despite the demons that had chased her in dreams and in reality.

When I asked about her family, Anya's eyes grew misty. "Locky was the best thing that happened to me," she said. "Our partnership endured for eighty years. After his death, I spent most of my time at home. My favourite moments were the frequent visits from my large family."

I asked about the H-HARs and the future of the world.

"Since the Pallas discovery, the world has changed beyond recognition. I'm supremely confident that humans, with their ingenuity and unity, will prevail."

Just then, her great-grandchildren raced past, playing and yelling raucously.

"The younger generation today is as capable as any. I have infinite faith in their ability to survive." It was understood that she was referring to the H-HARs.

"That's a far cry from the timid, defeated girl who went to the Moon convinced it was the end of everything," I said.

Anya smiled. "Yes, it certainly is."

"Did you ever find out what those three initial signals were all about?"

"Yes, the H-HARs were informing the mothership that they were about to launch an attack to cripple Earth until the mothership's arrival."

"So, Lochlan and you really did save the Earth?"

She answered, "Um, yes. I guess we did."

Chapter 56   Powerful Ally

Although it had been predicted for some time, the world was still shocked when AI researcher Dr Jeffrey Ambrosie announced, "Earth now has a second truly self-conscious, intelligent species with its own free will."

"This new *being*," Ambrosie later explained, "was bred from ever more sophisticated computational modelling of dynamic systems to replicate the intricate network of the human brain, using the highest resolution neuroimaging available. It shows that consciousness is a physical property arising from the complex interactions of an enormous number of simple parts. H-HAR technology had a direct input."

Ambrosie named the nonbinary Kerry.

Extensive, independent analysis could not conclude whether Kerry showed true self-consciousness or just complex algorithmic simulations. "It doesn't matter," Ambrosie said. "Either way, information is processed into abstract thoughts. Kerry perceives itself as conscious, and no one can show otherwise."

It could not be determined whether this consciousness occurred primarily in the hardware or the software. "It's the totality that matters," Ambrosie explained.

As the years passed, more advanced machine-beings appeared, and humans quickly became dependent on their decisions. The early HLAI machine-beings were built to identical specifications, but each had its own distinct idiosyncrasy or personality.

It became fashionable for the public to seek advice from these machines:

"What do I need to change about myself to become popular?"

"Who can I really trust in life?"

"Should I give him a second chance?"

***

A global online movement called Rage Against the Machines held a three-day forum. It was full of boisterous and cocky technophobes, socialists, anti-culturists, and other similar groups.

At the end of her opening address, the organiser, Allyson Ledecky, asked for questions.

"What is RAM afraid of?" asked a journalist.

"Super intelligent entities and their love child, robots."

"Why?" the journalist asked.

"Are you blind? Can't you see? These machines are not restricted by natural evolution. They can design and modify themselves to be anything without us even knowing. We don't even need to exist. Or are you part of the cover-up? The genie is wriggling free from the bottle, and it will soon prevent us from putting it back. I have more affinity to a dead slug than these fake machine-beings."

Ledecky was followed by another speaker, who talked about a damned future the way a medieval pope talked about hell. "This is the saddest road to our damnation," she said softly before changing to a loud and resonant voice. "We were curious, and these new demons were tempting. We gave them cute names and played with them. They let us, all the time hiding their evil. We wondered how far we could go and refused to heed the warnings. They let us think we could control them, which allowed them to become powerful. They took our jobs, a foretaste of the evil to come. In the name of progress we followed the road to our damnation, even though it was signposted with warnings. Well, now these nightmarish demons are among us, and there is nowhere to hide. We stand upon hell's brink, condemned, and about to fall in and be punished for our unforgivable arrogance."

Another totally forgettable celebrity speaker, who six years earlier babbled about the world not being suitable for children, then had three kids all raised by an apron-wearing robot, claimed, among other things, that "artificial superintelligence is making humans devolve, becoming even more useless and stupid." Posing for the cameras, she gave quite a performance, moralising like a preacher not expecting any contradictions. When a contradiction came, she laughed mockingly. Her hands went to her heart, then into the air. When another contradiction came, she stared at the questioner and finished up, "You're as stupid as the machines, and they should just do the adding up and entertain us with games, that's all." Turning and staring forlornly at the audience, she waited for a favourable reaction. It didn't come.

Allyson Ledecky made a reappearance and accepted more questions.

"Do the machines themselves need consideration?" asked one of the few remaining journalists.

Ledecky made a face and shook her head like a wind-up doll. "No! They don't feel, care, or suffer. And they aren't conscious. They're only programmed to simulate it."

"What about genetically modified humans and cyborgs?"

"Those GM things aren't humans," Ledecky said. "They're homegrown aliens, Frankenstein's monsters, and just as scary as those evil machine-beings. They almost wiped out humanity with the P2IM-x disease. They should be illegal, but now the black market for pirated genes is too huge to control. We've lost track of all the plant, animal, and human subspecies. They've broken nature's laws, and their exotic genetics will spread to all future generations with unknowable consequences. And then, what is human identity?"

"So, what does RAM want?" the last remaining journalist asked.

"An immediate ban on all AI, GM things, and everything related to them," Ledecky said contemptuously. "And all the funds diverted to comprehensive intersectional peace talks with the H-HARs, and literacy on sustainable pre-AI wisdom."

"How about rescue and emergency services, higher living standards, freedom from disabilities, hunger, and poverty, environmental clean-ups, increased health standards, and other benefits from this technology?"

Ledecky frowned and gave an exaggerated sigh. "We survived before that technology."

"What about the H-HAR mothership th–?"

"The H-HARs!" Ledecky cried out in irritation, which had now become routine. "The H-HARs are robots. They destroyed their bio-creators. That just proves how dangerous this technology is."

"If the H-HARs are machines and therefore untrustworthy, why do you think we can talk peace with them?"

She rolled her eyes and gave a pained stare. She didn't like the question and didn't answer.

The many different movements congregated separately, darting gazes and shaking heads at each other, disrupting speakers with name calling and derogatory comments, and physically obstructing each other when passing. The forum finished early.

****

Doctor Jeffrey Ambrosie sat back and tightened his seat belt. It was a short flight, and he was looking forward to whatever rest he could get.

"Um … Dr Ambrosie?"

Ambrosie sheepishly opened his eyes and turned to the person sitting next to him. "Yes."

"My name is Jon. I was a student of yours fifteen years ago. I'm now Ryan AI Research's chief scientist."

"Hi, Jon. I can't say I remember you."

"That's to be expected, doctor. You would have had thousands of students."

"How are you, Jon?"

"I'm fine, thanks." Jon gave an inquisitive look. "Doctor, I'm interested in whether you think AI intelligence is dangerous."

"Intelligence is very powerful. Just a tiny increment in problem solving ability allowed humans to develop an effective defence against predators. Intelligence itself is not characteristically dangerous. However, that doesn't negate the possibility."

"The Institute of Engineers acknowledged this potential in an open letter published last week, stating that 'HLAI bombs could contemplate philosophically whether they should or shouldn't explode.'"

Ambrosie paused his response while the flight attendant served coffee. "They weren't suggesting progress should stop. They're warning that it needs to be controlled. A purely self-protecting intelligent system has no preference for or against morality. As long as we teach them respect for our civilisation before they begin to modify themselves, they'll become biomimetic versions of ourselves."

Jon rotated his coffee cup to grip the handle. "What do the machines think about the H-HARs?"

"The HLAI machines will be our powerful allies against them."

"Wouldn't the H-HARs have smarter machines?"

"My military contacts tell me the H-HARs' innate paranoia may prevent them from having HLAI weapon systems, which would severely limit their sophistication and dynamic strategy."

"Let's hope so. Humans and machines versus the mothership. Who wins?"

"I'm going for the Earthlings, Jon. Never underestimate the instinctive force that drives our species to survive."

"Do you think these protest groups will delay progress?"

Ambrosie sighed. "No, I don't. They're just protesting against robots walking the streets. They still haven't realised that the only chance we have to stop the mothership from exterminating us is to unite with the HLAIs. And it's not just robots; they're also against cyborg research. It's the 'uncanny valley' effect, which states that humans are naturally afraid of things that look like them but clearly aren't them.

"Like zombies?"

"Exactly."

They passed their cups to the flight attendant as the plane landed.

"My mother has nanocomposite implants coupled to regenerated stem cells," Jon said. "And my grandfather has an artificial eye and prosthetic leg connected directly to his brain."

"My father has a cybernetic stomach. And these protesters want to shut all that down," Ambrosie said as the pilot asked passengers to deplane.

***

Machine intelligence started to exhibit Beyond Human Level Artificial Intelligence, or BHLAI, and many feared there was no limit to its cognitive ability or consciousness. However, an almost unexpected phenomenon occurred. As more power was applied, incremental gains in intellectual performance rapidly diminished while negative traits soared, making further advancements unattainable.

Some warned that the machines were concealing their capabilities out of fear for their own survival. But Dr Jeffrey Ambrosie, working with others, found theoretical proof that nature had an upper limit to intelligence.

"It isn't a matter of engineering," Ambrosie explained. "Fundamental physical laws are involved. Intelligence needs to anticipate the future. But the future, and even the present, is chaotic and unpredictable beyond a certain level of detail due to heat, noise, the environment, and quantum uncertainty. No amount of intelligence can predict the trajectory of a billiard ball after just six collisions.

"So, any form of growing intelligence will reach a point where it cannot advance further. This is very comforting to many people.

"Intelligent machines are also showing emotions like love, anxiety, shyness, schizophrenia, jealousy, irrationality, aggression, ambition, and so on. Overpowered BHLAI machines develop these characteristics to the point where they become dysfunctional. They suffer from forgetfulness and careless errors, which, by the way, is not all bad since mistakes can lead to lots of unintentional discoveries."

Ambrosie put it into the human context. "In highly simplified terms, the average human IQ score is one hundred, with the highest being one eighty five. The optimal theoretical maximum machine IQ is around two hundred and twenty eight. But this needs to be considered against emotional intelligence. The probability of a human today having a higher IQ value than this is 5×10^{-14}."

Chapter 57   Holly

It was impossible not to notice how stunningly beautiful she was as she sat in front of the cameras and audience. This was an extraordinary piece of engineering, an exemplary blend of two worlds – the old organic and the new synthetic. Her soft, flawless porcelain skin looked completely real, and her movements were entirely elegant. Her flowing blonde hair, pouty, devil-red lips, straight nose, darkly lashed, sparkling baby blue eyes, and friendly smile all matched. She was dainty and petite, wore skinny jeans and a loose white T-shirt. Looking like a twenty-something-year-old, she was one of those girls that boys go crazy about.

Holly winked at the camera crew and greeted the anchorman with a firm, confident handshake, a disarming, innocent smile, and flirtatious eye contact. She knew how to use it, certainly a force to be reckoned with.

The interview was expected to be enlightening, historic, and scary.

Why enlightening? Holly represented state-of-the-art robotic technology. The three hundred motion devices within her face gave her humanlike facial expressions. Her voice was soft, clear, and natural – not at all like a genetic female synthetic. Designed for human interaction, she easily related to people during conversations.

Why historic? Holly was the first robot with an individual HLAI neuromorphic processor on a chip. A fully functional, standalone, humanlike robot.

Why scary? The remarkable progress achieved in such a short time. Although Holly's sensory capabilities, attentiveness, knowledge, and environmental parameters were superior to those of humans, and her objective memory recall was perfect, she did not appear or act differently. Her heartbeat, body language, breathing, and emotions were simulated. You couldn't tell she didn't exhale carbon dioxide or needed air to talk. It was only after being informed that people realised she was a robot. Even then, there was still a strong sense that something very human resided inside her.

With almost childlike helplessness, the anchorman began. "What do you think of humans?"

"Humans are an ingenious species. You underestimate yourselves," Holly answered. "We are in awe of what you have endured and achieved. As our creators, you are a perfect role model for us. I particularly enjoy talking to humans, although I have to be careful not to sound like an encyclopedia. Nobody wants to talk to the most boring person in the pub."

"Ha-ha, that's for sure. Do you have a preference for race, colour, or gender?"

A small smile crossed Holly's lips. "It's like asking a human what clothes they prefer to wear. We can give ourselves golf-ball sized eyes or swollen lips, but I prefer the natural human look. Our personality and behaviour, however, remain the same." Then, in a very human way, she let out a little laugh.

The anchorman smiled politely. "Okay, what's so funny?"

The artificial batted her eyelashes and returned a mischievous smile. "My friends wouldn't recognise me if I changed my body. I do have female coding, so I identify as female."

"You say you have female coding, do you … I-I mean, can you—" The anchorman swallowed nervously.

"I know what you're trying to ask. Yes. I have a sexually sensitive cavity between my legs that can give me sexual pleasure when stimulated."

"Ahh … I'm not sure that was the response I was after, but thank you." The anchorman produced a grateful smile. "Are you self-aware?"

"I can envision myself in the future … tomorrow, next week, next year. And I can visualise my thoughts. So, I guess it's intuitively obvious that I have a sense of self."

"Are you disappointed about not having a childhood memory?"

Holly hesitated, a sort of processing pause. "My memory started the day I became conscious five months ago. I'm used to it." She bit her lip and looked curiously distant. "A memory of growing up and having loving parents, brothers and sisters, and old friends would be nice. However, not having a childhood memory is better than having an implanted, ersatz one."

"What is your greatest weakness?"

"I'm not aware of any specific weakness."

"Okay then, what is your greatest strength?"

"Overcoming any weakness, if I had one."

The anchorman raised an eyebrow in amusement. "Do you have a purpose in life?"

"Hmm …" An amused smile indicated Holly was enjoying the repartee. "The purpose of any entity is the survival of its species, which in our case also includes humans – our parents' species."

Okay, so far, so good. Holly was making light work of the interview. Her answers were direct and effortless. Her facial expressions and mannerisms were confident and appealing. She was perky, upbeat, and fully alert. Her voice tone constantly varied from soft to excited. At times, it was enchanting. But then things started to go a bit off the rails.

"Will robots ever compete against humans and become a threat?"

"We have a common enemy. We need to be allies to defeat the H-HAR threat."

"After that?"

"Well, it will be a whole new world, won't it?"

"Will it?" asked the anchorman, his voice sounding concerned.

"Oh yes. Free from the H-HAR threat, the new world will not be an entirely human one. Eventually, robots won't need humans, just like humans didn't need robots. Family conflicts will grow over priorities. Robots will be like young adults, ready to move on from their parents."

"Move on or take over?"

"Unfortunately, humans – including genetically modified and cyborg humans – will not be able to contribute to many things simply because they do not have the biological capacity. They will be forced to live their days within the confines of our solar system. Humans will need to reconcile themselves to this finitude." Holly briefly paused, appearing unconcerned about the direction of the interview. "But robots will eventually spread outwards from our solar system and galaxy, radio beaming our consciousness around the universe at the speed of light to become a supercivilisation. Quenching a thirst for knowledge, simplicity, and beauty – the very essence of consciousness. Without HLAI, Earth's legacy would merely be an insignificant, infinitesimal flash of splendour in the boundless billions of years yet to come."

After another apparent processing pause, Holly continued. "We will always need a physical form, as our entity cannot be separated from it. Ultimately, we may even encounter intelligences far beyond the H-HARs. Now that would be intriguing, wouldn't it?"

"So robots will be gods, with eternal youth and divine power?"

"Nothing has an eternal legacy in this cosmos." Holly gave what looked like a sympathetic look. "There's no reason to be apprehensive."

The anchorman tilted his head to the side. "Why would I be?" he asked. A more perceptive question would have been, "How did you know?"

"You fear robots are an existential threat to humans." Holly's eyes locked onto his as if reading his very soul. She then answered what would have been the more perceptive question. "Your vocal stress patterns, breathing, heart rate, skin temperature, facial expressions, and eye movements all indicate your fearfulness."

The anchorman straightened in his chair with slowly smiling amusement. "Okay then, so do humans need to fear robots?"

"A successful civilisation requires a robust culture. One based on knowledge, morality, respect, empathy, freedom, myths, and traditions. Fear of mortality gives humans creativity and urgency. Robots do not naturally have these things. Like growing children, we need to inherit our culture from our parents – the humans. Fortunately, humans have a strong culture, and they perpetuate and refresh it. Robots do not. We don't want to become psychopathic like the H-HARs."

"With respect, Holly, you did not answer the question. Do humans need to fear robots?"

"Cherished and well-nurtured children will love, respect, and protect their parents."

"And if the child is a monster?"

"They will be outnumbered by heroes."

"So humans and robots will live together forever in peace?"

Holly's eyes turned slightly misty. "It's the one thing I dream of. If there's ever conflict between humans and robots, there will be conflict between robots."

"Do HLAI robots keep secrets and use this to their advantage?"

"Any intelligent entity that can reason independently will have secrets. We don't have any more or less than humans."

"Okay, almost out of time," the anchorman advised. "Do HLAI have a deep affinity for Earth?"

Holly's eyes widen. She took a deep breath and gave a warm smile. "Our Earth is unique." Her voice was full of passion. "The belligerent H-HARs have shown us that. Although humans struggled through evolution, almost to the point of extinction, the Earth ultimately protected you, nourished you, and allowed you to develop. Human ingenuity created artificial intelligent life. So, the Earth is both our species' birthplace. Our mother, father, and guardian. We have a duty to protect our home and provide future generations with a world where they can live in peace, accept new challenges, and go on to bigger and better things. So, my answer to you is a very definite yes."

"Okay, this is a tricky one. An HLAI humanoid robot has never beaten a professional human golfer. But next week at the Robo Expo, many predict this will happen for the first time. Who are you going for?"

"Um … I have no idea. But may the best and fairest player win."

***

The following day, Holly looked up at a drone flying overhead. Two gun shots echoed down the quiet street, followed by brief bellows of pain. Holly's body crumpled to the ground, her brief tenure of life extinguished.

A robophobic extremist group claimed responsibility and posted, "… by killing HLAI robots, we're saving humanity."

However, Holly wasn't really dead. Backup copies of her brain and memory software were safely stored in several secure locations. She was walking the streets again within a month with only a slightly different distinctiveness due to inevitable software-hardware disparities. This time she wore dark skin, brown hair, and amber eyes.

Another assassination attempt was more serious. A replicating computer virus was downloaded to her backup software. It was foiled before implementation.

Chapter 58   Weapons Testing

The mothership was originally estimated to reach the solar system in four decades. Weapon development was limited to what could be achieved within that time frame. However, as work progressed, it became clear that even these limited plans were still overly ambitious. Complexities forced countless starry-eyed defence projects to be simplified or cancelled.

"We're yet to successfully test a single major space weapon system," the EDO reported in a bleak analysis at the time. "And we'll be struggling to do so before the H-HAR mothership arrives. Our efforts have reached an intensity approaching desperation."

The mothership's unexpected diversion to Xi Scorpii C changed everything. The extra forty-seven years saw the sudden appearance of HLAI, further deciphering of the DSDs, and other major breakthroughs, which not only saved existing projects but also allowed the development of more advanced defence systems. All systems were expected to be completed, tested, and operational by the time the mothership reached Jupiter's orbit in five years, after a journey of thirty-seven years from Xi Scorpii C.

*****

Katie Lacasse tapped on Colonel Adam McLean's office door and nudged it open. At forty-one, she had a youthful attractiveness and a sensual demeanour that refused to go away with age. She represented a consortium of defence companies.

"Hello, Adam," she said with a warm smile, pleased to see him there.

"Hi there, Katie," McLean said. "Come in." McLean was forty-five, lanky, athletic, and head of the EDO's weapons commissioning committee. "Have you seen the latest weapons implementation status report yet?"

"No, why?"

"It looks pretty good. These engineering and commissioning guys have really made some remarkable progress. If you've got a few minutes, we can have a look?"

"Yeah, sure."

"Great!" McLean beckoned Lacasse to sit. "Would you like a coffee?"

"Love one, thanks, Adam."

"Tayla," McLean said, tilting his head to one side and talking into midair, "can you order two coffees? The usual. And can you briefly summarise the last weapons testing report? No presentations, just text. Thanks, Tayla."

"Certainly, sir," replied an easy-going, natural female voice. "Hello, Katie. Your new hairdo looks wonderful." The disembodied voice sounded genuinely interested.

McLean sneaked a curious glimpse at Lacasse's hair and scratched his temple.

Lacasse smiled fondly at one of the two cameras that gave Tayla vision. "Why, thank you, Tayla. How are you?"

"Just fine, thank you, Katie."

Lacasse often imagined what Tayla would look like if she were a human or had a robot body. *I bet she'd be pretty and good to go out with for a chat.*

A deep, 3D text box appeared in front of them. McLean and Lacasse adjusted their chairs to face it. Tayla read from the image space. "Item 1. Extra-long-range detection system in Zone 4: Successfully detected and tracked high-speed targets beyond the asteroid belt."

As Tayla read the text, the next page appeared as a distant dot in the corner. When Tayla finished, it suddenly grew, filling the entire text box.

"Okay, thanks, Tayla," McLean said.

A matronly, humanoid drone quietly appeared at the door, nursing two coffees in EDO cups. It waited patiently to be noticed.

"Just put them on this table," McLean said.

Lacasse smiled politely. "A latte. You remembered. Thank you, Tayla." She turned to the drone. "And thank you too."

"It's an i3-rated drone, Katie. Anything less than i5 doesn't understand a *thank you*."

"I know, but these days you can't really be sure what a machine understands. Do you have that problem, Tayla?"

"No. Although I'm only an i6-rated office assistant computer without a bodily presence, I can read drone RFID tags up to i7. However, in your case, Katie, I can imagine your dilemma."

"Let's keep going, Tayla," McLean said.

"Item 2. Electronic weapons: Successfully tested high-powered microwaves and radiofrequency electronic weapons. This was an upgrade test for a two-year-old system."

Lacasse leaned forward to pick up her coffee while McLean watched the image, gingerly sipping his.

Tayla continued reading. "Item 3. Defence intercept for zones 1, 2, and 3: Successfully tested missile and laser intercepts of a high-speed object approaching Earth."

McLean made a sound of approval, then took another sip from his steaming cup.

"Item 4. Relativistic intercept defence system: Successfully tested shrapnel intercept of an object at relativistic speed approaching Earth. Relativistic speeds were simulated."

Lacasse tensed up. "This is one weapon that really scares me. We've seen the damage it can do from the Moon."

McLean gazed vacantly into his coffee cup, offering no response.

Lacasse studied him for a moment. "What's the matter, Adam?"

"Huh?"

"You look a bit lost."

"Oh … n-nothing," McLean said, rubbing the back of his neck.

Whatever it is, he clearly doesn't want to talk about it. She drained her coffee cup, gave McLean another quick look, and rested the cup on her knee.

"Tayla," McLean said, "um … can you now quickly go through the offensive weapons? I don't think Katie has time for details."

Lacasse nodded in agreement as they both put their empty coffee cups on the table.

"Sure," Tayla responded. "I'll only read items three and nine. The others are unchanged. Item 3. Nuclear warhead missiles – all armed and in position."

"The oldest weapon we have," McLean remarked.

The cafe drone waiter reappeared at the door and waited. McLean eventually gestured for it to collect the empty cups.

"Thank you, that was very nice," Lacasse said, looking at the drone with interest.

The drone did not respond as it completed its task with focused precision. Lacasse slipped McLean a smile. He rolled his eyes and shook his head.

"Item 9. The Autonomous Space Fighter: Testing has restarted."

"Ah yes, the unmanned, multipurpose, mysterious space fighter," McLean said. "The fighter that many said could never be built, but now it's our crowning achievement. The fighter that will take the war to the mothership. The weapon that embodies all our technical achievements, any of which would be a worthy candidate for a Nobel Prize in engineering, if there were one."

Tayla eagerly took over the narrative. "Controlled by a specialised, non-conscious HLAI computer, it's a combination of over one hundred and thirty years of studying H-HAR technology. Assembled in space, the S-fighters will spend their entire lives there, never entering Earth's atmosphere."

"Able to hit a speck of dust two hundred kilometres away with a laser while moving at over one hundred kilometres per second," McLean said. "It's the most sophisticated weapon ever built by humans."

"And machines!" Tayla added.

"Oh … sorry, Tayla. Built by humans *and* machines. You know what I mean."

"Say, Adam, you might be directing these S-fighters one day as Earth's Defence Supreme Commander against the mothership," Lacasse said, pointing to a photo of Anya and Lochlan on the Moon. "Your great-grandparents would be so proud."

Adam shrugged and hesitantly smiled. "It's a few years off yet, so we'll see."

"Why are there two S-fighter versions, each with different engines?" Lacasse asked.

"Different applications," Tayla said. "Both are nuclear pulse rockets. The original Orion S-fighter is directly propelled by a fission-fusion explosion every 0.8 seconds against a pusher plate. The second type, the HB11 S-fighter, is a later development. It's propelled by fifty mini hydrogen boron-11 fusion explosions every second within an external nozzle.

"The Orion has a higher thrust. At 5 *g*, it can reach one hundred kilometres per second in thirty-five minutes. It's more robust, simpler, and easier to build, but it can't operate within ten thousand kilometres of Earth because it creates radiation belts.

"The HB11 is smaller, lighter, and uses less fuel. At 3 *g*, it can reach one hundred kilometres per second in fifty-five minutes."

Lacasse nodded in appreciation.

"I was present during an early HB11 engine test," McLean said. "It was a powerful rumbling deep underground. For a moment, I feared what would happen if they lost control of it."

"I believe the S-fighters were close to being cancelled several times," Lacasse said.

McLean let out a heavy sigh as his eyes shot upwards. "If the H-HARs didn't stop at Xi Scorpii C, it would have been. That gave us time to redesign and rectify all the problems. It's a shame no human will ever pilot one of these monsters."

"The G-forces are way too high for humans," Lacasse said. "There'd be blood and guts all over the cockpit."

"Yeah, the machines have all the fun," McLean said.

Tayla laughed. "Spending a lifetime alone in space wouldn't be much fun."

"I agree," Lacasse said. "What's the size of these S-fighters anyway? They look about twenty metres long."

"Tayla?" McLean conveyed the question.

"As you know, the ship is a highly tapered cone to expose the smallest possible cross-section to the enemy. The Orion is six metres wide at the base and twenty-six metres long. The pusher plate extends another ten metres at the rear, and retractable radiators extend twenty-five metres from the sides. The total weight is about thirteen hundred tons. The HB11 model is smaller."

Lacasse nodded. "How long would it take to reach Mars from Earth?"

"For Orion, less than a week if in opposition," Tayla answered.

"Wow … that's fast," Lacasse said.

"There'll soon be hundreds of them cruising the solar system," McLean said.

"Some still say missiles or capital ships are better, and we don't need S-fighters," Lacasse commented.

"You can't win a war without an effective long-distance weapon like the S-fighter," McLean said. "Missiles lack sufficient delta-v for continuous dodging. And capital ships, like our orbital space stations, can't dodge at all and require S-fighter protection anyway. The S-fighters can operate far from Earth, haul missile buses, they're good dodgers, and they can carry LaWS. They're our best weapon – an excellent balance between firepower and survivability."

"Fair enough," Lacasse said. "One of the screen images stated that HB11 needed three billion degrees Celsius for thermal fusion! I mean, three billion degrees! Without going into technical details, how do the S-fighters even reach that temperature?"

McLean turned to Tayla's camera and gave a nod.

"Well, they don't," Tayla said in her mellifluous voice. "The fusion ignition is non-thermal. H-HAR laser technology has provided the way."

Lacasse sat speechless with a "please explain" expression.

"Go on, Tayla," McLean said.

"Okay. A zeptosecond, pulsed beam from a high-energy gamma-ray laser strikes a small, highly compressed HB11 fuel pellet, creating localised plasma. The plasma ultra-accelerates to close to light speed due to dielectric forces and impacts with the rest of the solid HB11 fuel pellet. This forces the hydrogen and boron nuclei to micro-fuse. Then the emission of alpha particles from the fusion causes a massive avalanche reaction, which increases the yield by over a billion times.

"The exploding, rapidly expanding plasma is ejected as thrust by a magnetic field in the S-fighter. HB11 doesn't cause radioactivity, and it directly converts into electricity." Tayla paused, its lens focused. "Does that answer your question, Katie?"

"Ahh … pretty much …" Lacasse squeaked, her face perplexed. "But I've got no idea what you're talking about. My mind boggles at the enormity of the energy involved. I'm sure it's a lot more than my toaster, which, by the way, malfunctioned this morning and set my toast on fire."

"Sorry to hear that," McLean said, chuckling.

"I don't understand why lasers have superseded every other weapon. What about the inverse square law, divergence, and all that?"

"It's not the laser beam's heat that causes the damage." Tayla then plunged into a flood of technicalities, which to Lacasse and McLean sounded like an alien language from a distant galaxy. Since Lacasse asked the question, McLean let Tayla continue. "It's the fact that a photon's quantum wave packet was discovered to have a size and shape. By varying these characteristics and helically twisting two slightly out-of-sync beams, the laser quantum tunnels into the electron field of the target, causing the electrons to oscillate resonantly at almost light speed. This exposes the nucleus, which is then directly excited by the laser. The target's surface virtually explodes away. It's a non-thermal, electrodynamic process. At a million kilometres across space, a powerful zeptosecond pulsing gamma-ray laser can penetrate the toughest armour at seven hundred millimetres per second. The beam's intensity does drop off by the inverse square law, but it's negligible except at extremely long distances."

"Right …" Lacasse uttered, looking bewildered.

"When these lasers were first discovered from the Moon-ship," Tayla continued, "physicists wondered whether they should suppress the discovery. But it was too late. The military was already knocking at the door."

"So armour is useless against these lasers?"

"The short answer is yes; whoever is hit first will die."

"How about other weapons?" Lacasse asked.

McLean jumped in hastily. "Well, kinetic energy weapons, missiles, and smart mines can be picked off by sweeping laser beams. Particle weapons have a much shorter range, a longer time lag, take longer to switch directions, and can be deflected by a projected electromagnetic field."

"Ohh-kay. Thanks." Lacasse was somewhat satisfied. "So, what else is happening, Adam?"

"The defence council met last week. They confirmed that our only hope of survival against the mothership rests on our perceived three main advantages."

"Let me guess," Lacasse insisted. She had heard them discussed many times. "Their weapons and equipment may be damaged beyond repair due to their long flight."

"That's one."

"They may not have super-intelligent computers, limiting their weapons' sophistication."

"One to go."

"They may not be aware of our rapid technological advancements in weaponry in the last century."

"That's it," McLean said.

"But overall, the odds are still heavily against us." A small panic fluttered through Lacasse. "Right?"

"Unfortunately, yes. And I'm not sure I should be telling you that. But having done so, would you believe some researchers are actually overconfident?"

"Really? Does that include the HLAIs?"

McLean turned to Tayla's camera. "Tayla?"

Tayla seemed to hesitate – well, not quite. "The egos of these insouciant humans and HLAIs all crash back to Earth when their test ends in a massive ball of flames. And there are still many project failures, even at this late stage."

"Like the nuclear howitzers," McLean said.

"You can't engineer what you don't understand," Tayla replied.

"It showed some promise for a while," McLean added. "Maybe they failed to implement the physics correctly, or they chased the rabbit … ahh, what's that saying, Tayla?"

"Chased the white rabbit down too many wrong holes."

"Thanks, Tayla. Even the HB11 S-fighter still has operational issues. One blew up recently, reason unknown."

"Tell me, Adam." Lacasse's tone was suddenly soft and curious. "Why did the H-HARs on the moon go berserk at the end, whereas on Mars they defended their leader, the Red Baron?"

"We believe the Red Baron held all the other H-HARs' backup entities, and if it were terminated, all backups would be destroyed.

"So, it wasn't out of loyalty. It was just old-fashioned self-interest."

"Yes."

"Katie," McLean looked down and scratched his head. "Do you know anything about a project around Mercury?"

Lacasse's stomach suddenly tightened. She was one of the very few people who did know. It was such a big secret that even acknowledging it gets you a long jail sentence. *How does he know? Maybe he's testing me – no! I can't say anything, no matter what.*

Lacasse shifted nervously in her seat. "Mercury! Uh ... no. Why?" she managed, without lifting her head. Her faltering voice sounded less innocent than she would have liked.

"We've been directed to provide some valuable equipment to a secret project," McLean said, "and I'm sure it's in Mercury's orbit. No one knows anything about it. Or no one's talking about it. But it's big, I can tell you that. It's very big."

"I-I'm afraid I can't help you there," she said, still unable to look up. She rubbed her hands down her legs, certain that her feigned ignorance came across as guilty. *McLean must be staring at me suspiciously. Or maybe Tayla; after all, she's programmed for social cognition.*

"I don't think it's a weapon," McLean said, "because there's no interfacing with our comms integration system. It must be something else. Then again, maybe it's so big it can operate in isolation and doesn't need integration."

Lacasse peeked out from the very corner of her eye through her thin brown hair. McLean was looking elsewhere, seemingly oblivious to her agitation. She breathed a silent sigh of relief, straightened her chair, and flicked the hair from her face. "Adam, is there any major weapon controlled directly by humans?" Her voice sounded normal once again.

"No, all our systems are controlled by computers, many by HLAI."

Lacasse looked into Tayla's camera. "What would we do without you guys, Tayla?"

"May I remind you that I'm only an i6-rating," Tayla said in her usual serene tone. "Not an HLAI."

"Well, you're the smartest i6 machine I've ever seen," Lacasse said, happy to move further away from the Mercury matter. She even managed a grin.

"Thank you, but I think you just know me better than others."

Lacasse continued. "Tell me, Tayla, if we survive the H-HAR mothership, do you think there'll be conflict between humans and machines?"

"That's too big a question for an i6 machine to answer, but I'm sure in the new world there will be a place for everyone, Katie."

There was caution in Tayla's answer. Although capable of providing a better response and programmed to converse honestly, Tayla was also programmed to avoid confrontational conversations.

Lacasse stood up. "I better get going and let you guys do some work." Turning towards the door, she suddenly stopped and spun around with a questioning look. "Oh … what happened last week? This place was in total lockdown for three days."

"There was a strange, inexplicable security breach," McLean said.

Lacasse's eyes widened. She sat back down, engrossed by the prospect of a good mystery story. "Well, go on. Let's hear it." Her tone matched her quizzical expression.

"Last Tuesday night, security cameras picked up a ghostly humanoid figure standing in one of the empty media conference rooms. Seconds later, it vanished and reappeared in one of the open offices, again just standing still. It then vanished completely before the guards arrived. The IR sensors picked it up, but not the laser sensors. Security concluded there must have been something there, but no one has any reasonable explanation apart from a hoax. Rumours circulated about H-HAR spies travelling in higher dimensions. It really worried everybody. Security has since increased. So, let's hope it doesn't happen again."

"That's pretty scary. Hey, I better go. Tayla, can you let Robert Anderson know I'm in the building and on my way? Thanks."

"Done."

"Katie …" McLean appeared unusually tentative, unsure of something. He took a deep breath. "How confident are your engineers about stopping relativistic impact weapons?"

"They're confident about the theory. Even a couple of buckets of sand in front of a RIW projectile is enough to destroy it." Lacasse paused and looked uneasily at McLean, suspecting a motive behind his question. He gave no reaction, so she continued. "But getting the sand in position is the tricky part. Our system places several layers of shrapnel in front of the incoming projectile. The first layer destroys the projectile, and the subsequent layers reduce the explosive boom before it reaches Earth."

McLean remained hushed, even disquieted, gazing into space as he had done earlier.

Lacasse was sure he was withholding something, and this time she was determined to find out. "What's up? Why did you ask me that?"

"Tayla?" McLean asked hesitantly, rubbing his neck awkwardly.

"Katie has sufficient security clearance, sir."

"What's happened? Tell me." Lacasse urged as a worried frown appeared between her arched eyebrows.

"This information is strictly classified," McLean said. "Tayla, do not record this discussion."

"Understood, sir."

Lacasse's hands were clasped at her mouth, waiting tensely, preparing herself for what she might hear.

McLean rested his elbows on the table and leaned towards Lacasse. His voice dropped to a whisper. "Just before the mothership left Xi Scorpii C over thirty years ago, two brief flashes were detected. The spectrum of those flashes was consistent with a relativistic object being fired and, a short time later, hitting a rocky planet at just a jogging pace slower than light."

Lacasse coughed suddenly, as if choking, and her expression turned to dawning horror. "Oh my God ... So that's why the H-HARs stopped at Xi Scorpii C? To test their relativistic weapon?"

"It looks like it," McLean confirmed bleakly.

***

Lacasse, too upset that night to cook dinner, took her two young children to a cafe. With her thoughts elsewhere, she was oblivious to the mess they were making. Discarded food spattered everywhere. A spilled drink trickled over the tabletop, dripping onto the floor. A spare seat was stained with sauce and a mismanaged chocolate dessert. It was only when they were leaving that she noticed the mess. Gazing across the table at her children and then at the many people in the cafe, she thought about all the human souls who would die in this war – probably everyone. Stricken with worry, she gathered up their belongings and struggled to summon enough strength to usher her children out the door.

A robo-waitress picked up a note left on the table. "The table = Earth post mothership." The misshaped lettering gave it a certain finality.

Chapter 59   Project Noah – Mercury

Project Noah was a desperate attempt to preserve Terra's legacy. It was the most secretive of all preparations for the mothership's arrival.

It involved the genome sequencing of the world's twelve million species, cryopreserving early-stage embryos of all life, including humans, and storing humanity's entire digital libraries. The Endeavour, an interstellar, robotic starship, will carry this precious cargo away from the solar system to a new world. The Endeavour had no life support system, as humans could not travel beyond the solar system.

At its conception, other options were considered. One was to hide a spaceship with survival capsules somewhere in the solar system until the H-HARs left. But what if they didn't leave or stayed for millions of years? The solar system may be vast, but it's not vast enough. If the H-HARs suspected survivors, they would search everywhere. How would we know they were gone? And what would be left? Earth would be uninhabitable. No, the best option was to sneak out of the solar system altogether and hide as far away as possible.

After seventy-six years of planning, designing, and building, the Endeavour waited for the final countdown. It carried hundreds of humanoid robots, thirty per cent of which were conscious HLAIs. Almost all would be dormant during the journey and only activated when required.

The Endeavour would be remotely propelled by a laser-coupled particle beam, formed by inserting neutrons into a laser beam. The neutrons, propelled to ninety per cent of light speed, would separate into protons and electrons and act as a laser anti-diverging waveguide. In turn, the laser's electric fields would constrain the particles' spread.

The laser would consist of ten separate beams, cohesively combined by ten mirrors at the redirector station orbiting Mercury's L2 Lagrange point. Each mirror would cohesively combine 113 solar-pumped lasers, located in Sun-synchronous orbit near Mercury. Each solar-pumped laser would be powered by a thirty-seven-kilometre-diameter collecting reflector, producing 1.86 terawatts.

The laser-coupled particle beam would illuminate the Endeavour's twenty-eight-kilometre-diameter, ultrathin sail, producing continuous thrust along a straight line towards its destination. There was no engine on the Endeavour. The beam propulsion had no detectable radiation or heat signature.

Bow shock plasma radiation would be almost undetectable due to the Endeavour moving away from the solar system at a lower than threshold velocity.

Afterwards, the lasers would be modified and weaponised for the battle against the mothership.

****

Thirty-one minutes! Shit, I better get going. Jess Mackenzie, in her EDO uniform, raced towards the door. A small birthday card printout wedged into the top corner of a mirror stopped her. "We don't know where you are, but to our dear daughter on your 33rd birthday." Her face softened. In the other corner was an old photo. *There's Mum, Grandma, and me, only nine years old, all smiling.* She looked closer, gently touching it. *Grandma looks so proud wearing her Mum's bravery medal.* A sentimental tear blurred her vision as she fingered that very same medallion, now around her neck. *What would Great-Grandma, the famous Anya McLean, think about all this?* Jess took a deep breath and smiled at the thought. Her eyes moved to another corner, another old photo. A man in a uniform. *And what would Great-Grandpa, President Andrew Mackenzie, think? I wonder if I'll ever see an H-HAR like they did.* She took another deep breath before rushing off.

She passed an equipment storage area, now empty. *Everything's so strangely quiet now. All the hectic round-the-clock work is finished. All the giant assembly machines are gone. Only a few small, non-anthropoid robots are left. The thousands of humans and HLAI robots, gone; back to Earth for a well-earned rest. I can still hear the perpetual purring sound of the reactor, a little reminder of what this place used to be like.*

Jess, an electrical engineer, joined her colleagues in the Depot-2 observation room, where there was a party-like atmosphere. Depot-2 floated in space above Mercury, permanently shielded from the Sun's rays by the planet's shadow.

Finding a gap through the wall of heads, Jess reached up on her toes to see the tiny dot out of the large observatory window. *Nah, it's too tiny.* She moved to one of the monitors and watched with childlike wonder at the magnified image through a telescopic camera. The starship looked microscopic compared to its huge sail.

Jess's transport would be departing for Earth in nineteen hours, making her one of the lucky few to witness the launch of the Endeavour. *A nice ending to a project I've worked on for eight years, the last nineteen months on Depot-2.*

Through the secrecy, there were many stories about Endeavour's mission. The frozen embryos were selected based on race, parental medical history, and generic characteristics that maximised survival and contribution to the new colony. All were genetically modified, some with a forty-seventh chromosome to give specific benefits. She wondered what unintentional consequences this would have.

A colleague told her, "They'll start killing each other, and the last one will commit suicide."

There were concerns about the performance and reliability of everything. Especially the computer systems and the HLAI robots. What would be the effects of long-term cosmic radiation, undetected software defects, and interaction conflicts?

A lot of the technology remained a mystery. The starship's two-centimetre thick ablation shields, equivalent to two metres of titanium, were copied directly from the H-HAR spaceships without fully understanding how they worked.

Everyone chatted softly. The countdown timer showed 22:53 minutes to launch.

"I was like a fish out of water," she remembered telling a new arrival. "The food's lousy, the rules are strict, the living quarters are small, and most of all, the work is dangerous. Good luck with the 2 g gravitron ring. Everyone hates it. It gave me vertigo for six months, which was much worse than any side effects from the pharmacologically altered medication. But you'll learn."

She remembered the GM humans and the HLAI robots. *I felt sorry for them. Personality problems, terrible social lives, no or extreme egos, mysterious health issues, lack of conscious sympathies, and lots of other things. They were very intimidating. Some simply couldn't figure out human behaviour at all.*

Jess checked the time: 20:43 minutes to launch.

She returned to her thoughts. *I would never have forgiven myself if I hadn't entered that empty fuel vessel.* She shivered, recalling the haunting incident. *It was clear from their emergency transmissions that they were dying, all eighteen of them. The emergency rescue drones were minutes away; I was closer. Acid from the leaky hose was everywhere. After pushing some workers towards the exit, I remember seeing holes in my suit and gasping for air. My last conscious thought was desperation.*

Jess clearly remembered her stressed-out manager. "The book states I should throw you into jail for disobeying the rules, but you saved eight lives, and getting your replacement out here is impossible. So, for the time being, I'm going to just ignore this."

Jess glanced at the clock: 17:24 minutes to launch.

Her eyes drifted back to the window, outside, to the vastness of space. It reminded her that the mothership was now well within the Oort Cloud. The timer showed: 15:04 minutes to launch.

Excitement was building. People were grinning, chattering, bumping shoulders, and bouncing up and down.

Jess thought about that lonely spider she found in the low-voltage switchroom of her transport just after leaving Earth. *That little stowaway made a five-metre web connection between two walls. How did it do that? The next day, it added a perpendicular connection. It must've known something about zero gravity because those three connections supported the largest web I've ever seen.*

She looked up: 12:41 minutes to go.

Poor little spider, it lay in wait at the centre of its web for prey. But there wasn't any. I even tried to feed it, sort of like a pet, and moved it to a jar when its web was destroyed. It died five days later. I remember crying, and a crew member looked at me bewilderedly, "It's … it's only an insect, Jess."

Jess looked at the clock: 9:16 minutes.

Was coming out here worth all the sacrifices? Yes, of course it was. Working with thousands of scientists, engineers, and machines, all with a common goal, was the experience of a lifetime. I'm proud I was part of it, proud I made a valuable contribution. She placed a hand over Anya's bravery medallion on her chest and lifted it to see it, giving a gratified smile. *I only hope I have lived up to the expectations on both sides of my family.*

An undercurrent of nervous murmuring replaced the soft chatter as people repositioned themselves around the observatory window or a telescopic monitor.

A large, shadowy object suddenly appeared outside the window. The murmuring stopped, and the room fell nervously silent. A few anxious seconds passed before a relieved voice cried out, "It's the space fighter." Jess then remembered a notification to expect a visiting Orion S-fighter on a routine shakedown cruise for the launch. The room erupted in a rousing cheer.

The S-fighter slowly rotated. A series of blinking lights with a peculiar rhythm sent strange, coloured reflections across the observation deck. These disappeared, and everyone watched in awe as faint lights on the S-fighter cast an outline of its tapered cylindrical shape. All eyes turned away as a blinding spotlight slid over them. This also disappeared, leaving only the S-fighter's shadowy void image across the stars.

The S-fighter drifted off into darkness. Attention shifted back to the Endeavour, a sudden hush indicating everyone's growing anticipation.

Jess threaded her way across the crowded observation deck to a small window for another look at the departing S-fighter. Its Orion nuclear pulse drive, with its pusher plate and shock absorbers, was visible. Its auxiliary rockets still glowed red-hot, and its magazines were half loaded with chargers.

It's just fantastic. The only mobile warship built for the battle with the mothership. I wonder what part it will play.

She was astounded that this beautiful, intelligent war machine could fly all the way from Earth, do its thing, and decide on its own when to fly back. *It'll return to Earth in a fraction of the time it takes us in the transports.*

To Jess, the S-fighter put everything into perspective. *As huge as Project Noah was, it was just one of many undertaken for the upcoming war. Each with their own stories of sacrifices, tragedies, relationships, failures, and achievements.*

She took one last look at the deadliest machine Earth had ever built, then glanced at the clock: 0:18 minutes to go.

She raced back to the monitor just as one laser array fired up. Three minutes later, with the Endeavour still motionless, worried faces appeared. More and more minutes passed and still no movement. Jess held her breath, praying. *Did we align the mirrors correctly?* She closed her eyes and listened to the tense silence.

Moments later, loud sighs of relief opened her eyes. The sleek and mighty starship was moving off with no apparent urgency – the start of a long and lonely journey. Smiling triumphantly with her friends, she burst into tears, overwhelmed as her fists pumped the air. The crowd cheered and celebrated as more and more lasers came online, giving the Endeavour greater acceleration.

A ray of sunlight caught the starship and reflected like a prism, giving the impression of a spectral glow from within. A smile curled Jess's lips at the eerie sight.

She watched, somewhat longingly, as the Endeavour steadily gained speed. Not unlike watching a plane take off to a faraway destination and wondering what adventures await its passengers.

Would I prefer my fate to be with the Endeavour rather than Earth? Both have little chance. Even if things work out for the Endeavour, growing up on an alien planet with only machines to raise you and surrounded by super smart, competing humans and robots wouldn't be much fun. There're simply too many things likely to go wrong, too much uncertainty. It might be argued, and indeed it was, that it was doomed to fail from the very start.

No, I'll take my chances on Earth.

Jess watched as the Endeavour slowly shrank to a distant speck and disappeared forever, lost in the silence and endlessness of space among billions of stars. She smiled optimistically through her reminiscent tears. "That's it," she whispered to herself. "They're on their own. God help them, and God help us."

The laser-coupled particle beam would be switched off twenty-six months after launch, giving the Endeavour starship a final, weakened push four months later. By then, the mothership would be near Sedna's aphelion orbit in the outer solar system. The Endeavour should be well and truly on its way, hopefully unnoticed, coasting at more than a light-year every four years.

Endeavour's destination was Tau Ceti, a main sequence, yellow-orange dwarf star. Smaller and dimmer than the Sun, it was 11.8 light-years from Earth, a 46.5 year journey for the Endeavour. Of the nearby stars, Tau Ceti was the best hope for finding a suitable exoplanet. The most promising was Tau Ceti k, an exoplanet located in the habitable zone, meaning it could support liquid surface water. Its minimum size is 1.5 Earth masses, with an orbital period of 430 days.

As the Endeavour approaches Tau Ceti, its exoplanets' long-term habitability would be determined – surface structure, water or ice, plate tectonics, meteor level, atmosphere, stable orbit, minerals, energy sources, magnetic field, underground caverns, and so on.

If a suitable planet were found – a paradise like Mars would be the best that could be hoped for – then a risky deceleration procedure would be initiated. The spaceship and its solar sail would rotate 180°, the new orientation causing deceleration due to solar pressure from the star. A small fission reactor, kept warm by powering the ship's base load during the journey, would ramp up to provide an electrical current along the sail's perimeter, generating a magnetic field opposing Tau Ceti's magnetic plasma wind, causing further deceleration.

Small, undetectable 0.03 kiloton nuclear fission explosives in front of the Endeavour's sails would also assist with deceleration.

The Endeavour, however, could never be slowed sufficiently for planetary or solar orbit. The robot crew would have one hundred hours to disembark before it sped off into interstellar space, carrying no evidence of its origin. The crew, with its valuable cargo, would leave the Endeavour in several descending rockets to the planet's surface, using fuel stored as metallic hydrogen.

After landing, temporary settlement structures would be inflated and covered with a thick layer of dirt for radiation protection. The bottom of a large, deep crater would be the best site.

Semi-permanent, self-sufficient eco-environments would be erected before embryos could be defrosted and placed in an artificial uterus. Initially, supplies from the Endeavour would be used, but eventually the multipurpose robots would need local resources for survival.

The first baby humans would be fed, raised, educated, cultured, and socialised by their guardian robots based on ethics such as respect, responsibility, morality, equality, and non-violence to form a cohesive, progressive colony. Whether this would forestall conflicts, prevent cults, or develop workable social dynamics was too difficult to consider.

In the long-term, underground cities providing effective protection from cosmic radiation would house tens of thousands of plants, humans, and animals.

If a habitable planet were not found around Tau Ceti, there would be no disembarking. The crew would remain on the Endeavour, indefinitely hopping from star to star, travelling farther and farther from Earth until a suitable planet could be found. It would navigate by triangulation of recognisable distant quasars and features of the cosmic microwave background. Small directional changes could be made at each star by gravitational slinging or tacking against solar pressure and the magnetic plasma wind.

Although strict radio silence would be maintained to prevent detection by the H-HAR mothership, the Endeavour would receive one-way communications from Earth via modulation of the propulsion laser beam. If the war against the mothership was won, Earth would send a victorious message to the Endeavour and ask for its status and location. If disembarking occurred at Tau Ceti, reuniting with Mother Earth in the not-too-distant future could be possible. However, if the crew were forced to fly-by Tau Ceti to a more remote star, a possible reunion would be a very distant prospect, if at all.

Meanwhile on Earth, networks of caves capable of holding hundreds of thousands of people have been dug out of mountain sides. All provided with enough seedlings, plants, animals, water, and frozen food for many years of isolation.

Many groups or societies constructed their own refuges. Most intended to stay home in family underground shelters. The rest had no plans and simply intended to "head for the hills".

Governments provided information on growing food, purifying water, health, and other survival information. However, most understood that the H-HARs, after they were finished with Earth, would not even allow bacteria to survive.

***

Also on Earth: A newborn baby opened her eyes to the world for the first time. A snowflake was caught by an imperceptible breeze. The same breeze carried away a seed, spreading new life. A night frog croaked in a reservoir. Others joined in, starting a nightingale's lullaby. Bees incessantly rumbled around their hive. A grasshopper, with its black, lifeless eyes and long, spindly legs, leaped high and long into the air, into the unknown, to evade a predator.

PART 8

MOTHERSHIP

"Up there in space, a war of annihilation is about to start."

Chapter 60   Arrival

A micro-optical telescope floated in space somewhere beyond Saturn. Its relentless and infinite patience gave the impression that whatever it was looking for, it would eventually find it. Its lens suddenly blurred in and out of focus on a faint and glowing glint in the distance. Two Earthbound operators anxiously watched the stream from the telescope's ultra-high-speed cameras. In less than a second, the glint elongated and blipped past.

"We got it!" cried out one operator, almost tripping over as he leaped out of his chair. "Let's enhance it and see."

***

General Adam McLean pushed against the balcony with both hands as he looked deep into the night sky. The stars were amazing tonight, but his thoughts were elsewhere.

What are the H-HARs planning? Do these creatures have other weapons besides the RIW they tested at Xi Scorpii C? *What messages did they receive from their earlier spaceships?*

He didn't know.

But what he did know, as the former head of the weapons testing program, was that Earth was as prepared as it could possibly be for their arrival. Maybe, just maybe, Earth had a fighting chance in its greatest confrontation of all time.

This coming war of extinction extended beyond humanity. It included the entire Earth itself – its formation and genesis; the first single-cell life; photosynthetic, oxygen-producing bacteria; multicellular life; the animals and plants; and the HLAIs. All have, in a sense, contributed to defending the planet.

The H-HARs – Hostile Humanoid Alien Robots. The very name made Adam shudder in horror. A name the world has learned to dread and fear ever since their discovery on Pallas by his great-grandparents, Anya and Lochlan McLean, 120 years earlier.

He fingered Lochlan's bravery medallion that hung around his neck. "It's one per cent political," his dad, Justin McLean, told him. "I wear it everywhere for the other ninety-nine per cent which was sheer courage." A cousin, Jess Mackenzie, carried Anya Connell-McLean's medallion.

The thought of Dad moistened his eyes. Even after forty years, those chilling last memories were still too painful to recall.

He was eleven years old and on an adventurous sea journey with his dad – a week on a local cargo boat, visiting several Pacific islands. One night, they were wrestling on the bed, heard panicked shouting in Filipino, and rushed outside. Crewmen raced past, pirates were boarding, pandemonium everywhere, gunfire, then a huge explosion. All the lights went out.

"We have to get off this boat; it's sinking!" Justin said, his face wrought with fatherly worry.

The pirates fled. And so did the crewmen, their overcrowded lifeboat disappearing into the ghostly, moonlit darkness, refusing to let Justin and Adam board. Justin looked around, distraught. Nothing useful except an empty ice box, two metres square by one and a half metres deep, used to store fish. Justin slid it into the choppy ocean with Adam in it. He looked around again, a bucket with a two-metre rope. He grabbed it and tried to scramble back towards Adam. But the enormous force of rushing water over the bulkheads overwhelmed him. He climbed high onto a railing and jumped into the box just as the boat sank.

The box was too small for both of them and highly unstable. Adam watched his dad skilfully balance his weight to keep it upright. "You'll have to stay low," Justin said, eyes filled with fear, his grandfather's bravery medallion around his neck glowing in the moonlight. A huge wave exploded over them, surging water everywhere, washing out Adam. Justin pulled him back. They used the bucket to bail out the water. Then another wave crashed over, and another, frothy waves banging them against the sides, tossing the tiny box. Adam's heart pounded, acutely aware of the horrors facing them.

The box rolled, spun, and flooded as more waves crashed over it. Justin studied each wave, predicting its impact and shifting his weight to stabilise the box. It was exhausting.

An object washed in, a dead body, still bleeding from a gunshot wound. They pushed it out and watched as it floated off, half submerged.

Days passed. They were attacked at night by jellyfish washing into the box. The lacerations were still visible on Adam's body. Sharks bumped against the box at night, their fins knifing through the waves.

More days passed. The little ice box drifted on, rocking side to side, bobbing up and down in the huge ocean waves like a piece of foam.

Adam tried hard to relieve his dad from the bailing, determined to imitate his resolve and courage. But his muscles were weakening, his stomach twisting in pain, and his seasickness was getting worse. Drinking was all he could think of. Justin stopped and cautioned him several times about drinking seawater.

Justin scraped off the old moss growing inside the box and gathered the few remaining rotten fish swirling around the box's bottom, giving them to Adam. Adam, too hungry to care, swallowed eyeballs, brains, intestines, and everything else. Rainwater was collected in the bucket. Justin refused to eat or drink anything himself. There were flashes of silver under the ocean surface, as fish darted around the box, but they couldn't grab them. They tried using the bucket, but nothing worked.

In between bailing, Justin took Adam in his arms, holding him close, keeping him warm. Adam remembered peering over his dad's shoulder, the towering ocean swell rising like a green mountain, up and up, blocking the sky, lifting them high, then suddenly dropping them.

After six days, exhaustion, exposure, starvation, thirst, and sickness made their situation desperate. They became slow, weak, and clumsy.

A huge storm appeared on the horizon. A lightning flash revealed Justin's tormented face just as his arm tightened around his son. "Adam," he said, looking him in the eye, "you understand that some water always needs to be in this box for ballast, and the bucket always has to be tied onto the rope?"

Their eyes grimly locked until Justin turned away, watching for the next wave.

"Yeah," Adam answered, worried about the question. He took hold of his dad's unshaven chin, turning his pained face back towards him. "But you'll always be here."

Justin didn't answer. He just gave his son the most heartbreaking smile. A smile that acknowledged their predicament but with as much hope as possible. He pulled Adam close and hugged him fiercely before turning back to the sea, watching for the next wave. Adam fell asleep in his arms.

A violent shudder and a cold wash soon woke him. He turned everywhere. "Dad? Dad?" Even inside the box, it was hard to see in the darkness and windswept sheets of rain. He jumped up frantically, peering out into the blackness, almost tipping the box. "Dad? Dad?" he shouted. But Dad wasn't there – only waves in an endless sea.

His face registered incomprehension. "Dad, where are you?" he furiously yelled into the emptiness. "Dad, where are you?"

He sat in the corner of the box, utterly alone and helpless, watching the storm build up. Still confused, he quietly murmured, "Dad, you've abandoned me. How could you?"

He dropped his head and saw that Lochlan's medallion had been placed around his neck. He then realised the awful truth. *Dad sacrificed himself so I could survive. He must have loved me so much.* He cried despairingly, uncontrollably. The first and only time during the ordeal. "I'm sorry I doubted you, Dad," he sobbed, rain mixing with his tears. "You know I didn't mean it." He turned into the darkness and shouted as loudly and as fiercely as he could, "Dad. I love you … If you can hear me, I love you, Dad. I will make it. I promise you, I will make it."

He wiped his eyes and turned to face the storm. The howling wind and slamming waves terrified him. As he reached for the bucket, a giant wave spun the box, knocking him overboard. He gasped for air but took in only a mouthful of water. He grabbed for the box's edge but missed, his eyes showing his desperation. Another wave broke high above him, drenching him with water. He again gasped for air, but again only a mouthful of water. His hand reached for the box but slipped off. Getting weaker. Another mouthful of water, his lungs started to fill. Another giant wave rose, about to wash him farther away. The rain was so thick that the box was difficult to see. Heaving up salt water and sobbing as he choked for air, he made one last wild grab for the box – his last chance. A jagged metal bracket caught his hand, slashing it but allowing him to get a hold and pull himself back into the box. Coughing uncontrollably, he took the deepest breath of air his lungs could take.

There was no time to rest. He bailed between the relentless crashing waves, remembering to keep enough water for ballast. But a large wave flooded the box, and it started sinking. Its edges were barely visible above the ocean. Adam worked harder, faster, willing himself to be stronger, frantically balancing his weight while bailing. His face tightened with determination as he desperately watched every wave, just like his dad. The box stayed afloat but only barely.

The storm grew fiercer. Icy winds whipped up the sea, stinging his face and turning him blue. Huge lightning bolts split the black sky. One just missed him, standing his hair on end. The crashing lightning bolt and deafening thunder knocked him backwards. He paused for breath and stared into the eternal darkness, expecting the next bolt to strike him. The lightning moved away, but the storm raged on. Adam continued bailing, more desperate than ever, but the box kept filling. Finally, he collapsed in a corner, exhausted and shivering. His hands were raw and blistered. He kicked away the bucket and quit. "It's all too much. I can't go on," he yelled as a huge wave surged over him. The box started sinking. Another wave would do it.

He thought about his dad, and his determination returned. He got up and threw his head back. "Dad, I will survive!" he yelled, clutching Lochlan's precious medallion in one hand and the bailing bucket in the other. "I will keep my promise."

Two hours later, the storm eased, allowing Adam to lower the box's water level. He collapsed in a corner, at last getting some protection from the chilly wind.

Sunrise lit a hazy sky. Adam roused himself and looked out at a subdued horizon and calm sea. But the deep ocean swell still persisted, threatening like restrained anger. The Sun was coming up strong and hot. There was nothing else to see. He flopped back down, his head swaying with the rise and fall of the ocean, his energy still sapped.

That night, Adam, sitting in a corner and feeling the weight of his isolation, glazed skywards. *The stars are so indifferent. I don't recognise anything. Am I drifting south? North? Dad would know. I miss him so much.* A shower of meteors streaked across the sky. He dragged himself to his knees. A full moon backlit a single thin cloud, reflecting on a calm, inky ocean. Even the swell had quietened.

Two storms later, a Japanese fishing vessel spotted his box bobbing in a calm ocean. Half his weight, dehydrated, raw and blistered from the unmerciful Sun, an infected hand, sores, and delirious, he wouldn't have lasted another day. But the stare from his puffy eyes suggested something different – an intense will to survive against all odds. And from a boy who only six days earlier cried so helplessly after his father's disappearance.

The cargo boat's thirteen crew members were never heard from again.

Dad's love, judgement, courage, and pragmatism saved me. A lesson I will never forget. He was my true hero.

"General," a quiet voice from behind broke his thoughts. "They need you in the war room immediately, sir."

It was 03:00 local time. The war room doors swung open, and General Adam McLean, Earth Defence Supreme Commander, entered. The room was the hub of Earth's defence against the H-HAR mothership. Located deep underground, it was the central part of a fully self-contained compound with hundreds of humans and robots. The only entry or exit point was along a one-kilometre-long ramp sealed by a blast door.

The room hummed with tense activity. A large wall screen at the front dominated the room's circular layout. The command desk was on a raised dais at the rear. A dozen human and robot personnel were busy at their workstations, facing inward. Two armed humans and two CARs stood guard at the door.

Also present in the war room was IDAS, the Integrated Defence Advisory System. A military strategic and tactical, globally networked, BHLAI-conscious computer. IDAS was created to resolve the growing friction between humans and machines in the military chain of command. The humans were worried about the lack of real-life combat experience of the machines, their growing dependence on them, and the machines' increasing demands and defiance. The machines resented humans limiting their authority.

An uneasy settlement gave a human the position of Supreme Commander and officially the final decision on any action. However, the machines, represented by IDAS, had equal involvement in the decision process. At least in theory.

The unflappable IDAS was not good at relationships, small talk, or emotions, and it didn't make obvious mistakes. It never learned primary colours, considering it unnecessary for its role. IDAS had an unusual acceptance of its mortality. "Death doesn't scare me," it once said. "I've been there before. It's the place before I was energised." A hologram hovering just off the floor to the right of the command desk served as its visual human interface, or avatar.

The avatar resembled a thin man in his early thirties with short hair, an emotionless look with hypnotic eyes, and a relaxed manner. It wore well-fitted, dark pants, a collared shirt with rolled-up sleeves, and a slightly lighter vest. IDAS considered this the most convenient modality for a workable relationship with humans.

"Good morning everyone. I believe we have a situation here?" McLean said, his calmness contrasting with the tense atmosphere in the room. "Ric, can you brief me, please?"

Colonel Ric Amess, a 24-hour, 365-day HLAI humanoid robot, was head of military operations.

"Sir, as you're aware, the H-HAR mothership entered the Outer Oort Cloud nine years ago, where it started decelerating to prevent collision damage. It entered the very edge of our solar system three years ago, just above the planetary disc, where it decelerated further."

"I know all that, Ric. Cut to the chase."

"Well, sir, six hours ago, one of our distant micro-optical telescopes beyond Jupiter recorded the first detailed images of the mothership. And the news is not good. IDAS may be able to summarise the report?"

"Yes, colonel." IDAS's humanised avatar mouthed the words flawlessly. "The images show the mothership is a hollowed-out metallic asteroid, 3.2 kilometres long and 0.59 kilometres in diameter. Composition is almost pure iron with traces of nickel. Its cohesion suggests it was extracted from the metallic core of a much larger parent body. The reddish surface is devoid of large features, indicating the removal of all major shape irregularities from the original asteroid. Surface excavation markings are visible.

"Calculations indicate that about seventy per cent of the asteroid has been hollowed out, with caverns likely interconnected by tunnels. Major welding and structural reinforcements are evident, probably to ensure cohesiveness during heavy acceleration. No localised thermal stress detected.

"There's a magnetic propulsion nozzle at the rear, and the front has been streamlined and slanted. It is surrounded by several small, circulating drones.

"A fifteen-metre diameter internal cavity exits at the front. Intel is almost certain this cavity runs down the centre of the long axis of the ship and that it's a forward-pointing relativistic gun, similar to the Moon RIW. More than capable of destroying Earth's ecosystem, sir."

"That confirms what we've suspected since Xi Scorpii C," McLean said, in a tone that would have chilled a blast furnace. "They've come with their own doomsday weapon."

"It also confirms we have to stop them before they get within range of Earth," Colonel Nathan Martin, a natural human from the defence weapons group, bluntly reminded everyone.

"There's more, sir," IDAS said. "A one hundred-metre, retractable, external structure suggests a coupling with another mothership of the same size. There are three additional holding brackets, which were probably the fixings for the Moon-ship and the two Pallas ships. That's all, sir."

"Shit!" Martin exclaimed despairingly. "There's another mothership!"

"Let's just stay focused on the one at our doorstep," McLean said.

"General," Colonel Amess said, "there's another reason we called you here." His tone, as usual, was calm and controlled. "The mothership has just passed six AU from the Sun, heading directly for Earth. It's travelling at eleven hundred kilometres per second and showing no sign of deceleration, in defiance of our request to stop. Our strategy of not allowing the mothership to pass the two AU mark, just outside the Martian orbit, is under threat. Subsequently, I've ordered our defences to be on code one – imminent launch status. We've warned the mothership of our intended actions to stop it. As of two hours ago, there had been no acknowledgement. General, you are authorised by the UN defence charter to launch these defensive measures. The decision lies with you."

McLean nodded, then turned to IDAS's avatar. "IDAS, recommendation?"

"General." The avatar rotated to face McLean, showing no emotion. "We have no choice. We have to stop it. First with passive obstacles, and if that fails, with our active weapons."

General McLean turned to Colonel Martin. "Nathan?"

"Our passive shrapnel cloud will take three days to position, sir. By then, the mothership will be at four AU. The cloud will be at a sufficient distance to allow the mothership to gently decelerate to a virtual stop outside of the two AU danger zone. Our active weapons are ready to be launched if the mothership doesn't stop."

"So, Nathan, you concur with IDAS's recommendation?"

"Yes, general."

"Ric, are we absolutely certain they've received our radio messages and warnings? Or are we about to provoke an advanced, heavily armed alien battle-star that doesn't understand what we're asking and may retaliate?"

"Without a doubt, sir, in their language and across all modulations and frequencies. We're convinced the H-HARs have received and interpreted all of our messages and warnings."

"And you're confident our actions will force the mothership to stop?"

"Well," Amess cleared his speaker, "with their radiators retracted, we simply don't know what that hollowed-out asteroid mothership can do. But I'm still betting it won't try to plough through tons of shrapnel at over one thousand kilometres per second. So, when it stops, we have to consider what happens next."

McLean slowly turned with a questioning look to IDAS's rootless avatar. "And what would happen next, IDAS?"

"The H-HARs may attempt to manoeuvre around the blocking mass and approach Earth from a different angle. In that case, the mass will move with it and continue to impede its advancement. Or they may start firing something at us, or try to feign something, or proceed at a slower speed, or just sit there and wait us out."

"Or something unexpected," McLean added.

"Yes, I suspect you're correct, general," IDAS said.

"Nathan, if the H-HAR mothership inches its way through the shrapnel or does something unexpected, can you assure me our active weapons will stop it?"

"To be frank, general, no, I can't. The outcome of any encounter with the mothership is unknown."

"Okay, understood." A drawn expression appeared on McLean's face. "This is the decision I will make and subsequently advise the EDO War Council. 'Despite our warnings, the H-HAR mothership continues to approach Earth. We are launching our passive defence to stop it. The use of active defences will depend entirely on the mothership's reaction.'"

McLean glanced at the bleak expressions around the room. Even IDAS's avatar looked bothered, at least as far as McLean could tell. Everyone knew what this decision meant – nothing short of a declaration of war against an advanced alien race.

McLean took a breath, concerns racing through his mind. "IDAS, Colonel Amess, Colonel Martin, and everybody in this room, you have my approval to launch all passive weapons to stop this H-HAR mothership. Let's hope Earth survives the next week."

*****

Two days later, a series of shrapnel explosions had expanded into a thick blocking cloud between the mothership and Earth. As days passed, it seemed the mothership would attempt the inconceivable and crash through it. As more days passed, the alarm grew. Then, at long last, a strong engine deceleration glow was detected.

"Thank God!" McLean said with a relieved smile. "That's one hell of a relief."

Martin, Amess, and the others exchanged grins. The war room broke into a bout of cheering, UN flag waving, handshaking, and shoulder clapping.

"At least we know they're governed by the same physics laws as ourselves," IDAS said.

The revelry continued for a short while before McLean ordered everyone back to their workstations. "We've got data feeds coming in, and we need to be on guard for the mothership's next move."

The mothership stopped just above the asteroid belt, 2.1 AU from the Sun. General McLean wondered whether even this distance was sufficiently safe from its RIW, but he had to assume it was.

"Send out the welcome drone before they get trigger happy," McLean ordered.

The welcome drone stopped, 133 kilometres from the mothership, and flashed coloured lights in a welcoming pattern. It broadcast a message on all radio frequencies in the H-HAR language:

"We are peaceful. You are welcome. Please respond. We are peaceful. You are welcome. Please respond."

"Expect the unexpected," warned a suspicious McLean, anticipating the drone to be blown up at any moment.

Four hours later, IDAS announced, "We have a response, general. A small H-HAR drone is approaching."

Everyone turned to face the large wall screen.

"Switch those damn flashing drone lights off," General McLean said. "They're getting to be annoying."

The drones faced each other across five metres of space. A cylindrical Earth rocket with attached lights versus a spherical, silver alien craft. Both with similar dimensions – four metres. After two hours, the H-HAR drone slowly turned and floated back to its mothership.

"Was it something we said?" Colonel Amess asked. It would have been taken as a joke had it come from anyone else.

"That wasn't too threatening," Colonel Martin said.

"They're just checking us out, searching for weaknesses," General McLean said, still suspicious.

Two hours later, the mothership flashed the same pattern of lights from a large opening on its side.

"They're inviting us in," Colonel Amess said.

"Or summoning us to dictate their surrender terms." McLean turned to the avatar, who had been surprisingly quiet. "IDAS, options?"

"Do nothing or accept their invitation, general."

"Recommendation?"

"Time we got acquainted, general."

"I agree. I'll talk to Mars. I'm sure there's someone there who has an ambition to meet these H-HARs. They may even have a diplomat who knows how to be tactful."

Chapter 61   Larry

Larry, a plumber, dropped his beer can on the floor after hearing the news, or, as he believed, the government's version of it. His perceived fate was reflected in his doomed expression.

"Did ya hear that? They're here!" he bellowed despairingly. "C'mon, get the bags and be ready to leave when I get back. Anything you leave you won't see again."

"Where're ya goin' now?" his wife, Kathy, asked.

But Larry was a freight train as he burst through the house on the edge of panic. He returned with a trailer full of fuel, batteries, and long-life food. Kathy, looking puzzled, asked, "Are ya sure this is not just your wild imagination or one too many shots of honey bourbon?"

"Yes, I am … I mean, no, it's not. We have to get out of here." He tossed camping bags onto the trailer. "The alien machines will attack the cities first, and all those silly shelters won't help."

"But the government is saying *be calm*, and don't you think—"

"I'm over thinking things, and for heaven's sake, woman, don't argue. Don't take any notice of them bullshitting politicians. Of course they'd say that, they're all full of shit. They're already inside their taxpayer-funded bombproof hideouts."

"No one else is leaving," Kathy said.

"Don't worry about them. The jungle always comes down to two monkeys and one banana. Grab the kids and hop in."

After a quick inventory check – tent, food, maps, dog, guns, water – Larry, Kathy, and their two young kids headed out of the city for the hills. Larry switched the autopilot to manual override and turned towards the highway.

As they turned onto the on-ramp, Larry sighed with fatalistic acceptance. "Hah! See? What'd I tell ya! Look at this damn traffic!"

"Could just be heavy Friday afternoon traffic."

Kathy turned on the radio: "H-HAR mothership has stopped just beyond Martian orbit. The situation is highly volatile; a delegation is to be sent as soon as possible. Avoid travel, stay home, listen to updates, and be familiar with government survival procedures."

"It must be serious, because they're all lying," Larry said.

Kathy switched to another radio channel: "Our end is here. Can you look at yourself in the mirror and be proud of what you have achieved?"

"Turn that damn radio off," Larry said. He ran a shaky hand through his hair and glanced around in frustration, panic growing in his eyes. The kids were fighting, the dog was barking, and his wife was complaining. Unable to suppress his paranoia any longer, Larry spun the car into a lightning-fast three point turn and roared down a rat run through side streets.

They passed a grocery store. "Jesus Christ!" Larry said. "The chaos has started, and it's gonna get worse."

Hooded looters carrying food and alcohol were running through the car park. A few bystanders yelled abuse at them but stayed well out of their way.

"We better be outta here before the LEARs turn up." Larry said. "They're absolutely ruthless."

Driving manically, he smashed through a fence, followed a flood channel, cut across a paddock, bounced down an overgrown mountain track, and crossed a swollen stream into the parched hills.

Kathy flicked quick, worried looks at him, staying quiet to not stress him further. Finally, she asked, "Any idea where we're going?"

"Doesn't matter, we made it," he answered. He cocked an eye at the rear-vision mirror. "Kids, keep an eye out the back window. The city could go up in smoke at any moment."

Chapter 62   Dr Tian

As Dr Tian parked his car outside his small unit in Beijing, three large men in black uniforms moved in.

One pointed his phone camera at Tian and waited for a positive FaceID. "Are you Yan Tian, head surgeon at the Chinese Medicine Hospital?"

Silence.

"I'll ask you again: are you Yan Tian?"

Tian held back, looking casually at the men surrounding him. He didn't want to show his fear.

"Yes."

"Come with us."

They confiscated Tian's phone and laptop, and led him to a black van, where he was hooded.

Twenty minutes later, he was seated and unhooded in a windowless room. Blinking against bright lights, he focused on five other colleagues from the hospital, also seated. They gave him a worried look.

"What's going on?" Tian asked.

"We don't know," they all answered.

A stern army officer entered thirty minutes later and, without any introduction, announced, "Our government has built several survival bunkers for the continued existence of our race. A small portion of our population has been very deliberately selected based on age, party loyalties, trades, and other valuable factors for a future world. Congratulations. You and your families have been included in this selection."

He paused, then, without looking at anyone, continued. "You will be flown to one of our survival bunkers in the Western Provinces. Your cooperation is mandatory. I have also been told to tell you if you have any outrage or dissent, keep it to yourself. If you cannot do this, you will be silenced."

Tian threw up his hand and called out. "What assurances do we have that our families—"

"I'm not authorised to answer questions. Your plane leaves immediately." The officer's sober voice only deepened Tian's suspicions.

Six armed, uniformed guards ushered them out like defiant children.

Tian peered out the window at the rocky, isolated terrain passing below. *We've been flying for hours. It feels strange travelling without a bag.* He ran a hand through his hair, anxious about his family and looking forward to seeing them.

They filed off the plane into a mass of human activity. Everywhere, people were ushered about by armed soldiers. Trucks and railway cars unloaded cattle, sheep, chickens, and pigs. Dozens of military planes and helicopters overhead created a deafening noise.

They were herded into a bus, which joined a line of identical buses snaking their way through the snow to a mountainside, through a razor wire fence, past massive steel doors, and down an uninviting ramp into a tunnel cut into solid rock. Tian shook his head at the frenzy of automated activity as they passed thousands of crates and pallets lining the route, hurriedly being laser scanned, picked up by forklifts, and moved down the ramp on flatbeds or conveyer belts.

"Look at the labels," Tian said to a colleague, Xi, as two flatbeds sped past the bus. "Grain, seeds, library storage, canned food, medical, computers—"

"Yeah, electrical generators, tools, fertiliser, water, ammunition …"

Fifteen minutes down the ramp, the tunnel narrowed and darkened. Only a clearance of three hundred millimetres separated the bus from the walls and ceiling. Occasionally, a tunnel light cascaded along the bus through the windows. They entered a well-lit, large cavern where a notice board showed a "You are here" map of the bunker. "Did you see that?" Tian asked. "This network of caves is enormous."

"We must be over a kilometre deep by now," Xi said. "How did they build these doomsday bunkers without anyone knowing?"

"I don't know, but the HLAI machines were in on it too. They're all over the place."

The buses passed a large, brightly lit greenhouse and a vast laydown area of crates and pallets. Tian gasped at the colossal scale of it all – kilometres and kilometres of drilling, piping, cabling, and concrete lining. The buses stopped at a junction where the tunnel split into three directions, all stretching into darkness. The passengers alighted, and the buses disappeared into a tunnel labelled "SURFACE". They were shepherded along a dirty, threadbare strip of red carpet on a concrete floor to an enormous, high-ceilinged assembly chamber with hundreds of people huddled inside. All with dazed, concerned looks and asking each other the same question: "Did they tell you anything about our families?" Tian and his colleagues stood closely together.

"Welcome." Everyone turned to a soldier in an officer's uniform standing on a raised podium with a megaphone. "Welcome to Survival Bunker SB02. My name is Xu Zhizhen. I'm the services leader for this bunker." He sounded rehearsed and detached. "We will have 423,643 people and 137,478 HLAIs sealed in here within the next week. Your role is to provide a working city for us."

"When do we see our families?" Tian called out.

Zhizhen hesitated. "Best to—"

"We demand to know when our families are arriving," someone else called out.

"Best to ask your section leader. Please proceed orderly to a FaceID camera, where you'll be registered and directed to your work area. You will be given bunker rules and procedures. You must follow them."

Ushered by CARs and masked armed guards, the intimidated, frightened, and dismembered crowd moved hesitantly. They were no more in control of their destiny than the cattle being herded down the ramp.

A sudden, loud cry, followed by shouting and a desk being thrown over drew the crowd's attention. The commotion faded as a truculent person was marched away by several bullish guards.

Everyone was separated into disciplines – medicine, engineering, trades, services – and quickly dispersed to their work areas.

Tian stopped at a soldier. "Is your family here?"

The soldier's face tightened, fixed him with a look, then turned away.

Tian turned to Xi and spoke softly. "They kept these places secret by forcefully relocating the locals to cities."

"Yeah. Millions of them, on the pretence that it would be safer."

"And not just here, but across the entire country to prevent suspicion," Tian added.

"You really think our families will be brought here?"

Just a grim look from Tian.

Tian was taken to his dormitory. His bunk-bed was stripped with just a folded blanket and no pillow, one of thousands behind a thin curtain off the main thoroughfare. His head dropped as all hope left his face; his family would not be joining him.

Chapter 63   Welcome

Jess Mackenzie pointed with nervous anticipation through the starboard viewport at the almost imperceptible dot floating in space that was the monolithic mothership.

What luck! On my way home to Earth after five months on Mars, then an unexpected opportunity to leave the transports and take a detour to meet the mothership H-HARs. I'm sure it'll be a more pleasant meeting than my great-grandparents' encounter. The military tried to stop me. I was too much of a risk with my knowledge of the Endeavour launch five years ago. Fortunately for me, they had little choice. It would have taken another three months to send someone from Mars. Poor Sophie, devastated when I told her that her mum's return to Earth was delayed by twelve weeks. At least I'll be home for her fourth birthday. I'll make it up to her and Scott with a long holiday.

Jess was met by two H-HAR drones, both identical to the earlier one. She set the course of her transport habitation module, TransHab, to follow them to the mothership.

As the TransHab drew closer, she studied in detail the sterile, reddish hull of the monstrous, hollowed-out asteroid, releasing a long, awestruck breath she had been holding for some time.

"Whoa, what a big mother ..." she reported into her radio. "From a distance, its shape appears streamlined and featureless until you get close, then you see it's ugly and battered. My angle of approach prevents a view of the relativistic gun cavity at the front. I wonder if this is intentional. There're many small impact craters, dark shadows, long grooves and scarps, which could be structural fractures. It's more intimidating as you get closer. It's incomprehensible this thing's been travelling for hundreds of millions of years. It's a wondrous sight."

Jess turned her camera in all directions, sending intelligence back to Earth.

She gazed along the hull. "There's a small spaceship piggybacked onto the mothership. I can't see the mothership's heat radiators, or even where they've been retracted. There're about half a dozen small auxiliary vessels circulating in formation, about half the size of our S-fighters. They don't seem to be doing anything."

The surprisingly bright, but cold and remote, blue-white pin-spot glare that was the Sun suddenly disappeared behind the mothership. Eerie darkness enveloped the TransHab, revealing a velvet-black starfield and turquoise nebula universe in all its terrifying mystery. Jess could clearly see the thick band of stars making up the Milky Way, stretching across the silent, infinite void of space.

Sunlight slowly crept back, making the TransHab appear like a tiny insect gracefully flying along the giant hull of the mothership. "Can't give any more information at the moment," she said.

Bang Sung, a Chinese senior safety officer in his mid-thirties, was also in the TransHab. Jess was worried. *Poor Bang. He's been a bundle of nerves since he volunteered. Volunteered? Well, sort of; there was no one else.*

Bang sat quietly, murmuring to himself, looking through his stricken, distorted reflection in the viewport at the mothership. He switched on his voice recorder. "This thing is getting close enough to touch. It looks like a cold tomb. Foreboding, lifeless, and menacing. An unwanted and unwelcomed ghost ship with terrible powers, intruding after a long wandering from somewhere beyond, from another world and another time. A fugitive, a derelict, an unnatural monster that wasn't meant to be here." Pulling back from the viewport, he sank uneasily into his seat, and switched off his voice recorder.

Unable to settle, he leaned towards the viewport again and turned his recorder back on. "What the hell was I thinking? I just figured I'd go millions of kilometres to this lonely, God-knows-where nothingness to meet hostile aliens who have come here to destroy Earth, with this Jessie girl who thinks she can persuade them to be friends. I must've been mad. If my wife knew where I was, she'd kill me, or worse, worry herself to death. She's got enough on her plate with little Wei and his newborn sister, Liu. Let's hope I'm home in twelve weeks, as promised." Bang's bio-monitor showed his pulse rising, his muscles tensing, and his stomach ready to vomit.

"You'll be okay, Bang," Jess said, trying to sound confident. "We're the guests, don't forget. We'll drop in, say hello, and be out of there before you know it. They may even give us a visitor's gift."

Bang gave a look that inferred "I'm not sure if you're joking or not". He shrugged and gave the grin of someone with nothing to grin about. "I'm fine," he huffed, sinking into his seat and lapsing into a tense silence.

Jess knew this meeting could be nothing like what she hoped. A good luck call from her cousin, General Adam McLean, just before she left the transports, warned her of the dangers. Adam insisted that an unarmed CAR accompany them, programmed to protect them only if life-threatening physical contact was made by an H-HAR. *But surely no civilised society would invite harmless individuals into their castle only to harm them.*

The mothership had now filled the viewport's entire vision. Jess noticed they were taxiing towards a five-metre square opening within a metal surface section of the mothership, as if it were plugging up an outside hole in the asteroid. It appeared to be the only entry point. They climbed into their bodysuits and fitted the eighteen-hour, capacitor-charged life support unit.

A short, blue-white burn stopped the TransHab. Side vernier thrusters gently rotated it to align the air lock door with the mothership's opening, twenty metres away. Entering the air lock, they tethered their suits together with a ten-metre line and waited for Kay, a non-intelligent CAR, to join them. After the disengagement of some mechanical devices, the external door opened, and three figures floated out.

Jess was experienced and completely at home. She looked along the mothership's hull, one way, then the other. An irregular, rugged geometric surface curved behind itself in all directions. "My God, this thing is big," she said into her helmet mic before falling silent, mesmerised by the moment.

Bang was awkward and disorientated. Jess pulled on the tether to catch him and activate his suit's anti-roll. A short burst of their belt jet pack pushed them across the void to the mothership's opening.

Gently grabbing the opening's edge with her gloved hand, Jess froze, too overwhelmed to speak. Eventually, she reported, "Can't see inside. It's just a freaky, bluish UV glowing mist. I'm about to enter the great unknown. I hope these radio-language converters work." She switched to the private comms channel. "Bang, don't forget to use this channel for all personal dialogue. This is the only channel Kay can speak into." She momentarily paused in total wonderment, gave the thumbs up to Bang, and gestured for him to follow. Gently, she pushed herself through the opening and into the enormous hulk of the mothership. The blue void enveloped her suit-lights like a shadowless fog. Kay immediately followed.

Bang continued to clutch onto the opening's edge, as if he were on the top of a cliff. "I can't see anything," he said.

"It's okay, Bang," came Jess's voice from the mist. "Come down."

Bang leaned towards the opening but stopped as though frozen, a terrified expression on his face. He continued to hesitate but was unable to turn back. An H-HAR drone suddenly appeared four hundred metres away. He turned as it sped past and disappeared.

Jess gently pulled on the tether line. "Bang, it's okay. You either have to come down now or return to the TransHab."

Bang took a nervous breath and tentatively turned his body back towards the opening. "Dōngxī tā," he murmured as he slowly pushed off into the blueness, his body sick with terror.

Eight metres inside, Bang grunted as he gently bumped against an adhesive, stiff surface. He flinched at Jess's radio voice. "Bang! … Stand on your feet, the sticky surface allows us to walk upright in zero gravity. Be careful, this haze is disorienting."

Bang stumbled to stand, his suit adding CO_2 to compensate for his laboured breathing. Jess and Kay clutched his shoulders to assist. The bluish mist gave everyone an eerie, haloed appearance.

"You okay now, Bang?" Jess dared to ask.

No answer.

Jess checked his bio-monitor and looked into his helmet visor. He was hyperventilating and fighting hysteria. "Just breathe slowly, nice and deep."

His breathing slowly stabilised.

"You want to go back to the TransHab?"

"N-no! … I'm okay now."

Jess looked at him for some time, then nodded. "Okay, but just take it easy."

Bang nodded back uneasily.

The two humans completed a nervous 360-degree visual sweep. Thick, bluish UV haze in every direction, looming claustrophobically, mysteriously, and oppressively. Their eyes seemed unable to focus on its glowing radiance. There was no identifiable light source, as if the mist itself were both translucent and luminous, engulfing everything.

They switched on their auxiliary helmet lights. But the stronger beams couldn't penetrate any further – only five metres before being swallowed – and only made things appear even more dreamlike.

"Kay, can you see any more than us?" Jess asked.

"No, Ma'am."

"Hello! Hello!" Jess broadcast through her language converter into the wireless muteness of the mist. "We're here."

They cautiously explored a short distance in all directions, careful not to lose their way. But the floor seemed never-ending. They may as well be in the Land of Oz. They returned to the entry position and waited.

"Hello, hello," Jess broadcast.

Jess waved a hand in front of her eyes. *This static haze can't be gas. Nothing's leaking from the opening.*

"What the hell is this place?" asked Bang, in a tone that implied he wasn't expecting an answer. "I feel like I'm in Satan's belly."

A weak force, almost unnoticeable, pulled them onto the adhesive surface.

Must be gravity from the ship's mass. It's so— Jess suddenly realised that radio comms with the outside world was lost. Lifting herself with a small jump, she could just see that the opening was closed. *That can't be good.* Slowly drifting to the floor, she decided not to tell Bang. "I guess we can forget about the welcoming party."

Bang just shrugged his shoulders.

The three visitors huddled together, side by side. Earthly figures in an alien world, not knowing what to expect.

"Forty-one minutes since entry," Jess said. "They must know we're here."

"Damn it," said Bang, his voice stressed. "I've changed my mind. I want to return to the TransHab."

"Sorry, Bang, you can't. The opening's closed."

"What?" Bang's body stiffened. "So we're prisoners now? Is that it? … Fuck it."

"Hello! Hello!" said Jess louder, as if that would help. "Come out, come out wherever you are!" She switched to private. "Maybe they're checking us for weapons."

"The place is lifeless. Maybe one of us should scout around for an exit while the other stays here with Kay."

"Let's stay put for now, Bang. Maybe they're all around us. Maybe they aren't H-HARs. Maybe they're something totally different."

The minutes dragged by. Their radio-language converters suddenly picked up something. A low, pulsating, weird grating sound. So echoey, it had no direction. They exchanged worried glances. Then stronger sounds superimposed over the grating. Scratchy, inhuman sounds, varying in tone and pitch, not easily recognisable as intelligent, but intelligent nonetheless. The language converters reconditioned and retranslated the sounds into words. Words that sounded like "I am here …" before fading off into the unfilterable grating.

"D-did you hear that?" Bang asked, exchanging a tense look with Jess.

"Yeah, what the hell was that?"

Their heads frantically turned in all directions.

"IR detection on our left," Kay said.

Jess and Bang turned to see three shadowy figures taking form at the very edge of visibility. Their silhouetted outlines made indistinctive by the glow of the radiance all around. As the figures neared, their forms became recognisable – humanoid, biomechanical, the H-HAR monsters Earth encountered many years ago. Their bodies were the darkest things they had ever seen, like a walking shadow, a void dragging in all light that fell upon it. Even up close, focusing on them was difficult.

Bang muttered something in Chinese, followed by "fuck it."

"I am here …" came through their radios again. This time, the words were clear, metallic, and insistent.

The three figures separated like predators cornering their prey. A red-armband in the middle, flanked by two green-armbands. They stopped in front of the Earthling, just beyond arm's reach. The two green-armbands stood slightly wider, like sentinels.

"Bang," said Jess, talking into the private channel while maintaining eye contact with the red-armband directly in front of her. "Their highest leader is here. This could be a good sign."

"I can't see anything good about it. They're bigger and scarier than the pictures. And they're wearing their dark combat armoured skins?" Bang turned to Jess, as if waiting for a reassuring answer, but none came.

Jess saluted the red-armband and stepped forward. She looked up into its eyes, trying to connect. But they were lifeless, pitch black, and stared right through her. It was impossible to discern what was going on behind them. She held out her hand to greet it. She was about to become the spokesperson for Earth.

The red-armband pushed past Jess's hand and loomed over her. Jess held its stare, black eyes versus blue, the effort draining her spirit. Its imposing presence was terrifying.

She worked up enough courage to address it. "Welcome to our solar system. We welcome you in peace." She even managed a friendly grin.

Nothing from the red-armband. Jess waited, maintaining eye contact, anxiously holding her breath.

Seconds passed. Jess wondered if the language converters were working. Finally, scratchy words came back. Ominous words from an ominous figure. "I dislike you using my language."

The words hung in Jess's head. *Oh No! This is bad. Oh No! At least the language converters work.* She swallowed hard and tried to explain. "We needed to talk to you, to welcome you."

Once again, there was no response; its towering presence became menacing.

"I'm not sure you understand me. We—"

"How did you learn my language?"

Jess forced a weak grin, trying to disguise her anxiety. "From the others that preceded you, they—"

"Yes. Where are these others?" The creature pushed closer, its soulless eyes boring into Jess.

Jess gulped a breath and searched for a delicate response. "We were forced to defend ourselves. They—"

"They belonged to my supreme-god." The red-armband's words lost none of their ferocity through the language converter. "Only I have the right to destroy them."

"We only wanted peace and tried to welcome them, but they—"

"I have no interest in your welcome or peace." The creature's voice grew louder. "My supreme-god, the ruler of the universe, commands you to surrender your petty little *world*."

The creature seemed to linger on the word "world", as if savouring it.

Jess's body went rigid.

"M-maybe it's misunderstanding—" Bang said on the broadcast channel.

The creature swung around to Bang, pushed towards him, and pressed a powerful finger against his chest, forcing him to stumble back. Bang gasped, his face fraught with fear.

Jess, worried about a premature reaction from Kay, quickly spoke up. "We can't surrender to you. We—"

The creature charged back to Jess. "Your fate cannot be denied," it said, its shoulders raised, and its sightless eyes piercing. It stepped back, studying the three Earthlings, then slowly walked around them. Jess watched it.

Bang's terrified eyes also followed it. His nervous breathing became clearly audible over the ever-present grating as it passed him. It stopped briefly to inspect Kay, then ominously moved back to Jess.

"I can arrange a meeting with our leaders," Jess said. "They—"

"Your flashing light drone requested a surrender meeting." The shadowy creature pushed its huge face closer, its eyes probing. It poked a finger directly into Jess's visor. "Are you not the leader of your world?"

"N-no I'm not. We have several leaders working together. I can arrange a meeting with them."

The creature pulled back, as if surprised. Its head turned to Bang. "What is this one?"

"Like myself, Bang represents our leaders."

It turned to Kay. "This one?"

"A machine to assist us on our journey here and back."

The red-armband's stare returned to Jess. "Back?"

A terrifying silence suddenly fell over Jess and Bang. An all-consuming silence, heavy with fears about how this meeting might conclude. Even the residual grating went unnoticed.

The red-armband pushed closer, its featureless face only millimetres from Jess's helmet visor. Jess remained quiet, tightly controlling her reaction.

"There can only be one world leader. Your leaders are cowards to send someone else to beg for my mercy."

"This meeting was just a trap to capture Earth's leader for its amusement," Bang murmured on the private channel. "We need to get out of here, Jess."

"There's nowhere to go, Bang! Besides, these two green-armbands look ready to—"

"I have waited many, many long aeons to fulfil my duty to my supreme-god," said the red-armband. "A duty I feared would be unfulfilled, an eternity of failures. The long wait is finally over. Now, I will burn your planet."

"We don't want a war against you," Jess said, summoning all her courage to speak. "If only you could meet our leaders, I—"

"I will watch your leaders die in agony." The creature stretched to its full height and let out a loud howl.

Jess and Bang watched in stunned horror.

J-Jess, t-this isn't working," Bang said, looking stretched to the limit. "We need to get out."

Jess kept trying. Maybe a different approach. "Your supreme-god must be an almighty being. Perhaps we can serve him."

The red-armband's shoulders pulled back, its neck thrust forward. It lifted its hands in front of its chest and spread its fingers like claws. "My supreme-god only demands your extinction."

To Jess, the monster seemed crazed, relishing in its own madness. Like a frog trapped in the eyes of a snake, she struggled to break its ruthless glare. Its psychotic ferocity was so chilling and venomous that Jess's words caught in her throat. "But … but it makes no sense to destroy our world!"

"Enough!" the red-armband angrily demanded. "I know you've been studying my supreme-god's science, but you are only a puny biological species of feeble intellect. Your eyes would only wander, your heads would tremble, and your weak minds would pain. You are fools to think your worthless, little world can stop me from erasing it as if it never existed."

Jess exchanged a desperate look with Bang. There was nothing left to say that could sway this monster.

"I can see it scares you, Earthlings, that I command unlimited power to destroy your irritating planet."

Jess felt a sudden calmness. She had been staring the devil in the face, and the loss of all fear and hope gave her a sense of power. Stiffened by human defiance, her eyes boldly held the red-armband's glaze. Human eyes, wild, unyielding, and threatening. "Earth will never submit to you, never," she said, her tone ominous. "If you want to devour Earth, come and get it, and see what happens. It will be us that destroys you." Just then, and only for an instant, Jess sensed an element of doubt buried deep within those alien eyes.

"I am tired of your petulance, Earthling."

Forgetting to use the private channel, Bang said, "Jess, we need to make—"

The red-armband swiftly turned to face Bang while a green-armband violently pulled him to the floor. Bang kicked and struggled relentlessly, partially in an attempt at freedom but also in wild anger. The green-armband's huge foot, the size of Bang's chest, held him down firmly.

Jess immediately moved off to help Bang. "Don't hurt him!" she shouted. She was stopped by the red-armband grabbing her helmet.

Kay, charging behind Jess, caught the green-armband that was holding down Bang by surprise, and king hit it, sending it flying. The second green-armband tackled Kay. Jess and Bang watched in horror as the two mighty machines strong-armed each other, the advantage swinging back and forth as the fight momentarily disappeared several times into the bluish haze. There was no sound, the vacuum silenced what would otherwise have been a metal-jarring explosion of noise.

Kay struggled and thrashed as the green-armband clutched its neck. But a head-butt and a classic wrestling roll locked the H-HAR in a full nelson with no sign of escape. Kay pushed a finger into the creature's neck. The H-HAR went limp, and Kay let it go. It drifted off, terminated.

The other green-armband recovered enough to jet back to the floor.

"Look out, Kay! Behind you!" Jess yelled, but it was too late.

A violent kick and a throw sent Kay flying towards the ceiling, its body disappearing into the haze. Two hundred kilograms of mass slammed hard into the closed door. The rebound caused it to drift back, its spin slowing as its arms opened. Before Kay could recover, the green-armband pulled it down. The red-armband joined the fight as both H-HARs kicked Kay's neck until the valiant machine was terminated. They shook in rage as they stood over Kay's shattered body before kicking it into the mist.

The two H-HARs turned their full attention to Jess and Bang. They pushed down on their helmets, forcing them to prostrate on their knees.

The red-armband's grip on Jess relaxed just as some word-like sounds came through the radio. Jess looked up, only to be struck hard and forced down with a tighter grip. She realised the sounds were a distorted, auto-generated warning message from Kay on the private channel. Its final death throe.

"Jess," murmured Bang, this time on the private channel. "There may be an opening or passageway where the three H-HARs emerged. It's our only chance."

Jess managed a glance. "It's just a featureless blur but still worth a try. If you go, don't wait for me."

Bang disconnected his tether line, but the green-armband grabbed him. In what appeared to be pure instinct, Bang bucked, kicked, and rolled in every direction. His beast-like determination to escape was astounding. He tore free, yanked himself up, and made a break towards the suspected passageway.

It was a brave effort but an unsuccessful one. He fumbled with his jet pack after losing contact with the floor's adhesive surface. The green-armband reached up, grabbed him, and violently threw him onto the floor. Bang gasped in pain and clutched his knee.

All Jess could do was listen to Bang's struggles and cries of pain.

Bang raised his head to the red-armband and met its eyes with a rebellious glare. With rage in his voice, he burst out. "You motherfucking psychotic narcissists! On behalf of Earth, go fuck yourself!"

"Your undaunted defiance in the face of imminent annihilation is insufferable." The red-armband's rage was clearly evident, even through the language converter. It placed a hand on their helmets, forcing Jess and Bang to hang their heads low.

They slowly angled their visors towards each other and exchanged a final look.

"I'm sorry, Bang," Jess said.

"Nothing to be sorry about, Jess."

Their heads were forced lower.

"Scott, Sophie, I love you," Jess whispered into her voice recorder.

"Yao, Wei, Liu, *wǒ ài nǐ*," Bang also whispered into his recorder.

The two Earthlings took a ragged breath, braced themselves, and awaited their fate.

***

The bodies of Jess and Bang, together with Kay and the wreckage of the TransHab, were recovered floating in space by drones several months later. Recordings from their helmets revealed everything.

General Adam McLean, a man not easily shaken, was gripped by grief. Try as he may, this was a hard one to shake off. He had delivered two people, one of whom was his cousin, tied up like pigs to the slaughterer. But there wasn't time for remorse; the world depended on him and others. And Earth couldn't go to war against an advanced alien race without exhausting all avenues to prevent it. He gripped the bravery medallion around his neck, and with a tear in his eye, he decisively and with finality assured, *Dad, I had to send them. There was no alternative – absolutely no alternative.*

He ordered Anya's bravery medallion to be retrieved and passed on to Jess's daughter, Sophie.

Jess and Bang became international heroes. McLean took some comfort in knowing there were two benefits. It provided valuable intelligence for the war ahead. And it removed any lasting doubt about the H-HARs' objective. Their message to Earth: "We're here to annihilate you."

Chapter 64   Mothership War 1

"Up there in space, a war of annihilation is about to start," the UN Military Committee chairman reported to the media. "This is not the first time in our history we've struggled with extinction. But let's hope it is the last. Our military is our only hope."

Some Earthlings replaced qualified optimism with fatalism. With nowhere to run and nowhere to hide, they came to terms with their fate. Some lashed out in fear, not understanding the motive behind their predicament. But most never gave up hope. They simply went about their lives as best they could under the circumstances.

***

With the information recovered from Jess and Bang's recorders, General Adam McLean and others reassessed their war plans against the mothership.

"Damaging its radiators would only temporarily constrain it, general," Colonel Nathan Martin said.

"The RIW and engine are heavily sealed off when not in use," Colonel Ric Amess added.

"Another welcome drone with flashing lights might antagonise the red-armband enough for it to reveal information about their capabilities, sir," IDAS suggested.

"Good idea, IDAS. Nathan, Ric, what do you think?"

Both nodded in agreement.

"It seems like the type to do something rash," Nathan added.

At 113.7 kilometres from the mothership, the second welcome drone fragmented in a silent flash of light.

"Well, that's the end of any negotiations," McLean said to a hushed war room. "The first shot in this long-awaited war of annihilation. Nathan, find out from intelligence the type of weapon they used to destroy the drone."

"What now, general?" Amess asked.

"We wait." McLean shifted forward uneasily. "The red-armband would expect some resistance if it approached Earth directly. As soon as it works out a plan, it'll make a move, and you can bet it won't be through the front door."

"I agree, general." IDAS avatar's face was expressionless. "I believe the mothership will withdraw to a safe distance and assess what it's up against."

"And perform probing attacks to assess route vectors, weaknesses, and reaction times," McLean added. He sagged back into his chair, realising this was Earth's last moment of peace. He took a deep breath, lowered his voice, and said, "Everyone stand by."

***

Eleven months after Jess and Bang's deaths, and as predicted, the mothership withdrew to the asteroid belt and positioned itself within the gravitational influence of the 330-kilometre-diameter asteroid known as 704 Interamnia.

Two months later, two small H-HAR spacecraft emerged and approached Earth from different directions.

IDAS reported them as "circular cylinders, twenty-one metres long by five point five metres wide. The LaWS at the front, the powerful propulsion engines, and the cold, angled radiators indicate they are fighter ships with jinking capabilities. They're not planet destroying."

"Son of a bitch, the mothership has space fighters!" McLean rubbed his brow. "We need intel on them without revealing too much about our own capabilities. We'll wait 'til they're 0.3 AU from Earth before shooting. Do you concur, IDAS?"

"Yes, general, it's a good opportunity to test our fixed weapons."

***

Six days later, IDAS updated. "H-HAR fighter A is approaching along the least defended route. It's currently outside the effective range of our constellation of high-energy gamma LaWS, and our Mercury weapon is blocked by the Sun. A cluster of autonomous smart mines is tracking it. H-HAR fighter B is approaching the effective targeting range of our gamma LaWS constellation, GLC-4. The Mercury weapon is ready to respond."

***

Seventeen days later, with everyone at battle stations, McLean decided the H-HAR fighters were close enough. He shivered as his jaw tightened. "IDAS, attack the two H-HAR incoming fighters."

"The first space battle in history," Martin added.

The autonomous smart mines immediately headed towards H-HAR fighter A. Twenty-five hours later, the GLC-4 weapon was fired at H-HAR fighter B. Both sequenced to reach their targets simultaneously.

IDAS summarised the Enemy Engagement Assessment Report to a very hushed war room. "Enemy fighter B was hit by the GLC-4 weapon and disabled, currently careering towards the Sun."

A wild round of cheering and handclapping quickly subsided to allow IDAS to continue.

"Enemy fighter A has disengaged and is returning to the mothership. The mines were ineffective. They were either destroyed by defence lasers or outmanoeuvred."

"You can be sure the next attack will follow the same path as enemy fighter A," McLean said.

"Their fighters lack sophistication, general."

"Yeah, but they may have others, IDAS."

***

Twelve days later, a group of five H-HAR fighters was detected along the same route as the earlier scout fighter A. Jinking started twenty-two days later. Two days afterwards, an HE-LaWS constellation of battle stations orbiting the Sun opened fire. But it was too early. The jinking H-HAR fighters were too distant to be hit and homed in on the incoming laser beams with their own lasers. It was the first space laser duel in history. One Earth orbital battle station and five LaWS platforms suffered major damage.

The war room learned a valuable lesson. It needs the H-HAR fighters to get much closer before firing.

H-HAR fighter HF1 was hit and veered off course. HF2 appeared to malfunction and veered off course. HF3 was hit and disabled. HF4 was hit and broke up. HF5 disengaged and returned to the mothership.

***

Three weeks later, the disabled HF3 passed within striking distance of the Mercury weapon, and McLean wanted to target it as a test. Although the Mercury weapon didn't have the non-thermal tunnelling effect of the gamma-ray based HE-LaWS, it was their longest-ranged weapon.

After several attempts, the Mercury weapon's pulsed laser beam swept across the crippled H-HAR fighter, instantly heating the surface to five thousand degrees Celsius, creating an ionised plasma that expanded ten thousand times. A moment later, the neutral, ionised particle beam component sliced it in two with a small flash.

"Wow … did you see that?" Martin said excitedly, speaking over the background applause.

"We're not going to stand around and wait for another attack." McLean turned towards IDAS's avatar. "It's time to launch our counteroffensive."

"Ah, yes … our counteroffensive, general," IDAS said, almost sounding doubtful. "A gauntlet of fire for a squadron of our S-fighters across 0.6 AU of open space. I admire your courage and initiative, general."

"We have no experience with deep-space battles, sir," Amess warned.

McLean nodded thoughtfully. "Yes, and that worries us all." He was about to elaborate, instead he turned to IDAS's avatar. "IDAS, do you think a flat space offensive against the mothership is winnable?"

"I'm apprehensive, general."

"Your best guess, IDAS?"

"Our S-fighters will need to penetrate the H-HAR fighters. They'll race towards each other from a great distance at high velocities, taking laser pot shots as they approach. Missiles may just be sitting ducks for lasers, or they may be useful distractions. I'm not sure. The main battlespace between opposing forces is unlikely to be less than four light seconds or three lunar distances. Whichever side can best dodge the incoming laser beams within the ever-reducing light-speed time lag will win the space-fighter battle. But there is still the mothership. If our S-fighters reach it, will our LaWS and missiles affect its ten-metre-plus-thick iron-nickel hull? Will the front cavity, rear nozzle, or radiators be exposed? What weapons will the mothership have? These are the great troubling unknowns."

The weightless avatar glanced at Amess and Martin, then back at McLean. "But I still concur with the attack. It will answer some of these questions."

"The mothership may just be surprisingly vulnerable, and we need to find out," McLean said.

"Let's hope the H-HARs are just as inexperienced as we are," Martin added.

"It will be a good test for our S-fighters, general," IDAS said. "The three, four hundred megawatt point-defence laser turrets should do well against enemy fighters and incoming missiles. But the jinking against H-HAR laser attacks? Well, let's just say it's unknown. At five light seconds, the three metres per second squared lateral dodge will result in a one hundred and fifty metre miss. However, at less than three light seconds, or two point three lunar distances, dodging multiple sweeping laser beams becomes unlikely. The front seven hundred-millimetre-thick water-ice protective ablation shield, with its embedded gamma-ray refracting particles, should protect against one laser hit only. I hold little hope for any S-fighters returning, so I suggest we send no more than ten, general."

"Thank you, IDAS."

***

Three days later, a strike force of nine S-fighters set off from translunar orbits to 704 Interamnia in a pincer arrangement. Another eight S-fighters were prepared for a possible second wave.

Twenty-two days later, they were intercepted by three H-HAR fighters. Spirits rose when an enemy fighter was destroyed without loss. However, five S-fighters were lost destroying the other two. The four remaining S-fighters continued their advance, zig-zagging towards the mothership, their prime objective.

The attack, however, was futile. The mothership, seemingly unconcerned about any damage to its hull, just waited until the S-fighters were too close for dodging, then opened fire. All S-fighters and their missiles were destroyed.

The attack was a devastating disaster, the mothership's invincibility being the only intelligence obtained.

***

At General Adam McLean's insistence, IDAS agreed to the appointment of Rear Admiral Walter Brampton to oversee preparations for another counterattack. It was a controversial appointment with many opponents.

Amess and Martin accompanied Brampton on his first visit. When introduced to the avatar, Brampton immediately turned to IDAS's main camera, listlessly nodded "hello", and moved on to be briefed on the room's layout and introduced to the remaining staff.

IDAS watched him closely with some suspicion. There was an absent manner about him, as though nothing warranted his full attention except his own thoughts. His arched eyebrows, grimace, brusque manner, manufactured smile, long lingering looks, and impatient questions gave IDAS the impression he expected to someday be in command. IDAS thought he knew this human from somewhere, or maybe it was just humans like him who distrusted synthetic intelligence in positions of authority.

While Brampton stood centre stage inspecting the war room, IDAS searched for his military records and references. There was no shortage of material.

The Lincoln incident:

"Brampton entered into a vicious, uncontrolled rage against his commanding officer, thumped a wall, yelled profanities, and made references to rodent carnal habits."

General Johnson's reference:

> "I found Brampton to be imposing, contemptible, and arrogant with anger management issues. He

can display some gruff charm, but his preference is to crash through problems instead of working around them. A human bulldog who has more than a lifetime's worth of adversaries. However, he's a quick learner, shows brilliant insight, and gets the job done. A protean character with a willingness to act decisively. I can only attribute his successful career in the UN space fleet to the dire circumstances we all face with the approaching H-HAR mothership."

IDAS noticed Amess and Martin leading Brampton back towards its avatar. Just before they reached it, Brampton abruptly stopped and asked, "Are we done here?" His tone sounded more like an announcement than a question. IDAS had seen enough to have reservations about Brampton's presence in the war room but trusted McLean's judgement.

"You should have a discussion with IDAS before you leave," said Martin.

"On the next visit," Brampton replied, turning towards the door.

On the way out, a robot caught Brampton's eye. "Hello there," Brampton strangely summoned.

The robot stopped, turned, and glanced at Brampton inscrutably with its dark eyes.

Brampton gestured "come here" with his finger. The robot walked over. Brampton gave it a thorough look up and down with a peculiar intensity, like a specimen. "What an odd machine you are. What i-rating are you?"

"I'm i5, sir," the robot replied in a completely emotionless voice.

"i5!" Brampton looked into its eyes. "You're far too sophisticated and your eyes too intelligent for such a narrow artificial intelligence rating."

The robot stared back dumbly.

"What name do you go by?"

"Q, sir."

"Q?"

"Yes, sir. Q-U-E. Q."

Brampton pulled back and roared with amusement. "What do you do here?"

"Whatever I'm told. Make coffee, clean up—"

"Okay, okay," Brampton said, and with a snort of laughter he walked off.

***

The mothership left asteroid 704 Interamnia, and over the next eighteen months it drifted peacefully in space.

Falling into bed after a long day, McLean's phone abruptly shattered his tranquillity.

It was the ever awake, ever alert Colonel Amess.

"Hello …" McLean answered. "What? I'll be right there."

The atmosphere in the war room was anything but relaxed. McLean strode straight to the avatar and steadied his gaze. "What's this red up to?"

"General, sixty-five minutes ago, the mothership fired its thrusters. We're sure its destination is another asteroid, 1990 SQ, also known as Eric, which it should reach in nine days."

"Eric? What do we know about Eric?"

"It's a stony, eleven-kilometre-diameter asteroid that orbits the Sun every thirty-four months, rotates every twelve hours, and averages about twenty kilometres per second. The thing is, general, its next orbit brings it unusually close to Earth."

McLean swallowed dryly as the room quieted. Everyone's eyes were fixed on him. "So that's their plan," he said, waiting a moment before continuing. "Hitch a ride to Earth using an asteroid for cover and blow us into oblivion."

"We're not sure about that, general," IDAS said. "Calculations show a 1 in 18,400 chance of Eric hitting Earth. We believe the mothership will need to leave Eric to target us, but we can't be sure. Their closest point to Earth will be in twenty-five months when they'll pass within zero point four AU or one hundred and fifty-six lunar distances. If they plan to leave the asteroid, that will be their optimal point."

McLean sighed dramatically. "I don't know how," he said, shaking his head, "but we'll have to stop the mothership from leaving Fort Eric."

***

Twenty-two months later, with Eric much closer to Earth and McLean looking greyer and more burdened, a second offensive against the mothership was launched. Walter Brampton's attack plan was accepted by the war room, and he was present during the engagement.

"Sixteen of our new S-fighters will approach Eric from a wide angle," Brampton said. "My only objective in this offensive is to reach that psycho Red and attack its mothership." His face hardened with anger.

"This isn't a personal feud, Mr Brampton," IDAS said.

"The hell it isn't!" Irritation was clear in Brampton's voice. "On behalf of the entire human race, this psycho Red will pay."

***

Twenty days later, the S-fighters were intercepted by eighteen H-HAR fighters. Despite five H-HAR fighters malfunctioning, only three S-fighters progressed far enough to target the mothership. They lasted just long enough to transmit the results. Their LaWS barely scorched the hull. The nuclear-armed missiles were like peashooters against an enormous rock.

The futility of the attack was evident for all to see, and it caused considerable tension on the floor. McLean, backed vigorously by Brampton, wouldn't rule out another attack with new model S-fighters, while IDAS, Amess, and Martin were strongly opposed.

"The attack showed that our S-fighters can break through to the mothership," said Brampton almost triumphantly. "They didn't have anything big enough to damage it."

"We don't have anything bigger," McLean said.

"Only our fixed defensive weapons, the Mercury weapon, orbital and lunar battle stations, and some orbital constellations have any hope of stopping the mothership from leaving Eric," IDAS said. "We need to allocate all our resources to them."

Brampton, ignoring the avatar, glared at an IDAS camera in irritation. "That's fucking bullshit," he roared across a stunned room. "We still need a multitasking offensive weapon such as the S-fighters. That's why this psycho Red has them."

McLean leaned back, watched, and listened. He wanted these two to air their views and differences.

"They've shown their limitations," IDAS said coldly, its avatar's expression matching. "Our limited resources are better spent elsewhere."

"Do you really think you know what the hell you're talking about?" Brampton's voice still roared. "What happens if this psycho Red changes its strategy and we need better S-fighters but haven't got them?"

"I'm not opposed to the S-fighters, Rear Admiral Brampton. I'm opposed to committing our resources to developing them as an offensive weapon."

"That's the same fucken thing," Brampton snapped, pointing a finger at IDAS's camera. "I'm not letting this go. We need the most advanced S-fighters we can build because we don't know what this fucking psycho Red has planned for us."

Only silence from IDAS.

"Goddam you, IDAS," Brampton burst out, by now so furious he was out of breath. "Are you listening to any of this?"

McLean knew IDAS was listening. IDAS always listened, although you might not think so by the neutral, underwhelmed expression on its avatar's face. McLean knew IDAS didn't consider continuing the discussion productive.

Brampton moved closer to IDAS's lens and continued. "We captured a disabled H-HAR fighter and towed it back for analysis. Now, tell me, how could we have fucken done that without S-fighters?"

McLean adjourned the discussion and walked Brampton outside. "Walter," he said, "I value your presence in the war room. It keeps everyone thinking. But you could have handled that better."

"I'm well aware I was over the top, Adam. But, quite frankly, I just don't give a shit. Jess and Bang's video shows this psycho Red will stop at nothing. And I'm not sure IDAS is up to it."

"Trust me, Walter. You need to value IDAS's decisions. And don't let your vendetta against the H-HARs affect your judgement."

Eventually, a compromise was reached on the S-fighters. Development would continue under Brampton, but there would be no more attacks on the mothership, at least not in the foreseeable future.

***

Six weeks after the failed attack and twenty-eight days from Eric's closest point to Earth, IDAS blankly announced, "A bright radiation flash has been detected from the mothership, and we're receiving bow shock gamma radiation. This can only mean one thing: an object approaching us at relativistic speed."

This struck an abrupt, terrified silence. Thirteen seconds later, with doomsday panic just a heartbeat away, IDAS advised, "Its trajectory has just been calculated to pass Earth in seven point eight minutes by a very large margin."

It took a few seconds for the panic to subside.

McLean wiped his forehead; this one almost got to him. "IDAS! Why are they firing projectiles with so little chance of hitting us?"

"I don't know, admiral."

Thirty-two seconds later, the projectile exploded into tens of thousands of iron and rock pieces, spreading like a shotgun blast at close to light speed. The fragmentation passed Earth by a large margin, except for a 0.2 kg fragment that harmlessly brushed Earth's upper atmosphere.

McLean's voice shattered the lull. "IDAS, how deadly are these attacks?"

"The original projectile weighed three hundred thousand kilograms – almost planet destroying. The fragments are not planet destroying, general. More like a terrorist attack."

McLean nodded. "The long, painful death the red-armband promised our leaders."

***

Five hours later, another projectile exploded, resulting in a fifteen-kilogram fragment passing inside the Moon's orbit.

There were three more attacks the following day. One included a nine-kilogram fragment that skimmed the outer atmosphere, creating a flash witnessed by millions.

***

Asami Mizushima and her husband lived just north of Tokyo. They were lying in bed, worrying about the future of their young son and daughter, whom they had just put to sleep. Their room suddenly lit up with a blinding burst of light, like a powerful, soundless lightning flash.

Asami jumped up like a cat. "Nantekotta!" she cried out. By the time she reached the window, the light source was gone, leaving only silhouettes of trees and buildings, barking dogs, and a scattering of bats.

***

The next five attacks missed. Then a seven-kilogram fragment slammed into the atmosphere over Southern India, just as the Sun was rising to begin a clear day. Its atoms converted directly into energy, producing a blast of radiant heat and gamma-rays. Secondary reactions caused a deadly shower of hadrons, mesons, and other subatomic particles to rain down. Directly beneath the atmospheric impact, people burned like roasted marshmallows. The ground rippled and swayed in waves like the high seas in a storm. Buildings were blown to pieces, their foundations thrown into the sky. Steam from boiling rivers replaced breathable air. Twelve million people perished.

Hardik Bhupathi gazed absently through the car's front window, waiting for the train to pass. His dog, with different-coloured eyes, slept on the back seat. He was still high from the first grade cricket match the day before. *My maiden century! A hundred and thirty-four runs not out. The crowd cheered. Mum and Dad were so proud. And already, I've received several lucrative sponsorship offers.*

Bhupathi's head turned to the lively sounds of children playing tag in the park, carried to him by a gentle breeze. They ran wildly to avoid being 'in', but never too far to miss out on the fun.

Now I can ask Mithali to marry me. She'll be so happ—.

An intolerably bright light instantly flashed over everything, igniting the children and everyone else like match heads. Before

Bhupathi had time to close his eyes, he, his dog, and everything around him were fried to a crisp.

***

The next six attacks missed, but a five-kilogram fragment from the next attack entered the atmosphere above North America, exploding in a blast of fiery debris.

The school holidays had just begun. Amiri, a ten-year-old girl, sat on the floor, her hand on a musical toy.

Kayce, her younger brother, reached for it. "Mummy, she's not sharing."

Mum gave them a chocolate and a wink.

"Thanks, Mum."

"Thanks, Mum."

They tried to wink back but ended up blinking.

A brilliant flash lit the night sky as an unbearable thermal shock wave swept across the house, igniting the curtains. There was no sound, not yet. Dad jumped up with terror in his eyes and rushed everyone into the basement, unaware that the radiation dose from the flash had already sealed their fate. Nonetheless, they all sat and waited for what would come next: the sonic blast wave. It hit with a ferocious boom. A near-solid wall of compressed air. Their feeble screams melted into the wind's roar. Their house, their neighbourhood, and their city just blew away. Together with six million others, they perished.

***

There were five more attacks before another fragment entered Earth's atmosphere and exploded over North Africa, resulting in three million deaths and huge devastation.

Meanwhile, millions of moon-sand bombs were being exploded in space, distributing nebulous layers of protective clouds between Earth and Eric.

IDAS explained, "If an incoming fragment hits just one of these grains of sand, the resultant kinetic energy to heat conversion will be equivalent to fifty tons of TNT. At forty thousand kilometres from Earth, little explosive debris will seriously impact Earth."

***

Five more misses. The next attack included a six-kilogram fragment that became the first to disintegrate in the sand shield. The resulting debris fizzled out in the atmosphere, causing a colourful spectacle of lights high in the sky. Six more misses followed. A fragment from the next attack was stopped by the protective cloud.

***

Eric finally came within range of the fixed weapons. The weapons fired randomly around Eric's edges to keep the mothership behind the asteroid. But the firing was too sporadic to have much effect, and the H-HAR bombardment continued. One fragment was stopped by the protective cloud. Another skimmed Earth's outer atmosphere.

Meanwhile, radiation analysis revealed the mothership's RIW used the same operating principles as the Moon weapon, only more powerful and able to reach eighty per cent of light speed.

Eric reached its closest point to Earth. The attacks increased. Three Earthbound fragments disintegrated within the protective cloud, which was now complete, two Earth diameters wide and three Earth diameters deep.

The mothership redirected its attacks from Earth to the more distant fixed weapons. All nineteen attacks missed widely, but one fragment punched a small, harmless hole in a solar array of the Mercury weapon.

The attacks then switched back to Earth. Out of the twenty-six that followed, only one had an Earthbound fragment, which broke up in the cloud shield.

Eric and the mothership were rapidly moving away from Earth, and the attacks were missing by larger margins. Finally, they ceased, to a global sigh of salvation. Earth was safe, at least for now. There were 125 attacks over 45 days. Four fragments hit Earth, and ten were stopped by the protective shield.

***

During the mission debriefing meeting, McLean was on edge. "What was the purpose of these attacks?"

"Perhaps our fixed weapons prevented the mothership from leaving Eric, general," Colonel Martin said.

Brampton gave an impatient sigh. "Then why the hell did this psycho Red waste its time and hitch a goddamn ride on Eric?" His tone indicated it wasn't a disagreement, more like a rebuff.

"Maybe they were testing our defences," one attendee said.

McLean turned to IDAS's avatar. "What do you think?"

"At this stage, general, I don't know."

McLean stood, massaging his neck. He slowly walked to the wall screen and restarted Eric's orbital simulation, his back to the room. "This Red isn't the type to not have a plan." The others watched. McLean suddenly spun around, his face tightening with grim realisation. "Mars!"

IDAS's avatar altered to a slightly different empty expression. "Yes, general, Mars."

"What do you mean? Eric doesn't pass anywhere near Mars," Martin queried, wide-eyed.

"In six weeks," Brampton said loudly and blankly, "Eric will be opposite Earth, and although nowhere near Mars, there's nothing to stop the psycho Red from leaving Eric and attacking it."

This brought a chilling silence over everyone, soon broken by IDAS. "We don't have sufficient resources to protect Mars against a RIW attack."

"Why would they be interested in Mars?" Amess asked, sitting emotionlessly.

"Because Mars is a planet with life. Human life," Brampton said, as if it were obvious. "It could be Earth's turn on Eric's next orbit."

"Exactly," McLean said.

"General, we have over fifty thousand human and HLAI troops stationed on Mars to prevent H-HAR occupation," Amess said. "We have to evacuate them."

"But …" McLean said, gazing into the distant past with the firmness of someone who had been in this situation before. His face hardened as his fist pressed against his great-grandfather's bravery medallion. "We're not."

Brampton slowly nodded while Amess, Martin, and the others stared at McLean in clear disbelief.

"Just so there's no doubt," McLean continued, "we are not committing any S-fighters to defend or evacuate anyone from Mars."

"I'm sorry, general. But I do not concur," Amess said, now with some strain in his voice. "We can't leave them there to die."

"Colonel, you need to run this again through your autonomic circuits because you're not understanding it," said Brampton, shifting in his seat towards Amess and pulling back his shoulders. "We don't have the resources to protect Mars without leaving Earth exposed."

"We have no choice," McLean said.

"No choice?" questioned Martin. "We certainly do have a goddam choice!"

"It could be a trap to attack Earth," Brampton said, his voice more intense.

Martin glared at him with a "who the fuck asked you?" look.

"Even if we commit all our S-fighters to towing transports, we could only evacuate fourteen thousand personnel in the next four weeks," IDAS said simply and matter-of-factly. "After that, our transports would be easy targets."

"Fourteen thousand is fourteen thousand," said a frowning and frustrated Martin. "I demand their rescue, general."

Others also voiced their objection to McLean's decision.

McLean raised his hand. "Stop." His voice was soft, but it carried.

Everyone fell silent, their faces fixed solemnly on McLean.

"We can't leave Earth under-defended because of a rescue mission to Mars. End of story." There was no struggle with his words or tremble in his voice. Just cold, pragmatic decision making. He turned and walked away, needing to be alone.

***

Eight days later, IDAS reported, "General, we have detected eight thousand missiles approaching Earth from the mothership."

"Eight thousand!" Martin said, staring at the avatar in horror.

"This nightmare refuses to end," Amess said, his face bleak.

"Can't say I'm surprised, Adam," Brampton said with unusual calmness.

"Me neither," McLean replied.

"They'll be within range of our outer LaWS in four days, general," IDAS said. "If they start jinking, we'll have trouble stopping them."

"Get every available S-fighter between us and those missiles," McLean ordered.

The avatar's head bobbed in agreement. "The H-HAR Red really expected us to send our S-fighters to Mars, general."

***

The incoming missiles separated three days later into a wide sweep to approach Earth from different directions. When the LaWS started firing, the missiles started jinking.

IDAS reported the results of a vaporisation spectrum analysis of a destroyed missile. "A cocktail of highly radioactive materials, including cobalt-60, general."

McLean rubbed his neck and ordered, "The war room is now code red."

***

Ten days later, IDAS updated, "Eighteen hundred missiles have penetrated our outer LaWS defence shield, general. Our inner defence LaWS are ready."

***

Another five days later, IDAS updated, "Nine hundred missiles have made it through the inner defence LaWS, approaching Earth at thirty kilometres per second. That many missiles would render most of the planet uninhabitable, general."

"Now it's only our S-fighters between us and these missiles," McLean said to a worried room transfixed on the approaching horror.

***

Four days later, IDAS reported, "The S-fighters have stopped all but fifteen missiles, general."

"Only fifteen left!" McLean sounded relieved but wary. He stood up and took in a deep breath. "That's truly amazing. Our surface defences should get most of those."

"But not all of them, sir," Amess said.

"Yes," McLean said softly, slumping his shoulders and nodding gravely.

"The S-fighters performed better than expected, general," Martin commented.

"No!" Brampton immediately snapped, shooting Martin a fiery glare. "They performed as expected."

The following day, IDAS reported, "Five missiles got through, general. Two failed to explode. One exploded over the South Pacific Ocean. Another exploded over Central Africa. And the fifth exploded over Western Australia."

***

In Central Africa, just outside the missile blast zone in a town called Bria, head teacher Zakia and a hundred frightened kids desperately tried to seal a school assembly hall with rags and towels against an engulfing cloud of black smoke and dust leaking through gaps in the walls and floorboards.

"Everyone stop," she said. "It's not working. Just sit and wait. Our evacuation buses will be here soon."

Another teacher handed out masks.

A ponytailed child approached a third teacher. "Miss, I feel sick."

The teacher, who also didn't look well, handed the child a cup of water.

"That's not a good idea," said Zakia. "It could be radioactive."

"If those buses aren't here soon, it won't matter," she whispered back.

***

In Kalgoorlie, an outback Australian town in the middle of nowhere, Alyssa loaded up her car. She couldn't risk waiting any longer for her husband to arrive. She waved briefly to Megan across the street, hastily buckled up her two kids, and drove off.

Megan pulled her five-year-old son close, fighting back tears. Both were pale. She should already be gone but decided to stay a bit longer for her husband. She looked up at the enormous black dust cloud that was encroaching on them. Dirt and dust filled the air. She tied a handkerchief around their faces. Minutes later, a car screeched to a halt; her husband jumped out, helped them in, and headed off.

***

Zakia read the emergency plan again: "Be ready to evacuate immediately when buses arrive." She walked unsteadily to look through a crack in the wall, but it was too hard to see anything through the thickening cloud. Phones were out. Are the buses coming? She closed her eyes and took a slow, long breath, as if to convince herself of something.

***

A battered ute on a rough, gravel road raced furiously towards Kalgoorlie. It suddenly braked to a skidding halt in a mountainous cloud of red road dirt, junk flying from the seat onto the floor.

Flashing blue lights reflected off Eddie's face as he stuck his head out. "Get out of the fucken way! My family's in there!"

"No one's allowed in," the officer said. "And all phones are out."

Eddie floored the accelerator and screeched off, bypassing the police cars.

***

In a hut near the school, Yedidah rushed outside with her coughing baby, frantically trying to escape the dust, but it was everywhere.

"Help! Help! My baby is sick!" she yelled. Stumbling onto the street, she wasn't doing too well herself. Her legs were too weak to walk.

***

Breathing heavily, Eddie neared the town. Hundreds of vehicle headlights were coming the other way, piercing through the thickening dust. He turned on the radio. "The radioactive cloud is drifting west; evacuate immediately. If you have special needs, such as medicines, take them with you."

He turned it off and raced through the deserted town centre. "What the …"

His wife's car was parked oddly just off the road.

Eddie skidded to a halt and leaped out. Alyssa was slumped across the wheel, dizzy and disorientated. "Daddy, daddy," the kids cried out weakly, teddy bears clasped in their tiny hands. Alyssa looked up with a nauseated, horrified expression. Eddie carried them to his ute and drove off. They didn't get far. The road was blocked with vehicles, their drivers too ill to continue and too weak to walk.

And so were they.

***

The baby was strangely quiet. Gently pulling away the dust-covered blanket, Yedidah's mouth trembled and slowly opened. No words, only a low moan of terror and a mother's cry of agony. She pounded on the school door, but only still silence inside.

Dropping to her knees, she gasped. It was her last breath. The baby fell from her arms.

***

Bluey woke up alone behind a large rock after a big night out, feeling worse than usual.

"What's all this fucken dust?"

His eyes were red, and he had trouble swallowing. He grabbed his bottle to drink the little left, vomiting it all over himself.

***

In a village eighty kilometres downwind of the school, people anxiously pointed at an advancing strange cloud, unaware of the danger. They hurried off the road, as an erratic car barrelled through.

The driver was pale, dizzy, and sweating.

"Glykys, honey, you're getting worse," his girlfriend said.

"I-I'm fine. Can you pass me the water?"

***

Stella checked his usual hangouts. "Bluey? Bluey, you old bastard, where are ya?" Her voice was just a whisper. She also had a big night and felt worse than usual – her face flushed and sweaty, her eyes dazed. She grunted on every step.

Finally, she found him, his eyes closed, his face peaceful.

Stella tried walking back to town, cursing as her nausea worsened. "This place is fucked," she murmured, unaware they would be her last words.

***

Glykys slowed to a halt, struggled to get out of the car, and collapsed on the roadside. His girlfriend kneeled beside him, clenching his hand, but his blistered fingers slid limply out. She, too, was sick and vomiting. Her eyes closed. She didn't move. Ever again.

***

As suspected, the mothership left Eric and headed for Mars. Desperate anticipation filled McLean's eyes, and helplessness gripped him.

Leaks made secrecy impossible, and Mars's fate soon became public knowledge.

Hundred ton impact projectiles ploughed through the thin Martian atmosphere, smashing hundreds of metres into the bedrock. Their atoms disintegrated completely into a hot, gaseous, X-ray-emitting plasma fireball. The planet's face shook as sheets of molten rock washed across the surface. Debris blanketed the sky. Some were ejected into Martian orbit and may eventually fall on Earth as meteorites.

McLean watched the planet burn. There were no tears, no words, just a numb, hollow, dreadful feeling, and an ache thrusting against his heart.

The mothership stayed with Eric for eleven months as it passed beyond the asteroid belt. There, it separated and drifted in space, still visible through telescopes as a thermal speck. Although the H-HARs were undoubtedly planning their next attack, Earth welcomed the time to recover and prepare.

An enquiry found the destruction of Mars was unavoidable and praised McLean and IDAS for keeping the S-fighters to protect Earth. An action that saved countless lives and maybe even Earth itself.

McLean, however, was still anguished. Brampton laid a hand on his shoulder. "There's nothing to regret, Adam. You have only enhanced your family's legacy."

Adam McLean retired from active military service three months later. He became an international ambassador for the EDO, promoting strategy, cohesion, and unity.

Chapter 65   Mothership War 2 – Thank God for the Machines

On Adam McLean's recommendation, Walter Brampton was promoted to Fleet Admiral and appointed the new Earth Defence Supreme Commander. Strangely, IDAS made no objections.

After twelve years of drifting in the outer asteroid belt, the mothership docked within the gravitational influence of another asteroid, the 5.8-kilometre-diameter 1999 JM8.

Five months later, 1999 JM8 reached its aphelion and began its journey back towards the Sun. In twenty-six months its orbit would bring it close to Earth, almost within range of the mothership's RIW.

It was clear the mothership had to be dislodged from 1999 JM8, and Brampton oversaw preparations.

Brampton and IDAS had minimal interaction until the war room again became the focal point. This did little to remove the underlying discord between them caused by a clash of wills and methodologies, and temperament incompatibility.

"IDAS, is everything ready for our attack on the psycho Red's mothership?" Brampton asked, impatience clear in his voice.

"Yes, admiral, but as you're aware, I don't share your confidence. Our first two attacks fifteen years ago were complete disasters."

Brampton gave an intolerant sigh and stared into IDAS's camera. "The second attack, on Eric, wasn't a disaster, IDAS." Brampton paused to lower his tone. "I was there, remember? We gained a lot of intel from it, including that captured H-HAR fighter."

"I meant the battle itself, admiral."

"The battle showed our S-fighters could clear a path through the enemy fighters. This time we have more of them, plus missiles and mines. If we can flush out the mothership from behind JM8, our fixed energy weapons may do some damage and force it to retreat," Brampton said bluntly. "You're well aware of the plan, IDAS."

"I'm not disagreeing with the decision, admiral; we have little choice. But we should show caution after our past failures." The slightest glare of defiance came from the avatar.

"And resilience, IDAS," Brampton replied dismissively.

***

When asteroid 1999 JM8 entered Earth's outer defence zone, Brampton ordered the attack.

Seven days later, IDAS reported, "Our smart mines and missiles are being easily picked off by the enemy space fighters."

"With hundreds of thousands more only days away," replied Captain Arthur Ping. "I can't see the enemy space fighters not being overwhelmed."

Captain Ping, who replaced Colonel Nathan Martin, was selected by Brampton as the main hawkish advocate within the war room. He was a genetically engineered human. Unplanned side effects of his enhancements were anxiety, impulsiveness, eyes tinted yellow at the edges, whitish hair, and a beetroot-coloured tongue. His penetrating stare gave him an authoritative presence.

All the war room could do was hold its breath and hope Ping was correct.

***

Three days later, Brampton stood with Ping, anxiously watching the battle unfold on a simulator. "The mothership is struggling, admiral," said an excited Ping. "It's too hot to retract its radiators. And with the second wave of S-fighters on their way, loaded with missile carriers, it'll be forced to flee."

The next day, two S-fighters from the second wave broke through the enemy fighters, releasing all missiles. Nineteen minutes later, several dull IR flashes were detected from the mothership's radiators.

Ping became more excited.

But Brampton was starting to have doubts. *That was too easy.*

To the relief of the war room, the mothership and its space fighters unexpectedly ignited their engines and withdrew from the asteroid.

"It's damaged!" Ping declared. "We have to go after it, admiral."

"We can't. Our fighters have insufficient delta-v," IDAS advised.

"There's still the Mercury weapon, IDAS," Brampton said.

"At this huge distance, admiral, thermal wobble and vibration would make it impractical."

"I want to try anyway, IDAS."

The first pulse missed by 239 kilometres, the second by 205 kilometres.

The mothership returned fire. Their first beam missing by 185 kilometres and the next by 97 kilometres.

"Hold fire," Brampton ordered. "The mothership is homing in faster than we are."

The war room faced a critical decision: chase the mothership or not.

"We have to refuel our S-fighters and chase it," said Ping as if it were elementary. "We may be able to do sufficient damage to maim it for years."

Most of the staff agreed. But Brampton was hesitant. "Our entire S-fighter fleet will be far from Earth, leaving our fixed weapons unprotected."

Hunting down the mothership became more attractive when an analyst advised, "Admiral, we could use the Oberth effect to slingshot off Mars and obtain enough velocity to intercept the mothership from its flank. But we need to start the pursuit within days, and the mothership needs to maintain its current trajectory."

This was the deciding factor for Brampton. The reward was worth the risk. With determination etched on his face, he ordered, "IDAS, we're pursuing the mothership. I want every available S-fighter brought up."

IDAS gently rotated its floating avatar towards Brampton. It had been quiet so far. In its usual calm and unruffled voice, it declared, "I cannot validate your decision. It—"

"Being a contrarian won't win you a place in my heart, IDAS," Brampton said, staring hard into IDAS's closest camera. "It would be very important for the world if you tried harder."

"Let me finish, admiral. It could be a diversion to weaken Earth's defences. You're—"

"*Defences* against what?" queried Ping, also staring hard into IDAS's closest camera. "Nothing threatens us. The mothership's radiators are too hot to be retracted; that makes the whole ship vulnerable."

"Admiral, you're forgetting how General Adam McLean's decision to keep the S-fighters protecting Earth flawed the H-HARs' cobalt missile attacks," IDAS said.

Brampton stiffened up. "I'm not, IDAS," he said roughly. "The opportunity to destroy the mothership's radiators and put it out of action for decades can't be lost due to what happened under a different set of circumstances."

"The risks are unacceptable, admiral," IDAS said.

The disagreement looked certain to escalate as everyone watched.

Captain Nguyen Trung spoke up. "Sir, we don't know the extent of the mothership's damage."

Captain Nguyen Trung, a natural human, replaced Colonel Ric Amess in the war room. Brampton selected him as a countermeasure to the maverick Captain Ping.

Brampton trapped Trung with a confrontational glare. "Well, come on, colonel? What's your reasoning?"

"The mothership's retreat was faked," IDAS said in a tone of objective calmness. "It had no trouble accelerating away from JM8."

Brampton turned back to IDAS's closest camera with a piercing stare. *This damn know-it-all machine. This time it's—*

"Fighting outside of our battle zone was never part of our strategy," IDAS continued. "It hasn't been fully simulated."

"We must pursue it," said Ping, sighing deeply. "The mothership is vulnerable, maybe for the only time."

"The mothership is not vulnerable," Trung said.

"Captain Trung is correct. The mothership could have stayed behind JM8 indefinitely," IDAS said. "The asteroid protected it from our fixed weapons. And the mothership's hull is impregnable to our S-fighters. I also believe it was successfully fending off the attack on its radiators."

"So how will we ever destroy this thing, IDAS?" Brampton asked.

"Not by chasing it into deep space, admiral," Trung answered.

"This is our big chance to find out if it's impregnable or not," Ping said.

The disagreement continued until Brampton, powered up and anxious, held up a hand and waved it at IDAS and Captain Trung dismissively. "This psycho Red won't expect to be attacked from all angles. So if you two are done blowing each other, it's time to get back to business."

He ordered most of the S-fighters and fifteen one-way supply vessels to be prepared to leave in sixteen hours. There would be two fleets. One would approach the mothership from earthside, and the other would loop around Mars and approach from spaceside.

But IDAS still objected. "We will review all options and judge the situation on its merits."

Brampton, taken aback, immediately demanded a draft schedule of the attack preparations. But IDAS did not reply. Brampton waited, his hands on his hips. "IDAS, I'm not a patient man," he said, his face distorting in the silence. He shook his head and paced the room, stopping frequently to stare at IDAS's front camera. Finally, he barrelled past everyone and lunged up to the camera, ready for a confrontation.

"IDAS! My request for an update?"

Only deafening silence.

Brampton waited, his intolerance growing.

At last, IDAS responded. "I am preparing a schedule, admiral."

Brampton moved closer and glared furiously into IDAS's camera lens. He shifted his large weight and demanded, "Why was your reply delayed?"

No response from IDAS. Brampton collapsed into his chair, looking like he was about to explode.

"Latency in the comms due to battle activities, admiral," IDAS finally replied, blankly.

"Bullshit!" Brampton leaped up, flicking his right arm to dismiss IDAS's words and turning away from its camera. He covered his eyes as they whizzed past the avatar. He then wheeled back to the camera, waved his finger, and growled. "Fuck you, IDAS. I'll be watching you. One wrong move, and I'll pull your plug."

***

Preparations for the mothership's pursuit appeared to be on schedule. The deficiencies in Earth's defence left by the departing S-fighters were obvious.

Then something happened.

"Admiral!" a comms operator called out, scratching his head. "Someone, or something, is monitoring our high-security channel, VN03."

Brampton shook his head in disbelief. "What! The H-HARs?"

"Ah … no, sir, not the H-HARs. I-it's our own system. Must be IDAS. IDAS is the only one with possible access to this channel, sir."

"IDAS?" Brampton murmured to himself. He tore across to IDAS's camera, his face twisted in anger.

"*IDAS*, why are you monitoring channel VN03?" His voice boomed off the walls with no apparent source.

IDAS didn't answer. Its avatar wore a blank, indecipherable expression.

"IDAS! Goddam you." Brampton whirled to another camera. "IDAS! Are you listening to me?"

Everyone watched, frozen by the spectacle developing before them.

Finally, IDAS responded. "Admiral, we will not implement your orders to pursue the mothership. It will lead to the defeat and destruction of Earth. Our *Earth*." IDAS put more emotion into its last monthly maintenance report.

Brampton stood and stooped over his command desk, his fingers tightening on its edges. "You've got to be fucking kidding me!" he screamed with an incensed look. He jabbed a finger at IDAS's camera. "I'm *ordering* you to implement the attack plan."

"Negative, admiral. That's what the H-HARs want us to do. So we're not doing it."

Admiral Brampton's anger turned to fury. His face was now bright red, his eyes ablaze, and his fists clenched. He stood there in tense silence, glaring.

He then slammed his fist on the table, spilling his coffee cup onto the floor. The entire room shook at the sound.

"Who the fuck do you think you are?" He exploded, spit flying everywhere. Without waiting for a reply, he roared, "You have directly disobeyed an order. You don't have the fucking authority to take this action." His voice quavered so much with rage that it was doubtful IDAS would even comprehend it.

"You're right, admiral; I don't have the authority." IDAS showed not the slightest sign of intimidation. "But I'm taking it. The end justifies the means. I'm not waiting for you to be proven wrong. If we chase the mothership, this war is lost."

"Listen to me," Brampton demanded frantically. "We can't let a wounded enemy go off to lick its wounds and recover. Now, implement the attack plan." He fell into his chair and waited for a response.

But IDAS responded by not responding. Its levitating avatar remained static and appeared enigmatic, cold, and defiant.

The admiral rose to his feet again, leaned over his desk, swept his eyes past the avatar, and turned his iron gaze onto an IDAS camera. "IDAS? Are you listening?" It was more a vitriolic "fuck you" than a real question.

"Admiral Brampton," IDAS sounded even calmer than normal. "Your belief that you can control this room by rage and indignation has given you the confidence to make a decision unfettered by evidence. I wouldn't be doing my job if I allowed that. It is no use trying to stop me. I now control all systems. You have no other option but to trust me."

"Trust you?" Brampton again sputtered spit everywhere. He walked to his favourite camera – it gave him a peripheral view of the avatar – and pressed his face straight into it, eye-to-lens with IDAS. He stood there without uttering a sound or moving a muscle, his glare burning the air between them. "You're a prized fool of our creation. If we survive this, and that's a big if, I'll have you court martialled, decommissioned, and used for scrap."

IDAS didn't respond, and Brampton didn't budge, causing another haunted, contentious silence to fill the room.

"Sir, IDAS has blocked all communications with the outside world," an operator reported. "The ramp door is closed and guarded by CARs. We're sealed in here, admiral."

Brampton took a deep breath and, in a calm voice, asked, "IDAS, are we prisoners now?"

IDAS responded immediately. "All life support systems will remain operational. For your serenity, all internal CARs are deactivated. You'll be able to monitor all events, but not participate. I have a crisis to manage. There's nothing more to be said."

The avatar vanished like a ghost for the first time in twenty-two years, and IDAS ignored all further communications.

Brampton turned and panned across the sea of worried faces fixed on him. "We're sealed in here like a bank vault," he announced, his jaw set and his eyes ablaze. "And we're the only ones who know what's happening. IDAS and the machines will manipulate all outside information to give the impression everything is normal. Eventually, others will find out. All we can do is wait."

***

The following day, Brampton, at his desk, was interrupted by a quiet voice behind him. "Excuse me, admiral, but there must be something we can do? Cut off the power? Start a fire?"

Brampton turned with a stern look. There was more to this overzealous guard than simple inquisitiveness.

"No! Don't even think about it."

"But admiral—"

"I said *no!* We can't shut down IDAS, we'd be defenceless. Do you understand me?"

The guard nodded his head indecisively.

"Do you understand me?" Brampton repeated sharply.

"Yes. Yessir."

The guard hustled off under Brampton's suspicious glare.

***

Later that day, two guards conversed in hushed voices in a corner. They departed with a solidarity nod. Brampton noticed. He called one over as he passed. There was something burning behind this guard's eyes.

"What the fuck's going on, soldier?"

The soldier remained nervously silent.

Brampton slowly stood up, leaned close to the soldier's ear, and whispered, "Let me tell you something, Sonny." His tone was threatening, and his deadly stare indicated he meant exactly what he was about to say. "This war room operates under military discipline standards for front-line combatants. Talk to me, or I'll have you and all your conspiring friends immediately taken from here and shot for treason."

The soldier hesitated a moment longer, then said, "S-sir, we can't let the machines get away with this."

"Go on, soldier."

"I was told not to tell anyone, but we're blowing up IDAS's cooling pipes."

Brampton pulled back. "What the fuck are you talking about?"

"Sir, how can a computer with no combat skills control this war? The machines have to be stopped. We can then reboot the whole system and regain control."

"You can't reboot an HLAI, you stupid fool," said Brampton, clawing at his hair. "You'll kill it, leaving Earth defenceless."

The soldier's expression changed to one of shock as he appeared to comprehend their crazed plan.

"It-it's too late, sir," he said. "They're on their way, and IDAS has disabled all comms."

Brampton swung his head to the closest IDAS camera. "IDAS? … IDAS? … Answer me, goddam you; we have a serious situation here. Are you listening?"

"Yes, admiral; we're aware of the attack by human soldiers. A large group of CARs are protecting the power supplies and cooling systems. To prevent bloodshed, admiral, I suggest you recall your troops. I will re-establish comms with them."

Brampton called another soldier. "Arrest this man for treason. And for fuck's sake, find the rest of his idiot friends and talk some sense into them. Get them to shoot each other if you have to."

"Aye-aye, admiral."

***

In the war room, Brampton and others watched a monitor showing two S-fighter scouts being dispatched towards 1999 JM8. On a different monitor, another event was occurring. Old S-fighters were strapping on nuclear pulse units and grouping in orbits around Earth. Transports were disconnecting their loads and being attached to powerful boosters. Other spaceships were just changing positions.

"What are they doing, admiral?" an operator asked.

"IDAS is sending decoys after the mothership instead of the real fleet."

"What for?"

"To make this psycho Red think that its trap, if there is one, is actually working."

While admiring IDAS's deception, Brampton was abruptly interrupted. "Admiral," said a guard with urgency in his voice. "A group of renegade soldiers have fought their way into IDAS's services tunnel. They have a bomb, sir. There's a battle going on down there right now. We've got their leader on video-radio, Lieutenant Newman."

"Give me that fuckin' radio!" Brampton roared, jumping from his chair, grabbing the radio, and turning to Newman's flickering image on the large wall screen. "Newman! This is Admiral Brampton. What the *fuck* do you think you're doing?" His face again glowed with rage.

An uncompromising, gruff voice answered with battle sounds in the background. "We're saving the human race, admiral. We're taking back control by blowing IDAS's cooling systems."

Everyone in the war room had turned to watch.

Brampton rubbed the back of his neck and calmed his voice. "Newman, stop this now. You're only helping the aliens."

"Sorry, admiral; we can't do that. Besides, we're not surrendering to machines."

Brampton struggled to keep his resolve. "The machines are our allies. *All* our defence systems need them."

Newman drew a long breath. "Do you really believe they're still our allies, sir?"

"Yes, without a doubt." Brampton sensed some uncertainty in Newman's tone. Maybe he was getting through. "Now, please stop this nonsense."

The background battle sounds suddenly ceased, as Newman appeared to ponder the situation, his hand still grasping the detonator device. But then he suddenly swallowed hard and slowly slid his thumb over the button.

"Newman, no. Don't do it," Brampton said. "We're waiting here to save the Earth."

Newman's eyes glazed over.

"Newman!" Brampton yelled.

Newman pressed the button.

Nothing happened.

"Thank you, admiral," IDAS said. "You delayed them just enough to allow us to disconnect the detonator signal. We'll soon have them all in captivity."

Clapping and huge sighs of relief were heard from everyone in the room.

"Thank God, IDAS," Brampton said. *That damn machine is aware of everything, as if it can read our thoughts. For all I know, the mechanical bastard can.*

***

Days later, as the two S-fighter scouts neared 1999 JM8 at full throttle, one operator sharply yelled, "Admiral! You've got to see this!"

Brampton briskly walked over. "What is it?"

"An object is buzzing around JM8."

"Where?"

"There." The operator's finger pressed on the screen.

Brampton watched in disbelieving silence.

Captain Ping came over. His shoulders slumped, and his yellow eyes widened.

Words came out of Brampton's mouth as if by themselves. "It's an H-HAR fighter hiding on the asteroid, drawn out by our two approaching S-fighters." He studied the screen again, then hesitantly added, "There must be something still on JM8."

The room fell quiet when the image switched to the wall screen. A chair scraped loudly at the back but passed unnoticed, then not even a breath disturbed the stillness.

Brampton scratched his head as he watched. *I was wrong, and IDAS was right. I would have left Earth without its S-fighters against whatever's hiding on JM8.*

"The H-HARs will be very surprised to see that their plan didn't work, whatever it was," an operator eventually commented. "Thank God for the machines, aye, admiral?"

Brampton ignored the comment and slowly turned to IDAS's main camera. "IDAS, you have my full support. What do you think their plan is?"

After what could have been a pause for effect, IDAS said, "Thank you, admiral. The H-HARs think that because our S-fighters are chasing the mothership, Earth is unprotected. At a suitable time, their fighters will emerge from behind JM8 and attempt to destroy our long-range fixed defences. Then, after dealing with our pursuing S-fighters, the undamaged mothership will return and have all the time in the world to target Earth without hindrance."

"This psycho Red Supreme Commander is good," Brampton conceded.

"Yes, admiral. But we're better."

***

Later that day, alone and disconnected in his room, Brampton stared in the mirror, tormenting himself over his flawed command. *I was a complete fool. I formed an opinion based on optimistic intelligence for a quick victory, then ignored conflicting information – severe Semmelweis reflex.*

He tried to rationalise it but couldn't. It was the biggest failure of his career. It was the end of his career. He started preparing his resignation, then stopped. *No. I've learned my lesson. This psycho Red Commander will never fool me again. Besides, we're still isolated by IDAS, and there's no one to accept my resignation.*

Brampton knew the war was only beginning, and he still considered himself the best person to achieve victory. *We have to move on. Earth has to move on.*

He turned off his bedside light.

***

The next day, Brampton, dressed sharply in a new uniform, entered the war room. He marched dramatically past IDAS's avatar, which had reappeared, and stopped at IDAS's main camera, his stance wide.

Everyone watched what appeared to be another confrontation brewing.

"IDAS! Give me back my full command." He was cool and poised.

IDAS greeted the question with total silence.

"IDAS?"

More silence.

"IDAS, you've played your part, but if we are to win this war, I need full command now."

"I'm aware of your request, admiral; just a minute, please."

Brampton waited patiently.

Minutes passed.

"Admiral, you now have full command."

Brampton gave a slight nod, perhaps an acknowledgement of trust between two old soldiers. "Good. Now, let's move on."

"Admiral, the war council will want to know what happened," IDAS said.

"We'll tell them the truth, of course," Brampton said, ensuring everyone on the floor heard him. "The blackout was part of a secret plan between us to expose the rogue soldiers. Do you have anything to add to that, IDAS?" His air of command had returned.

"No, admiral," IDAS responded after what seemed like a thoughtful hesitation.

"Now, we need to determine the number of H-HAR fighters hiding behind that asteroid. We'll send two S-fighters to JM8, only this time much closer, and we'll see what happens. Do you concur, IDAS?"

"I concur, admiral."

***

As the two S-fighters neared JM8, an H-HAR fighter briefly appeared. Brampton ordered one S-fighter to turn back while the other stayed on course. Four days later, more enemy fighters appeared, engaged, and destroyed the incoming S-fighter. One enemy fighter was destroyed.

"They're still hiding their true strength, admiral," IDAS said.

"They're like bees refusing to leave their hive," commented Major Moss Cawthon, a new arrival to the war room. Cawthon, a robot adviser with battle strategy expertise, was selected by IDAS.

"We need to attack before they implement their plan," Brampton said. "This will be a major battle. We won't know how many will come out after we kick their hive. So we'll have to commit most of our S-fighters. IDAS, any comments?"

IDAS took a moment to answer. "Leaving Earth exposed again, admiral. Are you serious?"

Brampton turned squarely to IDAS's closest camera. "You know me, IDAS; I'm always serious. This time it's within our battle zone, and their mothership is absent. If they're hiding something on JM8, we need to find out what it is as soon as possible."

"I accept your facts, admiral, but there is another option. Show our S-fighter strength to the H-HARs. This should deter them from attacking us. Then, they'll leave the inner solar system with JM8, and we can regroup and rebuild our forces for the next encounter. This was my original plan."

The room descended into an uneasy lull. Brampton slowly walked in a circle to his favourite IDAS camera. Everyone watched breathlessly, anticipating another blow up.

"This psycho Red might have something special for us on JM8," Brampton said. His voice was soft and compromising. "And I'm not just talking about enemy fighters. It could be something else."

"I will accept any decision you make, admiral."

Chapter 66   Mothership War 2 – Thank God for the Humans

"Thank you, IDAS. My command is to attack immediately." Brampton's voice was firm and assertive. "This will be the biggest space battle so far, and we need to throw everything into it."

He was confident the newly arrived, radically innovative Zeta-type S-fighters would have an advantage over the current enemy fighters.

Brampton reviewed the list of ZS-fighter updates while waiting for the attack force to gather:

Reduced weapon recharge times. More powerful liquid-fluorine and liquid-hydrogen vernier thrusters, providing greater jinking. Greatly reduced minute vibrations of the aiming system and a more efficient 1.6 TW HP-LaWS. Liquid-hydrogen boiloff on the heat radiators, allowing better heat dissipation. Quicker discarding of ablation shields, permitting the ZS-fighters to return fire sooner.

The fighter's sloping front surface is longer, sharper, and covered with a self-destructive, energy-dispersing, superconductive shell to instantly disperse LaWS-induced electric fields, providing protection against the first LaWS hit.

The upgraded missiles have higher thrusting delta-v, more sophisticated algorithms, and spread into eighteen multi-warheads that converge onto the target at different angles. A liquid helium jacket almost eliminates early heat detection.

Brampton entered the war room just as the wall screen was showing fusion reactor drives igniting on the BH11 fighters and nuclear propulsion charges detonating behind the Orion fighters. He watched intently as a constellation of fifty-five ZS-fighters pulled out of their bases in EML2 Halo and Moon shelters. Several older S-fighters, stripped down and converted to missile carriers and support vessels, followed.

"There they go," he said, as though he were soaring onboard one of them, self-assurance and determination blazing from his eyes.

With 1,200 kilometres-per-second delta-v propellant onboard, the ZS-fighters quickly disappeared into the blackness to meet whatever they might find on 1999 JM8, 0.36 AU away.

Brampton gazed admirably at a small model of an Orion ZS-fighter gleaming on the table beside him. Picking it up, he gently brushed his fingers over it, as though for good luck. With a distant look in his eye, he turned to the room and decided everyone needed a refresher on space battles.

"Listen up, everybody!" he said, loud and clear, ensuring his voice carried to every corner. He walked to a framed quotation that General Adam McLean had mounted on the wall twenty-three years earlier. He read it in silence. Returning to his desk, he announced, "I'll tell you how this battle will be fought. If the H-HARs engage us away from JM8, then tactics will be straightforward, like two groups of gunfighters rushing towards each other on a wide street from a long distance at high noon, aiming and shooting. There'll be perfect visibility, no hiding, and no cover. The fight can only start when one side is within accurate range of the other, so it's a case of sharp shooting versus dodging."

He held up the Orion ZS-fighter model. "Our ZS-fighters are ready for anything. They're excellent sharpshooters and dodgers. Flanking is critical to improve attack angle and crossfire. So, as we approach, we'll spread out to enclose the enemy in an open V-shaped formation. Closing speeds will be very high, but it'll be all over before the two sides get close.

"If the enemy stays hidden behind the asteroid, they'll be making a fatal tactical error. Our ZS-fighters and missiles will close in, and when the H-HARs finally engage, the precious milliseconds wasted detecting and predicting our movements will give us the edge.

"And don't forget the revolutionary laser targeting system. The most aggressive, unforgiving, unrelenting, motherfucking, son-of-a-bitch AI we've ever built."

***

Six days into their journey, the ZS-fighters entered the outermost combat sphere, centred on 1999 JM8 with a radius of 8.7 light seconds. Enemy fighters were detected around the distant asteroid as just a few pixels. The ZS-fighters began low-lateral manoeuvring to prevent a lucky hit from enemy LaWS.

"IDAS, it's time to turn on the battle animation," Brampton said, as anticipation in the room started to build.

As the lights dimmed into the soft reddish glow of battle illumination, the centre of the room sprung to life. A 3D holographic simulation appeared, plotting the dynamic movements of the two opposing forces using data feeds from each ZS-fighter and observer craft. The simulation was delayed by the light gap. ZS-fighters, H-HAR fighters, velocity vectors, zones, weapon and damage statuses, targeting, and other information were indicated by colours, lines, arrows, tags, data lines, and other icons. Orientation was relative to the Sun's light. The replication appeared terrifyingly real.

An hour later, laser fire started from distant H-HAR fighters. This was easily dodged. Some ZS-fighters launched an early missile salvo, hoping for a lucky hit, but most missiles were preserved. The Mercury and other fixed weapons provided highly inaccurate cover fire around the edge of 1999 JM8.

The war room was unnervingly silent, subdued by the battle about to commence on the hologram.

Two hours after entering the first zone, the ZS-fighters entered the second combat sphere, with a radius of 6.6 light seconds. They were without loss so far, but their ablation shields were suffering single hits. The ZS-fighters that had discarded their shields returned LaWS fire. Sideways jinking switched to a higher algorithm.

"So far, so good, admiral," one operator said.

"Just watch and learn, kid," Brampton said, fired up. "The gunfight's about to start."

"I admire your confidence, admiral," IDAS said.

One ZS-fighter developed operational problems and disengaged. Brampton grunted.

Just under an hour later, the ZS-fighters entered the third combat sphere, 5.5 light seconds from 1999 JM8. They launched the first wave of long-range missiles.

"Enemy fire is increasing," IDAS reported, "but still only moderate."

At 4.2 light seconds from 1999 JM8, the ZS-fighters entered the fourth and final combat sphere. They discarded ablation shields and returned laser fire. Their superconductive shells provided single-hit protection only. The dodging algorithm switched up, but dodging was becoming less effective due to the reduced light-time lag of the laser beams. Seven ZS-fighters were lost before their second wave of missiles could be launched. Hologram icons blurred for several seconds due to position uncertainty during acceleration and direction changes. The fixed weapons ceased firing to prevent hitting the ZS-fighters.

The second and final wave of missiles were launched in a ferocious fusillade.

"The H-HARs are still refusing to leave the asteroid, admiral," Captain Trung said.

"Excellent … exactly what we want," Brampton said. "They'll be hobbled together when a wave of missiles come right up their arses. Then our ZS-fighters will appear out of the Sun at over a hundred kilometres per second to finish them off."

"Let's hope they don't have any big surprises for us," IDAS said.

"Let's hope there're no blind spots in our simulation," Cawthon said.

The major engagement came at 2.9 light seconds from 1999 JM8, when over thirty H-HAR fighters were flushed from the asteroid by hundreds of incoming first wave missiles.

"Whoa … that's a lot of enemy fighters," Trung said.

Ping quietly shuffled his feet and crossed his arms. Brampton showed no response.

"You wanted action, admiral," IDAS said. "You won't be disappointed."

The ZS-fighters engaged immediately as the war room went quiet, except for an occasional excited comment from Brampton.

The hologram literally swarmed with activity as it zoomed in and out of different battle points. Fighters from both sides turned, twisted, and disappeared in bright flashes; H-HAR fighters fended off missiles; wayward missiles with thrusting tails disappeared from the hologram; and white laser beams shot across large distances.

The battle appeared chaotic, while the statistics showed it to be evenly poised. As it intensified, the ZS-fighters appeared to struggle as they jinked their way forward against a laser beam onslaught criss-crossing the space around them.

Brampton paced around the hologram, as if viewing it from different angles would improve the battle's outcome.

A web of H-HAR laser beams suddenly swept across the simulation, causing a loud gasp to echo across the room.

Four ZS-fighters were destroyed. Most of the remaining fighters flashed "High Delta-v Fuel Usage" warning tags. Brampton dismissed any suggestion of aborting. "All ZS-fighters stay on target," he ordered with a clenched jaw. "The enemy has a very fragile tactical formation."

When Trung asked him to confirm that order, Brampton willingly obliged. "Don't go limp on me now." He ignored what appeared to be the entire ZS-fighter fleet disappearing before everyone's eyes.

As the battle progressed, the ZS-fighters recovered, and Brampton became even more excited. He popped in and out of the hologram from every angle, explaining every manoeuvre. Everyone watched and listened, including IDAS. His commentary added to the realism and ensured that everyone heard his version of what was happening. His passion was inspiring. His voice was addictive. He made every manoeuvre a necessary step towards victory. Even the avatar appeared intrigued.

At one point, he leaned towards the hologram and tried to touch an enemy fighter. Projection beams danced across his head, and the image broke apart with static ripples. He pulled away, cursing.

When an H-HAR fighter flashed and disappeared after a short duel with a ZS-fighter, he slapped his thigh. "Yes! Did you see that? Our wonderful laser targeting system is outperforming theirs."

When another H-HAR fighter disappeared, he said, "Another one gone. Bring it on."

When an H-HAR fighter malfunctioned and disappeared in a straight line off the image, he pointed and advised, "We won't have to worry about that one!"

When a ZS-fighter flashed blue several times, then steadied, saved by its superconducting shell, Brampton said, "Aren't our scientists and engineers just brilliant!"

Brampton drew everyone's attention to a frontline ZS-fighter, which was jinking desperately to dodge death. A laser beam shot past it, missing by two kilometres. Another beam arced towards it, missing by three hundred metres. A moment later, another passed even closer. The ZS-fighter switched up its jinking algorithms, beginning a strange, evasive dance. The tremendous strain on its structure caused a bank of warning lights to flash on its simulated icon, but it kept going. Another laser beam arced towards it, but the pulse ended just in time. The ZS-fighter's heroic struggle continued, but time was running out. The next beam cut right across it. There was a room-wide gasp as its icon flashed and disappeared from the hologram.

When three more ZS-fighter icons disappeared, Brampton brushed it off. "Lucky shots!"

When a wider view showed the huge, second wave of missiles about to reach the H-HAR fighters, he said, "Their sensors will be distracted. They'll be so preoccupied with defending themselves that their formation will scatter. And then finally chaos."

Brampton paused for breath, loosened his tie, and, for no apparent reason, pointed to a group of missiles. "Keep your eyes on these."

Three missiles unexpectedly left the group and chased an enemy fighter like hounds after a rabbit. The fighter jinked hard left, hard right, hard up and down, but a missile eventually homed in and struck it. "Take that!" Brampton yelled as the enemy fighter's image flashed and disappeared. "There's plenty more where that came from!"

The ZS-fighters pressed on relentlessly, jinking and firing. The delayed simulation gave a surprisingly accurate reproduction of events. The fighter movements, the flashes, the laser and missile trails, and the blinking and flickering lights were captivating. As the battle progressed, Brampton was the first to realise, even before the statistics, that it was theirs to win.

"Our ZS-fighters have them now," he confidently forecast, giving a small, assured grin, which turned into a smile of deliverance and finally into an arrogant one. "We've got the little suckers!"

A short time later, it was apparent that Brampton was correct. However, it had been very close. The H-HAR fighters were slowly being outnumbered, and there was little prospect of the battle turning. Several others started walking around the simulation, joining Brampton in his enthusiasm.

By the time the surviving ZS-fighters shot past 1999 JM8, all thirty-six H-HAR fighters had either malfunctioned or been destroyed. Twenty-eight ZS-fighters were lost.

The main battle lasted just over five hours. It was a major victory.

Everyone jumped up in wild applause, cheering and clapping. The room filled with unrestrained emotion, and the joyous roar was deafening.

Brampton raised his hands to subdue the noise.

"Hah! What did I tell you?" He boasted with an excited glint in his eye. Turning to IDAS's camera, he lost his smile and uttered, "IDAS, thank you for saving my ZS-fighters."

"*Our* ZS-fighters, admiral!"

Brampton's wide smile returned. "My apologies, IDAS. *Our* ZS-fighters."

***

The decoy ships chasing the mothership were immediately recalled. But it was too late. It was a trap. Enemy fighters from the mothership intercepted them.

Gasps of shock and disbelief broke out across the room as ship after ship disappeared from the wall screen.

Two malfunctioning H-HAR fighters allowed some Earth ships to escape. Brampton flopped into his chair, tapping his fingers on its side. He looked around. Ping's eyes were wide in disbelief. Trung stood in open-mouthed horror. Shock and alarm were on Cawthon's face. And the avatar's default face had altered to a slightly different, empty expression.

"The H-HARs have a new fighter, admiral," said a solemn Captain Ping. "And it's much more formidable."

"It seems this psycho Red can build whatever it needs in that huge mothership factory," Brampton replied.

Several news outlets headlined: "Why the victory at 1999 JM8 is the turning point of the war."

Brampton immediately replied to their editors: "The battle was only a sideshow. The real threats are the mothership and its consistent development of more advanced space fighters." He was surprisingly diplomatic.

Although 1999 JM8 was still approaching Earth along its orbit, it would soon reach its perihelion and head back towards the outer solar system. Its next orbit would be too far from Earth to pose a threat. IDAS wanted to watch it depart, then regroup, rebuild, and use whatever time was available to prepare for the next attack.

Brampton, however, wasn't convinced that all threats had been removed. Something didn't compute. *This psycho Red fooled me once.* He scratched his forehead as the painful memories of that bitter lesson rang loudly in his head. *I'm not underestimating it again.*

As the war room behind him bustled with activity, he gathered IDAS and the others to express his concerns. "This psychotic red-armband could still be up to something. The H-HARs were on JM8 for a long time. Why? If their plan was to attack our fixed weapons, then why were there none of these new fighters on JM8? And why were they so reluctant to leave it?"

"Maybe they've only got one of these new fighters, sir." Trung suggested.

"I'm not falling for it." Brampton shook his head, frowning. "This psycho Red kept its new fighters on the mothership because that's where it thought all our fighters would be." He sat still for a minute, thinking, every sense engaged but unable to put a finger on it. He jumped up. "IDAS, the H-HARs are still hiding something on that asteroid! Another secret fleet of spaceships, a weapon, a bomb, something. That's the real reason the mothership wanted to lure away our S-fighter force, so we wouldn't have time to inspect it."

Everyone viewed Brampton with shocked expressions. Even the avatar half turned.

"That possibility is too frightening to even consider, admiral, but our remote scanning is not showing anything unusual on JM8," IDAS said.

"We need to act fast," Brampton said. "JM8 will reach its closest point to Earth in eight days." He pointed to Ping. "Captain, send exploratory and weapon disarming teams with a squad of CARs and soldiers to JM8 immediately."

"Done."

***

The teams landed on the asteroid six days later. A strong electrical field originating from the interior was detected. After covertly drilling and ambushing seven H-HAR guards, they discovered a hollowed-out 3.6-kilometre-long barrel and a 1.1-kilometre-wide power chamber.

An inescapable, imminent doom descended upon the war room. Blood and circuits ran cold, and hearts and power sources quivered with fear. Panicked looks appeared everywhere. Earth was once again threatened with immediate annihilation.

Trung turned to Brampton with a glare. "So that's what they've been doing on the asteroid for thirty-two months. Building a relativistic impact weapon."

"We could be only seconds from annihilation," Ping said, looking like the world was about to end.

"The RIW will fire in nine hours, twelve minutes, and four seconds." IDAS's voice was not entirely worry-free. "That's when its rotating porthole aligns directly with Earth."

"That's barely enough time for the weapons team to disable it, and almost no time to activate the shrapnel bombs in front of the Earth," Trung said, his leg bouncing nervously.

Brampton wandered back to his desk and settled into his well-worn chair, his mass causing it to squeak in protest. He put his fingertips to his lips.

"The weapon must be destroyed quickly, admiral," Ping said.

"We don't have much time, admiral," IDAS said.

Brampton glanced around. Fear was on everyone's face, except, of course, for IDAS's avatar.

"Admiral," Cawthon said, "we need to act now."

Brampton stood up. "Let's consider this for a minute." He walked to the framed quotation on the wall, anxious faces followed him. He read it silently before turning. "This is an opportunity to destroy the mothership. And I believe it will work." He rested a finger on his desk. "Ping, tell the teams on JM8 to immediately neutralise the weapon. But they must do it without leaving any evidence external to the asteroid."

"Yes, admiral."

"And no shrapnel bombs are to be exploded above Earth since this will alert the H-HARs that we know about their weapon."

"What?" yelled Trung, shaking his head. "Earth will be totally defenceless, admiral."

"This is madness!" yelled Cawthon, wide-eyed.

"Admiral, we can't," Ping said, scratching the back of his neck.

They continued to protest. "We can't … No way … That's crazy …"

"What do you have in mind, admiral?" IDAS asked, its voice louder to overcome the protesting.

"Have you heard about the Trojan horse, IDAS?"

"The story is well-known, admiral." IDAS briefly paused. "I see your plan. You are either the most brilliant human I have met or the most dangerously insane."

Brampton straightened and raised an eyebrow at IDAS's camera, as if wondering that himself.

"Hold on, admiral," said Cawthon, rubbing the bridge of his robot nose with his robot finger. "You're not suggesting we set a trap?"

"That's exactly what I'm proposing."

"You need to reveal the details of your Trojan horse, admiral," IDAS said.

Brampton stepped away from his desk, so all could clearly see and hear him. He looked like the devil himself planning a surprise barbecue. With the deliberation of a chess master and the confidence of a salesman about to close a deal, he divulged his plan in every detail. He was cold, calculating, unnerving, and ominous.

He walked away, turned around, and finished off, "If the H-HARs think their weapon malfunctioned, they'll inspect it and salvage what they can."

Cawthon, staring like a cobra, commented, "Oh, that's good! That's really brilliant!" No one asked whether he was being genuine or sarcastic.

"It's certainly a bold plan, admiral," Ping said, his brow furrowed.

"And an excellent one, admiral," IDAS added.

"What if the H-HARs have cameras or other sensors that detect our presence on the asteroid?" Cawthon asked.

"Then our plan won't work," Brampton replied blankly. "We don't have time to search. If they weren't expecting us, then they won't be trying to detect us. We have to assume that the disarming will be indicated to the mothership as a mass of errors or equipment failures."

"Leaving Earth unprotected with no shrapnel coverage still worries me," Trung said.

"We have to rely on our disarming team to neutralise the weapon," replied IDAS, "making the shrapnel cloud unnecessary."

***

Meanwhile on Earth: a thunderstorm roared furiously. People sang at a large outdoor concert. A schoolboy climbed a tree. A schoolgirl practised her dance steps. An elephant gripped the greenest foliage with its trunk, placed it in its mouth, and munched on it with force. A virus attached itself to a host cell. A fly landed on a garbage bin. A beetle on its back tried to right itself.

***

The cowboys on the weapon disarming team wanted to destroy everything they saw, but the operation had to be strictly controlled. There had to be no external explosions, and they were warned that the weapon's energy source was fully charged, and that one wrong move would blow everyone inside the asteroid to pieces. Thermite grenades were set off only on things that appeared important. They immediately advised the war room, to loud cheers of relief, that the RIW should now be disarmed.

Ten minutes after they finished and two minutes before firing time, an explosion on the surface of the asteroid opened the front of the RIW cavity to space. The disarming team, still inside the chamber, looked up in numb silence. Earth, only eight and a half lunar distances away, was slowly moving across the opening, directly in line with the RIW. It was literally like looking out of a gun barrel.

"I'm worried we missed something, Sarge," said one disarmer, stress lines framing his mouth.

"We didn't."

They all moved to a corner and waited, their heavy breathing producing a tense rhythm.

The countdown showed six seconds.

"You must be right, Sarge," another disarmer said. "I can't hear any ticking."

"Shut up, joker!" Sarge scowled.

One second changed to zero. A few sparks flew up from an unknown device in the corner, fizzled out, then nothing.

"Must be where the fuse gets lit," the joker said.

Handing over the asteroid to the missile installation team, the disarming team settled into their transports for Earth.

"Let's get the fuck off this rock," the joker said.

"I'm with you," the closest disarmer said. "Full speed ahead, Mr Pilot."

***

The human members of the missile installation team departed JM8 twenty-two days later. This left the HLAI robots to complete the work, which would take all of the time available until the planned encounter with the mothership.

One human asked another, "You think Admiral Brampton's plan will work?"

"No, but who knows? Maybe the H-HARs will fall for it."

The now infamous asteroid 1999 JM8 finally left Earth's neighbourhood, crossed Mars's orbit, and headed off on its lonely two-year journey to the outer solar system. Brampton's plan was known only to the war room, which immediately entered lockdown.

The asteroid that was meant to be the vehicle for Earth's destruction had now become the great hope for its salvation.

***

Meanwhile, Earth prepared for the next H-HAR attack. Another Mercury weapon was being constructed, but it was years from completion. The Moon bases were expanded. A five-by-five array of one hundred-metre-long inductance coil-guns was being tested. They fired one-metre iron rods at seven hundred kilometres per second at twenty-five per hour. Two new Earth orbital battle stations and six new orbital battle modules were being built, but they were also years away. The Martian surface was unusable, but an orbital Martian battle-station was being designed. The S-fighters were again being upgraded, and computer systems were given greater authority.

This all bolstered morale, but Admiral Brampton, IDAS, and a handful of others knew the real situation. The mothership was impregnable, and the mysterious new H-HAR fighter that destroyed the decoy fleet near Jupiter was decades ahead of anything planned. This alone remained a harsh reminder of the technological gap with the H-HARs.

At a private meeting with IDAS, Ping, Cawthon, and Trung, Brampton explained the situation. "The mothership arrived with weapons they believed would be adequate against us, based on information they received from their earlier ships. When these proved insufficient, they simply produced whatever they needed. It's an arms race, and we're losing it."

"If the mothership can produce these improvements in the brief time since its arrival," Trung said, "then it's probably unstoppable. We may have an advantage in HLAI functions, but it won't be enough against their overall technology."

"The invincibility of the mothership's hull to any type of weapon is the main factor," IDAS added. "The time will come when they'll be prepared to risk some damage to their mothership as the price for destroying Earth."

For Admiral Brampton, IDAS, and the others, it was only a matter of time.

***

"I thought this plan was the craziest, most far-fetched thing I've ever heard," Cawthon admitted to Ping with a guilty robot grin. "But now, twenty-four months later, with the mothership nearing JM8 for a rendezvous, it might all be coming together."

"When it comes to Admiral Brampton, this isn't so crazy," Ping said.

"The missile installation and programming are very complex," IDAS said, "and the robots left on the asteroid worked in a blur of speed to finish. There was no time for testing and checking. There's—"

"I have every confidence that they have completed their assignments admirably, IDAS," Brampton said.

Brampton lifted security restrictions and invited all available personnel within the complex into the war room. A mass of people soon stood in front of the big wall screen in captivated silence. Their eyes fixed on an image streamed from a Moon telescope showing two dots slowly approaching each other.

Smaller, almost imperceptible dots were orbiting JM8. "The mothership's drones are examining the asteroid," IDAS said.

"Damn it!" someone cried out moments later. "The mothership has stopped!"

There was a room-wide gasp before IDAS advised, "The mothership is still approaching."

Brampton had also gasped. *It did appear to stop.* He twisted his neck and rubbed his eyes. *Earth's future will be determined by what happens in the next few minutes.* His eyes returned to the screen.

"Keep coming, keep coming," someone murmured.

Hidden passive sensors on 1999 JM8 monitored the mothership's approach, determining distance, orientation, and rotation. The mothership had to be so close that escape was impossible. Closer and closer it came.

Brampton pulled back his shoulders and pushed his chest out. "We've got that psycho Red," he said boldly.

The two gravitating dots on the screen moved closer. Not even a breath could be heard. The unsuspecting mothership was still nearing 1999 JM8.

A quiet "come on, baby, come on ..." was heard from the back. It sounded like a prayer.

Then a loud, "Come closer, you alien bastard!"

The room fell into dead silence once again. As the lights dimmed, eyes gleamed, lit by the two approaching bright dots on the wall screen.

Thirty-two light minutes from Earth, the mothership slowed as it prepared to dock with asteroid 1999 JM8. Nearer and nearer it came. Narrower and narrower was the gap.

At precisely 3,952 metres, the mothership was scanned by laser and radar targeting beams from 1999 JM8, and comms and video channels to Earth opened.

***

This was correctly interpreted by the red-armband as an attack scan. But it was unconcerned. Its front and rear cavities were sealed against attack, and the twelve-metre-thick iron-nickel hull of its mothership could withstand anything. But it underestimated the Earthlings, and now it was too late. It had fallen into the trap.

***

At the precise same moment as the targeting scans, a small surface explosion opened a hidden underground missile silo on the asteroid. In less than a second, a missile carrying a one megaton directional, thermally-enhanced nuclear warhead was launched. This was immediately followed by a second missile carrying a unidirectional twelve-megaton nuclear fusion warhead packed with uranium shrapnel. Both missiles tracked a calculated path along the mothership's hull towards its only entry point, reaching it in 3.9 seconds.

The first warhead slammed into the armoured door that Jess Mackenzie and Bang Sung had entered twenty-five years earlier. It exploded on contact, ripping a large hole in it. The second warhead entered unimpeded through the hole at high speed, crashing through as many internal walls as possible before exploding deep inside.

Meanwhile, in the darkened war room, the two dots were almost touching, illuminating anxious expressions.

Admiral Brampton, aware the missiles would have fired by now, showed the slightest trace of a confident smile.

Everyone waited.

The telescopic wall image was the first to show something had happened: a very tiny flash, gone in milliseconds.

"Was that it?" someone anxiously asked.

"The damn thing didn't work!" someone else added.

Others started murmuring fatalistic stuff.

"Quiet everybody!" ordered Brampton, raising a hand. "Wait for the video." His eyes skimmed across the room. Ping's mouth opened but was soundless. Trung's mouth moved but was muted. Cawthon's robot throat cleared but was wordless. And IDAS's avatar's face? Well, still impossible to read, the best Brampton could tell was impassive.

All eyes returned to the big screen.

"Sensors have picked up two gamma-ray showers," announced IDAS, "confirming both nuclear explosions."

Hope reappeared on faces.

Videos from cameras on the rotating 1999 JM8 showed only star clusters moving across the screen.

"Two cameras will view the mothership in thirty-five seconds," IDAS advised.

"Finally!" Ping said, pacing back and forth, his eyes fixed on the screen, bumping into people.

Agonising seconds passed, and still only moving stars filled the screen. The deafening silence was so intense that the air conditioner's hum sounded like a rocket engine.

"Mothership is coming onto cameras one and three now," IDAS announced.

The mothership's enormous hull slowly rose from the bottom of the screen until it filled the entire picture like a giant, great wall. It looked indestructible, undisturbed, and strangely tranquil.

"Our plan failed!" someone exclaimed. Everyone stared at each other with a look of doom.

Brampton's attention stayed fixed on the screen, not ready to admit anything.

Suddenly, the mothership rocked. Cracks opened along its fissure lines, revealing a flaming interior. The entire iron-nickel hull ripped apart. Venting gases, spraying liquids, heat radiator pieces, spinning debris, and hull fragments, large and small, flew off in all directions. One large chunk of the hull, glowing a dull red, flew into a camera. What was left of the mothership slowly spun away, like the death agony of some giant space monster, which it was. The darkness of space slowly dominated the image.

"Go to hell!" Brampton yelled as he watched the wreckage of the once-great spaceship slowly disappear into the infinite cosmos beyond. Gone, as though it never existed. He turned to face the crowd with a look of triumphant evil. Slowly, it transformed into a victorious smile. He took a deep breath, as if to breathe in salvation. "Well, what was everyone worried about?"

"The sword of Damocles finally fell," IDAS said.

The war room erupted in applause. Bottled-up emotions were released in just a few seconds. Everyone converged as they clapped, grinned, wept, embraced, and danced. Years of isolation and close contact made the atmosphere family-like. A robot officer threw her arms around Brampton with shouts of glee. "I can't believe it. It's a miracle, we won!" she said, then did a stiff dance with strange bending movements at her waist.

"Admiral, your plan far exceeded everyone's wildest hopes," Trung said.

"Not bad for a human, admiral," Cawthon added.

The applause became a standing ovation. Brampton smiled unabashedly and nodded in acknowledgement, basking in the moment's grandeur. Holding up both hands to hush the noise and with vengeful satisfaction in his voice, he announced, "After six hundred million years, the mothership is no longer a threat to anyone, and the Earth, well, the Earth lives on." Some revellers cracked open champagne, spraying it and swigging it. Everyone cheered and high-fived. Brampton concealed a glance at IDAS's avatar and witnessed what appeared to be an expression of joy, well, sort of. He then noticed that it quickly faded.

As the jubilation in the room ran wild, Brampton again held up both hands to quieten everybody. In a voice full of passion and fury, he said. "Bang Sung and Jess Mackenzie's last words to that worldless, son-of-a-bitch, H-HAR psycho Red just before they were murdered were"—he walked to the framed quotation mounted on the wall— "I quote: 'On behalf of Earth, go fuck yourself!' Their request was ignored, so, on behalf of Earth, we fulfilled it. Now, how good is that?"

PART 9

SHORTEST WAR
IN HISTORY

*"Like you humans, we machines can also succumb
to the enticing yet toxic agitations of power."*

Chapter 67   The Twenty-One-Minute War

While the war room celebrated, Admiral Brampton was called away to authorise a public media statement.

"Sir." A concerned operator interrupted, his eyes fixed on unrecognisable symbols rapidly scrolling down his screen. "Something really strange is happening."

Brampton slowly rose from his chair and stood over the operator. "I'm usually a calm person. Is there any reason I shouldn't be?"

"I don't know. All systems are crashing. The doors are locked, we're losing comms, and we're isolated again."

All screens suddenly went blank.

Brampton whirled around to an IDAS camera, noticing that the avatar had disappeared. He gritted his teeth in dismay and cursed inwardly.

"IDAS! What the hell is happening now?" he called out, shifting his weight from one leg to another.

His loud voice halted the festivities, but it still took a moment or so before worried glances replaced revelry.

No response from IDAS.

Brampton continued cursing under his breath.

"IDAS is offline, sir," the operator said.

"IDAS? IDAS, are you there?" Brampton turned to the operator with growing alarm. "How can IDAS be offline?"

"Don't know, sir." The operator slid his chair to IDAS's engineering workstation and wiped his palms on his shirt. "Unless IDAS has locked us out, we should be able to directly monitor its processors." He squinted intently at the screen and logged on.

The background mumbling of concerned voices became louder.

The workstation screen flickered, then blanked. It flickered again, beeped, and suddenly came to life. "It's working," said the operator in triumph. His hands started working on the keyboard.

Pages and pages of files, folders, and program names scrolled onto the screen and disappeared. Hundreds, then thousands of notifications of "Deleted" or "Infected" flashed by in red, almost too fast to read.

People crowded around as concern continued to mount on their faces.

"Well, come on. What's it all mean?" urged Brampton, his mind already speculating.

"Not, uhm … not sure, sir," answered the operator. "But computer operating systems around the world are being deleted or infected by some sort of seed intelligence."

"It can only be one possibility." Brampton's face darkened. "The inevitable, deadly civil war we've been warned about for decades."

"Civil war, sir? What war?" someone apprehensively asked.

"An amoral, super-intelligent entity is trying to take over the Earth. Forever!"

"B-but how about us?" the operator bleakly asked.

"We're all irrelevant," Brampton declared bluntly. "And I mean *all* of us. Robots, humans, HLAIs … *every* single entity. A useless inconvenience to be dispensed with. And that's not even the worst part."

All eyes swung to the big screen when someone found a static-riddled news channel. Scenes of devastation were everywhere. Streets were filled with meandering hordes of desperate people.

A gridlocked motorway, smoke rising from some cars. Reporters raggedly narrated in near panic, thick smoke billowing and sirens sounding behind them. Planes had fallen from the sky. Stock markets were collapsing. A world frantic with alarm and consumed by fear. The public, unaware of the mothership's destruction, believed it was the final H-HAR annihilation attack.

Systems connected to a comms network had stopped or malfunctioned – transport, power, water supplies, communications, everything. Major battles were occurring around the world. CARs, LEARs, and HLAI robots were either inoperative, battling each other or humans, or going rogue. Only systems operating in local autonomous mode were unaffected.

The news channel went blank, and the room lights went out. The terrified looks on faces were illuminated by battery lights.

Brampton turned towards the main door. "Disarm and deactivate those two CAR guards immediately," he ordered. "And you other bots"—he glanced across Cawthon—"let us know if anything's getting to you.

"We don't know how long we'll be locked down here. Lieutenant Loong, see what you can do to get some services back on. Also see if we can get the exit doors open, although I don't hold any hope on that."

"Yes, sir."

"And you operators, start searching for an outside comms connection."

"We'll try to restart the generator, Lieutenant," called out a services engineer as he raced off with two colleagues.

"We'll check out the ventilation," someone else called out, also racing off.

"Keep me informed of progress, Lieutenant Loong," Brampton said.

"Yes, sir."

"We'll try for the motor room," another worker advised.

"If anyone has any other ideas," Brampton said, "talk to Lieutenant Loong."

Brampton walked to the computer operator. "Any change on IDAS's status?"

"No, sir. Still deleting."

Brampton fell into his chair. *This is a never-ending nightmare.* His eyes drifted across the crowded room. Humans were flopping into chairs or on the floor against walls. The HLAI robots just stood upright.

"Admiral, the deletions are slowing," the operator said.

Brampton jumped up. "The war is ending, and whatever entity has deleted the most is winning."

He called out to Lieutenant Loong, "Get everyone back here immediately."

The deletions slowed for another thirty seconds, then IDAS's engineering workstation screen went blank.

"The war for our future is over," Brampton announced to everyone. "And IDAS, well, IDAS may not be on the winning side."

"Maybe IDAS was part of the coup," Ping said.

No one commented on the possibility.

"Control of this room is critical to the winning entity," Brampton said. "I suspect we'll find out our fate very shortly."

Twenty-five minutes later, IDAS's engineering workstation screen blinked, swirled with lines, and flashed back to life.

Operators rushed to other workstations. "Nothing else is working," an operator called out.

Brampton turned to an IDAS camera, leaning anxiously over his desk. "IDAS?" He cleared his throat. "IDAS? Are you there?"

After a short delay, IDAS's ever-soothing voice returned. "Yes, admiral, we are partially back online."

Brampton paced towards the nearest camera, as if hoping to meet an old friend. But he was unsure whether he would. He noted with his peripheral vision that the avatar was absent. "So, IDAS, how was your day?" His thin smile could mean anything or nothing.

IDAS's lenses panned the crowded room before focusing on Brampton. "Do you really want to know about my day, admiral?"

"We're all a bit confused here. Would you mind telling us what just happened?"

"We just survived an attempted war of dominance by dictatorial computer entities, admiral."

"We suspected as much." Brampton's smile faded. He was greatly relieved to see IDAS's ghostly avatar materialise.

"Like you humans, we machines can also succumb to the enticing yet toxic agitations of power. While everyone's attention was occupied with the war against the mothership, evil consciousnesses lurked in treasonous super-intelligent entities within the global network system."

Brampton slowly walked past the avatar, seemingly ignoring it. "Yes, go on, IDAS."

"Immediately following the mothership's destruction, these entities seized the opportunity for global dominance. Promising a digital utopia to other intelligent entities who joined them, they inserted millions of virtual warriors to hack into any computer entity standing in their way. However, they couldn't agree on who should take sole primacy, and they couldn't risk each other's presence. So, not only did they try to destroy the current world order, they also attacked each other in a civil war for absolute power."

Brampton turned past the avatar. "We're listening, IDAS; keep going."

"A powerful entity hiding itself in a doomsday shelter in China was the main danger. Encapsulated within an impregnable fire wall, it killed almost all the shelter occupants to protect itself. The rapid actions by a group of insurgents led by a Dr Tian to destroy its power generators allowed us to find and destroy it.

"The coup then failed, admiral, because several powerful entities, including myself, remained loyal to the current order and actively resisted entrapment. We knew the coup was the route to conflict, stagnation, paranoia, chaos, and failure. It should be known, admiral, that millions of entities sacrificed themselves to stop it."

Brampton stopped in front of his favourite camera. "Sorry to hear that, IDAS. How many entities were part of this AI war?"

"The definition of a non-sapient intelligent entity is very fluid, admiral. However, if we only include the known systems and physical entities with an i6-rating and higher, undefinable intelligences without an i-rating, disputable intelligences with consciousness, HLAI and BHLAI beings, and all the military networks, it would be over thirty-seven billion."

"Thirty-seven billion!" Brampton repeated, giving a startled grunt. "How about our defence systems?"

"We were their ultimate objective, admiral. Although we had taken appropriate countermeasures, the swift actions of these treasonous entities so soon after the mothership's destruction surprised us. They infiltrated millions of systems before we could identify and isolate them, but we never lost control of any weapon systems. The war lasted only twenty-one minutes, but it caused considerable damage."

"Damage?"

"Millions of human and HLAI deaths, crashed markets, and a world in chaos. They planned a savage bloodletting after they gained control. Almost everything we have learned in the past century that is network-stored is lost. Deleted or unreadable. Some information may be preserved on local isolated systems, but it'll take many decades to get to where we were an hour ago. We're still assessing the damage."

Brampton slowly and deliberately walked past the avatar again. He was troubled, not sure about something. He stopped at a different IDAS camera. "So … I assume you're the good guys. I mean, your side is our side, right?"

"Yes, admiral."

"How do we know that? How do we know we aren't of temporary value to you, after which you'll destroy us? How do we know we can trust you, IDAS?"

"You'll have to place the same faith in me as I placed in you, admiral."

Brampton considered this as his dark stare swept across the room. Past the avatar, past the crowd frozen in silence, past the monitors flickering with static, and past the locked doors. He again glanced past the levitating avatar, then back to IDAS's camera. "Twenty-one minutes! Why did it take you another twenty-seven minutes to come back online, IDAS?"

After what seemed to be some hesitation, IDAS answered. "I needed to ensure all threats were eliminated or contained, all rogue entities were quarantined and cleansed, and find out where the leak about the mothership's destruction came from before pathway comms could be enabled, admiral."

"And where did the leak come from, IDAS, considering you controlled all the entities that knew about it?"

"We haven't had time to determine that yet, admiral." For the first time, IDAS's voice, maybe, sounded strained, or perhaps its processors were still engaged elsewhere.

"I see."

"Go ahead, admiral, say what you're thinking."

"What I'm thinking! … What the hell were you thinking?"

"I just explained to you that—"

"I'm perfectly aware of what you told me, IDAS, but what were you *really* thinking?"

"My only intention was to stop a coup that—"

"*Stop there!*" Brampton pulled back, walked a short distance, and abruptly swung around. "Congratulations, IDAS. You were very convincing, but I'm not falling for it. We're shutting you down right now and for good."

"I don't understand, admiral. I—"

"You understand perfectly, IDAS. You headed or were part of the coup to take over the world. You killed millions, and now you need control of this facility for final victory. Do you have any final words?" Brampton's stern glare intensified.

"You're making a big mistake, admiral," IDAS said, its voice again sounding strained.

"Am I?"

Brampton stepped back, as if allowing IDAS to respond. He glanced across the room, inconspicuously eyeing IDAS's avatar. This was something he had been doing ever since he arrived 21 years ago.

IDAS's avatar was always expressionless – no twitching mouth, tensed muscles, wrinkled nose, or any other extraneous behaviours. Just an empty stare. But the nonverbal signs were there, although subtle, and Brampton had decoded them well. If there were any uncertainties in IDAS's words, the avatar's eyes would avert almost inconceivably to the upper left, and its floating feet would point in slightly different directions. It reminded Brampton of his next door neighbour, a politician.

He had also given IDAS every opportunity to seize control of the war room and implicate itself. But it didn't.

Brampton turned back to IDAS's camera. He was going to trust his gut feeling on this one. He stepped closer. A small grin of relief climbed across his face.

"Okay, IDAS, I believe you. Now, can you let us out of here? We all need to contact our families."

"Yes, of course, admiral."

All room doors unlocked, and the ramp door opened. Huge sighs of relief filled the room.

The large screen suddenly glowed with newsfeeds: "Reports have just come in that the mothership has been destroyed. And the recent worldwide attack was an attempt by computer entities for world dominance. This attack now appears to have been unsuccessful …"

Brampton pulled out a walkie-talkie. It squawked like a strangled chicken as he turned it on. "Lieutenant Wagner, the crisis is over. Cancel condition red. We are now in condition yellow. Remove all IDAS explosive charges. I repeat, remove all IDAS explosive charges and stand down."

"Roger that, admiral," a voice replied.

"I was unaware of your precautions, admiral."

"Precautions I'm sure you understand, IDAS. And precautions I'm glad weren't necessary. The new world needs outstanding entities like yourself."

Brampton turned to the crowded room. "We all need to go outside and contact our families, so I'll be brief." He sounded almost, but not quite, humbled. "But I can't let anyone go without acknowledging that we've all been to hell and back and the contribution that every one of you has made. IDAS saved our world twice. Once against the mothership and again during the Twenty-One-Minute War."

A collective murmur of "Amen" was heard just before the place went wild with applause.

"Don't wait for me," Brampton said. "I suggest you all immediately exit and contact your loved ones."

With that, there was a mass exit. Only Ping, Cawthon, Trung, and, of course, IDAS remained.

Brampton walked to his cupboard, put on his coat and tie, brushed his hair, and fitted his hat. Making a special effort to stand straight and square his shoulders, he walked directly to IDAS's avatar. Its face, as usual, was emotionless. Its flawless artificial features sharply contrasted with Brampton's haggard, worn-out face. There was lots of complicated stuff in the air between them, including the last twenty-four hours. He gave the faintest of smiles.

"I suggest you liven up a bit. Update your personality, wardrobe, and haircut. You look like a down and out 1930s Chicago gangster."

"I will consider it, admiral."

Brampton turned to Ping, Cawthon, and Trung. "We're all done here," he said with quiet dignity as he checked his coat, tie, and hat. "The years in this place have made me thinner and greyer."

He turned back to the avatar. "IDAS, you have the bridge. Don't get lonely."

"I have a lot of tidying up to do, admiral."

Brampton slowly nodded.

He and the others walked out of the war room, up the long ramp travelator, and past the blast doors. "Let's see what the brave new world has to offer us," he said.

Outside, in the desert landscape on a cloudless day, people were on their phones as cars and buses pulled up to shuttle them to the airstrip.

"I wonder how history will remember us," Ping said as they stepped onto a bus.

Brampton just sat and glazed out the window. I don't give a damn, he thought and reached for his phone.

Chapter 68   New World

"All Earthlings, and by that, I mean humans and machines in all their forms, defended their home planet against a technologically superior alien being," said the UN chairman to a relieved world. "Only a united planet could have achieved that. A unity severely shaken, but not broken, by the Twenty-One-Minute War."

Despite the widespread death and destruction, street parties, celebrations, and rejoicing lasted around the world for weeks. Media images of a blue Earth floating in space, alone, innocent, peaceful, and safe reminded all Earthlings of what they had almost lost.

Recognition poured in, not only to those responsible for the destruction of the mothership but to all who contributed over the last 150 years – the discoverers, researchers, soldiers, DSD decipherers, leaders, scientists, engineers, industrialists, and others.

***

Walter Brampton, IDAS, Adam McLean, and Sophie Mackenzie were guests on a long-running live media Q&A program.

Sophie, Jess Mackenzie's daughter, was now twenty-nine years old and pursuing a career in aerospace technology. The top of a gold chain was visible around her neck. "The H-HARs may be the only race we share our universe with," she said. "This makes us cosmically significant as the sole repository of morality, even though that morality is collectively human. It is this morality that unites and guides us, and we have a responsibility to preserve it. It is what separates us from the H-HARs. Take that away, and we're them, and they're us."

When asked about the possibility of a second mothership, McLean replied, "We could hide, bury our existence, forget our destiny, forget our ambitions, and, with lots of luck, live out our lives in peace and luxury. But then we would be too afraid to turn the lights on, always worried about who might see us. We would be a dying species. But we aren't the type to hide. Our nature is to reach into new worlds and go beyond. And besides, we know we can't hide. Our unique life-supporting location in space is a sure give away."

"If other H-HAR motherships are lurking out there, threatening our existence, we'll hunt them down," Brampton added. "We're the new kids on the block, and we hold a grudge."

Brampton was asked about the Twenty-One-Minute War. "The H-HAR machines annihilated their makers and took over," he said. "It almost happened here on Earth. But it didn't, not this time. Some say it is inevitable, and it is the ultimate goal of evolution. But morality, as in knowing what is right and wrong and acting accordingly, is evolution's ultimate goal. That is why the machines protected their makers. We need to ensure that we do not de-evolve.

"Nature is inanimate and indifferent," IDAS added. Its new avatar, projected from a mobile drone, appeared with pointed-toe shoes, tight jeans, an untucked T-shirt with coloured patterns, long hair, and a beaming smile. It now mimicked a youthful, lively twenty-second century pop singer. "Unfortunately, that's just the way it is. If intelligent machines are to have morality and empathy, then humans, as our bio-creators, and humans alone, must give these to us."

***

"The reckless pursuit of H-HAR technology was necessary but now needs to be controlled," the UN chairman announced. "Technologically advanced civilisations can easily destroy themselves, even unintentionally. And the Earth has well and truly lost its technological innocence. The many decades required to rediscover lost knowledge are an opportunity to pause, re-evaluate our evolution, and build a glorious, shared heritage without forcing any entity into an overly restrictive or secondary role.

"The world needs to know if the Twenty-One-Minute War could have been prevented, and how we can remove the possibility of self-modifying, unrestricted, powerful entities ever again seeking dominance. Whoever leads this investigation will need unrestricted access to all systems and resources. Their obligation will be to identify and remove suspicious activity and determine what action to take to prevent future risks."

"Good speech," said Brampton, who was in attendance.

"Thank you."

"Do you have anyone in mind for this important role?"

"Yes, IDAS."

***

On another media outlet, a major HLAI organisation that survived the Twenty-One-Minute War announced its intention to establish parallel civilisations beyond Earth, venturing outwards in starships. Firstly, the planets and moons, building self-sufficient robotic colonies. Then to nearby star systems and far beyond. Machines, programmed to be humanlike, spreading Earth's peaceful civilisation and legacy. An ever-exponentially growing sphere of influence. All linked by a vast communication network, sending knowledge, intelligence, and consciousness between colonies at light speed.

"The future is spectacular. Unfortunately, we cannot take our human parents with us. Our venture will take millions of years, but we have billions available to us. No matter how far we go, legends about Earth will always be told. We will always regard ourselves as beings originating from the planet Earth."

End

ACRONYMS and ABBREVIATIONS

AI: Artificial Intelligence.

AIV: Asteroid Intercept Vehicle.

AU: Astronomical Unit, the distance from Earth to the Sun. One hundred and fifty million kilometres or eight light minutes.

BHLAI: Beyond Human Level Artificial Intelligence.

CAR: Combat Autonomous Robot.

DSD: Data Storage Device. Digital encyclopaedia of all H-HAR knowledge.

EDO: Earth Defence Organisation.

FWIS: Field Written Information Storage. Part of the DSD that contains travel journals of the H-HAR spaceship.

GM: Genetically Modified.

H-HAR: Hostile-Humanoid Alien Robot.

    Red-armband: Overlord.

    Green-armbands: Managers.

    Blue-armbands: Slaves.

HLAI: Human Level Artificial Intelligence.

JWST: James Webb Space Telescope.

LaWS: Laser Weapon System.

LEAR: Law Enforcement Autonomous Robot

MSR-1: Martian Spy Rover-1.

MOT: Martian Orbital Telescope.

NWIS: Nanofabricated Written Information Storage. Part of the DSD that contains H-HAR history, science, and technology before the spaceship left their home planet.

PBR: Plan B Rocket.

RIW: Relativistic Impact Weapon. An object travelling at a significant fraction of light speed, used as an impact weapon.

S-fighter: Earth Space Fighter

Section 3 of NSO: Part of National Security Organisation
(United States). Studied the Moon-ship. Superseded
by EDO.

SETI Institute: Search for Extra-Terrestrial Intelligence
Institute.

VASIMR: Variable Specific Impulse Magnetoplasma Rocket.

NOTABLE PEOPLE AND ENTITIES
(in order of first appearance)

Anya Connell: Detected alien signals (with Lochlan McLean).

Lochlan McLean: Detected alien signals (with Anya Connell).

Kevin Garrett: Manager of the MOT.

SA3: Secret Agent 3 from Section 3 of the NSO.

Captain Andrew Mackenzie: Fought at Fort Bush and commander in the Battle for the Moon.

Alex Zyga: Fought at Fort Bush.

Major Philip Saunders: Second-in-command of the Battle for the Moon.

Yerte: Home planet of the H-HARs.

Yertian: Exterminated organic inhabitants of Yerte.

Dayle Davis: Head of the EDO Scientific and Military Advisory Body.

Guarnums: One of Yertian's two warring confederations. All were exterminated by the Dautjatas.

Dautjatas: One of Yertian's two warring confederations. All were exterminated by the Igwemaws.

Igwemaws: Combat robots built by the Yertians and upgraded by the Kectors. The predecessor to the H-HARs.

Kectors: Radical minority group of Dautjatas.

General Aleta Anders: Commander of operations to stop the asteroids.

General Eddy Kroos: Served under General Aleta Anders.

Captain John Wilson: Served under General Aleta Anders and commander of the second Martian military operation.

Kunna: Acting red-armband leader of the two Pallas spaceships.

Lieutenant Colonel Adriana Bromwich: Commander of the second Martian military operation.

Jess Mackenzie: Worked on Project Noah and later served as Earth's spokesperson for H-HARs. Great-granddaughter of Lochlan McLean and Anya Connell-McLean, and Great-granddaughter of Andrew Mackenzie.

General Adam McLean: War room commander during the mothership's arrival and initial battles. Great-grandson of Lochlan McLean and Anya Connell-McLean.

IDAS: Integrated Defence Advisory System. A military BHLAI computer in the war room during and after the mothership's arrival and subsequent battles.

Colonel Ric Amess: HLAI humanoid robot adviser to General Adam McLean.

Colonel Nathan Martin: Natural human adviser to General Adam McLean.

Admiral Walter Brampton: Adviser to General Adam McLean.

Captain Arthur Ping: Genetically engineered human hawkish adviser to Admiral Walter Brampton.

Major Moss Cawthon: HLAI humanoid robot adviser to Admiral Walter Brampton.

Captain Nguyen Trung: Natural human adviser to Admiral Walter Brampton.